MONSTERS & GARGOYLES

Books One Two Three

LACEY CARTER ANDERSEN

To my amazing PA—thanks for taking this crazy ride with me.

~ Lacey Carter Andersen

Copyright 2019
Published by Lacey Carter Andersen
Cover Design by Rising Phoenix Covers by Andreea

This work of fiction is intended for mature audience only. All characters are over the age of eighteen. Names, characters, places, and incidents are either a product of the author's imagination or are used fictitiously. Any resemblance to any persons, living or dead, business establishments, events, or locales is entirely coincidental.

This book is protected under the copyright laws of the United States of America. Any reproduction or other unauthorized use of the material or artwork herein is prohibited without the express written permission of the author.

Want more from Lacey Carter Andersen?

Sign up for exclusive first looks at my hot new releases, exclusives, and contests from Lacey Carter Andersen!

Want to be part of the writing process? Maybe even get a taste of my sense of humor? Teasers for my new releases? And more? Join Lacey's Realm on Facebook!

Author's Note

The first part of this note is written to all of you research buffs out there. Read this before you start the story! I spent countless hours researching Greek mythology, along with many other cultures' myths and beliefs. This story does **not** accurately reflect all my research. I took liberties with this series. I picked through and chose which myths I liked and ignored ones that I didn't. I have nods to other cultures, and even created some twists of my own. I did all of these things for reasons. This is fiction after all! So take a deep breath, and accept it before you start, or this series might just drive you crazy.

For all my other readers, these are the first three books in a series of stand-alone reverse harem romances. There will be a lot of heat and a lot of humor. I really hope you enjoy it!

Medusa's Destiny

Chapter One

MEDUSA

I take another long swig of the bottle of booze in my hand. A nicely dressed couple walk past, shooting me a dirty look. I grin and take another drink. For a second I think I look freaking cool, and then I hit the trash can. Tumbling over it, I hit the ground on my back. The air rushes out of me, but I lift the bottle, satisfied to see I haven't spilled a drop.

I grin again and lift my other arm. Some old taco wrapper is sticking to my new leather jacket. *Great, just great.*

"Fuck," I mutter as I struggle to my feet.

This day just keeps getting better and better. First, I lose my job. Then, my best friend says I'm too much of a screw-up to keep in her life. And now? Now, I have old beans—and what I hope to god isn't meat—on my new jacket.

I just need to crawl in bed and let this crappy day pass me by.

As I stumble past an alley, I catch a flash of silver. When I pause, my superior vision picks out a woman pressed against the wall. Her breathing is rapid and her pupils dilated. Three men surround her.

I want to walk past. Damn everything to hell, I want to just ignore her.

Nobody appreciates my help anyway.

Closing my eyes, I tell myself this isn't my problem, but it doesn't matter. I'm already heading down the alley when I open my eyes.

"Hey!" I shout. "You guys just get out of here. I've got shit to do."

Everyone turns to me at once, but the greasy-haired guy holding the knife is the first to speak. "Nice sunglasses, cool girl. What? Too bright for you in this beautiful shit-hole?"

I smirk. "Trust me, asshole, you don't want me taking these glasses off."

I glance at the frightened woman to see that she's not exactly a woman. She's probably fifteen, but from her dark makeup and barely-there clothes, she wanted to look older.

"Now, this girl and I are going to take off, and you, fellas, can just go on with your night. Okay?"

This time, it's Greasy's good-looking friend who responds. "We're just having fun. Why don't you join us?"

He starts to move toward me with a big smile on his face. He probably thinks that smile is going to get me going, but I know his type. A pretty face often hides the most dangerous people, and this guy's dangerous. He's not as dangerous as me though. *Fucker.*

I take another sip of my drink. "I think I'll pass."

"Sorry," he says, his eyes narrowing. "I didn't really mean that to be a question."

My hand tightens on my bottle. This was seriously the last thing I wanted to deal with tonight, but if these guys needed me to beat the shit out of them, well, I guess I'll have to do it.

I set my drink down on the edge of a dumpster. "Come here, then. Let's get this over with."

There's the slightest flicker of doubt in his eyes, but he masks it as he slides up to me. He tries to grab my shoulder, but I move with lightning-fast reflexes, twisting his wrist and bringing him to his knees. A surprised squeak leaves his lips, and I enjoy the look of fear on his face before I snap his wrist. When he screams, I drive my knee into his nose, and a second later he's sprawled on the ground, out cold.

My gaze moves to his buddies. "Who's next?"

Greasy boy's knife moves from the girl to point at me. "What the hell are you? How the hell did you do that?"

I smile and head towards him at a lazy stroll. "That? Oh, that was nothing. What I'm going to do to you is going to make that look like child's play."

He slashes the knife out in front of him, his filthy face streaked with sweat.

I can't help but look at the girl. I can tell she wants to run, but I hope she isn't stupid enough to do it before I get the knife from Greasy.

When I get close enough, he stabs out at me.

I knock the weapon out of his grasp, and it hits the ground with a clatter. The sound radiates through the alley.

A second later, his quiet friend pulls a gun from his pocket, levels it at me, and pulls the trigger.

Bullets are fast, but unfortunately for these dipshits, I'm faster. I yank his friend in front of me, and the bullet hits him in the back.

Neither man has time to react before I send Greasy

flying towards his friend. Another bullet goes off, and they both hit the ground, with Greasy on top of him. A pathetic moan comes from one of them, but I'm not sure which one. I stride toward them, find the hand that's still clutching the gun, and crush the man's bones beneath my foot, along with the metal of the barrel.

He screams as I whirl toward the woman. She's trembling against the wall.

I want to say something, but what am I going to say? Don't spend your weekends with thugs? Go home to your mom and dad and be a good girl? *Why bother?* If what just happened doesn't frighten her enough, nothing I say is going to help.

So, I walk past her and pick up my drink. Taking another chug, I feel another wave of relaxation hit me. God I love tequila.

"Hey!"

I spin around.

The quiet thug hits me in the face, sending my glasses flying. I don't have time to warn him. To close my eyes. To do anything. Within seconds, he turns to stone, his face forever frozen in horror.

Closing my eyes, I kneel down and reach around until I find my special glasses. Slipping them back on, I look around the alley. The girl takes one look at me and turns and races away.

Slowly I stand. "You're welcome!"

I turn and start back toward my empty apartment, feeling strangely low. If I actually expected her to appreciate what I did, or thank me, then it isn't her fault. It's mine for being completely delusional.

Over two thousand years old, and I haven't accepted my place in the world. It's pathetic.

Because—news flash—no one ever appreciates it when

I help them. Yeah, everyone likes heroes. But scary monsters? Not so much. And that's exactly what I am. A monster. Medusa. A woman who can turn anyone to stone with just a glance.

Is it any wonder I'm such a screw up?

Chapter Two

MEDUSA

*M*usic blares. I scream, fall off my bed with a thump, and lay there staring at the ceiling. Did I really forget to turn off my damn alarm? Groaning, I grab my pounding head and barely make it to my feet. Yanking my alarm, I turn and smash it against the wall.

At last, the damn music has stopped.

I fall back into bed, and my eyes instantly close. Sleep tugs at me once more, even though I can now feel the bright sunlight prying at the back of my eyelids.

And then my phone starts ringing.

My eyes flash open. Grabbing it off my nightstand, I flip open my phone. "Someone better be dead—"

"Actually, that's exactly why I'm calling."

I freeze at the familiar voice. "What do you want?"

"What do you think I want, Melissa?"

I stiffen, trying to ignore my hammering heart. "Not a clue."

"So," he stretches out the word. "You have no idea why there are two dead men and a man who appears to have been turned into stone in an alley two blocks from your house?"

"Not a clue."

He swears. "This can't keep happening. Do you understand me? The Special Unit can only sweep so much of this crap under the carpet before humans start asking questions. Before you attract the attention of the wrong people."

"Yeah, yeah, okay."

"No, don't give me that. This is serious."

I put my hand over my face, my entire head throbbing. "Look, Peter, you dumped me, so don't start pretending you care about me now."

He's quiet for a long minute. "You're *Medusa*. I do care about you, just not enough to die for you."

I hate how much his words hurt. "Got it."

"Listen—"

"I've heard it all before. I'll watch myself, okay? Now, let me sleep off this hangover."

"Have you really been drinking again? I'm starting to worry about you."

"Again," I say, my voice crisp. "I'm not your problem anymore. Thanks for the heads up."

"Melissa…"

"Be safe out there, officer." I click my phone, ending the call.

I hold my phone for too long, rolling onto my side. I don't know how much longer I can take this feeling of nothingness. I don't know what's worse, the aching loneliness that doesn't seem to go away, or the feeling that nothing is ever going to get better. Peter worked so damn hard to make me fall in love with him, but the second he learned the truth, he was gone, just like everyone else.

The thing was... I wasn't just tired of hurting, of getting my heart broken. I was tired of everything.

Living forever sounds so fun in vampire romances, but that's when you have a bunch of hot guys fighting over you. Living forever as Medusa, a woman who turns people to stone with a glance, well, it's not all that fun.

I close my eyes, wanting to fall back to sleep. I love to sleep, because most of the time, my dreams are a hell of a lot better than real life. But unfortunately, now that I'm up, I can't.

Cursing my stupid life, I sit up and head for the shower.

I throw my clothes onto the floor and turn on the water. Stepping beneath the spray, I hiss, remembering that I still don't have hot water... yet another freaking bill I haven't paid. Teeth chattering, I scrub my hair and body as fast as possible, then shut off the water and get the hell out of there.

With a towel wrapped around my chest, I brush my hair and step out of the bathroom.

Suddenly, someone knocks at my door.

I ignore them, searching through my piles of clothes for ones that smell the least. But the damn knocking continues.

Cursing, I pull my glasses off the dresser, put them on, and head for the damn knocking. Throwing back the locks, I yank open the door.

A massive man is waiting on the other side. And when I say massive, I mean linebacker massive. He fills my entire doorway. Now, I'm barely five-foot tall, so I'm used to everyone looking tall, but this guy, he's tall for *tall* people. My gaze moves up from his narrow waist up to his broad shoulders and muscular arms, and then up to his face.

I suddenly find it hard to breathe. He's handsome, with

blue eyes so light they're almost grey, and short blond hair. *He has the face of an angel.* Because he doesn't just look strangely beautiful, he also looks… kind.

His gaze runs over my towel-clad form until at last, he stops at my face. A blush darkens his cheeks.

"Melissa Gorgon?"

I lean against the doorframe. "That's me."

"You're not what I expected," he says, staring at me as if I'm the first woman he's ever seen in his life.

Even though my damn head still hurts, I smile. There's nothing wrong with flirting with a handsome man. Blond gods don't drop from the sky every damn day, after all.

"Oh really? Well, want me to drop the towel and see if that's what you expected too?"

His blush deepens.

Maybe my life just got a little less crappy.

He leans closer. "Sorry."

I frown. "Sorry?"

Something hits me from behind, and my world goes black.

Chapter Three

MEDUSA

*B*linking awake, I try to move, only to discover I've been bound. My head snaps up as I'm instantly alert. I'm wearing a massive white shirt, I'm in a strange living room, and I'm tied to a chair. My hands are in front of me, in shackles, but ropes wrap around me, keeping me upright in the chair.

Mistake, assholes.

I flex, fully expecting to break whatever the hell has me tied down, but it doesn't budge. I try again, feeling the metal cut against my wrists, but nothing happens.

My heart starts pounding, filling my ears. How is this possible?

"She's awake!" My head jerks to the man in the doorway. He's the blond from my door.

"You're going to pay for this," I snarl at him.

He has the good grace to look guilty.

Another man squeezes past him. This one is just as big, but a little taller. He has breathtaking hazel eyes, messy brown hair, and a slight beard.

Every muscle in my body tenses as he walks toward me.

"So, do you usually have to tie up women to get them to your place?"

His eyes narrow. "Are you Medusa?"

I smirk. "It's pronounced Melissa."

"Cut the bullshit," he growls. "Are you her? The woman of legend?"

I shrug the best I can while bound to a chair. "Most legends are bullshit made up by people with tiny brains and too much time on their hands."

He comes to stand just above me. "Are you her?"

I give him a look I know is arrogant-as-hell. "I'm Melissa. A woman you and your buddy apparently kidnapped, so I think you're the ones with some explaining to do."

He leans down and puts one hand on the chair's arm. With his other hand, he reaches out and grabs the side of my glasses.

My pulse races. "Don't do that."

"Why not?" he challenges.

"*Don't!*"

"Why?" he starts to tug them down.

I squeeze my eyes shut and fight against my bindings.

He pulls the glasses off. "Open your eyes."

"No!" I struggle harder, my heart pounding.

I don't want to kill anyone. As much as everyone thinks I'm a monster, I hate it. I *hate* it down to my very soul. Killing assholes in alleys haunts me in quiet moments, but I can't imagine killing these two. For some reason, the idea makes me feel hollow inside. Gutted.

"Open your damn eyes!" He commands.

Frantic words bubble out. "I am Medusa. Please, put on my glasses. If I look at you, you're dead, do you understand me? Put my glasses back on!"

I expect him to obey me right away. Instead, everything grows quiet.

After a moment, I hear the blond speak from near the doorway. "I don't know many monsters who work that hard not to kill two people who kidnapped her…" His words are quiet, almost angry.

"What kind of game are you playing?" The man above me growls, leaning so close I can feel his breath on my face. "We both know what you are, so open your eyes and prove it."

I shake my head. For some reason, I can feel a panic attack coming. I *cannot* have a panic attack in front of these two men.

His hand is suddenly resting on my knee. "Open your eyes."

I freeze. "No."

His hand starts to move up my inner-thigh.

"What the fuck are you doing?" The blond says from across the room.

The dark-haired man keeps moving higher, and I'm suddenly horribly aware of the fact that I'm not wearing anything at all beneath this giant shirt that flops everywhere.

And then, he's ripped away. I hear something crash to the ground, but I still don't open my eyes.

"What the fuck!" the dark-haired man yells. "Harold, I was just trying to get her to show who she is."

My glasses are suddenly clumsily placed back on my face.

I look up into the face of the blond guy, who's apparently named Harold. "Thanks."

He looks… like he wants blood. I would have never thought the sweet, blushing guy who stood at my door could look so frightening, but he does. I guess I'm not a good judge of character, because I didn't think he'd be in on a kidnapping either.

"I'm sorry for Byron's behavior," Harold says.

I turn to look at the dark-haired man. He's getting up from the floor, where a table and lamp have been knocked over. Blood runs from his nose, and he looks pissed.

"She wouldn't open her eyes!"

Harold spins to face the other man. "So you made her think we intended to violate her?" He crosses his arms in front of his broad chest. "We were sent here to get a monster, not become one."

His words seem to vibrate through the room.

At last, Byron wipes at the blood on his nose, and the energy in the room changes slightly. "Next time you handle it."

The blond giant nods. "I will." Then, he turns to me. "So, you're Medusa?"

I nod, feeling wary.

He holds my gaze with his intense one, and for a minute I'm lost in the depths of his eyes. I feel lame, because a stupid thought floats into my head. *I've never seen that color blue before.*

The giant kneels down in front of me. "Well, Medusa, we need you to come with us."

"No way in hell." The words come out before my brain can process them.

Diarrhea of the mouth is a special gift I have.

He winces. "We... uh need you to."

"Thanks for the offer," I say, "but I think I'll pass."

Byron snorts behind the other man. "You're really handling this better than I did."

Harold shoots him a nasty look before he turns back to me. "The thing is, we need your help. And actually, you're the only one who can help us."

They need help from a monster? No one needs that.

"Why?" I ask, suddenly intrigued.

He takes a deep breath. "I can't tell you."

"Okay… well, then for how long?"

He gives a pained look. "We're not sure."

"Helpful." I sigh. "And where do you plan to take me?"

He shifts awkwardly. "Uh, we can't tell you that either."

I stare at him until he blushes again. "You make a compelling case, but I think I'm going to have to give an absolute no on this."

The dark-haired man comes up and puts a hand on the other man's shoulder, then draws him back. Suddenly, I'm face-to-face with this Byron.

My lips curl. "I hope you enjoyed feeling me up, because if you ever touch me again, I'll cut off your hands."

His eyes narrow, and he leans closer. "Two things, monster. First, I know what you are. You might have gained some sympathy with my friend because of that whole *I won't open my eyes* crap, but I know what you are. And two, I don't want to touch you. Just the sight of you makes me sick. So, no need to worry about that."

A thousand moments flash through my mind of times when people called me a monster. Days when people told me I made them sick, when men broke my heart when they found out my identity.

I act without thinking and smash his nose with my forehead.

He cries out and falls back. His hand touches his nose, his eyes widened in shock. It starts to bleed again.

"You—"

The other man cuts him off. "Medusa, we're sorry. We wanted you to come with us by choice, but time is of the essence, and the fate of an entire people rests on getting you to our destination."

"So," I swallow the bitterness in the back of my throat. "You're taking me against my will."

He nods, looking apologetic while he helps his friend to his feet.

The dark-haired man glares at me as he holds his nose, then goes to the window and throws it open wide.

"What, are we going out the window?" I ask sarcastically.

Byron smirks at me. "Actually, that's exactly what we're doing."

A sinking feeling grows in my belly. For some reason, it's like reality is finally starting to settle in. Somewhere in the back of my mind, I'd been sure this situation was temporary, that these two couldn't possibly hurt me. I'm an immortal monster, for God's sake.

But… something feels off, and I have a feeling escaping from them might not be quite as easy as I thought.

Chapter Four

BYRON

I am so angry. With myself, with Harold, and with the woman. I wasn't going to hurt her. I wasn't going to touch her. I just needed to know that she was as evil as the Elites said. Without being sure, how the hell was I going to carry out this mission?

How was I supposed to know she wouldn't open her eyes? Wasn't that her thing?

Pulling the tissues out of my nose, I stare at my reflection without seeing myself. All I can see is the woman. She's nothing like I expected. She's tiny, so tiny that I could hold her for days without tiring myself out.

And… she's unexpectedly beautiful. She doesn't have a head full of snakes, like I had expected. Instead, her hair is long and dark, full of waves, and she has the face of a goddess, not a monster.

An image of her naked form flashes into my mind, the last thing I should be picturing. I think of the moment when I dressed her in my white shirt. I'd told myself that it'd be easy for me not to look. That this was a creature that we were bound to fight against, to count as an enemy.

But… I don't know what the fuck is wrong with me. I tried not to look, but I'm a man, and she is stunning. All of her: her breasts, her smooth stomach, and her bare pussy.

I groan. I hate myself. It was only a second that I saw her before I yanked the shirt on and started buttoning, but it was enough.

She's attractive. *I* find her attractive. The enemy.

I am so fucked up.

Harold raps on the door. "We need to go."

I take a deep breath and glance down to see that my hard erection is visible through my jeans. Damn it! I untuck my shirt to hide the evidence, but I don't do a very good job.

Keep it together!

Opening the door, I stare at my best friend.

He runs a hand through his hair, which usually means he has something to say that I won't like.

"What is it?"

"Forrest called. He needs my help."

I stare at him. "You're kidding me."

He shakes his head. "You'll have to take her to Eros."

I cannot be alone with this woman. "Can't we just get Forrest together and then—"

"What, scared to be alone with me?" the woman says, looking toward me and pouting her lips.

My traitorous cock gives another twitch.

"Shut up!" I tell her. *How can she see through me so easily?*

Harold gives me a disapproving look. "You know the time constraints we're under. And I would take her, but you're the better fighter, if something goes wrong."

I want to pound my fist through the wall until I don't care about any of it, but instead I spout out, "Fine."

He nods. "Let's get her untied."

Harold is careful how he removes her from the chair,

careful that she can't escape. He leaves the chains on her wrists, but even with that, she runs for the door. I catch her easily.

She tries to fight against me, but all it does is increase my arousal to have the tiny woman thrashing against me while I pin her to my body.

"Stop it!" I finally command.

She stops, turns around, and spits on me.

I wipe her saliva off my cheek and push back the rage building inside me. "Do that again, and next time I won't be so gentle."

Harold gives me *another* disapproving look before he moves to the window.

A second later, he transforms. His skin turns the stunning color of wet stone as grey wings sprout from his back.

He turns to look at us before he leaves, motioning toward her with his head. "We'll meet at the location as soon as we're done."

Moving gracefully, he turns back to the window and jumps out, leaving me alone with our prisoner.

She turns to me, her mouth hanging open. "You're gargoyles."

I smirk. "Observant, aren't you."

Her nose scrunches up in a way I refuse to find adorable. "But gargoyles don't exist."

"Says *Medusa*."

She stiffens in my arms. "No, I mean, I thought you monster-hunters had died out long ago."

"Sorry, sweetheart, but we're alive and thriving." The lie comes easily. She doesn't need to know how our numbers have dwindled.

She's quiet for a long minute. "Are the rumors about gargoyles true then? Do you kill my kind to protect humanity?"

I can't answer her, so I don't. "Come on, I need your help with a friend of yours. Remember Eros?"

"Eros!" she says with a sneer. "He's no friend of mine!"

Ignoring her lies, I drag my prisoner to the window. "Yeah right, I'm sure your kind throw parties together or whatever."

She strains against the metal chains binding her wrists in front of her. "Eros was a god, if you'll recall. Not one of my kind, and now he's some kind of fucking siren of lust, luring unsuspecting humans to him. That is *so* not my thing."

My gaze moves to her delicious, pale legs. If she leaned forward in my shirt, I'd get a full view of her round ass cheeks. Like hell she doesn't lure men to her. This woman is a damned siren if I ever saw one.

When we reach the window, I shift into my stone-form. It only takes a moment for my skin to turn the same color as Harold's and for wings to sprout from my back. I stretch my wings wide, nearly groaning in relief at taking my true form.

"Come on, now," I tell her, in a gruff voice. "The sooner you help me, the sooner we can be done with each other."

"Fine," she says, spinning around, reaching her short arms out towards me. I'm mesmerized as I lean down and she puts her arms behind my neck.

When I stand up, she's forced to wrap her legs around my waist to keep from dangling from her chains. And then, I realize how completely screwed I am. This position… it's criminal.

You've got to be fucking kidding me. There is no way in hell I'm flying with this woman like this. No fucking way.

She shifts, and my erection gives a painful twinge. *Fuck. Maybe I should take on my battle form?* Battle form is when we're fully stone. It's not something we use often, because it makes us slower and more awkward. I'll never make it where I need to go in battle form, but then, I also won't be human enough to *feel* her and be turned on.

"Are we going?" she asks, in a voice that's too damned innocent.

What am I supposed to say? That I'm too turned on by her to fly like this?

I picture her on my back, her wide open naked pussy rubbing against my back. *That's not going to work either.*

"Didn't you say you were in a rush?" she asks.

I growl at her, then decide the hell with it and jump out the window. I'm satisfied as fuck when she screams. I guess the little hell-cat's afraid of something after all.

But then her legs tighten around my waist, and she's suddenly riding my cock. My oversized shirt is pushed up around her thighs and I know she's bare and open to me.

I'm so turned on I almost forget to flap my damn wings, but I do… right in time, and I take us up over the tops of the buildings. She keeps screaming, but I'm not worried about people seeing us. My glamour keeps us hidden from human eyes.

I'm not worried about the humans, but what am I worried about?

This delicious creature is squeezing her legs around me and rubbing herself so hard against me that it's only a matter of time before I come in my pants. I'm no inexperienced teenager, but I took a vow of celibacy. Which means it's been a long-ass time since I last buried myself balls deep into a woman.

I can change my damn pants, but I don't want this woman to know the truth. It's a matter of pride. Of keeping the upper-hand over my prisoner. As she breathes heavily into my ear, I hear her whimper my name.

My traitorous cock twitches again, hardening to the point where I don't even know if I'm flying in the right fucking direction, because I'm losing my mind. She wiggles against me, and my dirty mind starts to think of what she must look like spread wide right now. I'm sure she's tight and maybe wet. They say the line between fear and arousal is paper-thin, and I'm starting to wonder how true that is.

She whimpers my name again, and my hands shift.

Suddenly, they aren't on my shirt. My damn hands are on her ass. My shirt is too big for her, it moves in the wind above my hands.

I hate that I slide them around the curve of her generous ass. I hate that I hold her closer to my dick. When she gives a little bounce, I start to wonder if she's doing it on purpose, but there's no way. This woman is terrified. She hates me, and I'm sure as hell sure she doesn't find me attractive.

When she bounces again, my hands start to move her, bouncing her up and down on my cock. Her mouth presses against my neck, and I explode inside my jeans.

I'm shaking by the time my senses come back. Thank heavens that we're flying safely in the clouds. I was so lost to my desire we could've been flying straight into a plane for all I knew.

And now, for the first time in longer than I can remember, I feel oddly relaxed. Every nerve in my body is humming in satisfaction, and my muscles feel like liquid.

For a long minute, I fly quietly, hoping to God that this woman didn't notice what just happened. I hope she has no idea I'm so pathetic that I just came in my pants from having her spread body wrapped around mine.

She leans up and bites my ear. "Was that good for you?"

Damn it!

A string of curses explodes from my lips. "That was nothing!"

She pulls back, and I can just barely see her eyes through her sunglasses. Her eyelids are hooded in the sexiest damn way possible.

"You know, when your dick is the size of a bat, it's pretty damn hard to hide that you're aroused."

I glare at her. "Turbulence always does that to me."

She chews her bottom lip and my cock hardens again.

This is going to be a damned long flight.

Chapter Five

MEDUSA

Fucking Fates and their fucking sick senses of humor!
I smirk at the thought, because the Fates have *got* to have their bored hands in this mess. Who else could've created this insane scenario?

I'm Medusa. A powerful being capable of turning almost anyone and anything to stone… but not gargoyles. The bastards are immune to me.

And gargoyles? They're supposed to be gone. Vanished from this modern world.

So, all I can think is those three beastly ladies decided to have a good laugh and brought these assholes to my door. The perfect kidnappers for this monster. *And, of course, they're hot as fuck. And I'm insanely horny.*

None of this is cool. Not cool at all.

The next time I see them, I'm going to give those Fates a piece of my mind. But until then, I just need to figure out what the hell is going on. And what this gargoyle has in store for me.

We've been flying through an entire day and night.

Byron doesn't seem to mind, but I'm hungry, thirsty, and tired of pressing against his hard erection. It would be so damned easy to use him to get myself off. I'm so damned ready to have his big length inside of me that I'm leaking, and I feel so fucking swollen, it's ridiculous.

But I won't give him the satisfaction of knowing he's turning me on too.

Because I swear this guy has come three times since we started flying. Maybe I'm wrong. Maybe, like he said, it's just the turbulence, but his pants are wet, and it's not just from me.

His hands on my ass are so close to my heated core that it's driving me crazy, but sometimes he starts to move me against him, press me against him, and I feel the muscles in his body tense. The third time I watched his face, and he looked like a man coming. An angry man, but a man all the same.

Suddenly, we start to fly lower.

"Are we landing?" I ask.

He ignores me, which he has done for the last day.

It irks me.

As the wind starts to slam against us harder and harder, I begin to bounce against his dick again. His hands tighten on my ass, and I hope I'm making him frustrated, because my treacherous body is heating up again.

When we land beneath an apple tree, he doesn't release me for a long minute.

I look up at him, and he has the most tortured expression I've ever seen on a man. His eyes are dark, aroused. When his gaze moves to my lips, my breathing increases, and I feel my nipples harden against his chest. He's going to kiss me. I know it. He'll kiss me, and then we'll fuck like wild animals on this hilltop.

I can't believe it when he pulls my cuffed arms from around his neck and puts my legs down. My legs give out and I sink to the ground, unable to get my balance with my hands cuffed. The jackass doesn't bother to help me up. He just takes several steps back.

"That," he points to an apple tree, "is breakfast, lunch, and dinner, so eat up. And that," he points to a river nearby, "is your water for the day. And if you need to use the bathroom, find a bush. We take off again in twenty."

Without another word, he spins and stomps off. I glare at his retreating back. If I had any idea where we are, I would have made a break for it. Instead, I sigh and find a tall bush where I can use the bathroom. Afterwards, I wash my hands and stumble back to the tree, tired but not too tired to eat.

It takes some doing with my hands cuffed, but I pick a handful of apples. My hunger had started to fade, but as soon as I take a bite, it rushes back, hard and fast. The apples won't be enough—I need protein, dammit—but I eat as much as I can anyway. Enough to sate my hunger. *For now.*

Immediate needs taken care of, I start to relax, but I find myself aching for a nice bath, to clean off a day of sweat and filth from my skin. And, as much as I hate it, to ease my arousal in the cool waters.

I glance around myself, but the gargoyle Byron is nowhere to be found. The way Byron acts, I doubt he would come looking for me by the river's edge without announcing himself. I walk along the edge of the river until I find a little inlet. I unbutton my shirt, but then stop short when I realize I can't take it fully off with my cuffs. *Dammit!*

I sit on the edge of the river and sink in as far as I can

without getting the shirt wet. Once I brace myself, I start to wash. First, I splash my face, and I brush water through my hair to pull it back from my face. Finally, I slide my hands down my breasts, where my nipples are hardened into nubs, and down my stomach until I reach my hot core.

It couldn't hurt anything...

Looking around again, I listen closely until I'm sure I'm alone. When I don't hear anything, I slip my hand into my folds. I know it won't take long. My frustrations have built up to a ridiculous point. All I need is a couple strokes, and I'll be there.

Closing my eyes, I slide my fingers along my sensitive nerves, eager for my release. I move faster and faster, gasping for breath. I'm so close. So damn close.

Water sprinkles on my face.

My eyes fly open, and I'm staring face-to-face with a male water nymph. He's damned handsome, with eyes the color of the river, and dark blue hair. I already know he's a nymph of lust, because his gaze is fixed on where my fingers are buried inside myself.

Nymphs of lust are harmless, so I raise a brow. "Did you come to watch?"

His full lips curve into a smile. "I was watching. I came to join in."

I think of Byron and feel strangely guilty. "Sorry, big boy, but you'll have to be satisfied with watching."

His gaze moves over my body. He's hovering right over me, braced so he's not touching me, but I can tell what he's thinking. It'd take nothing at all for him to lie down on top of me and slip right inside.

Unfortunately for him, I won't allow it.

"Why are your hands bound?"

I stare at my chained hands and shrug. "I'm a prisoner."

He leans closer to me, so that his mouth is hovering just over mine. "Would you like to be my prisoner?"

Suddenly, he's yanked off of me.

I look up and see Byron, his face wild. He slams a fist into the face of nymph, and then punches him again, and again. The nymph is slim and half the size of Byron. If he keeps this up, he'll do some serious damage.

I scramble out of the water and grab the big gargoyle's arm. "Stop it right now!"

His eyes are still wild. His gaze moves over my bare body, and I blush, grabbing the sides of my shirt to close it; hiding myself from view.

To my surprise, that pisses him off more. He punches the nymph again, then grabs me and throws me over his shoulder.

I bang my chained fists against his back. "I'm wet! And practically naked!"

"You didn't mind him seeing you!" he roars.

I'm so shocked by his response I don't even know what to say.

He doesn't put me down until he reaches the apple tree and then he slams me against the trunk. I gape at him, completely unsure what he's planning.

His gaze moves to the shirt hanging open on my frame. He reaches out, and everything within me awakens, waiting for his touch.

It never happens. He buttons the shirt, one button at a time, starting at the top. His fingers slide against my skin as he does so. When he gets to the last button, his hand brushes my core, and damn it, I'm ready to have him inside of me.

Instead, he leans down and pulls my arms back around his neck.

My legs wrap around his waist, and he moves out from

beneath the branches of the tree. I have no idea why he's so angry, but he says nothing for a long time.

Regardless of what he says—or doesn't say—his hard erection presses against me for the entirety of our trip.

Chapter Six

HAROLD

"*E*xplain this to me again," Forrest says, really slowly like he thinks I'm an idiot.

He's the one who was taken prisoner by sirens, so who's the real idiot?

"We found Medusa, but she's… beautiful."

He drops the half-eaten stick of meat he's roasting over the fire. "How beautiful is beautiful?"

I don't want to talk about her anymore, because she's been haunting me since I first saw her. But then again, I kind of want Forrest to be as miserable and horny as I am.

"She's small—like I can't even imagine our cocks fitting into her tight pussy small. She's got these big breasts for a girl her size, and since she was wearing just a white shirt, I could see her little pink nipples through the fabric. And God, they were the kind of nipples every man just wants to suck. You know, put her on your lap and just suck for hours. Those kind of nipples. And she's got this whole body just made to be licked and nibbled on."

Forrest groans. "Have I told you how much I hate being celibate?"

I grin. "All the damn time."

Forrest pets his erection. "If you'll excuse me, I need a moment."

He rises, and I roll my eyes, only I'm fucking aroused too.

I swear to God we're pathetic. We hated becoming celibate. We hate living in a place where there are only three females anywhere close to our age. It was some kind of cruel joke that we were sent to find a monster and instead kidnapped the kind of woman we've been dreaming about sharing for years.

Despite myself, I pull out my cock and start to stroke it. I think about how delicious her pussy must feel. In perfect clarity, I imagined myself sinking deeply into her and pounding in and out until she crashes over the edge, screaming my name.

I come with a strangled sound, letting my seed decorate the floor of the woods. When I'm done, I pull up my pants, go to the river and wash my hands. When I get back, Forrest is already waiting for me.

"You're shameless," he teases me.

I laugh. "Like you're any better."

We sit in silence for a long time. Above us, the sky is decorated with stars. And the sounds of the crackling fire weaves perfectly with the sounds of crickets and owls. This is the life—freedom, with no one breathing down our necks or watching our every move.

"So," Forrest says, breaking the silence. "How are we going to kill this hot woman?"

I stiffen. Suddenly, the shadows in the woods seem deeper, darker, and I don't feel peaceful anymore.

"I don't know."

We both lie down in the grass, staring up at the stars,

and I know we're both thinking the same thing. Killing monsters we can do, but killing a woman? I don't think we can do it.

The thing is, we won't have a choice.

Chapter Seven

MEDUSA

I stare down at a city tucked away in the center of a tangled jungle. It's a strange mix of ancient buildings and modern wonders. Roads have been cut through the jungle to connect this place with the outside world, and from this high up, they look like black snakes weaving through greenery.

I know this place. *Although it's changed. A lot.* My mind goes back to hundreds of years ago when this was nothing more than a little village.

The people were kind… until they found out what I was.

My stomach twists. Somehow, even after so long, I can still remember some of the villagers' faces. *It's strange that they've all been dead and gone for a long time.*

That was another thing about living forever; you try to accept all the changes, but sometimes it kind of feels like a punch to the gut. Everything keeps changing, but you just stay the same.

But I guess nothing has been normal since I met these damned gargoyles. Which is… kind of nice.

I look up at Byron's face. He looks focused on the sky ahead of us, but I sense he's aware of my stare.

Who would have thought my enemies would be so damned hot?

Gargoyles used to be everywhere, in my younger days. Humans carved them, and their desperation brought the creatures to life. Monsters everywhere feared them. I even feared them, even though I'd never actually seen one. I remembered a time when just seeing a shadow overhead made my heart race.

But it had to have been more than two or three hundred years since I stopped looking for them in the sky, since I stopped worrying about them discovering me. Gargoyles just didn't feel like terrifying enemies anymore, more like nightmares from my childhood.

The presence of them should frighten me. They kill my kind. In fact, if I'm honest, I suspect that these intend to kill me. And I already know my powers don't work against them, even if I were inclined to try, which I'm not.

So why am I not afraid of them?

I want to believe it's because I know I have nothing to fear from them, but a small part of me worries it's because being around them makes me feel alive again, excited for life. I hate to admit that I'm eager to see what will happen next.

I must be more messed up than I thought. I'm practically chasing death.

We fly past the busy city until we reach a deeper part of the jungle. Byron begins to circle, slowly bringing us closer to the ground. I tense, wrapping my legs more tightly around him.

He swears, and his breathing grows more rapid.

In response, my own pulse speeds up. That ache comes back, the one right between my thighs, and I grit my teeth.

I'm supposed to be trying to frustrate this stoic gargoyle. Touching him shouldn't frustrate *me*.

We land in pretty much the only spot we can without his wings getting tangled.

My legs shake as he pulls my arms from around his neck, and I'm sure I'm going to crumble to the ground again. But to my surprise, the angry gargoyle holds me against him for a long moment, my chained hands pressed between us. I inhale, enjoying the smell of him. He smells like the wind and earth, all rolled into one. *Like freedom*.

For some reason, a shiver rolls through me. *Why does this jerk affect me like this?*

While he continues to hold me, his wings disappear, and his skin changes back to a human-like color. It might be my imagination, but his skin seems to warm beneath my touch. It feels pleasant… more than pleasant.

"Better?" he murmurs against my hair, and for a second I think the word is almost tender.

"Yeah," I whisper back, my breath puffing against his neck.

He practically leaps back from me, and it's pure luck that I manage to keep my balance. "Good, because we've got a lot to do and not a lot of time."

My hands tighten into fists. There he is again, Mr. Grumpy. "You keep saying that, but you still haven't said what we're doing or why we don't have a lot of time."

He strides forward and grabs my arm too roughly.

"Hey!" I jerk free of his grip. "I'm sick of this! Use your damn words!"

The flecks of gold in his brilliant hazel eyes seem to flash with warning. "You're my prisoner, I'll treat you however I damn well please."

My chin lifts. "Careful. I've been pleasant up until this point, but if you push it, I'll make your life hell."

Medusa's Destiny

"Pleasant?" he practically snarls the word. "Is that what you call nearly fucking a strange nymph when I take my eyes off of you for one second?"

I raise a brow. "Is that what's got your panties in a twist?"

He grabs for my arm again, but I step out of his reach. "Just shut up and come with me!"

"Not until you start treating me a little more nicely and answering some of my questions."

He stares, breathing hard. "I'm done with this shit. Push me a little harder and see what happens."

A challenge? I hide my smile. Boy, this asshole doesn't know me at all.

When he grabs my arm again, I let him.

He looks relieved. I give him a minute to haul me along. I wait for his shoulders to relax and his focus to shift to our destination. And then, moving with lightning fast reflexes, I spin, kicking him as hard as I can in the groin.

A guttural shout tears from his lips and his knees hit the ground, but I don't give him time to recover. I spin again and kick him in the face. He hits the jungle floor behind him, and I turn, racing to freedom.

I'm fast, but I don't know how fast he is, so I don't slow, even though my path is tangled and uneven. The shackles on my wrist make it awkward, but I manage. I barrel over branches and vines, moving further from the light of the clearing and into the shadowy darkness of the jungle. I hear him crashing through the tangled chaos behind me, and pick up my speed. It's even darker with the sunglasses on, but I don't dare take them off. Not ever.

My heart says he won't hurt me, but my brain keeps flashing through my experiences with him so far. Byron has a temper, and I'm pretty sure kicking him in the crotch really pissed him off.

I sense him, too close behind me. Turning slightly, I see him. *Shit!* He's almost caught me, and his face is twisted in rage.

My feet catch on something, and suddenly, I'm falling. Pain rips through my head as my skull cracks against something. For a second, everything goes black. I don't think I'm breathing. I don't think I'm still in my body.

Then I gasp. My vision comes into focus, and Byron's face is inches from mine. I stiffen and start to fight, even though I feel weak and confused.

He catches my hands and pins them against my chest. "Stop. You're fucking hurt."

I stiffen, but don't move as he releases my hands.

He reaches up and touches my head.

I gasp as my skull gives a painful ache.

His expression grows concerned. "You're bleeding."

Closing my eyes, I take deep breaths. "It's fine. I've had worse."

He says nothing for a long time, and neither do I. My head hurts like hell, and a headache is forming behind my eyes. I've got the sudden need to sleep. The thing is, immortals don't need a lot of sleep. Flying with Byron for the past couple days hasn't been hard. I've nodded off a few times, but other than that, I've been painfully awake. But now? I just want to sleep for a month. Because we might not need to sleep, but we still enjoy it.

"I'm tired," I say, and my voice sounds different, even to my own ears.

He shifts beneath me, and I realize he's got me cradled in his lap. "Then, sleep."

I shake my head, then hiss, because it hurts like hell. "You might kill me in my sleep."

He chuckles, and the sound rolls through me like a

wave, deep, beautiful, and completely unexpected. "I give you my word not to hurt you while you sleep."

The need to argue rises up inside me, but instead, I snuggle closer to him, and sleep pulls me under.

Most of my dreams are a pleasant escape from my crappy life. But this time, I dream about two gargoyles fucking me slowly.

This is definitely one dream I don't want to wake up from.

Chapter Eight

BYRON

I'm in big trouble. As Medusa groans in her sleep again and moves, brushing her naked ass against my erection, I'm having a harder and harder time remembering why I can't just bury my cock deep inside of her.

This woman is the most frustrating creature I've ever met before.

I mean, she attacked me. Attacked a gargoyle! We aren't just made of stone when we transform. We're known for being strong, fast, and powerful. She had to know she didn't have a chance in hell of escaping me.

It's like she did it just to piss me off.

My mouth curls into an unexpected smile, and I gaze down at her.

And then my smile fades, carefully pulling one of my arms out from under her, I reach forward and pull her skewed sunglasses off. I forget to breathe for a long minute. She's so damn beautiful, so unbelievably beautiful, even in the shadows of the jungle.

I cannot believe she's a monster. She's more beautiful

Medusa's Destiny

than any angel. Her long dark lashes tempt my fingertips. I want to touch them, to see if they're as soft as they look.

And I feel like a fucking jackass for even having such a dumb thought. Who wants to touch a woman's eyelashes? Who wants to stroke a woman's face to see if her skin feels as soft as they imagine?

I slide her glasses on and lean back against the trunk of the tree.

Me. I'm the jackass who wants to touch every inch of her.

If I just wanted to stroke her breasts, fondle the tips of her sweet nipples, or just bury myself inside her while I touch the soft folds of her body, that I could accept. I'm a horny gargoyle who hasn't touched a female in a good twenty years.

But her eyelashes and face? That pisses me off, because that means this isn't just arousal between us.

And I *hate* that.

Because when it comes down to it, I'll have to be the one to kill her. For the first time in my life, I don't know if I can do my job.

My brotherhood has a mission. Retrieve the monster, get her cooperation with two tasks that she is uniquely suited to help, and then take her to the sanctuary for one act before her final judgment. She may be our mortal enemy, but the survival of our people depends on her helping us. It doesn't matter if she is willing or not.

Which means I need to fix this thing between us before we reach our destination. I need to be a bigger jerk. I need her to act like a hateful bitch. I need to stop feeling my heart ache every time she looks in my direction.

I never should have stopped here. We've got time constraints, we can't delay, but here I am, watching her sleep. Because she scared me when she fell. Because, despite the fact that my gargoyle instincts should be telling me she's an enemy, I'm caring for her like she's an innocent under my protection.

Which makes absolutely no sense… my instincts have never led me wrong before.

I sigh. But for now, I run my free hand along her smooth legs, feeling my erection aching with need. I look down at her face and imagine what she'd look like laughing, or with her eyes wide as I make her come.

For now, I pretend that I haven't been sent to end her life.

Hours tick by. I nod off, holding her close, smelling her sweet lavender scent and dreaming of things that are stupid-as-hell, like waking up to see this woman naked, swelling with my child, and smiling at me.

Just stupid shit like that.

And then, I feel her stir in my arms and snap awake. The first thing she does when she awakes is feel for her glasses, and I sense her relax just a bit when she finds them in place.

I can't see her eyes beneath her sunglasses as they open, but I sense them. And immediately, I hide every dumb feeling and thought I have. The last thing I need is for her to know how I'm feeling.

"Better?"

She stretches in the sexiest damn way in the world, her perfect ass rubbing against my crotch as she moves. "Yeah. Head still hurts a bit, but I'm okay."

"Well," I clear my throat. "There's a hot spring on our way. We can stop there and clean you up a bit."

A smile twists her lips. "Are you offering to bathe me?"

I scowl. "Not a chance in hell, monster."

It hurts when her smile vanishes. "You're a real asshole, you know that."

Yeah, I am. "Just shut up."

Climbing to my feet, I keep her cradled to my chest. For some reason, I think of the moment her head hit the root. I'd been scared. More than scared. I'd panicked.

She wouldn't be getting hurt again under my care, not if I could help it. *Until you kill her, you idiot.*

"Are you planning to carry me the whole way?" she asks, looking irritated.

I picture her falling again. "I wouldn't have to if you weren't so damn clumsy."

She shoves at my chest, anger radiating from her. "Put me down."

"No."

"Put me down. Now!" she commands me.

I snarl. "No. Now, shut up. We need to get you clean before we see Eros."

She stiffens in my arms. "So, we're really seeing Eros?"

I scowl, mad I told her anything.

"I don't think that's a good idea."

I continue moving through the forest, determined not to look at her again. "I don't remember asking for your opinion."

Her hands grip the front of my shirt. "He's unstable as hell, Byron. And if we're heading where I think we are, he won't appreciate us in his temple."

"Well, fuck him, because that's where we're heading." *Damn it!* I glance down at her, annoyed when I see her satisfied expression.

"So, we're heading to his temple?" Her gaze grows thoughtful. "Why would a gargoyle want to see a god of lust? Aren't you guys incapable of getting hard or something?"

"You know damn well I can get hard!"

Her brow raises, and I want to scream that she got me to admit it. "So you *were* aroused?"

I say nothing. I'm tired of her mind games.

Her lips pucker. "So, a gargoyle who gets hard and comes while he flies wants the god of lust? Interesting."

I bite back my response.

"But I guess it makes sense. Maybe you're tired of exploding in your pants every time you fly."

"I do not—" I clench my teeth.

She looks even more satisfied. "So what is it, gargoyle? Does the wind turn you on or is it me, because you're giving a lot of mixed messages?"

I curse softly.

To my shock, a giggle explodes from her lips, and the sound is musical. Delightful.

My anger fades. Did I really just make her laugh? And why the hell does that fact make me feel so damn proud?

"Should I keep guessing as to why we're going to Eros?"

I break out of the jungle and come to my destination. I've only been here once, but nothing has changed. It's a waterfall crashing down into a pool of heated water.

She makes a little sound. "It's the same. So beautiful."

Beautiful? *It's just a freaking pool.* I look again, trying to picture it through her eyes. Maybe it is a little nice.

"You've been here before?" That surprises me.

For a second she looks sad. "A long time ago."

I want to ask her more. But getting to know her isn't exactly part of the plan. *Stick to the plan.*

I take her to the edge of the water and set her down.

She looks at me first, and then down at herself, her point clear. "Do you plan to undress me now or undo my cuffs so I can undress myself?"

An image of me slowly undressing her comes into my mind. My cock bobs eagerly.

Fuck.

I frown at her, remembering the sprint we just took through the jungle. "I'll undo your cuffs, but if you try to run for it, I'll hog tie you."

She holds out her hands.

Taking a deep breath, I close my eyes and touch the metal. The magical cuffs hum as I give my command, and I hear them hit the ground.

"Magic cuffs?" she says, sounding excited. "A god must have made them."

One did, but I don't tell her that. "Go get cleaned up."

She takes a step back from me, to the very edge of the water, then reaches for the buttons on my shirt.

Fucking turn around and walk away! I command myself.

But I stand absolutely still as she slowly undoes every single button, exposing more and more of her creamy, white skin. When she gets to the last one, she grasps the sides of her shirt, and I wait, pulse racing. I tell myself that she's a flight risk, that I have to watch her. The truth is that I want to see her. I *need* to see her again.

"Byron?" her voice is soft, husky.

My pulse races.

"Turn around."

I blink stupidly at her for a second. "What?"

"Turn around, you pervy gargoyle! If you want a strip show, you might want to be a bit nicer next time."

I scowl, hating how pissed off I am. I turn my back to her.

Her shirt lands on my head, and I yank it off, turning back around.

She's already splashed into the water and her creamy flesh is hidden from my view. I stare like some pathetic loser as she dives under the water and plays. She winces as she scrubs out her hair, and I'm transfixed by every move she makes.

At last, she tilts her glasses down, and her gaze meets mine. "You know, you might want to clean up a bit, too. It's been days since you last showered, and between the cum in your pants, and your manly scent… well, I think it wouldn't be the worst idea."

I scowl, hating that she's right.

I pull off my black t-shirt and toss it on a rock near the water, along with hers. As I start to undo the zipper and button on my pants, I find her staring at me.

"Can't control yourself?" I ask.

She shoots me an arrogant look and turns her back to me.

Satisfied, I strip off my jeans, boxers, sneakers, and socks. I set them on the rock, and wade into the waters. Ignoring her entirely, I wash.

When I hear her swimming, I can't help but look. She's going beneath the waterfall.

Like a magnet, I follow her.

When she swims beneath it, she tilts her head back so that the edge of the water hits her hair. I'm transfixed. She's like a water nymph, beautiful and tempting.

"Coming?" she asks, looking at me.

I move closer, standing beneath the falling water beside her. I'm tempted to pull her into my arms. I'm tempted to fuck her right here in this perfect moment, but I don't.

I don't.

The fact that I hold back… I'm pretty sure this will be one of my life's greatest regrets.

Yet, I can't. I can't fuck the woman I intend to kill. I can't break my vow of celibacy.

Soon, one of the female gargoyles will give birth. Once

she does, all the males will be allowed to mate her again. At least the males she desires, and she's made it clear that my brothers and I are at the top of her list.

We can finally touch a woman. We can finally try to have a child.

But only if we follow the rules. We can satisfy ourselves, but we can't have sex. The Elites believe our sperm is more powerful this way, and with our kind dying out, only the males who have controlled themselves can mate with a female gargoyle. Having sex with this woman would mean giving up twenty years of careful control. And it'd mean giving up my hope of ever having a child.

So, I hold back.

The moment passes. She looks away from me, and I swear there's disappointment in her eyes. With her glasses, I can't be sure.

"I'm done if you are," she says after a moment.

I nod.

We head back to shore. We're only a short walk from Eros' temple, and then the real work begins. A lot of people have tried to steal his fertility figure, but none have succeeded. But then, Eros is a seriously fucked up God who apparently has a soft spot for female monsters, so I think Medusa is our one chance at getting in the door without getting caught.

After that though, we still have to get lucky. I've heard the statue only appears when Eros is present, when he's using his powers to lure humans to him. So step one is getting Medusa inside. Step two is actually just being in the right place at the right time.

Because if I don't get that fertility figure, I'll let down my entire race. We need it to ensure the female gargoyles conceive again. I can't let them down.

I won't.

When we reach the shore, I freeze. Our clothes are gone.

"Fuck. Where are they?"

She sighs behind me. "Eros' people."

I whirl on her. "His *people*?"

"His magic lures humans to him. They come from the city to his temple, compelled by his magic. Many of them end up in this hot spring. Sometimes his people steal their clothes."

"So you knew this would happen?" I can't keep the anger out of my voice. I have a hell of a lot to do, and I'm pretty sure it'll be a lot harder to do naked.

And, when I glance at the tops of her breasts over the water, I reluctantly admit that she'll be harder to resist too.

To my annoyance, she crosses her arms angrily in front of her chest. "You think I want to be naked with you, asshat? Because I don't. I just figured his people would know we weren't human."

I shake my head. "And how would they know that?"

She shrugs.

I grit my teeth together. "Well, this is just great."

"Relax. I'm sure there are clothes scattered all around his temple. We're going there anyway."

She's right. "Fine, but keep your hands to yourself."

She snorts. "Yeah, right. I'm not the one who is constantly hard."

Turning, she heads out of the water. I hate that I watch her every move. I hate that I love the way her wet hair hangs down her back, and I hate how much I love the sweet curves of her round ass.

I leave the water too, and reach down, snagging the cuffs. She glances back at me, and her eyes widen. "You can't be serious."

"Just in case," I mutter.

Then, her gaze moves down.

I know she's staring right at my hard dick. And there's not a damn thing I can do about it.

"Gargoyles are always hard," I tell her defensively.

She laughs. "At least you've got something to be proud of." Turning, she looks toward the jungle. "It's that way, right?"

I'm feeling a little too happy about her complimenting my junk, so it takes me a minute to respond. "Yup."

Then, we start the longest hike of my life, as I walk along, dick hard, and a beautiful naked woman in front of me.

And did I mention that I'm celibate?

The Gods must be laughing their asses off at me.

Chapter Nine

MEDUSA

Just as I expected, we do find clothes scattered around the outside of the temple, but it's evening by the time we're dressed. I managed to find a yellow sundress, and Byron squeezed into clothes a size too small. The green shirt barely buttoned over his broad shoulders and leaves spaces exposed between each button. The khaki shorts had to be left unbuttoned at the top, and to my enjoyment, they leave absolutely nothing to the imagination.

It takes all my willpower to look away from the hunk of a man, but I'll be damned if I let him catch me staring again. Instead, I turn my attention to the sunset above the trees. To my surprise, the sky is strangely beautiful tonight. I lift my sunglasses and peek below—I can't remember the last time I actually watched the sunset and noticed the way the reds and oranges stand out against the dark blue of the sky in the evenings.

My mind goes back to my apartment, my ex, and my empty life. It's kind of strange that it took being kidnapped by gargoyles to realize just how bad things had gotten for me. When I get back, if I get back, some things are going to change.

I feel Byron staring from beside me. "What?"

"You know that your gaze doesn't affect gargoyles. So why do you worry about your sunglasses so much? It's just the two of us."

I shrug. "Habit I guess. If someone were to come up and startle me, and then die because of it, well… I couldn't live with that."

I lower my sunglasses. Shields back in place. "I've been thinking about what I'm going to do when I get back home."

His expression grows troubled. "You got people worrying about you?"

Folding my arms over my chest, I look at the sunset again. "Peter's probably going a bit nuts, but other than that—"

"Who's Peter?" he asks, frowning.

"He works for the Special Unit." *And he broke my heart.* "And he worries about me."

"You have a boyfriend in the Special Unit?" He looks shocked.

His reaction hurts. *Medusa has a boyfriend?* How unbelievable! Who would want to be with that disgusting monster? *Who indeed?*

Even though he's kind of right,

My chest hurts as I glare at him. "Surprised?"

"Surprised?" he repeats, and his entire chest seems to swell. "And what about the nymph you were about to fuck? Would your *boyfriend* be happy about that?"

The venom in his voice sends rage boiling through my blood. "None of your damned business!"

I hear his teeth grind together. "Forget it. I shouldn't have expected differently from one of your kind."

Your kind. "Asshole."

He turns away from me and starts walking. "We've wasted too much time here. We need to get into the temple and out of it without Eros spotting us, so keep up and keep quiet."

"Yes, sir!" I respond sarcastically, but stand up to follow him. "And what exactly are we doing in his temple in the first place?"

He doesn't answer me. *Of course not.*

I stomp through the jungle. "You know Eros will kill us if he thinks we're there for anything but complete debauchery, right? And gargoyles kind of have a reputation for ruining that kind of fun."

He continues ignoring me.

Whatever.

As we get closer, we hear the temple music. It grows in volume and rhythm with each step forward, some strange song with unidentifiable instruments and loud bass that thumps even the ground beneath our feet. We exchange a look, then continue through the jungle a little more slowly until we reach the temple.

It's made of grey brick and looks simple from the outside, but I can feel the power of the glamour washing over the structure. The glamour is strong, stronger than anything I could create.

Then, I hear laughter.

We both freeze and watch as two humans emerge from a path to one side. The man and woman are touching, grabbing each other, and stumbling toward the temple.

Frowning, I close my eyes, feeling for magic. There, just on the edge of my awareness, is Eros' magic. It has little effect on immortals, but it's strong enough to lure humans anywhere close by straight to him.

"Come on," Byron whispers.

We step out of the shadows and a brilliant golden light suddenly illuminates the massive door that leads into the temple.

I look to Byron. "Should we be worried?"

"Just be careful. We get in, get what we need, and get out."

My eyes widen. "We're stealing from him!"

He shushes me, grabbing my arm. "Are you trying to get us killed?"

"No, but apparently you are! I'm not doing this."

His eyes narrow. "You're not doing anything except staying where I can see you while I get what I came here for."

"Fuck," I mutter. "You're insane."

"Just keep up." He holds the cuffs up. "Or these go right back on."

I don't want to do this, but I obey. He might think it's because he has some control over me, but he doesn't.

The thing is, Eros is completely insane, and he has been known to impose awful punishments. If he finds a gargoyle in his temple, he's going to be suspicious. I have a feeling that I can help the situation if needed. I am a decently attractive woman, after all, and Eros is the god of lust. I'm sure he'd love to find one of my kind in his temple, as long as he thought I was there to feed his powers. For some kind of hot sex.

I stay with this stubborn, asshole gargoyle, not because I have to, but because I don't want him getting killed. Even though he's a jerk.

We creep up the steps. The instant our feet touches the first step, the temple transforms. Instead of looking like ancient stone with green moss growing slowly up the abandoned structure, it looks the way it did when it was first built. With polished stone, and a beauty that swells from it.

When we move inside the entrance, we both pause. White stone pillars are in a circle on the outside of the massive room. In the center, a pool of crystal blue water bubbles. Along the outside of the pool? Humans fuck on the dozen or so beds that form a perfect circle.

My jaw drops.

I shouldn't be so surprised. Eros is the god of lust after all, but I didn't expect this for a second. A few humans having sex on the floor? Yes. But a dozen of them on white, fluffy beds with clear curtains around them? Not so much.

It's probably a glamour. All this beauty and elegance stinks of a glamour, but it's a very convincing one.

"There!" Byron whispers.

I follow his gaze. Across the room, in a little alcove with a small light beaming down on it is an ugly little statue. The man-thing has a twisted face, large breasts, and a cock that's longer than the little statue itself.

"That's what we're risking our lives for?" I hiss under my breath.

He ignores me and takes a step forward.

I catch his arm. Eros' people emerge from the shadows of the little rooms tucked in the darkness beyond the pillars. They're tiny creatures, painted in gold, with little loin cloths covering their junk. They carry stone mugs with blue liquid that they pass them out to the people. The humans stop their activities long enough to drain the drinks, then the little creatures take the empty cups back.

"Drugs?" Byron whispers.

"I bet they have a drop of ambrosia in them."

A drop would do nothing to an immortal, but a human? It was like a horny pill, keeping them aroused all night long.

"Come on," he murmurs, then leads me carefully

around the outside of the room, trying to keep us in the shadows.

Shit. I guess we better just hope no one spots us. Great plan… really great.

To my shock, we reach the statue without being spotted, and Byron hands the figure to me. I stare at it in confusion. He points at my dress.

Is he serious? Oh right, his outfit's already bursting off. He has zero chance of concealing it there.

Glaring at him, I grab it and stuff it under my dress, cradling it near my belly like a baby.

Then, we turn and start back. Which is exactly when the shit hits the fan.

One of the little creatures is suddenly in front of us, staring in excitement. He takes Byron's arm and pulls him toward the center of the room. I try to take a step back, but two more of the creatures are behind me, pushing me forward.

It's hard to breathe. Do they know what we are? Do they know why we're here?

And are we lucky enough to be here without Eros?

They take us to one of the beds. The only empty one.

For a second we both blink stupidly, and then Byron spins toward me, grabs me, and shoves me down on the bed.

I give a shriek of surprise, and then he's on top of me, careful of the statue.

There's no time to react, no time to think, when Byron's lips suddenly touch mine. For a minute, they're crushing, frantic, and then our kiss changes. His mouth gentles, and it's like the air in the room changes too. I hold myself still, and slowly feel myself relax. His lips are nice. Warm. Shockingly gentle.

I sigh and lift one of my hands to tangle into the back

of his hair, drawing him closer.

He pulls back from the kiss. His face is inches from mine. And for a second I'm lost in his intense gaze. His hazel eyes, a beautiful scattering of gold across a greenish-blue, seem to draw me in.

For the first time, I'm tempted to touch his face. To run my fingers along his scruff of a beard. I want to know if it feels as rough as it looks. And I want to know what his expressive eyes will do if I touch him.

I feel his hand move up my outer thigh. I can't breathe for a painful second as his fingertips graze the skin of my hip, and then, I nearly jerk in surprise as he grabs the figure against my stomach.

Regret makes my chest ache. That's what this is all about. The figure. Putting a show on for Eros' people, so they don't know why we're here. The look I thought I saw in his eyes… the way I thought the kiss changed… it was all a load of shit.

He moves the statue so it's lying to the side of us, still in my skirts. Then, he rises above me and undoes his shirt.

I hate how my gaze clings to the hard, fine lines of his chest and stomach. And when he strips off the shirt and puts it beside us, all I can see are the muscles of his arms. Big, strong.

If he wasn't Byron, if this wasn't all an act, I'd reach up, curl my hands around his arms, and touch the tempting muscles like I owned them, like he was mine.

He reaches for the statue again, and hides it in his shirt beside us.

I see the relief on his face when he's done, and he settles over me a little less tensely. His gaze focuses back on me, and for the life of me I don't know what he's thinking. Probably something about me being a monster again.

Instead, he places his arms on both sides of my head,

capturing me beneath him in a way that makes every muscle in my body heat up.

"What now?" I whisper.

"Fuck if I know," he says, but his gaze is on my lips.

It takes a second to remember to breathe. "I guess just stay like this until they're not looking."

"Yeah." He shifts again, and I'm pleasantly aware of his erection yet again.

Closing my eyes, I picture it. Gods, no wonder this man was so cocky. He's huge. Perfect. Long and thick and unlike anything I've seen before. He's got the kind of dick that a woman dreams about riding to ecstasy.

Damn him. I wish he had a tiny nub. I could stop fantasizing about some shriveled up, crooked mess.

"Why don't you have snakes?"

My eyes fly open. He's still staring. "Snakes?"

"In your hair?"

I laugh. "That's just a myth. Like gargoyles being monstrous."

To my surprise, his lips curl into a studly smile. "Are you saying I'm handsome?"

I raise a brow. "You know damn well you're good looking. I'm sure the gargoyle ladies are all over you."

His smile fades. "Not so much."

"So you're not constantly banging?"

He looks even more miserable. "No, it's been a long time since I…"

"Banged?" I smile, feeling a bit better. "Is that why your control is so shitty?"

He makes a sound, almost like a laugh, and then he stiffens. "Not all of us are in relationships."

Staring down at his chest, I bring my hands up from my sides, placing them between us. "I didn't exactly say I was in a relationship."

"Your boyfriend—"

"My ex."

He looks smug again. "So that's why you were considering *banging* the water nymph?"

I smack his chest. "What is with you and this nymph?"

"I don't know." And his voice takes on a strange tone. "I guess I thought after you'd spent the day riding my dick, I wouldn't immediately find you naked with a nymph."

"You're jealous!"

His gaze narrows. "I'm not!"

"You so are!" I laugh. "Oh my goodness, you're jealous of a nymph!"

"I'm not!" he growls.

But I can't hold back my laughter. "Oh come on, did you really think I was going to just start having sex with a stranger? He just interrupted…"

I clamp my mouth shut.

But it's too late. He grins. "Interrupted what?"

I can see him searching his memories. And I know the second he remembers, because his expression grows triumphant. "You were getting yourself off!"

My damn cheeks grow hot. "Whatever. I'm a big girl. I can do what I want."

He settles himself more deeply between my thighs, and my entire core hums at his erection pressing between my legs. "So, maybe I'm not only one who enjoyed our flight."

I find myself stroking his chest. "I think Eros' magic might be affecting us a bit, because I don't think I remember you ever being this talkative. Or charming."

"I'm charming?" he grins. "I don't think I've ever been called that before."

A strange chattering comes near our heads. We look to find two of Eros' people holding out cups. We take them, chug the drinks, and give them back.

Medusa's Destiny

I freeze, licking my lips. That tasted familiar.

"Was that straight ambrosia?" Byron asks, a strange note to his voice.

My thoughts grow fuzzy, and I let out a little breath. "That doesn't make sense. A cup of ambrosia would kill a human."

The world grows brighter. Turning my head to the side, I see Eros standing in the shadows. The god wears a golden robe, like some kind of playboy. It's tied loosely, revealing his furry chest and aroused dick. And, he's watching us, a twinkle in his eyes that I don't like.

Byron groans above me, and I turn back to him.

His eyes are squeezed shut. His jaw locks, and I swear he's fighting something.

"Byron?"

His eyes snap open, and I'm overwhelmed by the raw desire in his gaze. "Fuck it."

I don't have time to react. His lips descend on mine, and I'm lost. His lips taste like heaven, a smoky sweetness that makes me burn from the inside out.

I grab his hair and pull him closer. And this time, he doesn't jerk away. His kiss deepens. His hands move to my hips, and he pulls me harder against his erection.

All thoughts are gone. Just a need to have this man inside me.

I wrap my legs around his back, and he groans above me, breaking our kiss.

His hands slide beneath my dress, and in seconds, he's lifting it off of me and tossing it next to us. His expression is desperate as he leans down, his mouth closing around one of my nipples. I moan, holding him closer as feverishly licks and sucks, while his hands roam over my breasts.

This man is something else. Because it's like he's starved for my breasts. He licks, sucks, and nibbles on them. Every time I think he's finished, he presses his face in the valley of my breasts, and breathes as if he's trying to control himself, his thumb rolling my nipples, then, a second later, he returns to them. I've never been lavished like this before. And I love every second of it.

But he's not the only one who gets to have fun.

I tug his head back, then run my hands down his chest to his pants. He watches my every move, his eyes dark and full of need as I slide the zipper down on his shorts.

I swear to the gods that when I pull his long shaft free our bodies shudder together. Stroking him up and down, I hold him like I own every inch of it. I drink in the look on his face. The one that says he's overwhelmed with need.

My hands curl more tightly around him, and my speed increases as I pump him. His long shaft feels as hard as metal beneath my touch, and my mind spins with the image of riding this beautiful cock.

He shudders again above me, swears, and pushes my hand away.

Shedding his shorts, I think he's going to plunge into me. I *want* him to plunge into me.

Instead, his head drops between my thighs and I gasp as his lips press into my folds. It's unreal. A dream. A fantasy I'm going to wake up from, dripping wet.

He's so good. Oh so good. His touch gentle, coaxing my arousal higher and higher. He brushes his lips inside of me, electrifying me. And when he starts to lick, I cry out his name, feeling myself about to lose control.

"Byron," I pant. "I need you."

He raises his mouth, and I'm amazed by how he looks at me.

Moving up my body, he lays on top of me again. Grabbing my wrists, he moves them so they're above my head, then presses them to the bed.

"Want me to fuck you?"

I nod.

"I need you to say it," he growls.

"Fuck me."

He leans forward and bites my ear. Then, hot breath panting against me, he whispers. "You keep your eyes open. I want you to know it's me inside of you. Me fucking you."

Goose bumps move across my skin, but all I can do is nod.

Putting both my wrists into one of his hands, he reaches down with his free one and grabs my hip. My legs lift and curl around his back once more. Immediately, I gasp. His tip is at my entrance. He dips himself lower, right into my wet folds.

I can't breathe. It feels incredible.

His tip shifts, sliding in my wetness, but not entering me. I move my hips, brushing myself harder against him. His breathing increases, and then he's easing into me.

My body quivers. He's massive. Barely squeezing into my tight channel. If I wasn't so wet, so ready, there's no way I could take this big gargoyle.

But I am ready. And the size of him, along with my slickness, creates the most delicious friction.

If he wasn't holding down my wrists, my entire body would be lifting off this bed. But instead, he keeps me in place as he slides deeper and deeper.

When he gets to his hilt, he kisses my ear "Your pussy is the tightest fucking thing I've ever felt, and I'm going to make it mine."

I nod, and he kisses down my throat.

When he pulls back out, my eyes fly open and lock with his. And then, he's plunging back in.

I have no words. No thoughts. Nothing.

This feeling is unreal. It's bringing me to life. Awakening within me things that I thought were dead.

When he moves his hips, thrusting in and out of me, I'm lost. I cling to him, letting this big gargoyle take me closer to the edge with each movement. I strain against the hand that pins me down, but there's no escape. I'm his. His to do with what he wishes.

And what he wants… it's exactly what I want.

In and out. In and out. A perfect moment I never want to end.

But the end is near, bright and real. Each second I'm brought closer and closer until at last, I cry out, and tumble over the edge. I'm nothing but nerves. But pleasure.

This feeling… it's like a beautiful death. Or maybe a rebirth.

The woman I was is gone, replaced by this bright light. A being of just feelings.

He shudders above me, and I feel him explode inside of me. His cum is warm and delicious. He continues to move inside of me, his sticky sweetness coating us both.

After several long seconds, he collapses on top of me.

We lay that way for a long time, and then he slowly lifts his head up and looks at me. He doesn't say a word, but he doesn't need to. He felt it too. Whatever this is. It's powerful.

Instead, of speaking, he reaches down and starts to stroke my clit.

"Byron!" I gasp.

"Now, you're going to turn around, and I'm going to fuck you all over again."

My body quivers in anticipation.

This is going to be a long night. And I don't mind it one bit.

Chapter Ten

FORREST

I'm crouching in the shadows of the jungle, with Harold breathing down my neck. "Where the hell is he?"

"I don't know," Harold whispers, looking to the bright temple. "But he should be out by now."

This isn't good. Byron is a soldier. And he's damned good at his job. If he hasn't come out yet, it's because something went wrong.

Two people stumble through a path in the woods, laughing drunkenly. They head into the temple, and disappear.

I sigh, standing up. "I think we need to go in."

"How?" Harold asks. "If Eros catches us, he'll mount us to the top of his temple for eternity. If we're lucky."

I look at my brother. "We just try to blend in."

His brows disappear into his blond hair. "I'm not pretending to want to have sex with you."

I laugh. "Fuck, that's gross. No, we just act like his magic is calling us. We'll figure out what to do next once we get inside."

Harold runs his hand through his hair. "I guess I don't have a better plan."

"Darn right. Let's go."

We try to act like two people drunk on the lustful magic that draws the humans to this place, but Harold does an awful job. Me? I'm not so bad.

When we are almost in the room, we see the two people who came in ahead of us. A tiny creature taps their shoulders and hands them drinks. The two chug them, and then go right back to making out.

I wait until Eros' little creatures leave, then start forward through the entryway and into the massive room. We stand in the shadows for a moment, staring around the room. There are a lot of humans having sex on beds around the room, and even a few fucking in the little bubbling tub in the center of the room.

But where's Byron?

And then... I see him. And I can't stop seeing him.

A woman is on top of him. No, not a woman. A goddess. I know her immediately as Medusa, not just because of her dark glasses, but because of her description.

Her hands are in her dark hair as she rides my brother. Her eyes are closed, and her head is thrown back. She's got the kind of face that men dream of, but my gaze slides past it to her breasts. They're beautiful. Just big enough to fit in my hands. And even though she's a small girl, I don't think I'd need more than her beautiful pink-tipped breasts.

I imagine myself sliding between them. *I bet they'd wrap my cock just perfectly.*

And then, I look further down. Over her smooth stomach to her pussy. My brother is inside her. She's bare, open, and I can see how wet she is from here.

Gods damn it, I'm going to lose it. I've never wanted a woman like this before.

But I'm celibate. Like my brother! Well, like my brother *was*!

And yet, if she came to me and wrapped those legs around me… I wouldn't turn her away.

One of the little creatures presses a mug into my hands. I drink it without thought, aware that's what a human would do in this situation, and barely feel it as they take it back from me.

Harold gives his empty drink back to the creature and comes to stand next to me. "What is he doing?"

"*Her*, apparently."

"But Byron isn't like that. He's focused. Dedicated." He grabs his head. "Shit, is your head spinning?"

My head isn't spinning, but my vision is blurring. I move to the woman as if compelled by a force greater than myself. I sense Harold moving beside me, and suddenly, we're both standing in front of her.

Byron's gaze swings to us. "What are you waiting for?"

Her head turns to us. "Harold… and you're…?" her question is broken off by a moan.

"Forrest," I mumble, curling my hands to stop from touching her.

Her lips quirk. "Well, I think you boys are overdressed."

I freeze. *Did I hear her right?* "You want us inside of you?"

She smiles, presses her hands onto Byron's shoulders and rides him harder. "Better hurry "

I swear to the gods I've never gotten my clothes off that fast. But in seconds, I'm naked. And so is Harold.

The bastard doesn't hesitate for a second. He climbs on the bed behind her and positions himself at her ass. At first I think he's going to plunge right in, but instead he runs his hand down her back while he reaches for her ass. His thumb presses inside of her, and she groans and bucks against him.

I'm so fucking turned on I think I might lose my mind. But then, she lifts her head, grabs my dick, and pulls me closer. When her tongue licks my tip, a string of curses explode from my lips. This woman isn't a goddess. She's a damned siren, luring me to my doom.

Unlike those freaking sirens who had to imprison me to keep me from leaving.

And yet, as she begins to lick my balls I don't give a damn. I dig my hands into the back of her hair and pull her closer. When she takes my shaft deep into her throat, I growl and thrust all the way in.

She chokes around my shaft as Harold thrusts into her from behind. For a second I think about pulling back, and then she starts to hum. I'm in fucking heaven. Or maybe hell.

I'm thrusting, and she's taking every damn inch of me. And my dick is shaking with a need to explode. In that second I'm glad I masturbated just a few hours earlier, or else things would be over long before they started.

And yet, she's so freaking good. Her hot mouth seals around me like something made for draining a man's seed.

I grab her hair and force her to take me deeper, feeling my head spinning as I get closer and closer to the edge. Watching my brothers inside of her doesn't help my control. They thrust in and out, taking her like madmen as she moves against them.

It's strangely erotic. Feeling her sucking me, while I watch them fuck her. When she scrapes her teeth gently along my shaft, I fucking explode, filling her with my cum.

This god damn siren doesn't mind one bit. She sucks me clean as she orgasms with the two dicks inside of her, then, finally, lets me pop out of her mouth.

Collapsing between my two satisfied brothers, she gazes up at me.

"Want to try it in the water next?"

I think the three of us more than made up for our twenty years of celibacy. We took turns fucking her. We fucked her at the same time. Hell, we fucked her upside down.

And then, we climbed into bed around her, holding her as if she was our whole world.

"I think I love you," Harold whispered, kissing her neck.

She laughed softly. "All right, big boy. All right."

I don't know what I thought would happen next, but hours later I opened my eyes. My head no longer swam. The temple no longer blazed with a golden light. Instead, we were lying on a massive, flat stone. Not a soft bed. Sleeping humans were lying on the same stone beds. All the beauty and magic of the night was gone. All that remained was the sun's early morning light just barely illuminating the temple.

Rubbing my head, I untangled myself from the pile of naked limbs and stare at our bed. Medusa was a beauty between us. Her glasses askew. Her hair tangled around her like a lover. She was the most incredible creature I'd ever come into contact with.

And yet, last night some ambrosia made us throw away twenty years of celibacy.

The thought makes me feel as if I've swallowed a stone. We had a plan for the future. We'd finally get a chance at impregnating one of the female gargoyles. Of having a child.

Shit. What did we do?

It was strange. I feel sick at the idea that our plans are ruined. But did I regret my night with the woman?

I didn't know.

And that bothers me.

But how will Byron react? He was going to be angry. Having a woman and a child had been his obsession for years.

Damn it, well, I guess we have to handle this, either way.

"Byron? Harold?" I whisper, shaking the two gargoyles. They winced and wrap themselves more securely around the beautiful woman.

Sorry guys, we have to get back to reality.

Shaking them again, I watch as Byron's eyes slide open. Without hesitation, he shoots awake, panic in his eyes. Looking down at Medusa, his eyes widen.

He shoves away from her, waking both her and Harold.

"What's wrong?" she mumbles, sleepily.

"We fucked you, that's what's wrong!" he shouts.

Some of the humans start to stir.

They're going to have a lot of questions. Questions we don't want to answer.

"We need to get out of here," I say, feeling panicked.

Medusa scrambles off the bed, grabbing her dress and putting it on in a rush. Then, she moves away from us to hover near the entrance to the temple, her arms wrapped around her body in a way that's strangely vulnerable. I have the sudden urge to go to her and pull her into a hug.

Yes, we were all facing the fact that we'd lost our future.

But she'd been drugged by freakin' Eros too. Had she even wanted to sleep with her kidnappers? The question makes me feel sick.

I rise, dressing and stuffing my feet into my shoes. Adjusting my t-shirt, I move to her. "Medusa?"

Her shoulders stiffen, and she doesn't look back at me. "Yup?"

The bravo in her voice seems at such odds with her

hunched shoulders and tightly clenched arms that I don't know quite what to expect.

"Are you okay?"

She turns, and I know she's staring at me, even though I can't quite see her eyes through her sunglasses. "Of course, why wouldn't I be?"

I move a little closer, watching the sun rising about the jungle top. "Maybe because of all the sex and drugs?" I try to keep my voice light and teasing, hoping to put her more at ease.

"You're three hot gargoyles. I'm the monster. If anyone's regretting last night, I'm thinking it's the three of you."

I'm shocked by how cruel her words are to herself. "You're a beautiful woman who got drugged into sleeping with three men she barely knows. You have a right to be upset."

Her shoulders shake a little, and I curse myself for being so blunt. "Whatever, it's fine."

"It's not," I tell her, and I'm surprised by the anger in my voice. I'm not an angry guy. I'm a guy who likes to joke and laugh. "If I ever see that fucking Eros, I'm going to punch him in the face just for you."

To my surprise, she laughs. "I think that might be the nicest thing anyone has ever said to me."

"Then you must be surrounded by a lot of assholes," I blurt out.

She finally releases her arms and turns to look at me. She's so damn beautiful in the morning light. "What, have you been stalking me?"

I feel my face wrinkle in confusion.

She leans closer. "Because the only men I know are assholes."

My smile comes easily. "That can't be true."

We both jump a little as Byron pushes between us, muttering curses.

She looks at me again and raises a brow.

For some reason, I start to laugh. In seconds, she's laughing too.

The pressure on my chest lessens. I didn't like the thought of her regretting her night with us, with her hating me.

Harold comes slowly behind us. "We need to get out of here."

I stiffen. "But the artifact—"

"We got it."

He can't seem to look up. His blond hair is an absolute mess, and he looks like he wishes he could force his massive frame to be less noticeable.

And I know why. Because suddenly all the beauty of this morning is gone.

We've gotten what we need here. We have more to do, but each step brings us closer to home.

Which means Medusa doesn't have much longer to live.

Chapter Eleven

MEDUSA

*B*yron won't touch me. He won't go anywhere near me, and his rejection hurts on a level that's absolutely bat-shit stupid. I've lived a thousand lives. I've had a million moments of heartache. And some moments that were really, really bad.

I shouldn't care that he's rejecting me now, that he regrets our night together.

But it still hurts.

When it's time for us to go, Byron reshackles my wrists, and I'm shocked that I wasn't thinking clearly. I should have tried to make a break for it. I shouldn't have allowed him anywhere near me with these things.

But they've fucked all my logic out of me.

"Where are you taking me now?"

"I'm not taking you anywhere!" He snarls at me, clenching that fucking ugly artifact more tightly.

I open my mouth to ask him what the plan is then, when he shoves me toward Harold. "You take her!"

His words are more a blow to me than his touch. *Was being with me really that bad?*

I don't care! I tell myself. If he thinks I want to be anywhere near his dumb ass, then he's as stupid as he looks.

Harold, on the other hand, is being strangely shy. When I lift my arms and put them around his neck, he avoids my gaze and places his hands lightly on my waist.

"Are you ready?" he asks, too softly.

"It's not like I have a choice," I tell him.

His brilliant blue eyes lift to meet mine, and I'm lost. For his massive size, this Harold really is a gentle giant. The way he looks at me, as if I'm some pretty girl he has a crush on, warms my bitter heart.

"I'll go slowly," he tells me.

A second later, his flesh turns to hard stone, and his wings spread out behind his massive frame. I take a deep breath and jump to wrap my legs around his waist.

I hear his teeth grit together, and then, he leaps into the air. As his wings flap harder and faster, we rise higher above the jungle. I look at the greenery beneath us with a strange mixture of feelings. My night with the three gargoyles was easily the best one of my life. But knowing that, at the very least, Byron regrets it, makes me feel terrible.

Even more like an ugly freak.

I press my face against Harold's chest, and as we fly, I'm ashamed to say silent tears run down my cheeks, whipping away in the wind. I don't know why this should be any different. I've felt undesirable and despised my entire life. So I'm really crying over nothing.

Just the same old crap.

When hours and hours later, we land gently, I'm almost sure I was asleep. But when Harold untangles himself from my grip and sets me down in the grass, I realize we're in an orchard. Immediately, the only thing I can smell is oranges. Inhaling deeply, I don't even care how stupid I look. I lie back on the grass and stare up at the clouds, feeling… not relaxed, but something I can't quite place.

Harold comes back a second later, blocking my vision of the clouds. "Orange?" he asks, holding it out to me.

I smile at the sweet sincerity in his voice and struggle to a sitting position, using my cuffed hands.

To my surprise, he peels my orange for me before handing it to me, and then sits down next to me, so close our thighs touch. We eat in silence for a while, comfortably. Enjoying a quiet moment before I have to go and ruin it, of course.

"Where are the other two?"

He slows in his eating. "I let them get a little ahead of us, so we could stop without them bugging us."

Ah, well that's kind of nice.

I smile. "Thanks."

"I just…" he seems to struggle with the right words. "I felt you crying."

My smile vanishes and suddenly I'm not hungry anymore. "Sorry."

"You're apologizing for being upset?" He laughs, and it's a kind laugh. One that rings through me like a beautiful bell. "Everyone cries sometimes. I just wanted to know why."

I shrug. Usually I lie about this kind of shit. But for some reason, I don't really feel like lying today.

"Byron seemed pretty upset about last night."

Harold stares at me, waiting. And for some reason, there's no pressure behind his silence, just a willingness to let me talk.

I chuck the remainder of my orange on the ground and glare at where it falls. "This isn't the first time someone's regretted being with one of my kind. It's stupid that it bugs me."

His brows draw into a line on his forehead. "This isn't about you."

He looks as if he's debating with himself.

Poor thing can't even bring himself to be mean to someone he considers a monster.

"It's okay. I know what I am. I know how others see me."

He shakes his head. "No, I meant it when I said it isn't about you." He pauses for a long minute. "The thing is, our people are dying out. And the priority of our Elites has become solely focused upon building our numbers."

"Why are there so few of you?"

My mind ran through every possibility, before Harold answered my question.

"Not many humans carved female gargoyles, and female births are uncommon. And—"

"So," I interrupt, not able to keep my mouth from running, "gargoyles are either created or born, and either way there aren't a lot of females, so your kind are dying out."

He nods. "And because of that, there are very specific requirements for any males who will be given a chance to impregnate one of the few gargoyle females. One of which is for us to remain celibate…which we've successfully managed to do for the last twenty years. But, because of our night with you, we're no longer allowed to have a mate or child."

"What?" I can't hide my shock. "That's stupid. One night with me shouldn't cost you everything. I mean, we were drugged."

He shrugs. "It's simply our way."

"No," I tell him. "You three aren't going to say a word

about what happened between us, and you're not going to lose everything."

He stares at me as if I'm crazy. "We can't lie."

"Why the hell not?"

"Because—"

"Eros drugged us. You guys wouldn't have slept with me otherwise."

It takes him a long time to answer. "It's okay. I just wanted you to know that Byron isn't mad at you. He just gets mean when he wants to push someone away. He tried that with me, years ago." He smiles as he says the last part.

Harold rises and gathers more oranges, ending our serious conversation. He peels two more oranges while I watch him, fascinated yet again by how such a big man can be so gentle. With a shy smile, he hands one of them to me and sits back down.

While we eat, we chat about the most normal things. He asks me about life among the humans. We talk about my many jobs, my friends—I even tell him about my ex. Never did he seem to judge me. Instead, he asked questions, seemed interested, and made me feel… special.

At last, he grew quiet. "We have to keep going."

"To…"

He seems to consider my question for a second. "Eventually, to our home."

"Why?"

His shoulders stiffened. "Because, we need your help."

I hate that I know he's lying. I hate that I know there's more going on here than I understand.

That alone should send me running from these gargoyles, searching for a chance at escape.

But instead, I take the hand he offers me, raise my arms to wrap around his huge neck, and snuggle closer as we rise into the sky.

Because I want this feeling to never end. This sense, almost like… almost like I'm loved, or at the least cared for.

And the second I return to reality, this is gone forever.

I'm not naïve. I don't think they're taking me somewhere to shower me with hot sex and candies. The thing is, I'm Medusa. I've lived for a very long time. If these gargoyles wish me harm, they aren't the first ones.

So maybe—just maybe—going with them is worth the risk.

Chapter Twelve

BYRON

I can't believe I lost control like that. I can't believe I lost *all* control. And the worst part of it all? It wasn't just the drugs. Yeah, they didn't help matters, but I've been on the edge since I met this woman. It's like my brain packed its bags and took a vacation and my dick is screaming, "Fuck her! Fuck her so hard she never remembers another cock but yours!"

And shit, I think my dick is an asshole, because I don't think Medusa suddenly only wants me. But my cock? It only wants her. It wants to sink right back into her. It wants to plunge right back into her mouth. It wants to see if we can make her scream out in pleasure as I plunge into her tight ass.

My head keeps reminding me that we have a female gargoyle, Ashunda, who has made it clear we're the next males on her list. In a couple months she'll have her baby, and then she's going to be in our bed night after night until she gives *us* a baby. It's everything I've ever wanted.

And yet… my stupid cock doesn't even perk up at the thought of beautiful Ashunda.

No, but it hardens into a pole every time my thoughts turn to Medusa.

I'm so fucked. So completely fucked.

Then there's the other thing, if we tell the Elites about our… misstep, everything is ruined anyway. Even if Ashunda is disappointed, we won't be eligible mates anymore. She'll have to go onto her next choice.

I can't wait another twenty years for a chance at a mate and baby. I just can't!

The wind stirs beside me. I see Forrest has finally caught up to me.

He raises a brow. "Did you decide what to do?"

"About what?" I snarl at him.

"Do we tell the Elites about what happened?"

I exhale slowly. "No. We were drugged. It didn't mean anything. We keep our mouths shut."

"And do we tell Marcus?"

Fuck. We've never kept a secret between us before. But, he'll tell. "No."

Forrest whistles softly. "You must really want Ashunda."

"Don't you?" I bite back at him.

He's quiet for a long minute. "I don't know. I mean, sure, if she's our only choice. She's self-absorbed and not very bright, but beggars can't be choosers."

I glare straight ahead. "Do you have a point?"

Again he pauses, but the mischievous look vanishes from his face. "I like Medusa. There's just something about her…"

"Her monstrous powers to manipulate men maybe?"

He laughs, unkindly. "How the hell did she manipulate us? She was drugged too, according to *you*."

"But she got what she wanted. She's under our skin. Making us question what we're doing."

Forrest shakes his head. "You're ridiculous."

"Am I? Because you're talking like you're ready to throw away a perfectly good female gargoyle, for what? A monster? A woman there's no future with? You and I both know that the second we take her home, she's done. So whatever the hell you're thinking about, stop it."

"For a guy who spent the night fucking a beautiful woman, you're in a shitty mood."

I flap my wings harder and separate myself from him. We're going to be seeing Marcus soon. As much as I hate it, we need to get on the same page first. If he knows what happened, he'll tell. And we can't lose everything because of one night.

My thoughts turn to Marcus. I picture his dark hair and his harsh face. People say I'm an asshole… until they meet Marcus.

And then, I imagine him and Medusa.

Against my will, my fists clench. My heart's racing. Once we reach our next destination, Marcus will be there. And I can't let anything he does to our prisoner get to me. So why does just the thought of it turn my stomach?

We stop flying just before nightfall, near a barn on a hillside that looks like it has been empty for a long time. Forrest goes to a nearby city for food, and I wait and watch the sky until Harold and Medusa arrive.

I don't look at her. I can't look at her, but I see Harold. He's already under her spell.

The little woman strides past me and into the barn without a word. Every muscle in my body feels tense. If this was another place and time, if we weren't monster hunters and her a monster, I'd ease this fight between us with a good fucking.

But instead I cross my arms over my chest and glare at Harold. "Took you long enough."

He shrugs. "We stopped."

"For what?"

"A snack. A rest. She's not accustomed to flying all day."

I glare. "And since when do we try to make our prisoners as comfortable as possible?"

He sighs, loudly. "She's not a man-eating minotaur. She's not a sea monster, crushing boats. She's just… a woman."

"That's what she fucking wants you to think!" I shout. "Do you think if she could turn us to stone, she wouldn't have done it by now? You've read the history books! She's left a wake of stone people behind her. She's a killer, hidden in a shapely body, I'll give you that. But she's a killer all the same, so pull your head out of your ass and remember it!"

To my shock, he advances on me. "You keep telling yourself that and maybe you'll start to think it's true! But I want you to think for one second what would have happened if she hadn't been okay with our night together. I want you to think about what it was like for her to wake up this morning and know she was drugged into fucking the three of us."

I swear, everything inside of me turns to ice. "Does… does she regret what happened?"

He stares at me. "She's a monster, right, Byron? So does it really matter to you?"

Harold follows her into the barn, knocking my shoulder roughly as he passes. I don't react. I'm rooted in place.

We are gargoyles. We protect humans. We protect

people. We have never hurt a woman in all our long lives. The thought of it—sickens me.

I'm striding into the barn before I can think about what I'm doing. Harold is sitting on a barrel of hay next to her. They both stop talking at my approach. I stand in front of her, not knowing what I'm going to say before I say it.

"Do you feel like you were… taken advantage of last night?"

I can't see her gaze through her sunglasses in the shadows. "No, relax. I know what that feels like, and last night wasn't like that. We were all drugged. But I don't think any of us did something we didn't want to. Am I right?"

It's like I can finally breathe. "You're right."

But someone has hurt her like that? A protectiveness roars awake inside of me.

I grasp her arm gently and pull her into a standing position. I can sense her confusion. I don't think, I just pull her against me and wrap her in a hug.

She's stiff in my arms, but I stroke her hair anyway. Not realizing I was shaking until that moment.

"I'm fine," she says, softly against my chest.

Pull it together, Byron. I slowly pull back from her. And then, we're just staring at each other.

"Food's here!" Forrest shouts, walking into the barn with several bags.

The spell broken, we move away from each other. Everyone sits on the barrels of hay eating Chinese food. Forrest makes jokes. Medusa laughs, and Harold watches it all, looking happier than I've ever seen him before.

And I eat my food that tastes like regret. Knowing that we're using this woman. Knowing that we have one more dangerous task for her before we deliver her to her death.

What the fuck are we supposed to do when I can't even stand the idea of her hurting?

We are so screwed.

Chapter Thirteen

FORREST

We talked before we left the barn and agreed that neither Marcus nor the Elites would know about our night together. For some reason, it doesn't ease my tension. The idea of being free from our commitment to our people somehow felt right. I didn't want to use Medusa as an excuse, but I liked that it made everything feel easy.

Today, I get to fly with her to our next destination in Greece. I'm not looking forward to getting there, or seeing Marcus, not when I have her riding me in the air.

Twice I almost asked her if I could drop my pants and just start fucking her in mid-air. I think she'd enjoy it, and I know my swollen dick would too. But I think we got a free pass on our drugged night together. If we did it again, we'd have to accept that we broke the rules and deserved the consequences. Even though I wouldn't mind it one bit.

Her hand strokes the back of my neck. My gaze snaps back to her.

"You looked lost in thought," she says.

My eyes lock onto her mouth. "I was just remembering what it was like when you sucked my cock."

Her cheeks turn red. "And?"

"It was fucking amazing."

She shrugs. "Well, I've had lifetimes to learn just how to give it to a man the way he likes."

My dick swells uncomfortably in my pants. "I hope you didn't have too much practice, because I'd like to think mine is the first you've had."

She rubs against me, and I groan. "Is that right?"

I'm losing my god-damn mind. "Gargoyles are known for being a bit... possessive."

"Really?" And her brows rise above her glasses.

"Uh-huh." I'm breathing hard. "Some even call us jealous creatures with insatiable appetites for pussy."

She lets one of her hands drop from around my neck and slide down my chest. I stop breathing, watching as her small hand slips lower and lower until she's gripping me through my pants. "I'd say based on this, there's probably some truth to the rumors."

I thrust into her hand, and she grips me tighter. "You're driving me fucking crazy."

Very slowly, she starts to stroke my dick. "Are there any rules about someone getting you off?"

I'm in heaven... or maybe hell, I'm not sure which. "Not a one."

The next few minutes are spent with me trying to keep flying, trying not to send us spinning into the god damn ocean while she strokes me through my pants. When I finally come, my entire mind goes blank for a second, and then my vision becomes strangely bright.

"You really know what you're doing with a cock," I tell her, panting.

She leans up and bites my ear, her breath warm against my skin. "My turn."

When she takes my hand and slips it between us, I swear I've become her servant. Her worshipper. She is now my god damn goddess, and I'll fall on my knees in front of her any time she wants.

I touch her wet folds, and she moans into my ear.

Listening to her harsh breathing as I stroke her slowly, teasing her wetness, is enough to make me hard again. When she starts to grind against me, panting my name, I'm about to say fuck everything and tear my pants off. My fingers plunge into her, and then she begins to rock against them.

Her hands grip my shoulders tightly, and then she orgasms around my fingers. Riding me like a god damn horse. When she finally collapses against me, my fingers still buried inside her, I kiss the top of her head in absolute wonder

The gargoyle side of me is screaming that this woman now belongs to me, which makes no sense. I'm not a virgin. I've fucked a lot of women in my life.

But I've never felt this way before.

I reluctantly pull my fingers out of her hot pussy, smooth her dress down, and fly a little faster, realizing we've fallen far behind. "You're kind of amazing," I tell her.

She looks up, and her sun-kissed face looks flushed "Thanks, you're not bad yourself."

The rest of our flight is spent with me holding her as closely as humanly possible, and trying to make her laugh. I'm careful not to tell her too much about the gargoyle way of life. I'm not completely nuts after all, but I also want to get to know her, and for her to get to know me.

I don't have a clue why.

Maybe it's because I know there's something special about her. I also know our time together is limited.

When we finally reach Greece and set down in a park within the city, something has changed. Medusa seems uneasy.

"Where are we?" she asks.

"Greece."

Her arms wrap around her chest again.

"You okay?" Gargoyles can't help themselves. Our drive is to protect the innocent. And Medusa is screaming of innocence right now.

"I'm fine," she says, but she won't look in my direction. "But what are we doing here?"

Harold and Byron come from one part of the large park. I can sense Harold's unease, but Byron is back to pretending like he's a badass. His face is pulled into a frown, and his hands are clenched.

"Marcus will meet us there." Byron doesn't look at her. "But first we need to find some new clothes and try to blend in a little."

I glance at Medusa. Her little dress is beautiful, but definitely a bit dirty, and she isn't wearing shoes. And the rest of us? We don't look much better.

"Probably a good idea. So, where to, boss?"

Byron looks like he's trying really hard not to roll his eyes as he turns and leads us through the park. I shift, my skin turning tan, and my wings disappearing. Now all of us can be seen by the people we pass by in the park. And it's definitely a good idea that we change our clothes, because we're getting a lot of suspicious looks.

The three of us find whatever will fit us at the first clothing store. Jeans, t-shirts, and some basic jackets make us look a little less like we just spent a few days sleeping in barns and fields. Byron also purchases a leather backpack,

Medusa's Destiny

which he shoves the fertility statue and cuffs into before slinging it onto his back. We take Medusa to a clothing shop next to ours. She selects her clothes a little more carefully and slips into a changing room.

We're lounging around feeling out of place, with a nervous sales lady flittering around us. After living as long as all of us have, we easily slip into the local language, but even without the language-barrier three massive men make the woman nervous. *Or maybe it's the way Byron is glaring.*

I'm pretty sure the tightly-wound gargoyle is about to lose his shit when Medusa comes striding out of the dressing room. "This will work," she said, walking past us to the shoe area.

But the three of us? We can't stop staring. She looks fucking beautiful. The dark jeans she wears hugs her in all the right places, and her white tank-top is partially see-through. She wears a lacy white bra underneath, but the combo is strangely alluring. Because the way she acts… it's like she has no idea how hot she is.

She grabs a pair of socks and has the sales lady bring her a tiny pair of boots that somehow fit her small feet. At last, she stands up. "Ready, boys?"

Harold doesn't say a word. He goes to the cash-register and pays for her stuff, and then we're all hurrying out of the store.

I rush to catch up to her.

"You're looking good."

She smirks. "You're not so bad yourself."

I don't know why, but I take her hand. For a second her hand is stiff, but then she relaxes it and curls it around mine. I know it's stupid, but I like this feeling. Like we're a couple enjoying a day out together in the city.

"This place looks so different than I remember," she says softly.

I'm kind of surprised she didn't visit Greece more. She's Greek after all. Wouldn't she visit her hometown every so often?

"When were you here last?"

She stiffens. "More than two thousand years."

"Geez."

While we walk, she seems to grow more and more uneasy. Her steps grow slower. Every time she looks at an old building, she pauses for a really long time, her expression far away.

At last, Byron turns to glare back at us. "Come on, Marcus is going to be there soon, and we don't want to be late."

"Where are we going?" Medusa asks again, but the attitude has left her voice. She just sounds… worried.

Byron glares as we catch up to him. "No questions."

People glance our way and move around us. I almost tell Byron he's making a scene, but he seems to realize it. Turning, he continues walking.

We move up the hill now, heading for our destination. Medusa moves slower and slower until at last she stops completely. People move around us, but her gaze is panicked.

"Where are we going?" she repeats, and I'm right, she sounds scared.

Byron stops ahead of us and glares back. Before I can answer, he's storming towards us. "What the hell is the problem?"

"We're going to Athena's temple," I finally tell her.

Her hand pulls from mine, and she steps away from us. Her hands move up, gesturing as if to push away from us. "I won't go there."

"Why not?" I ask.

But Byron is quick to respond. "You'll go where we tell you to."

"I won't," she says, taking a step back.

A few people glance our way, moving around us on the sidewalk.

"Medusa," he hisses, almost under his breath.

And then, to our shock, she leaps off the sidewalk and races toward the trees that cover the sides of the hilltop that lead to the temple. It takes all of us a second too long to react, and then we're hurrying after her, careful not to alarm the humans. When we reach the safety of the trees, we bolt after her.

Byron is the first to reach her. He snags her around the waist, and they almost go tumbling to the ground. Suddenly, she's kicking and flailing in his arms.

We reach her. All of us exchange the same, *what the hell is going on?* Look.

"What's wrong?" Harold asks, and he sounds upset.

"I won't go there!" she shouts.

At last, something seems to click with Byron. He sits down, pulling her into his lap. She tries to hit him, but he catches her wrists. Their eyes meet, and to my surprise, Byron doesn't look mad, he looks confused.

"We need to take you there," he says, very slowly.

"Why?" she asks, and the word sounds torn from her throat.

"There's something we need there. And you know men can't enter her temple."

"Tourists go there all the time!" she says, her words desperate.

"You know we aren't visiting the ruins…" he explains quietly.

Most Gods and Goddesses can glamour their temples to

look like the past. But when they want to, they also have places that they consider sacred or important that have more powerful magic. Their worshippers, and other Immortal creatures, can literally step into these places like stepping back in time. Everything is the way it was in the place's glory days.

Often it's this other world that the Gods and Goddesses reside in, sliding from the past to the present like time travelers. And yet, usually it's just the place that's enchanted. Outside of that, it's only the present that rules.

And that's where we must go. To Athena's temple in the past.

There, she has another artifact, one that was stolen from Artemis, the goddess of children and childbirth. If we take it, it can give us extra protection to ensure the pregnancies we do have will result in healthy children.

The problem is that none of us can enter the temple. Only women can, since Athena is a virgin goddess. To walk into her temple as men would draw instant attention from her worshippers.

"We need you to go in and take something," Byron says very slowly. "It's in a hidden room behind her throne. The necklace hangs from a statue of her. It has a red stone. And, it's very important."

"I know the room. I know the necklace, but I won't take it."

"Medusa, this isn't a request. It's an order." Byron speaks the words, but even I don't believe them, because he's busy pulling her shaking frame closer.

"I can't," she says, pressing her face into his chest.

Byron looks at both of us. "Marcus should already be here."

I tense, having almost forgotten. For a minute, all I can picture is Marcus coming upon us and seeing us like this. Marcus is one of the best monster hunters of our kind.

He'll be disgusted by our affection for Medusa. He won't understand why we're here hugging her instead of forcing her to do our bidding.

"We should go," Byron says, surprising all of us.

He rises as if in a hurry, and I realize what's happening. He's made a decision to get us out of here before Marcus sees Medusa. We want to understand why she's so upset, and we won't be able to do that with him here.

We don't go back to the sidewalk. We walk through the trees on the hill, concealed from the humans.

Ahead of us, a man steps out of the shadows. We all freeze.

Marcus takes a step forward. His dark eyes, locking onto each of us in turn until he comes to Medusa.

"Good, you have it." He strides forward, then pauses. "Where are its cuffs?"

"In my bag," Byron says, his words tense.

Marcus moves around him and takes the cuffs out of the backpack. He grasps her hands, too harshly, and clamps them back on.

And Medusa must be very upset, because she doesn't even react. She looks far away, lost somewhere we can't reach her.

"Now," Marcus says. "Does the monster know what it needs to do?"

"Her name's Medusa," I say, and I know I sound defensive.

His emotionless gaze flicks to me, then away. "Does it know what we want it to do?"

I see the muscles in Byron's gaze clench. "She doesn't wish to go into the temple."

Marcus only hesitates a moment. "Since when do we give a fuck what monsters want?"

None of us answer.

The muscles in his jaw tighten. "Put her down."

Very slowly, Byron obeys.

She stands in the middle of us, looking tiny and vulnerable. Her wrists are bound. Her muscles tense. And I'm glued to her, trying to understand the change in her.

"Monster, you will go into the temple and steal what we require," Marcus says, looming over her.

"I won't," she tells him, her voice soft.

He murmurs the spell, and a second later she cries out, sinking to her knees.

Every muscle in my body is tense, ready to attack.

"Marcus…" I know the word sounds threatening, because it is. He sure as fuck better not hurt her again.

Marcus grabs the chain that links her cuffs and hauls her to her feet. "Do you think that hurt? With just a few words, I can have these magic cuffs tighten until they sever your hands. Is that what you want? Shall we see how much pain you can take until you obey me?"

She spits in his face.

He hits her, and before her body crumples to the floor, we're on him.

Byron has him by the throat, pressing him against a tree. And I've got my fist drawn back, ready to beat him to a pulp. Harold has gone to Medusa, kneeling at her side.

No one breathes.

"Someone explain to me what the hell is going on!" Marcus demands. He's still an alpha, even when he's pinned against a tree by his throat.

I'm not sure Byron has even heard him. His entire chest is rising and falling rapidly, and the anger in his gaze terrifies even me.

I don't drop my fist, but I answer. "Medusa isn't the monster everyone says she is. She's… a person. We know we need her, but she's scared of the temple. We're not going to send her without knowing why."

Marcus laughs. "I knew I shouldn't have sent you three without me. You've fallen for her shit so easily, it's shocking." His gaze is cruel as it sweeps over us. "I bet she's got a tight pussy to have you all this wound up."

I punch him. Hard.

It wasn't a conscious decision. It was a reaction, a primal need to protect the woman in my care.

Gritted words I didn't plan leave my lips. "Don't talk about her like that."

His eye already looks swollen as he focuses on me. "You hit me?" he sounds shocked.

"Damn right!" I say, my voice growing louder. "You aren't an asshole. You're just completely wrong. She isn't a monster. She's a woman. Think about that and ask yourself if you're comfortable with what you're saying."

"What about the hundreds of people who she's turned to stone over the years?" his words are quiet now, and I can tell he's evaluating us.

None of us have a good answer.

"No one wants to hear the truth."

I turn. Medusa has struggled into a sitting position. The entire side of her face is swelling. It looks so painful that everything inside of me twists. How the hell could Marcus hit a woman? How could he hit *her*?

"We want to hear the truth," I tell her, and mean it.

Medusa curls her knees into her chest, and her eyes fill with tears. "I *am* a Monster. I *have* killed people."

"There! See, I'm right!" But Marcus doesn't sound satisfied, he's staring at the crying woman.

Harold sits slowly beside her. "That doesn't make sense. When we took you, you made an effort not to turn us into stone. If you're some heartless killing machine, then why did you do that?"

Tears keep tracking down her cheeks. "Do you guys really not know?"

We all exchange a confused look.

She laughs, but the sound is filled with heartache. "You went to kill a monster without even knowing how I became this way."

"We thought you were born this way…" I say, confused.

Her lips twist into a smirk that's so at odds with her tears. "I was mortal. A worshipper of Athena in the very temple you guys are trying to drag me into." She takes a ragged breath. "Until Poseidon saw me and decided he wanted me. So on the floor of Athena's temple he… he… took me against my will."

I've never wanted to kill a god before, but in that moment, I want to kill Poseidon. I'm blinded by a need to kill him. I know the bastard gods have a history of taking what they want, but I've never seen the effects of their actions before until now.

Medusa rubs at the tears on her face. "Athena was so outraged that we defiled her virgin temple that she cursed me. Any man who looked upon me would be turned to stone." She shrugged. "There's more to the sad little story of how a mortal woman turned into an immortal monster, like years spent on an isolated island alone. But I've covered the most important parts."

"I'm so sorry," Harold said. He tries to touch her, but she jerks away.

"It's fine," she says. "It's literally been over two thousand years since I became this fucking monster. It doesn't bother me, okay? I just can't… I can't go into her temple."

Silence stretches between all of us. What are we to do? What can we say?

Of course we can't send Medusa into the place she was raped.

But we've also all realized something at the same time: Medusa isn't a monster. Not on any level.

She's just a woman cursed by the gods. So what do we do now?

Marcus pushes Byron's hand away. "I need to speak to the three of you." He looks at Medusa. "Stay here. If you try to run, you should know you'll never get those cuffs off."

She doesn't even look at him. She just buries her face into her knees.

The four of us slip away into the trees just a short distance away.

Marcus sighs. "All right. We need to talk."

Chapter Fourteen

MARCUS

Well, fuck me. There appears to be one monster in these woods, and for the first time in my life, I'm pretty sure it's me. Not the crying woman I hit.

I mean, she could be lying. She could be a *really* good liar. Most monsters are. But I've killed dozens of monsters in my lifetime, males and females, and I've never fallen for their tears or pleas before. I think I'm usually a really good judge of character, and this Medusa… nothing about her screams that she's a liar.

"Did she really purposely *not* turn you guys to stone?" I ask, crossing my arms over my chest.

Harold nods enthusiastically. "And Byron was threatening to… hurt her." He shoots Byron a look.

The other gargoyle looks like he's going to be sick.

There's more going on here. But I just don't have time to dive into everything this second.

"Fine, until we know what she is or isn't, we'll be a little more gentle." I reluctantly agree.

Forrest shoots me a dirty look. "And no more *hitting* her."

"Or using the cuffs to hurt her," Harold adds.

A second later, Byron says softly. "And we can't make her go into the temple."

I've never seen them like this before. It's like… like…

I look at each of them a little more carefully. "Are you guys in love with her?"

My question is met with silence, which says more than their words ever could.

My head feels light for a second. I'm their alpha. The four us are meant to share a woman. Gargoyles choose their Brotherhood of Stone, knowing how few female gargoyles there are, and how hard it is for us to breed. Not every brotherhood has an alpha, but I'm without a doubt theirs. And yet, I've never felt on the outskirts of our group before.

But right now I do.

They've fallen in love with a woman… a monster we're supposed to use and kill. And I've become their enemy. I'm the voice of reason telling them this is stupid, even if my words don't say that exactly.

I'm going to have to fix this. *After* we've accomplished what we came here to do.

"We still have to get into the temple," I tell them. "How do we expect to do that without her?"

"Force our way in," Byron says with a shrug.

I raise a brow. "So basically unleash a bunch of bloodshed in a goddess's temple? The goddess of *war?* Seems like a bad idea to me."

Byron gives me his stubborn-as-fuck look. "Well, we aren't sending her in there."

"Then tell me another solution that won't end in us all getting cursed or killed."

"I'll do it."

I whirl to see Medusa standing near us. She looks surprisingly small and vulnerable. And the gargoyle in me has an innate need to offer her my protection. But I don't. Not until I know who we're dealing with.

"You're not going in there," Byron says, and there's no room for argument when he speaks.

She draws herself up as tall as her tiny frame can manage. "I decide what I can handle, and I can handle it."

"Medusa," Harold's voice is gentle. "You just had a breakdown at the idea of it."

"I did not!" And there's some fire in her voice. "I just needed time to wrap my mind around it. You guys sprang it on me!"

"That was not just about being surprised," Forrest says. His tone is light, but his body language is screaming that he's upset.

She marches up to us. "So basically, you're all going to get yourself killed fighting in Athena's temple rather than have me deal with a little emotional baggage? You guys aren't being logical."

For some reason, her words hit me as strange. "You're our prisoner. If we all get ourselves killed, isn't that a good thing for you? Why are you volunteering to help us?"

She turns toward me. I wish I could see her eyes beneath the shadows of her sunglasses. But the shades of the tree are too much. "Didn't anyone ever tell you not to look a gift horse in the mouth?"

"I like to know the reasons behind a person's actions," I tell her.

"I'm sure you would, asshole, but you're not going to. So decide what you want to do."

It's strange how much nothing is going the way I planned. And I planned everything, down to the smallest detail. Each of us had a role to play in order to return in time to save our people. It was a risk assuming that a monster would help us inside this temple, but I'd had plans on how to force her to. Mostly they were plans involving torturing her until she obeyed.

But I didn't plan on this place being so upsetting to her. I didn't know that anyone would care about her feelings, and I never thought a monster would volunteer to help us.

Sending her in feels like a liability. In my mind, I ran through each scenario on how we could get the necklace, like sliding chess pieces into place. We had to trust her. It was the only way any of this would work. Even though I didn't like it.

"Alright, we send her in."

All three of the gargoyles speak at once, varying degrees of anger and shock.

I raise a hand. "She can do it. Trust her."

That silences them for a moment, and then Byron says, very slowly, "What if she breaks down? What if she gets caught?"

We'd abandon her to the goddess's wrath.

"We'll cross that bridge if we reach it."

None of them look happy, but Medusa gives a little nod and spins on her heel toward the temple. "Let's get this done."

We follow after her, my gaze sliding between my men and her. This woman, and their relationship, is a puzzle I haven't yet figured out. But I will figure it out.

Mark my words.

And if she's using them, playing us, I'll kill her without hesitation.

Chapter Fifteen

MEDUSA

In my entire fucking life, I've never been the kind of person to back down from something. My reaction to this temple shocked me to my core. I'd known I'd avoided Greece because of the bad memories. I knew I avoided boats, islands, and the ocean because of my years spent in exile.

I didn't know that coming here would cause the memories to rush at me like that, pushing me into a full-blown panic attack.

And man am I embarrassed. It's been thousands of years since I was a human. It's been hundreds of years since I realized that I took no fault in what happened to me. It was the fucked-up system of the gods, a system where gods raped whomever they wanted, and goddesses punished the victims as if they held the blame.

I want to enter this stupid temple to show that I'm over what happened, to show that I'm stronger than they think. Stealing the necklace? I know how much Athena loves her little trophy. The idea of taking it from such a bitch makes me happier than anyone could imagine.

But still, the risk of getting caught and punished again would keep any sane person from entering the temple. The thing is, if these gargoyles decide to go in fighting, Athena will know instantly, and they'll be tortured and killed in ways they could never imagine.

The goddess of war is a cruel woman with an ego bigger than her temple.

I reach the sidewalk leading up to the temple and slip in with the tourists. A couple look at my chained hands, but no one says a word. I sense the gargoyles behind me, and I make sure my steps are measured. I don't need them to know the emotions this place boils up inside me.

My thoughts slip to Marcus. He has short hair, a military cut, and dark eyes. His body is far more muscular than the other gargoyles, but in a really controlled way. For some reason, I can picture him being the kind of person who plans every second of his life.

I instantly dislike him. People like that are control-freaks, and control-freaks and I don't get along.

There's no doubt he's hot, but… I look down at my cuffs and remember how hard they'd squeezed, so hard it felt like my hands were going to be torn from my wrists. A little blood darkened the edges of the metal, and I imagined my wrists were swollen and nasty looking.

And then there was my face…

This guy was an asshole, and I wondered how he would complicate things from here on out. I had no clue, but my gut told me that his presence wasn't good.

"Stop," Marcus growls in my ear, grabbing my elbow a little too roughly.

I jerk my arm to pull away from him, but he spins me around.

Instantly, we come face-to-face. His expression is

neutral, but there's something in his eyes that makes me feel like I'm being judged.

I feel him touch my wrists, and then the handcuffs drop. He grabs them and hands them back to Byron to hide in his bag.

Harold gasps near me, and I look to see he's staring at my wrists.

Looking down, I frown. Yes, they're bruised and nasty looking. The edges of the cuffs cut my skin, but it isn't too terrible.

My mind goes back to the island I was kept on so long ago, of the many battles I fought there against heroes who wanted to make their name in the world by killing me. Everyone remembers the statues of warriors covering the island, but they weren't there to see me dragging myself across the ground after a fight, my gut torn open. They weren't there to see the many nights I wept, a battered pile of flesh after yet another fight I'd just barely survived.

No, in those days I was completely alone in exile. I suffered, *real* pain, not a scratch like this.

"Does it hurt?" Harold asked.

I jerk a little, coming back into the present.

"This is nothing," I laugh, but the sound is hollow.

Forrest is suddenly at my side, brushing my hair back from my face.

None of the guys speak for a long minute. It's strange, as if they don't want this Marcus to know they give a shit about me. That hurts.

I mean, I get it. I'm not a fucking moron. No one wants to say they might care a little about a worthless monster, but I don't know, they're big guys. Gargoyles. I didn't think they'd cower so easily. Why does this Marcus guy have so much power over them? I'm still trying to figure it out.

"Do you have any questions before you go into the temple?" Marcus asks, his gaze searching my face.

I shrug. "Nope. But you fellas relax. Either I get your precious necklace, or I die. Either way is a win for you."

"Medusa—" Byron begins, but he doesn't finish his sentence.

I wink at him. "Don't worry about it. Just stay here with your boss."

He looks like he wants to say something, but I spin on my heel and head for the temple. *I can do this if I don't look directly at the entrance.* I try to forget about the gargoyles walking behind me. I try to forget about everything except getting in and out.

When we reach the top of the hill and the ruins of the temple, we separate from the crowd of visitors going in and out. We move to the side of the path, beneath the shade of a tree. I finally force myself to look up. At first, there's just the white ruins. I hear cars honking not far from us, and the smell of gasoline and food perfumes the air.

Closing my eyes, I will myself to see the glamour, to peek into the past. Nothing special happens. There's no explosion or a magical whoosh. Not that I expected one.

When I open my eyes, I'm standing in the past. The concrete sidewalks and tar roads are gone. A dirt path leads to the majestic building. The trees covering the path are overgrown compared to the modern era, when trees were taken down to make things nicer and neater.

Only a few travelers are walking to the temple, wearing either white togas, or the scratchy homespun clothes of the poor. All of them are carrying gifts for Athena. Some have small things in delicate packages, while others carry baskets on their heads or in their arms.

"We'll wait here," Marcus says.

I stiffen and turn.

My gargoyles seem completely out of place, tucked in the shadows near the temple. Harold and Forrest look nervous. Byron looks upset, while Marcus is simply watching.

It's now or never, bitch.

Turning away from them, I hold my head high as I start up the remainder of the hill. Just in front of me, the white temple looms. Its massive pillars are polished, almost glowing in the afternoon sunlight. A priestess of the temple kneels on the marble ground, polishing and cleaning the steps and floor.

My belly clenches. *How many countless hours did I spend doing the same?*

Hold it together!

I step around the woman, seeing my leg peek out from the white toga that's glamoured my modern clothing. The priestess looks up and smiles at me. I give her a slight nod and keep going.

Inside, the air of the temple feels heavier, perfumed with the smell of leather and flowers. I freeze, my heart pounding. I've never forgotten that smell, and I'll always associate it with the temple of the Goddess of War.

Maybe this would be easier if I had.

I keep going, barely looking at the worshippers who stand near the columns leading into the main room. This building is not particularly beautiful in comparison to the massive temples that dominate this city, but this temple wasn't built as a thing of beauty. It was erected in a part of the city vulnerable to attacks. It's small and sturdy, with thick pillars that look more practical than decorative.

It was a place for people of the city to come to fight off attacks, and it's the perfect tribute to a Goddess of War.

When I finally allow my gaze to move to the wall where

Athena has been etched in marble, I freeze. They make her look like a thing of beauty. My lip curls. She isn't the least bit beautiful. She's a bitch with power.

And that's all.

Offerings surround the massive carving. People kneel before it, their own offerings set before them. Priestesses move about them, touching people's heads, and speaking to them in low tones.

Fucking idiots. They spend their lives believing Athena gives a damn about them when she doesn't. She's a goddess. She doesn't care about anyone except herself.

I move away from them and watch cautiously as I move into the shadows and slip into the doorway. With sure steps, I weave through the little maze of halls and doors. Pressing on a brick, I grit my teeth as the wall slowly slides away. Moving into the darkness, I slide the door closed behind me and enters the room forbidden to all but Athena's priestesses.

Here, a massive golden statue of Athena dominates the room. The necklace hangs on her hand, with its beautiful blue gem, and its little carvings of babies.

I don't hesitate. I walk straight to it. I climb up her statue, bracing myself on her hips, boobs, and weapons, then snatch the necklace from her outstretched hands. Breathing hard, I leap down and clasp the necklace on, twisting it so that the only thing people can see is the golden chain around my throat.

Ignoring the butterflies in my belly, I leave the way I came. When I'm nearly to the main room, a priestess carrying a water pitcher nearly runs into me.

"You're not supposed to be back here!" the young woman says, her brows high in surprise.

I give her an innocent look. "I got turned around, such was my wonder at the great and mighty goddess."

She smiles. "It is no surprise. Even I feel overwhelmed by the power of our lady at times." She points to the doorway behind her. "Just that way and you'll find yourself back where you began."

"Thank you," I whisper, inclining my head to her.

I pass all the fucking stupid worshippers. I hurry down the middle of the path lined with pillars. In front of me I see the sunlight that illuminates the steps that mean my escape.

And Athena appears in front of me.

She wears a long robe, so white it hurts my eyes. The glow that surrounds her in gold might have once had me collapsing to my knees, overwhelmed by her power. But instead, I see past it, to the dark-haired woman with dark eyes. I see a woman with an average face and average beauty, at best.

"Medusa," she greets me, smiling. "It's been a long time."

I try to force a smile, to not think about the necklace that's poorly concealed at my throat. "Athena."

She laughs. "No bow? No respectful greeting? You've changed since you were a little human who thought the world of me."

"I changed after my rape and my curse." The anger in my voice surprises even me, and I realize I'm trembling in rage. "I loved you like a mother, and you—"

She laughs again and waves me away. "Oh yes, I forgot about my little curse. Look at those sunglasses—what a smart idea. I guess with them you're no longer restricted to that island of yours."

I shake my head, all logic flying out the window. "I will not stand here, not even with a fucking goddess, and pretend any of this is okay. You ruined my life! You ruined any chance I had at love, or children, or happiness."

She raises a brow. "You were a priestess to a virgin goddess. You would have never had those things."

"I could have been happy!" And now I'm shouting. "You punished me for something one of you gods did! I didn't have a choice! You think I wanted that old, ugly bastard to pin me down? Do you think I wanted any of it?"

She raises her chin, and a fire comes to her eyes.

Oh fuck, I've screwed up. She's going to curse me again. She's going to make my life even worse.

Athena moves closer to me. She reaches out and touches the chain of the necklace at my throat, and a raises a brow. I can't breathe. She's going to kill me now. There's nothing I can do to stop it.

She sighs. "Thousands of years ago we gods weren't nearly as enlightened as we are today. Perhaps I—overreacted with your curse. Had such a great thing defiled my temple in these modern days, surely I would certainly make a different choice. So, Medusa, my child, I will forgive your tone and anger, and I will bestow upon you the gift that you long for."

Tears fill my eyes. She's finally going to take back this curse. I might not live forever, but I could live a good life. Then, I can actually die. Not just go on and on, suffering for eternity.

"Thank you," I whisper.

She places a hand on my chest and it glows with her golden power.

"But if ever you enter my temple again, I'll kill you. Enjoy your gift." The golden glow runs over every inch of my flesh until the light is so blinding that I can see nothing but her face. "My necklace is yours."

And then, everything goes black.

Chapter Sixteen

MEDUSA

I collapse onto my knees in the street outside of the temple. The sounds of the modern world explode around me, but I can't seem to move. I can't seem to do anything but stare in front of me. She said... she said she'd right her wrong. I thought… I thought she'd make me normal again. That I'd no longer be a monster.

But she gave me this fucking necklace instead?

I can't… breathe. My chest feels tight, and tears blur my vision.

A necklace? A necklace I don't even want.

And she left me like this.

"Medusa?" Harold's voice cuts through the fog of my panic.

I turn and meet his gaze, gasping in breaths.

His expression hardens, and he sweeps me into his arms.

I know the others are around us as we walk back down the steep hill. But I can't look at them. I'm too busy sobbing, trying to breathe, and being swallowed by my grief.

When they take me into some kind of apartment, Harold asks me what I want.

"Take the necklace," I say.

Harold's face looms over me. "Medusa..."

"Take it," I gasp. Suddenly, I feel like it's choking me. I grasp at it with shaking fingers. "I can't breathe. Take it off! Take it off!"

Harold grasps the necklace and snaps it off my throat. And I draw in a breath.

I struggle out of Harold's arms, and I move away from them. They're all staring at me like I'm nuts. And maybe I am.

Turning, I run from them, spot a bathroom, and race inside. I lock the door, flip on the shower and crumble into it. The water's cold, but I don't care. I just cry and cry.

If it hadn't been for the necklace, I might be human now.

I grasp my stupid glasses and toss them onto the shower floor, hating them with every fiber of my being. Drawing my knees up to my chest, I descend into a kind of sadness I haven't experienced in thousands of years. It reminds me of the day they cast me onto that island, alone and afraid.

Young and sheltered, I'd spent the time since I was a young girl serving in Athena's temple. I had never been alone. I had never slept outdoors, never made a fire. I looked around that god-forsaken place, and my heart broke. I felt... lost.

Like I do now.

And it's stupid. Nothing's changed. I was a monster yesterday, and I'm a monster today.

So why do I feel like everything's changed? Maybe because I faced something I've feared since I was turned into this *thing*. I saw Athena again.

But if I hadn't been stealing the necklace… if I'd just gone to face her… right now I'd be human.

I hope those fucking gargoyles understand what I gave up. I hope they know that shiny piece of shit stole my only hope at ever having a real life.

"But of course they don't. And of course they don't care."

Every muscle in my body tenses. I just faced down my demons. I risked my life. All for men who hold me as their prisoner. All for men who still can't promise me they won't kill me when my use to them is gone.

I don't know how long I sit in that shower before I turn it off. Stripping off my soaking clothes, I drop them into the bottom of the tub, pull on my putrid glasses, and wrap a towel around my body. When I go out into the tiny bedroom of the apartment, I see a white shirt has been laid on the bed, one that has *Greece* written on the front. I dry myself and put it on, then go out to face the gargoyles.

They ordered food. It's laid out on the table they all sit around, but no one is eating. When they spot me, all eyes are glued onto me.

"What?" I ask them, glad I sound angry and not heartbroken.

"Hungry?" Forrest asks.

I'm not, but I also know I haven't had a lot of proper meals lately, so I nod and take a seat. Harold silently makes a plate of food for me, and then we all eat.

Part of me wants to ask a lot of questions, but I'm also retreating inside myself. I know it's a defense mechanism. I just want to curl up on the bed, and drink until I fall asleep. Maybe someday I'll get a therapist to help me with it. If I live that long.

We finish eating, and I stand up, intending to find a bed and drink myself to sleep. Just like I wanted.

"Just a moment," Marcus says, and his tone is a little less harsh.

My gaze meets his dark one, and I can feel him evaluating me. "You need something?"

"We need to talk," he says.

I want to tell him to go fuck himself, but instead I sit back down. "Make it quick."

He raises a brow, and I can sense anger bubbling beneath his surface. "You know what we are and what you are. That makes us enemies."

I try not to look at the other gargoyles. I know they won't defend me, and I shouldn't expect it. "I understand gargoyles see the world in black and white. People are either good or bad, but monsters are always bad. Nothing else matters."

He leans back in his chair and steeples his fingers in front of him. "And you think that's wrong?"

I smirk. "I know it's wrong, but I also know that after hundreds or thousands of years, you guys aren't going to change your tone because of one monster who doesn't seem to fit the bill."

"Did any of us say you don't fit the bill?"

Suddenly, I rise, my hands shaking. I go to the tiny kitchen and tear through the cabinets until I find a bottle of cheap vodka, half empty.

"Liquor isn't a good idea right now," Byron says, and there's a warning to his tone.

I glare at him behind my glasses and unscrew the top. "Liquor's always a good idea."

Taking several deep swigs, I don't stop until I feel the warmth and relaxation moving through me. Then, I pull myself up onto the countertop, so that I'm facing them, and drink more slowly.

My gargoyles look concerned. Marcus has his same annoying expression, like he's evaluating me.

"We need to know what happened in the temple."

I take another drink as my stomach clenches. "What's to tell? I got the necklace. Isn't that all you care about?"

A flash of hurt comes and goes on his face in an instant. "We need to know if we've angered the Gods. We need to know if anyone saw you."

Did anyone see me? *You fucking asshole.* "Yeah, *fucking* Athena *fucking* saw me. Did you think she wouldn't?"

Someone draws in a surprised breath.

Any kindness I saw in Marcus' expression vanishes. "That's a bullshit lie."

My heart starts thumping, filling my ears. "Don't call me a liar."

"Marcus—" Harold begins, but the asshole cuts him off.

"She loves that fucking necklace. There's no way she'd let you leave with it."

I laugh, a dry, angry laugh. "Oh, she let me leave with it. The bitch."

"Monster…" Marcus begins, starting to stand.

Forrest stands too, putting a hand on his shoulder. "She's not a liar."

Marcus laughs. "You three actually believe a goddess let her steal from her without a punishment?"

"It was a punishment," I say, and now I know it's true.

All of their gazes fall on me.

"She realized she was wrong to curse me. And so, she agreed to give me the one thing I wanted more than anything." I feel tears sting my eyes. "She gave me that fucking piece of jewelry rather than end my curse."

I feel tears roll down my cheeks, and I grab the bottle

of vodka and take another long sip, trying to stop the meltdown that I know is coming

Then, Forrest is there in front of me. He takes the bottle and sets it on the counter before he wraps me in his arms. "I'm so sorry."

I grab the fabric of his shirt, and bury my face into the material. I hate that they're seeing me weak, but I've never had someone to comfort me when I was sad. This feels so good. It doesn't matter that I'm not even sure these gargoyles like me or see me as a person, it's better than being alone.

"Alright," Marcus says. "We believe you."

"Fuck you," I mutter, the words choked by tears.

"Now, does anyone want to explain what happened between the four of you?"

I'm shocked when Byron speaks. "We slept with her."

I open my eyes at the sound of a chair scraping against tile.

"Is that a joke?" Marcus spits out.

Byron meets his gaze. "No."

Marcus rubs the thin layer of hair on his head and starts to pace. "So all of this is for nothing? We can't take a mate. We can't have a child."

I huff out a breath, and feel the liquor really settle across my brain like a warm blanket. "We were all drugged with ambrosia. They didn't break their vow. It wasn't their choice. And don't worry, I'm not going to tell anyone, so we can just pretend it never happened."

"Pretend it never happened?" Marcus asks. "We can't do that! And what's more, ambrosia might hit us like drugs, but you four knew what you were doing."

I open my mouth to defend them, but Byron answers instead. "Yeah, we did. And we don't regret it. She's beautiful, and unique, and we like her."

Marcus launches into a rant, but I barely hear him. I lift my head from Forrest's shoulder, and look at Byron. His expression is unreadable, but he watches me.

I'll never figure that one out, so I turn back to Forrest. He smoothes the wet hair back from my face and tucks it behind my ear. "Like you didn't know."

For a minute, I'm overwhelmed by him. He's so handsome, with his deep green eyes and model-good-looks. That mouth, made for smiling and for kissing.

Maybe it's the liquor. Maybe it's the day from hell that I've had. The week from hell. But I reach up and pull him closer to me, catching his mouth with my own.

For a minute he holds himself stiffly, as if in shock, and then his mouth softens against mine, and our kiss deepens. His tongue moves into my mouth, and I moan and press myself harder against him.

I remember that I'm wearing nothing but a shirt, and not even my underwear protects me from him.

"What the hell are you doing?" Marcus shouts. "Have you lost all sense?"

He yanks Forrest back and I nearly topple off the counter.

Forrest has the good grace to look embarrassed. "There's just something about her—"

"Maybe she has the power to seduce," Marcus says, crossing his muscular arms over his chest. He looks at me as if I'm the devil.

I hate that I notice he's muscular. I hate that I see a tattoo sticking out from beneath his tight grey shirt, and that I have to curl my hand into my palm to keep myself from reaching out to touch it. Now that I'm thinking about it, my drunken mind can't think about anything else except touching that tattoo… and seeing what it is.

"Is that alright, Medusa?"

My head jerks up.

I feel my cheeks heat. Did they see me staring at Marcus? "What?"

Byron shakes his head and sighs loudly. "Marcus needs for us to meet with a nearby gargoyle. You'll be alone for a little while…"

Marcus huffs. "She won't be alone, I'll be here. And I wasn't exactly *asking* you three to obey my command."

Yet, as confident as he sounds, my gargoyles are staring at me, waiting for me to speak. "I'm a monster," I tell them, "I can handle one asshole."

Forrest and Harold head for the door, but Byron heads straight for me. He places his hands on either side of the counter, and his expression is serious. "Just obey him. He won't take your attitude quite as kindly as we do."

I lean forward and bite his bottom lip really gently.

He makes a sound that's a mixture of surprise and approval.

I pull away from him. "Also, did you really just imply you've been kind to me? I want the record to show you've been a grumpy jerk since the moment I met you."

He huffs angrily, but his gaze is locked onto my lips. "Just be good."

"Yes, sir," I say, with a salute.

For a minute I actually think Mr. Grumpy is going to laugh, or maybe kiss me, but he turns toward the balcony. They throw the doors open wide and one after another, the three shift into their gargoyle forms and leap into the night.

I stare at them, filled with a strange longing I don't understand.

I hear metal sliding against leather, and I turn to see that Marcus has pulled a dagger free. It looks sharp and deadly.

"Time for the two of us to talk."

Chapter Seventeen

MARCUS

I don't know how the fuck to approach the beautiful monster the others seem to have fallen in love with. All I know is that after tonight, I either need to get on board with this romance, and find my place in it, or I need to come up with a plan to kill her quickly when she's of no use to us.

The dagger feels cold in my hand as I move closer to her, and then come to stand just inches from her. Even on the counter, the tiny woman still looks small. Actually, she looks perfect, sitting at just the right height to be fucked.

Holy shit, where did that thought come from?

Maybe it's the fact that I know the others slept with her. It makes me feel… strange. We're supposed to share a woman. I'm on the outside of this, which hurts my pride in a way I never expected.

Or maybe it's because I watched her kissing Forrest. The way he touched her, the way she touched him—that was amazing. The sexual tension between them had filled the air like an intoxicating perfume.

While the others have struggled with their celibacy, I

haven't. I simply willed myself not to think about women. Every time I imagined thrusting into a wet pussy, I did something else. I worked out. I practiced my fighting skills. I kept myself busy.

But suddenly, I have no desire to break down into pushups, or go for a long flight. That's not what I want. That's not what my body needs. Somehow, it seems ridiculous that I convinced myself otherwise.

There's the way she was looking at me—this beautiful creature finds me attractive too.

"You wanted something," she says, her voice husky.

Oh fuck, she even sounds horny. Like something out of a fantasy.

"I want to know why they have fallen under your spell." I search her face for an answer, and I can't see past her glasses. Tearing her glasses off, she gives a surprised gasp, and it's like a wall crumbles between us. Her eyes are... blue, clear and deep like the sacred waters of our lands. I didn't expect that, and I didn't expect them to be so expressive. I no longer have to guess at her feelings,

"I need answers," I tell her.

One corner of her mouth quirks up. "Honestly, after how long they've gone without sex, I think they would've fallen for anyone who spread their legs for them. So don't worry, chief. I'm nothing special. When the time comes, they'll treat me like any other monster."

Something unexpected rises up inside of me. "They've resisted a lot of beautiful women over the years."

She shrugs. "Well, I guess all they needed was a monstrous freak."

The gargoyle within me hates the way she talks about herself. She looks so tiny, so unsure, but then she insults herself like she truly thinks that's all she's worth. Nothing.

"You aren't just a wet pussy to them." I realize that I mean the words as I say them.

She laughs. "Oh no, they had my mouth and my ass too."

I feel my cock harden, straining within my pants. I get the sudden perfect image of her mouth wrapped around my dick. Then I imagine the way it'd feel to part her ass and slide inside of her.

I'm breathing hard. "I know what you're trying to do."

She raises a brow. "What's that?"

"You're trying to turn me on."

Her gaze slides down, and mine does too. Suddenly, we're both looking at my erection.

"Wow," she mutters, "don't try to blame that python on me. That's all your doing."

Suddenly, I resheath my fucking dagger and grab the bottle of vodka next to her. I take a few swigs, trying to calm myself. I shouldn't be aroused by her acknowledgment of my erection.

When she pulls the bottle from my grasp, I can't stop staring at her.

She smirks at me. "Careful, big boy, not everyone has my tolerance for liquor."

When she puts the bottle to her own lips, I imagine it's my cock in her mouth instead. "You'd be surprised," I tell her.

I take it back from her and take a big drink, just to prove her wrong.

The liquor hits me like a wave, warm and comforting. I set the bottle down. *She's right. Maybe I should've gone slower.*

I lean a little closer to her. "Explain it."

"What?" she asks, licking her lips.

"What's so special about you? They were ready to fight me just to protect you. *Me,* their brother. They wouldn't even fight for a female gargoyle. And then there's Byron, watching you with him is like watching a miracle. He likes you. And he doesn't like anyone."

Her eyes widen in shock. "It isn't like that. It was one drug-induced fuck session."

"Liar," I whisper.

She shakes her head. "Trust me. No one has ever loved me. No one could. I'm a monster. I'm a dangerous creature who will only ever bring them misery. That's not just me throwing myself a pity party. That's literally what they've said." Her eyes fill with tears. "My ex said he cared about me, but not enough to die for me. That pretty much sums up my love-life."

I place my hands on either side of her on the counter, aroused by this complicated creature. "But you can't hurt us, little monster. Your stone-glare… it's nothing to us."

Her expression is weary. "But it doesn't change what you think of me."

"It doesn't?"

She nibbles her bottom lip and my erection strains harder. Unable to help myself, I lean forward and capture her lips.

For one minute she holds herself stiffly, but then she melts beneath me.

I groan, and my arms circle her back, pulling her closer.

I just need one quick kiss to see why the others are lost in her. That's all I need. And then, I'll pull back. I'll stop things before they get too far.

But the longer we kiss, the more my logical thoughts swim away. Our kiss deepens as we move against each other, teasing each other with our tongues, testing each other.

When she moans, and her hands slide around my neck,

I pull her closer. Her legs wrap around my back, and then my erection is pressing against her pussy. My hands move down her back to grab her ass… which is exactly when I realize she isn't wearing underwear.

Something inside of me snaps.

I grasp the bottom of her shirt and toss it off.

Our kiss breaks, and she gasps my name.

I don't think. I just push her back, pull her legs over my shoulders, and press my mouth against her pussy. She gasps and arches her back. Her hands go into my hair, bringing me closer.

I lick my way deeper into her folds, then use my hands to part her wide. She moans and bucks against me, but I move slowly and carefully. It's been so long since I enjoyed the taste of a woman, so long since I felt one orgasming against me.

Every sound she makes spurs me on, makes my pants tighter and more uncomfortable. When I start to rub my mouth against her clit, she goes wild, and I reach for my pants, undoing the button. I pull down the zipper and pull my dick free, stroking myself as I lick her.

At last, she rises off of the counter. "Oh, fuck me, Marcus. Please, fuck me."

God, I love my women submissive, begging for my touch.

I rise from between her thighs and wrap her legs back around my back. She arches as I suck her nipples, stumbling toward the bedroom. We make it to the wall before she shifts slightly, and my tip slides into her wet folds.

Pressing her against the wall, everything inside of me tightens. I watch her beautiful face. Her expressive eyes. As I press inch by inch deeper into her. I enjoy the way her nails dig into my shoulders as she pants *yes, yes, yes*.

And it takes everything inside of me, every drop of

Medusa's Destiny

willpower to keep from exploding inside of her. But I won't. I won't embarrass myself or come before she's enjoyed her pleasure.

I keep going until I'm balls deep inside of her.

Pausing there, my lips move from the hard peaks of her breasts and up to her neck. I suck every inch of her, leaving my marks. I claim this woman who now belongs to me. To us.

I begin to thrust in and out of her as the nerves along my shaft scream in pleasure. The intense feeling radiates through every sensitive inch of my flesh and fills my mind with nothing but her. Nothing but an awareness of my dick sliding in and out of her tight channel as she squeezes around me.

I'm aware of her legs tight around my back. Of her nails digging even deeper. Of her moving against me to take my thrusts harder and harder.

When her inner-muscles squeeze around me, a string of curses explodes from my lips, and then she's orgasming, bouncing wildly against my dick like a creature in heat. Her pleasure does crazy things to me. I clench her tighter, thrust harder, and explode, filling her with my seed.

I move in and out of her, enjoying feeling myself spurting for several long seconds before our thrusting slows, and she crumbles against me. My entire body shakes as I hold her tighter and take us to the bed. I lay back, keeping myself inside her.

Her head rests against my heart in a way that's strangely intimate.

I find myself stroking her hair, strangely content. Perhaps it's just that I've finally spilled my seed after so many long years. But the thing is… I'm not sure. This woman, she surprises me.

I'm going to have to consider what all of this means. How it changes things.

But for now, I simply let my eyes close. I like the way it feels to have my dick still inside her tight pussy. I like her lying on top of me, her breath even and peaceful.

My breathing slowly matches hers and I slip into sleep, not even caring what the others will think when they come home to find us like this.

It's not like they can say a thing. They've already fallen under her spell.

Chapter Eighteen

BYRON

I love the feeling of the wind sweeping around me, especially when my mind is so turbulent. I knew Marcus would be disappointed in me for my weakness. He's always seen me as his second-in-command. He trusts me to steer our brotherhood into making the right choices, into doing what was necessary for the survival of our people.

My mind goes to my father. The leader of our people. Suddenly, my heart starts to race faster. I push my wings harder, leaving Harold and Forrest behind.

Most gargoyles are created, not born, so families are made between those of us who become close. But my father was made by the same human as I was. He was placed on another corner of the clock tower in the little town we watched over.

The other gargoyles in our town were destroyed during the last war. They'd been asleep too long and unable to awaken at the screams of fear of their humans, but my father and I awoke. And when there was no one left to protect… we left. I went my own way in the world, searching for more of our kind.

And he created the sanctuary.

My father was a harsh man. Yes, he could be cruel at times, but without him, gargoyles would be extinct. Too many had lost themselves in their stone-flesh, never to awaken again. The few who remained survived because of him.

But, soon he would die.

I tense, soaring through clouds. I try so hard not to think about it. Emotions make us weak, make it hard to focus on the task at hand. So why was he all I could think about now?

Far below, I almost miss the meeting place. I swoop down to the ancient ruins and land lightly on the top. The bag on my shoulder suddenly feels too heavy, and I have to take a deep breath to keep myself calm.

Forrest and Harold land loudly behind me.

"They aren't here yet," Harold says, slightly surprised.

I shrug.

"I'm kind of glad, because I think we need to talk." Forrest leans against the building, his expression troubled. "Once they have the statue and the necklace, we've done the most important tasks to help our people…"

Yes, the necklace and the statue is what we hope will save our people. But Medusa herself might be the only answer to saving my father, and the other Elites.

"It's not enough," I tell him, knowing exactly where his thoughts are going.

"The Elites have lived for a long time—"

"I won't be responsible for sealing my father's fate," I tell him, a warning in my voice.

"But you're okay with Medusa dying?"

My fists clench. "I didn't say that."

Harold puts his hands up, as if to stop our impending fight. "Who says it has to be one life or another?"

"They do!" Forrest and I say together, and then we glare.

Harold sighs and looks toward the moon, speaking in a practical tone that I despise. "If we don't bring Medusa to the sanctuary, all the older gargoyles die. But then when her use is over, they'll kill her."

"Exactly what we just said." I turn my glare onto him.

"But what if we negotiate for her life?" His words drop between us.

Forrest stands straighter. "You really think they'd negotiate for the life of a monster?"

"We can ask for a Blood Moon Judgment."

I inhale sharply. My thoughts circle back to the last time one was called. "That still doesn't guarantee her life."

"We have three months before the Blood Moon. If they can't hurt her in that time, they can get to know her… and just like us, they'll see she isn't dangerous."

"It's a risk," Forrest says, his expression far away.

"And our entire brotherhood would have to agree to request it from the Elites." I think of Marcus. "I doubt that will happen."

Harold turns his light blue eyes onto me. He has a way of softening even the hardest heart. "We can convince them to see things our way. If we're all on the same page."

I think back to the last Blood Moon Judgment. Blood Moons are rare, occurring about twice every three years. Requesting a Blood Moon Judgment is a risk. It angers the Elites and makes them less inclined to support the brotherhood that asks for it. The last request was made more than fifty years ago… and the brotherhood lost their judgment, their standing in the community, and eventually left their home altogether.

"So this plan rests on the belief that we can convince Marcus to side with us, put our brotherhood in jeopardy, and convince a group of old, angry gargoyles that Medusa isn't a danger to humanity. That's one sound plan."

Harold raises a brow at me. "Do you have a better idea?"

I don't, so I keep my mouth shut.

We spot the two gargoyles before they land. Max and Arthur are not nearly as large as we are. But they're twins, crafted from the same maker, and both have a good spirit.

Max shifts back into his human-form and grins at me.

I shift as he approaches. He grabs my hand and pulls me into a "bro-hug," as he likes to call it. "When I heard you guys were successful, I wasn't surprised. The others though… they were sure either Eros or Athena would have turned you into dust by now."

Forrest laughs as he hugs Arthur. "Please! We told those gods we were taking what we wanted, and they could go fuck themselves."

Arthur throws back his head full of shaggy, dark hair and laughs. "So you guys grabbed the stuff and ran?"

"Exactly," Forrest says, with a smirk.

"So where are they?" Max asks, and our smiles vanish.

I let my bag slide from my shoulders and carefully open the top. Harold helps me pull out the statue and the necklace.

Arthur whistles low. "*Damn!*"

Max takes the necklace gently from my hands and looks at the broken clasp. Briefly I remember tearing it from Medusa's neck, unable to stop myself when I saw her panic.

"How did it break?" Max asks.

Harold answers before I can. "Stealing from Gods is harder than you think."

Max's grey eyes lock onto us, and I can see he knows we aren't telling the truth, but he's a good guy. He'll keep it to himself. "I guess the necklace works, with or without the clasp."

Arthur takes the statue and pokes at the giant dick. "They must have carved this after seeing what I'm packing."

Forrest slaps him on the back and points at the figure. "No man, you're looking at his nose. *That* down there is his cock."

They're grinning like idiots, which calms my tension… at least a little. I forgot how nice it was to be around the others.

"So tell us about the monster," Max says. "Is Marcus able to keep her prisoner on his own?"

"I'm sure he's doing just fine," I say, dryly.

Max raises a brow and meets my gaze with an unspoken question in his eyes.

"Has she killed any humans on your mission?" Arthur asks, sounding excited.

Harold answers, his voice tense. "She isn't like that."

"Like what?" Arthur grins. "A killing monster?"

"Yeah." Harold's eyes narrow. "Did you know she wasn't even born a monster?"

I feel every muscle in my body tense. I don't feel like that's our story to tell.

"How so?" Max removes his bag and pulls out soft leather. He begins to very gently wrap the necklace.

"She was a human once. She used to serve in Athena's temple, but she was raped by Poseidon. Athena cursed her in punishment."

Max freezes in his task. Arthur's amusement at the statue flees. None of us can stomach the idea of a fragile human being hurt, but women? We have a particular weakness for them.

"So how did she go from a human, punished for being a victim, to being a killing-machine?" Max says, finishing wrapping the necklace and putting it in his bag.

"Who said she was a killing-machine?" Forrest sounds like he's trying to keep his voice light. "She's just a creature with an unfortunate ability."

Max stands and puts the bag on his back. "You guys aren't going rogue, are you?"

I grab him by the shirt and shove him backward. His lower back hits the edge of the building, and his top half hangs over the edge.

Forrest swears and grabs me by the shoulder. "Stop it!"

"Let him go!" Harold says.

Someone grabs me with surprising strength and yanks me and the little fucker back. But I don't let go of Max.

Arthur is suddenly peering at me, his expression thunderous. "Let go of my brother."

"He ever accuses us of going rogue again, and I'll break every bone in his fucking human body. Understand?"

"Got it." Max says the words, but there's rage in his eyes.

I release him and step back. Harold and Forrest are immediately between me and them.

Max kneels down and picks up the statue from where it was dropped in the fray. "Luckily it didn't get broken." There's an accusation in his words that I don't like.

"Next time you should choose your words with care," I growl at him.

Max's anger fades, and he cocks his head and looks at all of us. "I was joking. I've known you guys for too long to throw around an accusation like that. I know damn-well you aren't fucking monster-lovers. Just watch it—for a minute you sounded like you sympathized with a beast that's been turning humans to stone for thousands of years. If you arrive home talking like that, you might find yourselves turned to dust before you think."

My fists clench, and I take a step closer to him.

Forrest whirls to face them. "Thanks for the heads up."

Max wraps the little statue and puts it in his own bag. "We'll get these back as fast as we can fly. The ladies will appreciate it. The Elites already created a shrine where the women will lay and the magical artifacts will be near them, to offer them protection and help. You'll receive a hero's welcome when you return, bet on that."

"Thank you," Harold answers, and maybe they don't sense the tension in his words, but I do.

We stiffly give another bro-hug, and then shift back into gargoyles and take off into the sky. When they're little more than shapes against a moon-lit sky, I turn to Harold. "Still think they'll give Medusa a fair chance?"

Forrest shoots me a dirty look. "We can always choose the alternative—to let the old men die."

I glare at him. "Or to let her be killed."

But even when I speak the words, I know I can't allow either death to occur. My soul could never recover from it. If we can convince Marcus, we'll risk our lives and reputation with a Blood Moon Judgment

How fucking wonderful…

Chapter Nineteen

HAROLD

I don't know what to do. Every moment of my day is consumed with thoughts of Medusa. Her laugh. Her smile. Her bravery, even when she's terrified.

For some reason, seeing her so haunted, so broken, completely shifted my world. With hurt women, I feel a need to protect them. To keep them safe.

With her, I want more than that. I want to kill a God for her. I imagine myself destroying Poseidon, piece-by-piece. I imagine myself ripping him to shreds, in the most painful way imaginable.

And then? I imagine myself returning to my sweet Medusa and keeping her safe forever. Holding her. Showing her that some men can be trusted. That some men know how to treat a woman.

The surge of emotions sweep me under, and all I can think about is the *after* then—the moment when I remain by her side forever. No matter how much I try to think about anything else, my mind keeps returning to her.

As we fly back to the city and away from our meeting place with the messengers, I realize something else. When I return, I'm going to make love to Medusa. Not because I'm drugged up, or horny, although I am, but because I've made a decision.

I am not just going to save this woman's life. I'm going to make her mine.

And I don't care what I have to do to make that happen.

The wind picks up, and I realize just how aroused the thought of her has made me. My erection strains uncomfortably inside my pants. My rebellious brain takes me back to our night in Eros' temple, when I fucked our sweet woman in every possible way.

There's something unimaginably incredible about being a big man fucking a tiny woman. It isn't just that every hole in her body is tight, squeezing my dick in protest. It's that I can bend her, move her, slip her between us with ease. It's that I can dominate every part of her.

Now I'm officially losing my mind. I need to take her, and I don't give a shit what the others think. The second I return, I'm parting her sweet ass and slipping right inside.

If she'll have me.

I feel my muscles tense. All along we've been thinking about dealing with the consequences of caring for a monster, of protecting a monster, of having sex with a monster. But what if we don't matter to her? What if it was just sex for her?

The idea makes my stomach twist and my fists clench. It's true—we haven't really treated her well. She's our prisoner, after all. We kidnapped her, we hurt her, and we forced her into a dangerous situation.

I wouldn't blame her if the second she got a chance, she ran as far and as fast from us as she could.

But I can't let that happen. Not when I feel this way

about her. I need to show her that she matters to me, even if the others aren't yet on board.

The lights of the city come, and we soar over it all until we reach the balcony of the apartment. Then, we gently land, one at a time, and shift into our human-forms before going inside.

I'm surprised to find the apartment strangely quiet. Marcus is nowhere to be found, and nothing is disturbed. My heart races. Even gargoyles have enemies… perhaps they've found us here. Perhaps a monster came who was more powerful than Medusa and Marcus together, one they couldn't stop.

I move to the bedroom, and freeze.

Marcus and Medusa are together in bed, naked. She's lying on top of him. Her beautiful ass facing me. The kitchen lights highlight the curves of her body in a strangely intimate silhouette. "What the fuck?" Byron mutters beside me.

"Well, damn!" Forrest says.

And we all just sit and stare, unsure what to do or say. Marcus—our fearless leader—couldn't resist her either? Maybe we have more of a chance than I thought of convincing him of the Blood Moon Judgment.

I want to explore that thought more fully, but there's a naked Medusa in front of me.

"What should we do?" Byron asks.

I shrug out of my shirt. "I don't know about you two, but I'm going to see if they're ready for Round Two."

Forrest gives me a shocked look, but then he starts to undress too.

I slip into the room and stare. Marcus' cock is still firmly inside her pussy. I wonder what she'd think of her ass being filled by me?

Moving behind her on the bed, it shifts beneath my

weight. I run a hand along her spine, stroking her back and hips. She sighs and wiggles on Marcus.

He mutters, "shit," and his eyes pop open.

He looks from me to the naked woman on top of him.

She lifts her head sleepily and glances back at me.

I hold my breath. What will she say?

"You going to stand there all day? Or put it in my ass?" she mumbles.

A shudder moves through my body. "Yes, ma'am."

But I know better than to plunge into a tight asshole. I want my little woman screaming in pleasure, not in shock.

Marcus seems to understand. He pushes the hair back from her face and pulls her down for a kiss. A little moan leaves her lips, and he curls his hands around her breasts.

I position myself behind her, but don't enter. I focus instead on touching her skin, her back, her hips. And then, I move her on top of Marcus, watching his dick slipping in and out. Getting more and more wet by her juices.

Grasping my dick, I slide myself in her wetness.

She's shifting and moaning, taking Marcus harder with each stroke.

When my pulse fills my ears, and my dick is coated in her juices, as well as my own precum, I part her ass. Slowly slipping inside is like the sweetest torture in this world. She grips me tightly, awakening my flesh. Pleasure ripples through me.

When I come to my hilt, a shiver moves through my body. *Keep your control*, I tell myself.

Forrest and Byron enter the room, naked and erect. They come to stand at her sides. I grasp her waist and pull her so that she's sitting on us. I have to adjust to move back to let her come down fully on top of my erection.

She makes a little sound of protest, and then their dicks are in her face.

Immediately, she grips them and begins to stroke. They each grab one of her breasts in a possessive manner. When Forrest flicks her nipple, she gasps and leans toward him. He swears as she takes him into her mouth. And my own arousal builds at the sight of her sucking him off.

Using her hips for leverage, I move Marcus and I in and out of her in a rhythm that's pure pleasure. When she lets Forrest's dick pop out of her mouth, she immediately turns to Byron's dick and takes him deeply.

Feeling myself inside her and watching her pleasure my brotherhood is like heaven.

When her inner-muscles start to tense, she begins to ride us. And holy fuck, I'm lost to her. She rides us in a frenzy of movement, and my brain can't process anything except her tight body wrapped around me.

When her head throws back, and she shouts a string of nonsense, I come, exploding into her tight ass. Forrest and Byron don't disappoint. Their cum shoots out, coating her breasts, and I feel Marcus coming seconds later.

We're all breathing hard. Trying to regain even an ounce of our brainpower.

She looks down at her chest. "Fuck boys, I've never enjoyed being painted, but that wasn't half bad. Now, who's going to clean me off?"

We all volunteer at once.

She laughs.

But Forrest is the one who scoops her up and takes her to the shower.

The three of us lay side-by-side on the bed.

"So you fucked her?" Byron asks, amusement in his voice.

Marcus sighs. "I couldn't help myself. It wasn't just her beauty. Or the fact that you three were falling in love with her—"

"There's just something about her." I finish.

Both men nod beside me.

"We've decided we can't kill her, or let them do it." Byron's voice is hesitant as he speaks.

Marcus doesn't respond for a long time. "So your plan is to run?"

"No," I interrupt. "We're going to request a Blood Moon Judgment."

He stiffens. "We won't win."

And I say the words I didn't realize until now. "If we lose, we fight our way out. We take her with us. We leave that world behind us."

Again, he's quiet for an uncomfortably long time. "And all of you are willing to accept the consequences of this decision."

"Yes."

"Then," he clears his throat. "That is exactly what we'll do. Either all of us survive or none of us do." His words have a finality I don't like. It's as if he's weighed the possibility of us fighting dozens of gargoyles and escaping with a monster, and decided we won't win.

"Life is too short to be lonely," he says after a moment.

I stiffen, surprised. I didn't realize he was lonely.

"But tonight I think we work off twenty years of celibacy." There's a smile in his voice. "We can deal with our unlikely future tomorrow."

Even though our plan will anger our people, will have them calling us monster-lovers, and make them believe we've betrayed them, I smile. I've never looked forward to a night more than this one ever, not in thousands of years.

Chapter Twenty

MEDUSA

"My vagina hurts. And my ass. And my throat."

Byron's hands tighten around me as we fly through another thick cloud. "Sorry about that." But he doesn't sound too sorry.

He sounds a little proud of himself.

I snuggle closer against his chest. "I wasn't complaining. If all my holes are going to hurt, I can't think of a better reason for it."

He laughs, a surprisingly husky sound.

I look up at him as I feel his erection against me. "How can you be horny? *Again?*"

I'm pretty sure the big gargoyle would be blushing, if he wasn't stone. "It's the wind."

"Still sticking with that turbulence crap? I can't decide if you're brave or an idiot."

He smirks down at me. "Has anyone ever told you just to stay quiet and be polite?"

"The ones that have got kneed in the groin."

He shakes his head. "You are the most frustrating woman I've ever encountered."

"You're not the first to tell me that."

"You talk all the time," he says, but there's humor in his tone.

I smile. "It's probably because of my time in exile. When I got around people again, I just couldn't stop myself."

Something subtle changes in his demeanor. "You were exiled?"

Oops. That's not exactly a sexy story.

"Boy, you guys really need to research your monsters more before you kidnap them. Haven't you heard all about the stories of me on Horror Island? The island covered in statues of dead warriors?"

His hands pull me even closer. "I guess I knew about it. At least I knew warriors had been sent to kill you, and all but one of them had ended up dead."

"Perseus," I say his name softly. "He was the only warrior to ever escape my island alive."

"Why did you let him live?" His tone is neutral, but I can sense tension behind his question.

"I never wanted to kill any of them. I was alone on my island, a young woman trying to survive after being raped and cursed. Men would sneak up on me, I'd turn, and they were dead. But Perseus was smart. He used a mirror to see me without getting himself turned to stone."

"I remember that story. But didn't it end with him cutting off your head?"

I smile, remembering those days as clearly as if they were yesterday, because they changed my life forever. "That's what he told people to get them to leave me alone. Instead, he made my first pair of sunglasses. He stayed on the island with me for a while and taught me how to fight.

He told me about the world, the Gods, and the monsters. He helped me to understand how I could survive in it, without ending up dead." For some reason, tears form in my eyes. "He was also my first love."

Byron stays silent for a long time, and I wonder what he's thinking. "So what happened to him?"

I shouldn't tell him. I've never told anyone this story before, but I do. "He was a king. He had responsibilities. He couldn't just sneak off with a monster. There was a woman—Andromeda—we stumbled upon her. She had been offered as a sacrifice to a sea monster. I turned the beast into stone and saved her life. Perseus freed her. That gave him a chance at a real life.

So, I left. People worshipped him as a hero for killing the sea monster. They believed he used my severed head to kill it, and he married Andromeda. They lived a happy life until he died of old age."

"You're a better person than I am."

I startled and glanced up at him. "And why's that?"

"I could never let someone else end up with the woman I love."

There was something strange about his tone. Something that made me uncomfortable. Maybe because the pathetic part of me was hoping he was talking about me.

Yup, I'm a loser.

"It was the right thing to do," I told him. "Being with me was dangerous. And like every other man I've ever been with has said, just not worth their lives."

Byron snorts. "Sounds like you've dated a lot of cowardly bastards."

"I'm *Medusa*," I tell him, like he's lost his mind.

He leans forward and brushes a light kiss against my lips. "I know."

I snuggle against him, my mouth tingling pleasantly

from his touch. There's just no words for the way I feel right now... maybe content? I don't know what tomorrow will bring, but I'm going to cherish this moment. If there's anything I've learned in life, it's that happiness is fleeting.

I'm not sure how long I sleep when I'm startled awake by Byron's voice. "We're here."

Slowly sitting up, I see that Forrest, Harold, and Marcus have all closed in around us. I can sense their tension like something palpable.

"Where are we?" I ask, feeling nervous.

"Our home."

I stare far below us. There's nothing but a massive tangled forest. "That's where you *live*?"

"Let's go," Marcus orders our group, not bothering to answer my question.

He goes first, follow by Forrest, then Byron and I, and Harold behind us. With each second that passes, I feel more and more uneasy.

And then, below us, I see something shimmering in the morning light. Like a massive translucent bubble surrounding hundreds and hundreds of acres of woods. We fly lower and lower, and I see a little opening in the bubble. We shoot through it, and I gasp.

Inside, the air is warmer, and everything is different. There's a tropical feel to all the plants, and a crystal blue river flows through the entire enclosure and feeds into tiny pools with waterfalls. I spot houses built into the tops of the massive trees. Some are spread throughout the enclosure, but I see a collection of them all in one area, not far from the largest waterfall. There, perhaps a dozen little houses dot a clearing in the woods beneath the treehouses.

"What is this place?" I ask Byron, in awe.

"Our sanctuary. The home of the gargoyles. It's a place protected from the outside world."

"I love it," I say, and I mean it.

He stiffens. "You do?"

"It's beautiful."

I can tell my compliment makes him happy, but the tension radiating through our group doesn't dissipate.

"Things are going to get worse for me, aren't they?" I ask.

He takes too long to answer. "We have a plan to protect you, but you'll need to trust us."

I look at the handsome gargoyle that holds me, and then my gaze scans over our group. All the men are watching me. *Do I trust them?*

"If you want to leave—" Forrest begins.

I guess I trust them more than anyone else I've met. "No, I can handle it."

But I'm pleased he even made the offer. Forrest might seem like all fun and games, but I can tell he's ready to kick ass when he has to. And right now he's got that look—like he wants to beat the shit out of someone for me.

Which is sweet.

"The prejudice against monsters runs deep here," Harold explains. "We're going to fight for you, but we want you to be prepared."

I laugh, trying to sound confident. "This isn't my first rodeo, boys. Everywhere I go someone wants me dead. Someone despises me. It'll be a walk in the park."

None of them look convinced.

"I'll trust you guys that you won't let me die, but you guys trust me that I can take what they throw at me, okay? We can't have brawls breaking out with you and your people because of the things they say or do. That won't help anyone."

Marcus raises a brow. "You're just going to take it?"

"You bet."

He does that annoying thing where I know he's analyzing me again. But then I remember our night together, and I realize he's not nearly as annoying as I first thought. He's just one of those guys who is wound so tight that when you get him in the bedroom, he snaps like a horny rubber band. I mean, hell, he was insane last night. I don't think I've ever heard a man talk that dirty to me… or say the f-word that much.

And it really turned me on.

Oh, and then there are his tattoos. The one on his arm was the most bad-ass looking pair of wings, and the rest of his chest was covered in even more.

Yeah, Marcus has a tight ass. But he's not as much of a tight ass as I first thought.

So, I wink at him. "Relax, I got this."

Byron holds me a little closer as we soar over the amazing jungle. I see tiny fairies drifting through the trees. Sparkling fish flip and dive in the waters of the river. The flowers seem to bend toward us as we fly past.

I realize for the first time what I didn't know before: this place is magical.

I wish I could stay here forever. Magic makes you feel different, full of hope and possibilities. Magic exists out in the real world, but places like this are rare… and they certainly aren't places I'm allowed inside of.

When we spot gargoyles ahead of us, I think they're going to fly out to greet us. Instead, they shoot away toward the village.

My happy feelings crumble and my nerves scream back to life. I told my gargoyles I could do this. So I need to. I will. I *have* to.

By the time we reach the village, there are dozens of gargoyles on the ground. We land not far from them, but my men don't move. They remain in place, still in their stone-forms.

"Welcome back," someone greets.

The man looks entirely human… but older than any human I can imagine. His wrinkles have wrinkles, and his eyes are so pale, I'm almost certain he's blind. His back is bent at an uncomfortable angle, and he inches toward us using a staff carved out of dark woods. When he nearly reaches us, he stops and cocks his head. His strange pale eyes fall onto me.

"Good, you got her!"

Murmurs rise up in the people behind him. Groups of gargoyles cluster around three very pregnant females, who look human. They stand as if warriors, protecting the women from me. But there's also curiosity in their expressions as they try to look around my men to see me.

"Bring her to the hall," the old man orders, then turns and starts right back the way he came.

We follow him slowly. My men say nothing. We pass the groups of gargoyles, and I can't help myself.

"Hey, I'm Medusa. I'll be your prisoner this morning!"

No one laughs.

"Tough crowd," I say.

A lovely woman with pale yellow hair meets my gaze.

"Is it tough to be surrounded by all this testosterone?"

She raises a brow, and her lip quirks, but she doesn't answer me.

We shuffle to the largest building in the tiny town. It's made out of stone, unlike the other ones, with moss covering nearly every inch of its walls and roof. The two big doors are thrown open, and I'm surprised by the slight chill that swallows us as we enter the darkness.

The old man reaches the room and struggles up the stairs of a dais, before seating himself on a simple throne.

Three ancient people are seated to each side of him, three women, and three men. All of them watch our group with suspicion, as we come to stand before them.

"Let's see her," the old man orders.

Byron's grip tightens around me for one second before he slowly puts me on the ground.

My legs tremble ever-so-slightly, which I'm sure has more to do with our long flight than my nerves. At least that's what I tell myself.

"Why aren't her hands bound?" the man says, and his angry words echo around us. "What's to stop the monster from simply reaching up and removing her glasses, killing us all?"

I answer before the others can. "How about a thing called a moral-code? You know, the same thing that keeps your gargoyles from just snapping weak humans' necks."

There's thunder in the man's eyes. "Bind her hands."

Marcus steps forward. "That's not necessary. She's agreed to help our cause."

A woman speaks from beside the old man. "I'd hoped that Max and Arthur's account of their interaction with you was incorrect, but it seems we do have cause for worry. The four of you are treating the monster as less a prisoner and more of a guest, which suggests she may have manipulated you into trusting her."

Marcus crosses his big, muscular arms over his chest. "Only a fool would use excessive force with a willing prisoner."

The older humans lean toward one another and begin to whisper. I don't know what my gargoyles are thinking, but their actions are making me nervous.

At last, the oldest man's gaze lands on Byron. "We can't wait any longer. Each moment brings us closer to death."

He nods and moves to my side. "Father, I understand. And Medusa is ready to help."

Father? This old man is his father? I didn't even know gargoyles had fathers… and this guy looks human. So how did that work?

"So, how do her powers work?" the old man asks.

I answer instead, hating to be talked about like I'm not here. "I remove my glasses, and any humans or weaker magical creatures are turned into stone. Pretty simple."

The old man glowers at me. "Can't you get her to shut up?"

My men stiffen, but say nothing.

"I'm sorry, I didn't realize you lacked basic manners." There's a bite to my words. "You'd think after helping you get Eros' statue and Athena's necklace, that you'd at least treat me like a person."

His mouth curls up in disgust. "I think somehow you've forgotten your place, so let me remind you. We are the protectors of mankind, hunters of monsters. And you are a disgusting creature the world would be better without. Helping us on our mission doesn't change that."

I open my mouth, but Byron cuts me off. "How do we want to do this?"

His father looks angry as he takes a deep breath. "I'll go first, so we can see if it even works."

"No," Byron says, his word final. "Someone else—"

"I won't ask my people to risk their lives if I'm not willing to." The old man stands. "I'll go first."

"Go first with what?" I ask.

For a second I think he won't answer me, but then the old man's gaze holds mine. "You're going to turn me into stone."

I can't breathe. No, I don't just go around turning people into stone. No matter how much of a jerk Byron's father is, I can't be responsible for taking his life. Not only does the idea turn my stomach, but this man is Byron's family. If I kill him, he'll never see me as anything but a monster.

"No," I refuse.

The old man smacks the end of his cane on the stone, the sound echoing loudly in the room. "You will do as I say."

My hands clench into fists. "I know what you think of me, but I won't have your death on my conscience."

A man laughs. My gaze goes to him. He has pepper-grey hair and yellow teeth. "And what about all the others you killed?"

I glare at him. "I don't kill for fun. I've only done so when I didn't have a choice."

The man with the yellow teeth grins, and a chill runs down my spine. "Oh, how lovely. A monster with a moral code."

Harold gently takes my arms and turns me to face him. "We're not asking you to kill him. We're asking you to try to save his life. Remember, most gargoyles are immune to your powers because we can turn into stone any time we want. But with these people, we think your powers can more than work on them, we think they could give them immortality."

Save a life with my curse? *Yeah, right.* "I think you have my powers all wrong."

He smiles, and there's sadness in his stunning blue eyes. "Hear me out. Something's happening with our older gargoyles—"

"She doesn't need to know that!" Byron's father shouts.

Harold continues, as if the old man never spoke. "They're losing their stone-forms, and without them, they're aging rapidly. Using your powers is our only chance at turning them back to stone and saving their lives. We think that if you turn them to stone, then it may re-activate their ability to change."

Something chokes my throat. *I could use this curse to save people? It's… it's not possible.* "And what if it doesn't work?" I whisper. "What if it just kills him?"

He pushes the hair back from my face. "If you don't try, he's got maybe weeks left."

"A few weeks are better than nothing," I tell him. "Trust me."

I look back at the older humans, and sympathy blossoms within me. At one point they were immortal, frozen in time in healthy bodies. They must be terrified.

And maybe… maybe I can help them.

"Please," Harold begs. "Just try. We wouldn't have brought you here if we thought you'd fail."

I take a deep breath. I can *try*. Maybe if I can save them, they'll see me differently. My gargoyles won't have to fight to justify why my life should be spared. These old gargoyles will see with their own eyes that I can do more than just kill.

"Okay, I'll do it," I say, squaring my shoulders.

"We weren't giving you a choice," Byron's father says, his voice shaking. "You're our prisoner, and you will do as we say."

I stare at them, and something changes within me, something I know is a result of the four men at my side. Men who seem to care about me.

"And I want to make something clear to you. There are people who believe gargoyles are evil, that they are cursed beings. There are people who fear mermaids, sirens, witches, nymphs, demi-gods, gods, and every other magical being. But after all your lifetimes, you must have come to realize that there are good and bad in every group. That you can't just decide an entire species is bad. So, yes, I'm a monster. Yes, you hunt my kind. But I want you to know here and now that not all of us are bad. I'm helping you today, not because I fear you. Because believe me, you're not the first group to kidnap me. I've endured prisons. I've endured torture. I've endured things that none of you could ever imagine. And if I didn't want to help you, nothing you could do would force me to."

The man with the yellow teeth sneered. "Nice speech, monster."

A few of the old people laughed. I can feel the tension in my gargoyles.

"I just had to say it," I say with a shrug. "But I know empathy can't be taught, so it is what it is. I'll try to save your life, and you guys go right on hating me. I'm sure it's easier that way for all of you."

"Let's get on with it," Byron's father says, but there's something unreadable in his expression.

The older man stands. He seems unsteady on his feet. Byron sprints forward and moves to take his arm. His father pulls away, then shakily steps down the stairs on his own. Byron hovers behind him, his expression concerned.

I watch them, and something twists in my chest. Byron loves his father. Of course he does. But it was hard to see it under his tough exterior. Now, however, as he hovers behind him, I see it.

I don't know if any bored Gods are watching us now, but I pray they save this angry gargoyle's life.

Do you truly pray? The unfamiliar voice echoes in my head. The power of a God humming in each word.

Someone is listening. Someone is watching.

I haven't prayed to the Gods since I was exiled, since I still believed in something. But I slowly sink to my knees, and clasp my hands in front of me, bowing my head.

Yes, I pray. I pray that I have the power to save these gargoyles. To do something good with my curse.

I wait for a long minute on my knees, my eyes squeezed shut. But there's nothing. No voice. No response.

Regret makes my heart clench. The words I thought I heard... they must have been a trick of my mind, the desperate hope of someone who was terrified, someone who finally found people who could see the good in her. Someone who knew that if she killed this man, four handsome men would never see her the same again.

When I open my eyes, I'm surprised to feel a tear flowing down my cheek.

A curious request of a monster. The voice comes again, but this time it sounds amused.

I don't move for a long second, waiting to see what more he'll say, but the voice is silent. Then I realize the God I've prayed to could just as easily be here to watch me kill this gargoyle as he is to help me save him. Fucking Gods.

I brush the tear away and climb to my feet. Which is the first time I realize that the entire room is silent, that every eye is on me.

No one knows what to make of my prayer. I can see it in their faces. But hell, I don't know what to make of it either.

Byron's father stands in front of a massive window made of different colored glass. It makes up an image of a gargoyle on top of a building, staring down at a city with a sunset behind him.

The old man stands alone. Byron is back by my side.

And the Elites are to our side.

My legs shake as I take a deep breath and move closer to him. He watches me warily, and when I'm just a few feet from him, I pause.

"What's your name?"

He looks hesitant. "Elite Edgar."

I smile. "Here's what I need you to do, Edgar. I need you to put all your energy into hoping this works, because I'm scared. And I need one of us to be brave."

His eyes widen in surprise. "All right."

I take another deep breath and reach for glasses, but freeze. Looking behind me, I search out Byron. "Is there anything you want to say?"

He opens his mouth and then closes it. "No, because this is going to go just the way we plan. My father and I can talk afterwards."

His faith in me is like a warm hug. "Thanks," I say, and the word is barely a whisper.

He nods, his gaze holding mine.

I turn back around. "Ready?"

The old man looks pale, but nods.

And… I slide my glasses off.

Chapter Twenty-One

MEDUSA

*E*dgar turns to stone, but not the way others have before. It starts in his face as his expression freezes into one of fear. His pupils fade as his skin turns grey. It moves over his throat, shoulders, chest and arms. I watch the stone as it moves over him like a virus.

Horror steals my breath. I've killed him. I've failed. This man is not a gargoyle. He's just… another dead man turned to stone by a monster

When the stone spreads down his legs, and I know all the life has drained from him, I collapse onto my knees. "No," I whisper.

Tears fill my eyes, and I pull my glasses back on. I'm weeping, and I feel stupid. Why did I hope for anything other than what's happened before?

My gargoyles are suddenly kneeling around me. Marcus pulls me into his lap, and I cry harder.

"I killed him," I say, and then my gaze meets Byron's. "I'm so sorry!"

He reaches out and takes my face into his hands.

There's so much pain in his expression. Pain I caused. "It wasn't your fault. You warned us. We made you try."

"It didn't work," the yellow-toothed human says, and his voice is filled with regret.

"We're doomed," another of the men say.

A woman starts to cry. And then, one of the women points behind us, to Edgar. "Wait..."

Every muscle in my body tenses, and I turn back around. Cracks have formed in the statue of Edgar. The sound of stone breaking fills the air, and suddenly, the stone explodes off of him. A gargoyle stretches out of the mess of broken stone, like a creature that has shed its skin. His large wings flutter, and he roars so loudly the ceiling shakes.

Then, his wings slowly fold onto his back, and for the first time I see his resemblance to Byron. It's uncanny. He still looks older than his son, but more like a wise father, rather than an old man.

"It worked," he says simply. "Our way of life is saved."

My men hug me. People are laughing.

"Now, for the others," he tells me.

This time when I stand and move to the older people, I don't feel scared. They move to stand in front of their simple thrones and look at me. I'm overwhelmed by the hope in their eyes. I'm not their killer...I'm their savior.

I've never felt like this before. Wanted. Needed. Important.

"Ready?" I ask them.

They nod, smile, and say their confirmations.

I smirk. "Get ready for your hot gargoyle bods."

Pulling my glasses down, it's the first time in my life that I feel joy as I watch the six people turn to stone. Byron's father, and my gargoyles, move to my side, as I slip my glasses back on. The older people are all frozen in place, all the color of stone.

"You've saved their lives," Forrest says.

He wraps an arm around my shoulders, squeezes, and pulls me to his side. I'm so happy. There are just no words. Is it really possible that I have a greater purpose in this world? That I can be of use?

When the stone begins to crack and crumble from the people, there are suddenly six younger, healthy-looking gargoyles, stretching their wings and roaring in triumph. A few shoot into the air and circle the inside of the building, before landing once more.

A sense of celebration fills the room.

Edgar gives his son an awkward side-hug. "I knew we could count on you to save us."

Byron shakes his head. "It wasn't us. It was *her*."

The pleasure drains from his face. He steps away from us and seats himself back on his throne. His change of demeanor shoots through the room, and the other Elites follow suit, sitting back in their own chairs.

"Now, about this monster—" he begins.

"She just saved all your lives!" Forrest says.

"Yes, she did. But that doesn't change what she is."

"Are you fucking kidding me?" he shouts.

"Watch your tone!" One of the Elites snaps back.

Edgar leans back in his throne, and his gaze levels with mine. "You have spent a lifetime killing and wreaking havoc on mankind. The punishment for your crimes is death."

My throat closes. I knew this was coming. Why did I think my actions might change their plans? Might change the way they saw me? I feel light-headed.

"You can't do this," Forrest says.

"Monster lover," the man with the yellow teeth shouts.

Forrest leaps forward, but I catch his arm. He looks between me and the elder, his gaze wild.

"Don't," I tell him.

"He can't talk about you like that," he presses, and every muscle in his body is tense.

"We talked about this," I say. My gargoyles can't fight an entire village of gargoyles, and I won't have their deaths on my hands. "I can handle this."

"You can handle what? Your death?" he shouts at me.

I give him a sad smile and touch his face. "I've got this."

Marcus pulls Forrest back, and his gaze slides to the gargoyles. He gathers himself and stands before them. When he finally speaks, his voice is deep and solemn. "We request a Blood Moon Judgment."

A few of the Elites gasp.

"Marcus—" Edgar begins.

"We request a Blood Moon Judgment," Marcus repeats, a challenge in his voice.

Edgar looks to his son. "This is madness. If you do this, you'll lose. Not just the judgment, but your standing in this community. You will be forever seen as monster lovers. You will never be sent to hunt one down again. You'll never be allowed to take a woman, or have a child. You'll be outcasts within your own community."

My heart races. "Guys—"

"We've made our decision," Byron tells them.

His father closes his eyes. "Very well." Then, he opens his eyes and raises his voice. "The monster will be imprisoned until the Blood Moon. On that date, your brotherhood will be given an opportunity to present your reasons for sparing her life. If you lose, you give up everything, and she still dies."

"No," I say out loud. "They won't change their minds. Don't do this. I've lived a long time. I can—"

"It's done, and we don't regret it." Forrest takes my face and tilts me up to look at him. "Do you understand? This is our choice, our fight. You've done everything we've asked, and more. You've done enough."

"I can't let you—"

"The choice has been made," Marcus says. And when I look at him, I'm surprised to see admiration in his gaze.

"Take her to the prison," Edgar orders.

Two gargoyles stand from the dais, and they move beside me. The yellow-toothed man reaches for me.

Byron springs forward and growls low in his throat. "Take her there. But don't touch her."

The man drops his hand, and Forrest releases me. I move between the two strange gargoyles, and we walk toward the door. I can't believe I'm willingly allowing myself to be imprisoned. It goes against every instinct within me, but I can't walk away. They told me to trust them. If this is the only way we can be together, then so be it.

When the end comes, if we lose, at least I'll die with their love.

That's something I never imagined having.

I look back at them one last time. All four men look like they want to chase after me, like they want to hold me in their arms.

My heart squeezes. The doors open, and I step out into the sunlight.

Chapter Twenty-Two

EDGAR

There were so many ways that I imagined this day going, but I never thought that in saving my life, I'd condemn my son's. He has fallen in love with a monster. His standing in our community is gone. Not only has he lost his honor, but he has lost the faith of all of us.

How could he make such a dire mistake?

"They will need to be watched," Galena speaks softly to my side.

It's just the two of us in the throne room now, me and Galena, my most trusted advisor. I sent the others away after a time. Their excitement about returning to their old bodies, combined with their disgust at our gargoyles, was too much. I couldn't think.

"Agreed," I tell her, even though it makes my chest ache in a strange way.

My son and his most trusted friends must now be watched. We don't have faith that they won't try to free the monster.

Somehow, I've failed him.

Galena takes my hand in hers in a way that feels almost practical. "I can't imagine what you must be feeling."

No, she cannot.

"But this Medusa…" she begins.

I know what she's going to say. I replay the events since the monster appeared before us. It does not make sense. She is unlike any monster we've encountered before.

Her kind are tricky, vile creatures who are capable of doing anything to survive.

But—and I swear to the gods that I will not voice these thoughts to anyone—she seemed so genuine. Even in my stone-form, I saw her cry when she thought I was dead. I could *feel* her sadness and regret.

"What do you know of her?"

Galena is quiet for a long time. "Very little. Until recent events, I believed her dead."

We'd received communication from a detective in The Special Unit in her city. He'd informed us of her killings, and the need for the city to be rid of her. The revelation had been a blessing to us, and we hoped for a chance to save our lives. We had told Peter we would take care of it.

We had sent the team we felt best suited for extracting her and retrieving the artifacts.

"Each pregnancy takes longer to achieve," Galena begins, and I already know where she's going. "If the artifacts do not help significantly, we're doomed. These three babes may be the last of our kind. And with us turning human in our old age… our people will simply cease to exist."

"Unless the babes are female."

She sighed. "We haven't had a single female child in three generations."

"And so what are you saying?"

"Perhaps we should not kill this Medusa. Perhaps we

should simply keep her indefinitely as a prisoner, so that she may renew us each time we turn to stone."

"No."

She releases my hand. "How many times have you said that the survival of our people trumps all else?"

"If we stop having babies… if we need the help of a monster to remain immortal… I would sooner let our people die out. We would have no hope at new babes, at any kind of a future, except one that hinged on a monster's abilities."

"Edgar, be reasonable."

I clench the handles of my chair. "The decision has been made."

She doesn't understand. The three females will give birth very soon. If there is not a girl among them, our fate is likely sealed. That's even if the babes survive. It took ten years for these pregnancies to take root. The last three pregnancies resulted in one early miscarriage, one stillborn child, and one healthy boy.

I pray every day that we have three healthy babes this time and that the magic of the statue and the necklace will give us what we need to continue as a people. But I've calculated our odds… and they don't look good. I believe this is the end of us.

We have been renewed. For how long, I don't know. But truly, all we needed was to know the sex of the children. My only purpose for continuing to live was to see if our people have any hope at all.

If we don't, we should allow ourselves to grow old, to become human, and to die. There's no reason to stretch it out and to fight against the inevitable.

Even if this Medusa bothers me on a level I don't understand, she's still a monster. Eventual death is preferable to relying on an enemy to save us.

So, we shall see.

"Do you think they love her?" Galena asks.

I stiffen, and remember their faces. "Perhaps."

"Then, we should do all we can to keep them from her. To remind them of their true loyalty—to us."

I nod. "If we keep them from her, I fear their patience will come to an end, and we'll be forced to do something that we'll regret. But we can make it hard for them. We can do everything we can to distance them from her."

"Perhaps reminding them of Ashunda will help. Seeing that soon she will be free to choose them, as I know she wishes to do."

They'll know she'd never choose them now.

"We can try."

But as I stare blankly into space, I know a few things. No matter how this ends, I will lose my son. You cannot kill the woman your child loves, no matter that she's evil, without his hatred consuming him.

I just hope that in three months, on the night of the blood moon, they will have come to their senses.

Because one way or another, blood will be shed that night.

Chapter Twenty-Three

FORREST

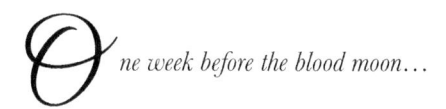

One week before the blood moon…

"Please, just let me see her! Even if it's only for a minute!" I know I'm begging, but it's been one month since they allowed us to visit Medusa, and I'm desperate.

I'm going to lose my mind if I don't see her soon, if I don't know she's safe.

Arthur looks uncomfortable. He knows why I've come now. The typical guards are assholes who've ignored our pleas. But Arthur is covering for them, now that their female is in labor, and he has a kind heart. He and I are friends.

"I'm not supposed to…" he says, but there's something in his voice that I don't like.

"Is she okay?" I ask.

He avoids my gaze. "She's a monster, and a prisoner."

"That's not what I asked."

After a minute, he sighs, and his grip on the handle of

his sword loosens. "The others wouldn't want you to know, but the guards even feel sorry for her. For a while, they'd come in and play cards with her. She'd tell them stories. I think… I think they even liked her. But things started to change about a month ago."

My heart races. "Change how?"

He looks uneasy. "She stopped eating. She's been… sick. Throwing up a lot. She gets paler and thinner. The others didn't tell you, but they've requested that the Elites give her time outdoors. They have requested that she be allowed to see Galena in hopes of healing, but each time, they've been denied. The guards didn't want to do anything to risk their female's health or their standing in the community, for their child's benefit. But I think they were glad to let me take over."

I feel sick. "Why?"

He runs a hand through his dark hair. "Because they knew I couldn't see a female like that and do nothing."

"What have you done?" I ask, a little hope blooming in my chest.

His gaze holds mine. "It's not what I've done. It's what I'm going to do."

I frown, but before I can ask, he continues.

"This evening, just before the sunsets, I'm going to walk the perimeter. The guards within the prison will be taking a break to eat, and I'll be the only one here. The others are busy helping the new moms."

Two of the gargoyles had given birth to healthy sons. And the third was laboring. No one could remember ever having this many babies in the village, and everyone was scattering to care for them.

The Elites had sent our brotherhood on every errand under the sun, to care for the babies' needs. We have retrieved every supply imaginable from neighboring cities, and even though we knew they were trying to distract us, we did as we were told. We've just recently returned.

"What are you saying?" I ask, even though I know.

He holds my gaze. "You'll only have a few minutes with her. You'll need to get in and out without being caught. And if they find you, my name stays out of it." He looks troubled. "Try to get her to eat. Maybe it's just sadness. Maybe you can lift her spirits, before she wastes away."

I can't help the fear that sweeps me under. How ill is Medusa? And what could be wrong with her? Immortals rarely got sick. But the fact that even the others are concerned makes me uneasy.

"At sunset," I tell him.

He nods.

I clasp his arm, and he clasps mine.

"For what it's worth," he continues. "I was angry when I learned that you guys had fallen for her. I felt betrayed. But after spending time with her, I get it. And so do the others. I still think you'll lose the blood moon judgment, but I think a few of us plan to speak on her behalf. Even a few of the female gargoyles have spoken with her, since she has more knowledge of babies than they do, and… I think they may even see her as a friend."

I'm surprised by everything he says. It sounds as if we were the only ones restricted from seeing her.

I leave, flying as quickly as I can to our home. It's further from the village, in a massive tree near one of the smaller waterfalls. I land outside the door, and open it. I'm angry as hell, but I also have hope for the first time in months.

The others are waiting for me. They look up as I enter. Harold stops cooking over our little stove and Marcus and Byron stop sharpening their swords at the table.

"They didn't let you," Marcus sounds angry.

"Of course they didn't," Byron sneers. "I don't give a fuck anymore, I'm going to see her."

"One more week," Harold presses. "We just need to be patient for one more week. If we can show that we can obey the rules, that she hasn't turned us against them—"

"They'll still kill her." Byron sheaths his sword and places it on the table, his head bowed.

We're all being tortured without her. It's been three months of absolute hell. The few times we saw her... made us realize how much that we loved her. After being apart, we know how much we need her. She's the only female for us.

We've already decided that if they rule against her on the Blood Moon Judgment, we will fight. Even if it was to the death.

I take a deep breath. "We can see her tonight, if we want."

Harold freezes. "What do you mean?"

"Arthur will be the only guard for a little while. He said that we can sneak in and out to see her."

"Thank the Gods," Marcus mumbles.

Everyone looks relieved, which is why I hate what I have to say next.

"There's something else." The air changes. "She's sick."

They look at me like I'm stupid.

"Sick how?" Byron asks, really slowly.

"Arthur said she hasn't been eating. And that's she's lost weight... and she's been throwing up."

Something dark moves over Byron's face. "For how long?"

"About a month. He said the guards have been worried

enough about her that they asked the Elites to allow Galena to look at her."

"And my father said no." He rises very slowly from his chair. "So, our female has been alone in a prison cell, throwing up, and not eating, and no one thought to tell us? No one would even permit a visit from the healer?"

I nod, holding my breath.

He turns, paces for a moment, and then goes to the wall and begins to punch the wood until it splinters. When he draws his arm back again, Marcus catches it. Byron's knuckles are bloody when he whirls to face our leader.

"I'm going to kill them."

Marcus looks between his injured hand and his face. "No, we're going to save her. If she's in as bad of condition as they say, we're going to save her tonight."

Some of the anger drains from Byron's face. Marcus pulls him into a hug, and they clench each other tightly for a long moment.

"She's going to be okay." Harold removes the sharpened swords from the table, placing them on the weapons shelf. Then, he places bowls on the table and ladles out the stew. "She's immortal. And like she says, she's survived a lot. She can survive this too."

Byron pulls out of Marcus' hug and stares at all of us. "But she shouldn't have to. Having four gargoyles to protect her should mean that she's safe, and loved, not suffering alone. It kills me that this is all our fault! She did nothing to deserve this!"

And that's it... the reason we can barely function, the reason none of us can laugh without her. That's the reason we barely eat, and we've withdrawn from our people.

She is ours to protect, and we're failing her.

Something no gargoyle should ever have to endure.

"Sunset isn't far away," I tell them. "We should eat and gather our weapons."

They nod, and the chairs scrape against the wooden floor as we settle at the table. But all we do is stir our stew, and no one talks. We are all thinking the same thing. Not far from us, the little woman who holds our heart doesn't eat. How can we?

Chapter Twenty-Four

MARCUS

We stand at the edge of our village, watching the sun. We've heard the announcement. Ashundra has given birth to a boy, and everyone believes that we're to thank for the three healthy babies. Everyone believes that the necklace and the statue have brought this good fortune. The women have taken turns wearing the necklace since we brought it, and they all rest frequently in the room set aside for the statue. But for our efforts, everyone thinks we would have lost at least one babe.

It's strange to both be celebrated by our people and abhorred by them. They claim to be confused by our love for Medusa, and yet, I've seen it in their faces. I, unlike my brothers, have kept careful tabs on everything that's been going on. No, I didn't know she was sick, but I did know the other gargoyles have been visiting her.

At first when I listened cautiously into conversations, they spoke of her with disgust and disdain, but their tones have changed, and I know why. They can only spend so much time with her before they know she isn't what they've been told.

I just pray it's enough to turn the minds of the Elites during the judgment.

"It's time," Byron says.

I observe two guards leaving the prisons, toward the main building, where dinner is being served. We wait until the doors close behind them. The streets are strangely quiet, with everyone either caring for the new mothers, or eating in the great hall.

It's now or never, I think, and I take a deep breath.

I hope and pray that Medusa isn't as sick as Arthur described her.

We try to move casually through the village, but our steps are fast. When we come to the bars that cover the door of the prisons, Arthur is there on the other side. He unlocks the door and then he hands me the keys. "In and out," he says.

I nod. "Thank you."

He remains in place, so that anyone who might walk by will see him there, guarding everything as if nothing is amiss.

We unlock two more gates before we come to the cells. Hers is on the end. The slightest light from the little windows near the roof of each cell allows the red glow of the sunset to light our way.

We hurry to her prison, and I pause as I reach it, searching for her. And then, I spot her. She's lying on her bed. She's curled around her stomach, one hand hanging off the bed. Her skin is pale and her face is sunken as if starved.

Something inside of me screams in terror. She looks dead. I logically know she's not, but she looks that way. My hands shake as I put the key in the lock and turn it.

"Holy shit," Forrest whispers in horror beside me.

As soon as I get the door open, we all spring inside.

I gather her in my arms beneath her thin blanket. And I'm terrified by how light she feels.

"Medusa?" I whisper.

Her eyes are open, but she's staring off without seeing.

"How the fuck did this happen?" Byron sounds like he's about to lose it again.

There's no time for panic or fear. This is worse than I ever imagined. I thought we could obey the rules and have a chance at the Blood Moon Judgment, but there might not be anything left of her to save by then.

I hate the idea that we must betray Arthur, but we do. We need to get her to Galena, no matter what the consequences are. We need to find out what has an immortal this sick.

"We've got you," Harold whispers, smoothing her hair back from her face.

She doesn't react.

I stand, and my brotherhood immediately flanks me. Their swords make the slightest whisper of noise as they unsheathe them.

We move past the empty prison cells and open one door after another.

When Arthur turns around, he doesn't look surprised.

I stiffen. How are we going to hurt him?

"Just make it look good," he tells us.

Then, he turns his back to us.

Byron moves behind him, and hits him on the back of the head with the hilt of his sword. Arthur drops to the floor, and we pull him to the side. Now, no one will believe he helped us. His standing in the community will be safe.

Thank the Gods for Arthur.

We open the last door and start across the village. Galena's house is at the edge, near the water. It's also on the ground, luckily for us.

We hope that she has returned home from helping with Ashundra's birthing.

Halfway to her house, we hear a door open and the explosion of conversation. We freeze. My gaze goes to the door of the dining hall. Two gargoyles are walking, chatting with each other. They look up, then do a double take and stare at us.

Fuck.

"They're escaping with the prisoner!" One of them shouts.

He races back into the dining hall, and we turn and rise into the air, shooting across the village to Galena's house. Behind us, more shouts fill the air. Galena's house grows closer and closer. We just need to reach it and bar the door. Then, we can buy her enough time to help Medusa.

We hear the gargoyles pursuing us and can sense them in the air, not far behind. Without slowing, Byron crashes into Galena's door, and I shoot inside. My gaze sweeps from the fire, to her shelves of medical supplies, and healing bed in the center of the room. The healer? She's nowhere to be found.

Fuck.

I turn back around, stepping outside where Harold and Forrest guard the door. "She's not here."

Tension sings through them as a dozen gargoyles land in front of us.

"Move," Byron orders them.

Benjamin, leader of the guards, pulls his sword from the sheath on his back, and the other gargoyles follow suit. "Give us the monster. Don't be fools."

"She needs to see the healer," Harold says, his tone desperate. "She's sick."

Benjamin wrinkles his nose. "Are you really willing to die for her?"

Our answer comes as one. "Yes."

The guards leap forward, and I step back, pulling Medusa out of harm's way. Forrest, Byron, and Harold clash swords with them. Their movements are that of well-trained warriors, as they keep the overwhelming number of enemies at bay. Even when swords strike their flesh, leaving behind marks in their stone-forms, they don't hesitate.

The sounds of battle fill the sanctuary. Birds lift from the trees, and the glow of the fairies change from golden to red. As the sky darkens, the sounds of war take over.

Suddenly, someone shouts. "Stop!"

The guards freeze and move back.

My men are breathing hard, standing in front of me to protect my precious burden.

Byron's father pushes through his warriors, and his gaze burns as it falls on us. "What is the meaning of this?"

"She's sick!" Byron shouts. "And you left her in there dying—"

"Her kind can't die from illness," he says, and there's no kindness in his voice. "She might suffer, but—"

"Fucking asshole!" he shouts. "Since when do we allow women in our care to suffer?"

More gargoyles have appeared in the doorways of the buildings. Some fly down, landing not far behind the guards. The entire village must be out. I see Galena emerge from the birthing room, cleaning her hands on a towel. The two females, with small infants, leave other buildings, staring curiously as their men gather around them.

"She is not a woman! She's a monster!" Elder Edgar shouts back at his son.

Harold's soft voice comes, but this time it seems to ring all around us. "Is she really the monster here? This *woman* risked her life to get that statue. This woman faced her own demons—her own memories of being brutally raped—to steal the necklace, from a goddess no less. And who, even knowing that coming here might result in her death, came to help us. She went willingly to our prisons. In return, we left her sick and suffering. She's not the monster here. We are."

Edgar steps forward. "Do you all truly believe that we'll change everything we think of monsters because you fell in love with one? Monsters kill humans. We hunt them. Nothing has changed."

I don't know what comes over me, but I push past the others. "I know how easy it is to see things as black and white. Hell, my life was easier when I did." Despite myself, I look down at her. "And then, I met her. She was born human and cursed by the Gods for being a victim of their cruelty. She actively chooses not to kill, even though it's within her power to do so. I know it'd be easier to just lump her in with the creatures we've killed, but we can't. Not in good conscience."

"She's not going anywhere," Edgar says, but his tone isn't so confident.

"We just want her to get help, that's all."

Galena steps through the crowd. "Bring her inside."

Edgar grabs her shoulder. "You can't be serious!"

She rolls her eyes. "Look at her. She's hardly dangerous! And besides, I owe her one."

Tension continues between all of us as Galena leads me into the house and tells me to lay her on the bed.

I do.

"Now," she says. "Get out."

I shake my head. What if Galena hurts her?

She meets my gaze. "You have my word she'll be safe, but your brotherhood is on the edge of something dangerous. You're their alpha. Go out there and buy me enough time to figure out what's going on."

My head spins, and I feel fear unlike anything I've felt before as I look down at my Medusa's sunken, pale face. I walk back, stumble out the door, and it closes at my back.

Taking several deep breaths, I pull my sword free and go to stand with my brotherhood. We face down the people we called friends, people that we considered our family.

Some of them regard us with anger, some with interest, and others—with pity. But I don't care. I don't care about anything, as long as she's safe.

Time ticks away. Crying babies are taken back inside. The air grows colder and the moon rises. And still, the warriors face off with us and the Elites gather. Waiting.

And then, Galena steps out of her home.

The light from her fire illuminates all of us.

We look back her, holding our breath, hoping that Medusa will be safe.

"Well," she says, very slowly. "I've found the cause of her mysterious illness."

We hold our breath.

"She's pregnant."

The air whooshes out of us. My brain freezes.

"She's about three months along, and given the size of the child, I have no doubt it's a gargoyle." Steel laces her voice. "If she is not treated with the utmost care, if she's not fed according to her cravings, if she's not given sunlight and happiness, the child will die, along with the mother. The fetus is taking everything within her, consuming what it needs. And it's still not enough."

The news that our woman is carrying our child wrecks

me. Hope rushes through me at the same time as absolute horror at what our people have done to her.

We have to see her, to touch her and hold her. The fact that she's sick and dying is enough to destroy us, or give us a new reason for living.

But we can't go, not until we're sure they won't simply rush us and kill her.

We turn to the Elites, waiting.

I don't think they've ever looked more uncertain and shocked in all the time I've known them.

"She's still a monster," Gary says, his yellow-teeth clenching together.

"Are you fucking kidding us?" It's Arthur. He's holding a rag to his bleeding head. "A gargoyle child is the most precious to our people. There should be no question what happens now. The woman joins our people, and her baby is cared for by us, just like any of our children."

"She's a monster!" Gary repeats.

The females have returned outside. They stride forward, clutching their sons to their chests. Everyone goes silent.

They come to stand in front of us and turn to face the Elites.

Ashundra speaks for them. "You'll hurt her over our dead bodies."

Another woman glares. "Idiot men."

The third female places one hand on her hip, and her gaze slides over all of them. "Attacking a *pregnant* woman? You should be ashamed!"

Their words shock everyone. We're breathing hard. My hand grows sweaty on the hilt of my sword. *Will they listen with the females on our side?*

Arthur and Max push through the crowd and come to stand beside the women.

Max speaks, his voice carrying. "Many of you have met Medusa, spoken to her. You know what she did for us. You also know her curse has no impact on us. Where do you stand? With her and her child—with Marcus, Harold, Byron, and Forrest's child—or with your hatred of monsters?"

The head of the guards sheathes his sword. "I won't kill a pregnant woman."

The other guards follow suit.

We stare at the Elites.

Edgar finally speaks. "For now, she's granted sanctuary. While she's pregnant. After that, we'll discuss her fate."

We feel relief unlike anything we've felt before.

Arthur grabs my shoulder. "Congrats. You're dads!"

We… we *are* dads. We have a tiny baby inside our woman. Inside our sick woman.

And they *will* survive. No matter the cost to ourselves.

Chapter Twenty-Five

MEDUSA

*S*ix months later…

"Seriously, guys. I can't eat any more." I look down at our little table. There's a half-eaten chocolate cake, ribs, mashed potatoes, pickles, a cherry pie, and salmon.

My big belly is bursting, and still, they're trying to feed me more.

"Just another bite," Harold pleads, holding up a fork full of pie.

I sigh, and eat it, just to make him feel better.

His entire face lights up, and I almost laugh. It isn't hard making them happy nowadays.

"I'm getting fat," I tell them, swallowing the pie.

Byron scowls. "You are *not* getting fat. You're getting healthy."

"I was healthy twenty pounds ago," I say, and mean it.

Ever since I left the prisons, and they moved me into their home, I've been doing better. Instead of eating that

Medusa's Destiny

nauseating crap they fed me at every meal, my gargoyles literally race out to get whatever I crave.

At first I couldn't walk, but they carried me around the forest. They helped me bathe months' worth of grime off my body and hair. They took me to visit the fairies, and to play with the magic fish. They've catered to my every whim—without comment or complaint.

I got stronger. I could walk again. I could eat more and more.

Now, I know I'm out-of-the-woods, and yet they continue to baby me.

"Guys, I'm huge. I haven't been able to see my feet in weeks."

Byron huffs. "That's because our baby is growing big and strong." He kneels down beside me, and places his head on my belly. After a second, he looks up, his expression *very* sincere. "The baby wants more food."

I laugh and punch him playfully. "You stop that right now! I'm twice the size of the other women when they were pregnant! The last thing I need to do is to keep eating. This baby is already massive!"

All my men are grinning. Harold goes right back to fussing with the baby crib he built, making sure it's securely next to our bed for the millionth time.

"It's perfect," I tell him, laughing.

He blushes. "The baby should be here any day. I just want everything to be perfect for him or her."

I look at their home. It looks like a baby store threw up in it. "I think we're good."

Forrest walks by me and places a kiss on my cheek. "Just let him fuss, or he'll go back to driving us all crazy with those damn baby books."

"What?" he frowns at us. "We need to know not just what to do during the birthing, but when the baby is actually here. I bought a new book about gentle parenting, and I really like the idea of teaching instead of punishing—"

Forrest groans.

But Harold just continues. "No time outs, just time ins. We would talk them through challenges, rather than disciplining them."

"I can't listen to this anymore!" Forrest shouts, throwing his hands up.

I start to laugh again, but it cuts off as a pain shoots through my belly.

"Are you all right?" Marcus asks, and then they're all at my side.

Marcus adjusts Athena's massive necklace around my throat, then places a hand on my belly, as if he can tell what's going on inside of me.

"I'm okay," I tell them. "You just stuffed me. I think a walk might help."

They immediately gather around me to push my big pregnant body out of my chair.

It's almost comical, but the truth is, I'm not feeling great.

Forrest carries me down from the treehouse, and we go to the village. The five of us walk together, slowly. I keep hoping the pain will fade, but it only seems to intensify.

Damn that last bite of pie. I knew that I shouldn't have eaten it.

The female gargoyles sit on blankets in a grassy area in town. Two of the babes crawl around, while their protective fathers stand guard.

They wave when they spot us. We make our way towards them.

"How are the babies?" I ask, trying not to wince.

Ashundra answers without hesitation. "Still not

sleeping through the night. Probably because *certain* men rock him every time he makes the slightest noise."

I force a smile. "Damn those jerks."

She laughs.

"Well," Elery says. "Little Shawn is now getting into everything, so they've locked down our house with every baby proofing thing imaginable. I can't even use the toilet without going through a dozen locks."

Autumn grins and looks at my men. "Little Mitchell is the same way. You just wait!"

"We can't wait!" Harold exclaims, making everybody laugh.

I hiss as pain shoots down through my belly.

"More pain?" Byron asks. "We should see the healer."

"I'm fine," I reassure him. "Just too much pie… and cake."

Ashundra rises and comes over to study me. "You don't look so good. Go check with Galena, just in case."

I start to protest.

"What if the baby's in trouble?" Harold asks.

His question makes me stiffen. They don't need to remind me how many things can still go wrong.

"Maybe we will go see her… just to be sure," I say.

We make our way to Galena's. Even though they all want to carry me, I refuse. I can still walk, despite what they think. A few male gargoyles nod at me as I pass, but their gazes linger a little too long. I swear to god, my men all tense, like they're about ready for an actual beat down.

I laugh. "You guys realize I'm like twenty months pregnant, right?"

"Nine months," Harold says, sounding angry.

"But if they think you'll be up for grabs once the baby comes, they're going to get to experience my foot in their asses," Forrest says, his voice loud enough for them to hear.

Geez. Like I'm a catch. Even here.

But I kind of like seeing them jealous.

"I thought that's how things work here," I say, innocently.

Byron sweeps me into his arms, and his mouth crushes mine.

I sigh and soften beneath his kiss. My lady-bits heat up, and I wonder if we have time to stop at our place for a quickie before we see Galena.

He pulls back from our kiss, leaving me panting. "Sorry, but we've decided we're not going to share. You got a problem with that?"

I tap my chin, as if thinking. "Maybe you guys can remind me of your skills later, and I'll—shit," I gasp as another pain hits me.

It lasts for too long before I can draw in a breath.

For the first time, I'm a little worried. What if something *is* wrong?

They race to Galena's house and push open the door.

She looks at us and rolls her eyes. "Again? Boys, I'm sure she's fine."

"Actually, there might be something wrong this time," I say, trying not to sound nervous.

Her annoyance vanishes. All the many times they've dragged me in here, I've never been worried.

"Lay her on the table."

They do, and she shoos them out of the room while she checks me.

At last, she smoothes down my dress, and her gaze meets mine. "It looks like you're going into labor."

My breath hitches. "Now?"

She nods. "It could last awhile. But you're far enough along that I'm not worried."

When she calls my men back in, they hover around me, looking anxious and excited.

Fearful, I lay back and wrap my arms around my chest. "I'm not ready for this."

Harold pushes my hair back from my face. "It's going to be okay."

I shake my head.

Byron squeezes my knee. "You can handle anything. And besides, we're right here. You'll be okay. Just trust us."

I look at each of my men, scared out of my mind. I guess if this is going to happen, at least I have them.

But I don't tell them the truth—I've never been more terrified of anything in my life.

Chapter Twenty-Six

EDGAR

I look up as Galena enters the great hall. All of us are seated, waiting to hear the news. Did the child survive the birthing? If it did not, we'll have to move quickly to kill her before her men can interfere. If the child survived? We'll have to decide how long to let her live.

She comes to stand in front of us. I'm a bit surprised she hasn't joined us on her throne. "It's done."

My pulse races. "Out with it. Did the child live or die? Is It normal? Dangerous like its mother?"

She stands taller. "Medusa had twins."

Elizabeth gasps and stands. "Twins? That's… impossible."

"Did they survive?" I ask, my gaze snapping back to Galena.

She nods. "Both children survived… and both children are female."

A chill moves down my spine, and every hair stands up on my body.

"It's a blessing from the Gods," Elizabeth whispers, covering her mouth.

Heath turns to me. "This changes everything."

I meet his gaze. "It changes nothing."

The atmosphere of the room is charged, like the moment before lightning strikes.

Heath speaks to me slowly, as if I'm a fool. "We cannot breed with Gods, or demi-gods, humans, or magical creatures—but apparently, we can with monsters. And their new genes might give us the daughters we need to survive as a species."

I feel my muscles stiffen. Is that what they all believe? They all think that we should welcome monsters into our homes with open arms? Can they really be so stupid? This was one... unexpected pregnancy that changes nothing.

Galena clears her throat, and I turn back to her. "Her children are the healthiest that have been born into our society in longer than I can remember. They're large, sturdy, and already very aware of their environment."

"Did you use your Sight?" I ask, holding my breath.

She nods. "When I touched the children, I knew. I knew that they were the answer to our prayers. Either we breed with monsters, or our people die out."

I lean back in my chair. This can't be true. Yet, Galena's Sight has never failed us before.

"There are other female monsters," Elizabeth begins. "Perhaps if they can fall in love with our men, they can be less dangerous. They can become a part of our people the way Medusa has."

"We can't just suddenly tell our people that we're no longer monster-hunters! Their purpose will be gone." Gary stands, glaring at all of us.

I fold my hands in front of my mouth, thinking. Do I trust Medusa? No. Do I want monsters to suddenly join our society? No.

But I'd be a fool to say so. I've seen a change in the

others, month after month. They like Medusa. I feared what they would do if we tried to kill her.

And yet, I also can't take away our purpose.

Nor let our people die out.

"What if we didn't come out and tell them that we've changed our stance on monsters?" I say. "What if we send our potential brotherhoods to capture female monsters? What if we give them tasks that will allow them time to get to know the females? By the time they return, they will either be able to tell us the women are dangerous, and we can't reproduce with them, or they'll form a bond. And we can reluctantly agree to allow them here, on certain terms."

Galena relaxes in front of me. "As long as all the women are safe, including Medusa. We will not lure breeders here, simply to kill them when they aren't of use anymore." There's a bite to her words that reveals just how angry she's been with me for even considering still killing Medusa.

"Agreed," I say. "We'll keep our location hidden, so if they cannot do as we wish, we can turn them free once more, without fear of them extracting revenge."

Everyone seems in agreement that my idea is the way to go.

Except Gary and I. We know the truth. We know there are gargoyles among us who may begrudgingly allow Medusa to remain here, but who will also never see monsters as one of us. If any of the women don't work for what we need, we'll set them loose— and we'll send our men to kill them.

The others don't need to know the truth.

"Go," I tell Galena. "Care for our daughters. They are, after all, the fate of our people."

Elizabeth nods. "And we should tell the others. And celebrate!"

They leave in a rush of happiness, but Gary and I remain.

When the doors close, he doesn't look at me as he speaks. "We won't let any monster leave here alive, right?"

I smile. "Not a single one."

Chapter Twenty-Seven

HAROLD

I haven't slept in three months, and I've never been happier in my life. Our daughters, Bella and Trinity, are absolute miracles. We cannot get enough of them. We cannot get enough of their smiles, or their chubby cheeks. We change diapers. We sing songs, and we cherish our beautiful wife—who gave us a family.

Who filled our house with love.

I rush across the grass, heading for a bush on the other side of our village. It has Sweet Berries—fruit my wife says taste like cupcakes. She's asked for a big bowl of them, and I live to serve her every need.

She's amazing. She nurses the babies on demand, bathes them, soothes their tears. If she asked for the moon, I'd give that to her too.

I'd give her anything. She deserves *everything*.

Max, Arthur, Steven, and Clark leave the main hall, looking excited. I pause when they reach me.

"Something happening?"

Arthur grins. "We're going monster-hunting!"

For some reason, my stomach tightens, knowing now that not all monsters are bad changes how I see the world.

"Who?" I ask.

Max leans in, as if sharing a secret. "Keto. She's a mermaid, the mother of all sea monsters. She's supposed to be very dangerous."

"Well," I search for the words. "Good luck."

Steven laughs and puffs out his hard chest. "Believe me, we won't need it."

I go to get the berries, but look back at them as they soar to their home near the edge of our sanctuary, beside the biggest lake. I hope they come back safely.

But it must be my beautiful woman and my amazing daughters, because I also hope they fail in their mission.

Chapter Twenty-Eight

MEDUSA

I can't believe both babies are asleep. Seriously. I love the little angels, but this mama could use a break. I swear they've got their father's energy... which is just exhausting.

Galena slips quietly into the room. I give her a smile I know is tired-looking.

She creeps over to their cribs, looks down, and smiles. That's one thing. Even though I'm getting a little stir-crazy, staying in one place for this long, it's kind of amazing. Everyone treats me, and my daughters, like we're miracles.

My guys say it's because of how rare daughters are, and because they're basically one of our few shots of making sure gargoyles don't become extinct. But either way, it's nice to know my girls will be completely beloved and protected by an entire race.

Galena sighs softly and comes to where I'm sitting in a rocking chair. "Go on then, go take a break. I got it."

I tense, excited at the thought of freedom, but also nervous about leaving them. "You sure?"

She smiles. "I can handle two sleeping babies."

I nod and force myself to stand and grab my stuff, then stuff it in a bag and fling it over my shoulder. I give one lingering look at them, then slip out the door. My guys have built a ladder onto the treehouse for me, so I don't have to wait for one of them to fly me down. Even if they don't like me using it.

Starting down the rungs, I have one second to gasp, before someone plucks me off. I turn and spot Forrest, who's grinning like a madman.

I shake my head. "Quit doing that!"

He laughs. "Who's watching the kids?"

I hesitate. "Galena."

I feel him stiffen. "Surely one of us can—"

"She's trying to give us a break," I emphasize, hoping he can read between the lines. "Didn't you guys go to *bathe*?"

He shifts me in his arms, and I can see his frown. "Are you sure she can handle them?"

I almost roll my eyes. "At least long enough for us all to *relax* together."

He nods, his expression far away. "I guess."

We fly to the most private waterfall, and I feel a rush of excitement when I spot my guys already bathing in the waters. They look up at us as we land, and my pulse picks up. Man, it's been awhile since I saw so much of their skin. So much muscular arms and muscular chests

"Who's with the babies?" Byron immediately barks.

"Galena," I tell him calmly.

He immediately heads for the shore. "I can go—"

I sigh and place my hands on my hips. "You'll stay right there. The babies will be fine without us for a few minutes."

My guys exchange a look. Byron sinks back into the water, but he looks irritated.

Okay, it looks like they aren't going to figure this out without some help.

I reach for the bottom of my shirt. "She's going to give us some time to get cleaned up on our own." I pull my shirt off. "To get a break from the babies." I reach for my comfy pants and pull them off too. Even though I can feel all eyes on me, I pretend not to notice as I strip off my underwear and bra. "And enjoy some time. Alone."

Splashing into the water, I sigh as the warm water rushes over me. This is what I've been waiting for. Well, this, and some dick. A lot of dick.

It's been two months since I gave birth, and I've been given the green light for some action. And I'm so glad… I was about to lose my freakin' mind. But if my guys think I'm going to beg for it, they have another thing coming.

I grab some of the flowers that bloom near the water and crush them in my hands. Immediately, I'm overwhelmed by the sweet smell. Like chocolate.

This place… it's fucking amazing.

I rub the flowers together until they foam in my hand, and then I run it through my hair and sweep it over my flesh. Trying to be casual, I glance at my guys out of the corner of my eyes. Sure enough, they're all watching me.

Moving onto my breasts, I lather the soap over the mounds, and linger over my nipples, before I sink down into the water and wash it off. When I emerge, someone is directly behind me. I spin to find Byron staring down at me.

"Need any help?"

"Help with what?" I ask, innocently.

He raises a brow. "Getting washed up."

I shrug. "No, I'm good."

Reaching behind him, I grab more flowers, crush them

up, and continue cleaning myself. My stomach… and lower.

His gaze follows my progress.

When I sink under the water, I'm suddenly face-to-face with his aroused dick. Unable to help myself, I take him in my mouth and start to suck. His cock swells in my mouth, and I suck him slowly before finally coming up for air.

He's panting as I emerge. His eyes darkened by desire. "That was… unexpected."

I reach out and curl my hand around him. "Well, when a giant dick gets that close to my face, I have to do something about it."

Forrest moves closer. "If you're looking for a giant dick…"

I grin and look down. Sure enough, he's hard and absolutely delicious looking.

I reach out and start to stroke him, too. Forrest sighs loudly, and closes his eyes, his hips moving slightly with each stroke of my hands.

Someone grabs me from behind. I gasp and turn to see Marcus. He gives me a pointed look. "Did the healer say that we can…?"

"Yup," I say.

I feel him shudder behind me. "She's sure you'll be safe?"

"Yup." I gently rub my ass against his erection.

He reaches around and grasps my breasts, holding them in his hands. I lean back against him and continue stroking my gargoyles.

When Harold comes to stand at my other side, he tilts my head toward him, and his lips seize mine. His touch is harsh and demanding, his tongue sweeping inside as if to claim me. Marcus' fingers pinch my nipples, and I moan against Harold's lips.

I haven't stopped stroking my men when Byron reaches forward and parts my lower lips. My legs shake as he strokes me gently, slipping into my folds, and dancing along my clit. My nerves scream with each touch of his fingers.

Oh yes, I knew this would be good, but I forgot just how good. How in the hell did I go so long without sex?

Harold breaks our kiss. And Byron lifts my legs and wraps them around his waist.

From behind me, I feel Marcus spreading my ass cheeks. Byron captures my mouth again as Marcus slowly pushes deep inside of me.

My nails dig into Byron's shoulders, and I pant into his mouth, the hard peaks of my nipples brushing against his skin.

When Marcus reaches his hilt, he grasps my thighs and pulls me back from my other men. He lies down on the shore, his dick fully buried into my ass. Byron quickly lies on top of me, and presses his tip into my pussy.

I'm breathing hard, feeling overwhelmed. My nerves are singing, my pleasure building. Having them both inside of me again feels like nothing else. As Byron sinks deeper, the feelings intensify.

Harold tilts my head back, pulling me from Byron's kiss. He and Forrest stand to the sides of my head. Within seconds, Harold angles his cock down and pushes himself into my mouth. His movements are possessive and intense as he dips in over and over again, each time going deeper.

I'm shocked when Forrest tilts me slightly, and then my lips widen as he slips himself into my mouth too. The fit is so fucking tight. But I'm aroused out of my mind, feeling two dicks pressed together, fighting for dominance in my mouth.

They each grab one of my breasts tightly, and they press in deeper, hard and faster.

Marcus and Byron start to fuck me. Not gentle, not making love, but fucking me hard and fast. I'm completely at their mercy, not even able to do more than shift to take them deeper. I'm just sandwiched between them, the luckiest fucking woman in the world. Four big cocks inside of me, four men deliciously capable of pushing me to the edge.

My orgasm builds higher and higher. It grows so intense I'm almost nervous to let it go, to give in. But I don't have a choice. Pleasure sings through me. Two giant dicks pump in and out of my mouth. Two giant dicks pound into my pussy and ass.

My men start to swear. I feel them swelling.

Feeling my men so close to their own orgasms sends me over the edge, and I come in an overwhelming explosion of sensations, keening wildly around the shafts in my mouth. My orgasm triggers my men and the grip me tightly as they fill every part of me with their delicious cum.

My men come too, gripping me tightly, filling every area of my body with their delicious cum. None stop pumping, not until I've sucked the dicks in my mouth clean, not until Byron and Marcus have spent every drop of their seed.

Exhausted, we collapse and lay together on the shore, our bodies partially in the water. Two dicks still inside of me.

"That was... nice," I say.

"Nice?" Byron raises a brow. "That was fucking epic."

I shrug, trying not to grin. "It was pretty good."

Forrest lies back, his hands behind his head, looking pleased as hell. "I guess she might need another round to decide."

"That could work," I say, laughing.

In this moment, I'm ridiculously happy. I have two

babies. I have four amazing men. Basically, I have a better life than I ever thought possible.

"Shit!" Someone exclaims.

I look up to see Benjamin, the head of the guards staring at us with shocked eyes.

"Fucking look away!" Byron shouts.

Benjamin's gaze jerks to the trees. "Uh, Galena said the babies woke up."

I sigh. I guess we'll have to wait a little while for round two.

Benjamin slinks back into the trees, and I watch as my big, naked gargoyles climb out of the water. *Oh my, those are very nice asses.*

Marcus catches my gaze and grins. "See something you like?"

I laugh and shake my head. I can't believe I once thought being a monster meant I couldn't be happy. My happiness fades, and I think about the other female monsters. Those ladies are like my sisters. I wish I could find a way to bring them this kind of happiness too.

Stepping out of the water, I dress. When the babies are old enough, maybe we can travel a little. We could visit everyone and give them a little hope.

Harold sweeps me into his arms, and I shriek. "Come on, we've got babies waiting!"

My thoughts return to my beautiful children as we launch into the air. I don't know if they'll be fully gargoyles, when they get old enough to shift, or if they'll be something else, but I know they'll have my love and the love of their four protective fathers.

And what more could two little girls need?

Keto's Tale

Chapter One

KETO

I swim through the waves, my tail leaving a trail of blood behind me. With each movement, pain radiates through my entire body. My teeth chatter, and my stomach turns. I look back one last time, but my enemies are long gone.

But I didn't kill them all. Right? Of course not…

That's the thing about mermaid hunters. They're like cockroaches. Every time you step on one, ten others come crawling out. If I could swim until I could reach a mermaid healer, I would, but I'm not sure how much longer I have before I pass out. I know a safe place up ahead, if only I can reach it. Lucky for me.

My lips curl into a pained smile. *Yeah, right, I'm super lucky. The luckiest bleeding mermaid-slave in the sea.*

I spot the island up ahead that I've been trying to reach. I swim around to the other side and come closer until I reach the sandy bottom of the shore where I know she'll see me. Using my elbows, I climb toward the island like a dying creature. For a second, my head surfaces, and I just lay, propping my top half out of the water, breathing deeply.

My arms shake and my body aches, but none of it matters. Because I survived... without being trapped in a cage. *Again*.

I shudder. That's the best I can hope for.

At least I took down a few of the bastards in the process.

Yeah, most of the other mermaids are smarter than I am. They stay in our cities far beneath the surface of the water where they have lives, friends, and families. More than that, they're far from the humans who obsess over their existence.

But me? I'm despised and feared by my own kind. They want nothing to do with me, and so I spend far too much of my time close to the surface of the human world.

And unlike most mermaids, I've developed a fondness for breezes, sunshine, and the feeling of warm sand beneath my skin. I still avoid humans whenever possible, but I like sunning myself on desolate islands, eating the fruit from the trees, and experiencing surface weather.

If only this world was as safe as it is beautiful and strange.

Closing my eyes, I will my fins to shift and my legs to appear. The agony that comes from my injured tail makes my vision go black for too long. The brightness of the sun burns through the darkness, and I open my eyes, wincing. My face is partially covered in sand. I'm lying on the shore, my body partially submerged.

I need to climb out. I need to get help.

"Keto!"

Tilting my head, I see Lamia emerge from beneath the shadows of the thick trees on the otherwise barren island. The lower-half of her body is that of a serpent, bright green and scaled. She slithers rapidly across the sand and her serpent-half shifts into legs as she kneels down at my side.

"What have they done to you now?" Her voice wavers with unshed tears.

She pulls my head onto her knees. And her face hovers above mine. As always, I'm overtaken by her beauty. She has black hair down to her waist, and her pale green eyes shine in contrast. "Who was it this time?" she asks.

I shift, wincing in pain at the movement. "Mermaid hunters."

"Fuck," she mutters.

"Sometimes I wish I could just hide like you do."

The second the words leave my mouth, I want to turn back time. A flash of hurt comes over her face. I know what she's thinking. She wishes she could leave. She wants to know that she won't hurt anyone, but she can't be sure. And she refuses to ever kill again.

So she's here, a willing prisoner, left with nothing but the memories of her dead children. Meanwhile, I'm the jerk who complained about my freedom.

"I'm sorry," I say.

She gives a sad smile. "It's okay. I'm just glad you could reach me."

Her gaze moves to my legs, and her eyes widen.

"Harpoon," I tell her, as if she can't already tell from the massive, bleeding wound.

She sets my head back gently on the shore and slips down into the water. Lifting my injured leg, she studies the wound, while I try my best not to scream in pain. My fingers claw into the sand, and I bite my lip until I taste blood.

"I can heal it," she whispers.

Placing her hands on both sides of my injury, she closes her eyes. First, I feel the familiar tingle, but then the burning comes. I whimper as tears slip down my face. I sense my bones knitting back together, my muscles healing, and my skin closing.

At last, she sags over me. My leg still hurts, but not nearly as badly.

I sit up and help her sit up too, with an arm around her shoulders.

For a minute we both remain still, staring out at the sunrise.

"Why can't they just leave you alone?" she asks, her soft voice filled with anger.

"They're assholes."

She laughs, and I treasure the sound as something priceless and rare. "Yeah, they are."

"But they're still better than my brother."

She sits up more steadily, and I drop my arm from around her. Her gaze moves to the collar around my neck, and the weight of the metal seems to grow heavier.

"Now that's one person I wouldn't mind killing."

I grin at her, glad to hear her joking. I must have caught her on a good day. "You and me both."

Something subtle changes in the water. Perhaps the temperature? Or the speed of the waves?

I turn to Lamia. "Something's wrong."

She frowns. "What?"

"I don't know yet."

She whirls around just as men emerge from the shadows of her trees. *The hunters! The ones who survived!*

My heart races.

The leader smiles. Each man holds an automatic harpoon.

"Come on then, mermaid, don't make us kill your friend." His finger twitches on the trigger of his weapon.

Lamia stands, and the men's eyes sweep over her tiny

dress in a way that sends the hairs on the back of my neck standing on end.

"Leave my island, now!" she orders.

I stand slowly, favoring my injured leg. The men's eyes sweep over my naked flesh in that way that makes me uneasy.

"Sorry, sweetheart," the leader says, "but someone will pay a very generous price for your little freak. I'm just not willing to give that money up."

"You're going to die here," Lamia says, her voice soft and sad.

He laughs. "Excuse me if I'm not afraid."

"Lamia," I whisper.

If we back up slowly and stay in the water, I'll call my creatures. They'll tear these men to pieces, and we'll be safe. I'm ready, but before I can act, I realize that it's already too late. I can see it in her eyes. Lamia has already decided that they'll die by her hands.

I don't want her to do it. She hates killing. It hurts her in a profound way.

These men just aren't worth it.

I grab her arm and haul her one step back into the water. Instantly, I feel my connection to the sea like something powerful and tangible. It spreads out through the cold waters in all directions. A deep awareness of the sea creatures makes tingles spread along my skin. Not far, one of my beasts lurk. I nudge his mind, and his eyes spring open.

He begins swimming toward me in a flurry of movement. Soon, he'll be here. And he'll rip these humans to shreds.

The men are closing in around us. They think they're being subtle, but they're not.

I count seven of them, all dressed in simple, modern

human clothing. They carry their automatic harpoons confidently, as if their weapons will protect them from me.

They've seen what I can do, how I can control the waters and the sea creatures, but they think I'm powerless on this island. *They'll see how wrong they are soon.*

"I'm not some mindless beast, some creature to be hunted," I tell them. "Capturing me is the same as any human woman—it's kidnapping. Do you guys really feel good about that?"

The leader smirks. "I'll feel good when I look in my bank account. That's all that really matters."

Lamia takes a step closer to them, shrugging away from me when I try to pull her back to my side. "So, it's all about the money to you?" she asks.

The man smiles. "No, sweetheart. It isn't. When I think about what they're going to do to her, I get hard as stone. The idea of them pulling her apart piece by piece until they know what she is gets me every time. The thought of her tail lying like a piece of fish on a table, the idea of her heart, eyes, and brain dissected like a monkey—that's why I do this. The money is just a perk."

Images flash across my eyes. I remember the tiny cage so small I could barely move, the little tools used to rip scales from my flesh. I'll never forget the needles filled with substances that burned their way through my body.

Memories of the one and only time I was caught.

I'm breathing hard. It's nearly impossible to focus on the situation before me. I want to cry, to slip beneath the waters and hide until I can't remember, until my memories can't hurt me anymore.

Instead, I tighten my hands into fists and glare. My memories might hurt, but not as badly as being caught again.

Lamia slides closer and closer to them. Their weapons

jerk from me to her. They look uneasy. And I can imagine they're wondering why she isn't afraid… why she's heading right for them.

I hope they don't realize the truth before my creature can reach me.

Come on, I urge the little hydra. *I need you.*

His purr of acknowledgment moves through my mind. He's close. *So* close. But not close enough.

Lamia continues her trek toward them until she's just ten feet away from the leader.

Oh fuck, this is not going to end well.

The man smiles at her, and again his gaze moves over her in a creepy way. "Either you're not very smart, or you're terribly brave. Either way, I get the feeling no one will miss you if you disappear. Maybe my men and I will simply take you with us… for entertainment."

I frown. *What does that mean?*

But Lamia seems to understand. Every muscle in her body tenses. And I know what's going to happen before it does.

She'll kill again. It'll be all my fault.

"Lamia, I got it," I call, desperate to stop her even though I know it's too late.

A second later, she shifts. Her legs disappear, replaced by her snake-half.

I see the men's eyes widen. I know what they're thinking—they've found another fantastical being to capture. If only their greed didn't cloud their fear.

She makes a sound, a small hiss under her breath, and leaps. Instantly, she comes crashing into the leader. Her fangs have elongated, her scales blossoming on her skin.

One man shoots his harpoon. She easily avoids it, using the leader as her shield. The harpoon goes through his chest, and out the other side. His mouth opens, and blood pours out.

Another man shoots. She uses the body again, and a second harpoon goes through his shoulder.

Shit!

I can't wait any longer. She's good, but there are too many of them and only one of her.

Calling to the waves, I bring them high over my head behind me and send them crashing into the man closest to the shore. He screams and falls as the water drags him back. I sense him struggling beneath the water, but I ignore him.

I lift the waves again. The second man leaps out of the way, but I send my water after him. It claws into him like a hand, and drags him back into the ocean with his friend.

Four men remain.

Lamia leaps onto one of them, and her eyes are wild. She uses her fangs to tear out his throat and then sinks her teeth into the mess, feasting on his blood. I look away to the remaining men. One of them has leveled his harpoon at her.

My muscles tense and my hydra explodes out of the water, chomping the man in one bite.

The little hyrdra, Haskul, is beautiful as he throws back his head and eats the man. Another dragon head explodes from the water, and he feasts on another of our attackers. Before the other man can escape, my hydra sends its tail into him. He goes flying, hits the trunk of a tree with a sickening sound, and lies unmoving on the sand.

She warned them that they'd die here. If only they had listened. I shake my head. I feel a little bad about their gruesome deaths, but it's also nice to know they won't be hunting me again anytime soon. *Or any other innocent creatures.*

One of the hydra's heads turn to me. I move to Haskul,

and he leans his massive snout down. Similar to a dragon, his blue-scaled flesh shimmers like diamonds. I pet him gently as he purrs.

Another dragon head nudges me from behind. I laugh and turn around to pet him too. My two-headed hydra is sweet. He's still little more than a child, but he's dangerous when angered. Luckily for me, he's one of the many beasts who sees me as its mother—the mother of all sea monsters.

"Thank you," I whisper.

Then my thoughts stray to how these hunters got here. "Can you search for any boats in the area? Or more humans who smell like these? If you find them, you have my permission to kill them and destroy what you find."

The hydra rubs against me one last time, then slips back into the waves.

Turning, I look back at Lamia. She's feeding on the dead men, drinking their blood. Her face and chest are covered in the scarlet liquid, and her eyes are wild. Her fangs pierce their skin deeply, and her jaw is wide.

My heart squeezes. It's been so long since she killed last, since she gave into her desire for blood. And I'm the one who brought this to her door.

Fucking hell. She deserves better.

"Lamia." I start toward her.

She looks back, blood running down her chin. "Leave! Now!"

I shake my head. "It's okay!"

"Leave!" she shouts. "You aren't safe here! I can't control myself."

I freeze, my emotions warring within me. "I'm not afraid of you."

Sadness fills her eyes. "I'm afraid of me... please."

I can't seem to walk away from her, but I also don't step

forward. She's my friend. I'm not afraid of her, but I also know what it feels like to see myself as a monster, to want to be left alone.

"This was my fault," I tell her. "If I had known the men were still hunting me—"

"It's not your fault." Her voice is soft. "This is what I am. What I'll always be, no matter how hard I fight it."

"No, Lamia—"

"Yes," she says. "Now go, please."

I step backward until my feet hit the water, but I look at her one last time, covered in blood, tears sliding down her cheeks. "I'm not afraid of you. You hurt those men to protect me. Not because you're dangerous."

"Keto—"

"I love you," I say. "I'm going to check on the hunters' boat and make sure they're gone and we're safe. Okay? Then, I'll be back."

After a long moment, she nods.

I turn and leap back into the water, my feet shifting into a tail. When I reach the other side of the island, I rise above the water and instantly spot the little boat… or what's left of it. My hydra has torn it to pieces, leaving wreckage floating in the water around it. I smell blood in the water.

Any mermaid hunter who survived our first two battles didn't survive this one.

I turn to head back to Lamia, before she completely spirals out of control.

Suddenly, the metal collar around my neck tightens. I claw at it, trying to breathe. I struggle beneath the waves, clawing harder and harder on instinct. My vision blackens, and my thoughts slur together. When I think all is lost, the collar loosens. I breathe, sucking in and out rapidly until my vision slowly returns.

Keto's Tale

I'm glad I'm in the ocean. Glad to know that my tears are blending into the water.

My brother has called again. Like the slave I am, I have no choice but to go.

Or else next time he might not stop until I'm dead.

Tremors wrack my body as I think of what death is like for an immortal goddess. I think back to the last time I died. I woke in the Underworld, reliving each moment of my death, remembering the excruciating moment my head was severed from my body. The memories didn't stop the whole time I made the climb up from Hades' dark realm back to the world of the living.

It's like a nightmare that won't end, because the second I emerge from the Underworld, I'm still my brother's slave. Only, in the time I was gone, he killed as many of my creatures as possible, without me there to protect them.

All of it was to teach me a lesson, *a lesson I've never forgotten.*

One day, even if I continue to obey him, he won't stop. He'll kill me, and there's nothing I can do to stop him. I'll experience death again. Knowing that haunts me whether I'm awake or asleep.

So, I must go. I must obey him.

I try to turn back around, to tell Lamia so she won't think I abandoned her. But as I try to swim in the opposite direction from my brother, the collar tightens again. I go as far as I can until I can't breathe. More tears slide down my cheeks as I swim away from Lamia.

The collar finally loosens. I look back at the island. I can't see her.

This will destroy her. She'll think I left because of what she is and what she did. I know how that feels… it's awful, like a tearing in your heart that doesn't seem to stop.

I'll make it up to her, when I've done whatever awful thing my brother wants me to do now.

I can't remain any longer, wishing things were different.

Rushing through the water, I swim past my sweet hydra. One day my brother will end my life, but if I can help it, that day won't be today.

I just have to be fast enough.

Chapter Two

KETO

My brother wasn't in his palace beneath the sea, but I can sense that he's near. And unfortunately for me, I know exactly where. I rise above the waves to his island, a place covered with the treasures of hundreds of wrecked ships. *His pathetic obsessions.*

As I reach the edge of the water, I close my eyes and let my magic shimmer over me. A second later, my tail's replaced by legs.

I walk awkwardly on my long legs and climb the mountains of gems and gold, all of which he forced me to acquire for him. I've destroyed countless ships over thousands of years. I hear the sailors' screams, sometimes during the day, like a sound carried by the wind or the waves, but mostly I hear their screams in my dreams at night.

All of them were innocent humans who did nothing to deserve my wrath. They probably had wives and children waiting for them at home, loved ones who will never get closure, never even see their bodies.

The humans will tell themselves that the ocean is a

cruel and unpredictable mistress. If only they knew it was me controlling the waves and storms. I send my creatures to the ships to tear them to pieces, while my brother's minions collect the sparkly stolen items like greedy children.

I kick at the mountain of wealth, sending coins scattering. *What a useless mountain of nothing.*

"Angry, sweet Keto?"

I stiffen. Aphros comes from behind me, and I stiffen, waiting for his touch.

It comes lightly upon my back, and then he's in front of me. A big man with long blond hair, green eyes, and a soul filled with darkness and poison, he's also my brother's second in command. I hate him down to my very core.

"My brother called for me."

He frowns. "He didn't mention it to me."

That's interesting… he tells the asshole everything.

"I should go." I want to tear away from his touch, to punch him so hard his teeth fall out.

He laughs and pulls me against him. "Don't hurry away, my sweet Keto, stay and lay in the coins with me. Let me help you see the gods."

I grit my teeth. I despise his touch. We've had sex before, but it was unpleasant and not something I want to repeat. I can't directly tell this man *no*, but I can avoid him.

"Do you really want to be responsible for making my brother wait?"

His smile fades away, and anger fills his eyes. "Sometimes I think you don't like our time together."

I want to slit your throat and watch the blood pour free. "You know the King of the Sea's needs come first."

I hope I don't sound sarcastic as I say my brother's self-proclaimed title. Because we all know the truth: I'm far more powerful than either of these pathetic gods.

Keto's Tale

Amphitrite may be the Queen of the Ocean, but I'm the Mother of All Sea Monsters. If she didn't avoid me so carefully, she and I alone would rule these seas.

And, of course, the whole me being a slave thing keeps me from ruling anything.

Aphros leans down and inhales near my throat. "Alright, but be quick with your brother. My cock hardens for you."

Ugh. I pull away from him and continue my path to my brother, not looking back. Every moment with Aphros is awful. I only hope I can escape quickly enough to avoid him later.

When I reach the top of the pile, I continue walking, even as the coins shift and slide beneath my feet. The afternoon sun beats down on me, but I can't enjoy the sensation of warmth on my skin. I'm about to see my brother and learn what new, awful task he has in store for me.

A short time later, I hear the giggle of nymphs.

Sex and gold, that's all he cares about. I've never understood the addiction to either. Gold means nothing. And sex? That had been little more than a painful, uncomfortable experience. I could go the rest of my life without gold or sex.

If only that was an option...

Gold, lacy material has been strung over and around a circle of trees. In the center of them, my brother lies tangled in more of the silky material, with a dozen naked, giggling nymphs.

"Phorcys!" I call, trying to keep the hatred from my voice.

He glances up. I can see that women are moving beneath the material, so I jerk my gaze up to his face.

My gut tightens. I hate how similar we look. He has the same high cheekbones, arched brows, the same dark eyes, full lips, and bright auburn hair as I do. I hate that we have anything at all in common, but especially our looks.

"Sister." His greeting is arrogant. "You look well."

I'm naked. As a mermaid, the fact that I don't wear clothes makes sense, but when I stand before my brother as a human, I feel exposed and vulnerable.

"Why did you call for me?"

He pushes his lips out in a pout. "Why is it that you never seem happy to see me?"

"What's with the crap?" I snap, in no mood to play this game after the day I've had. His eyes narrow, and he shoves the nymphs beneath the covers and stands up. "I wanted to make today civil, but I guess my angry sister could never allow that, could she? Come with me."

I follow slowly behind him as he takes us across more gold and then to the far end of the island to a small beach covered in golden sand. With each step we take, I grow more uneasy.

My brother is a simple man, and usually his commands reflect that. Create a storm. Destroy a boat. Bring waves of impossible heights to destroy human beaches. The fact that he says nothing makes me worry even more. "Have you ever journeyed into the Atlantic Ocean?" he asks, crossing his arms behind his back.

"You know I haven't. No mermaid would dare enter the Sea Dragons' territory." *Why is he asking me this?*

"And what do you know of the Sea Dragons?"

My pulse races. "They are Shifters, beings as old as the mermaids. They have vowed to rip apart any mermaid who sets tail in their waters."

He turns to me, his lips curled in amusement. "You're right, my sister."

"Why are you asking me about them?"

"Come with me." His legs shimmer as he enters the water, and within seconds, his tail appears.

I follow after him, my own tail forming as I dive into the water.

He leads me down, around a coral reef brimming with life and a stunning array of plants covered in more gold. When we reach a place where light barely penetrates the darkness, he stops before a wall of waving green seaweed. I sense a cave just beyond the plants.

He pushes through the plants and I follow behind him, squinting and trying to make out anything ahead of me. I'm shocked when he grabs my forearm and yanks me into the cave. My back hits the bars of a cage, forcing the air from my lungs.

It takes me a second to react, which means I'm too slow to keep the door on the cage from slamming closed. Leaping forward, I slam against the cage door, but it doesn't move. Panic rushes at me in waves. I don't do well in cages. The humans kept me in cages when they ran all their tests.

"What—let me out!" I shout into the water, my words as clear as if I we're standing on land.

He smiles, an awful smile. "I'm afraid not, because then my little plan won't work."

"Plan?" I ask, swimming around the small space, slamming myself against the bars, pulling at them as my panic grows.

"Yes, see, there is a prophecy that only a mermaid princess can sate the lusts of the Sea Dragons and return the oceans to the merpeople. So, I intend to test that prophecy with my very own princess sister."

I look back at him. "No, please. Please. Don't do this."

He cocks his head. "You're begging me? Really?" Slowly, he swims around my cage. "In all the years since I placed that collar around your neck, you never once asked me to remove it. Not once. No matter what I did to you. Could it be these Sea Dragons have frightened you enough to finally ask me for a favor?"

I don't care that he thinks my panic is because of the Sea Dragons. I have to get out of the cage. Now! "Yes, a favor. Please!"

He leans in close to me. "The thing is… I just don't care enough to help you."

Turning, he starts back out of the cave.

"Phorcys! I'll kill you for this!"

Without looking back at me, he laughs. "We'll see who ends up dead."

His favorite sea beast, a blood-thirsty creature with the body of a mermaid and the face of sharp-toothed lion, grabs one of the bars of my cage. Three more of the creatures enter the cave and grab the other ends. Picking my cage up, they ignore my screams and curses, dragging my cage through the currents and toward the open ocean.

Fear seizes my heart. I throw myself against the bars of my cage once more. All logic disappears, and I become nothing more than an animal, doing anything and everything I can to escape.

I can't think of the sea dragons. I can't think of anything except the need to escape this prison. As the bars close in around me, I start to scream.

And I'm not sure I'll ever be able to stop.

Chapter Three

KETO

I don't know how long I spent rocking back and forth in this cage. I don't know when I stopped rocking, but now I'm curled up in the bottom of the cage. I'm cold, and the colors of my tail have dulled. Instead of the beautiful pinks, purples, and blues, my tale is a hundred shades of gray.

This has never happened before.

There's blood everywhere, from my shoulders, my head, even my hands. I vaguely remember bashing myself against the bars of the cage, but it's fuzzy.

My brother's minions have slowed. That means I'm probably in the sea dragons' territory, but I'm not afraid. I'd rather be anywhere but trapped in this dreadful cage.

I'd rather be dead.

A helpless tear disappears into the waves.

Just as I'm about to give up hope, I feel something wriggle beneath me. I open my eyes and look beside my belly. It's one of my smallest creatures, Cryshon, and also one of the most powerful. He's round and golden, with tiny fins all around him. His huge eyes look at me with pity.

My stomach tightens. Technically, my creatures can go to the sea dragons' territory, but Cryshon shouldn't be here. Things will get bad, and I want him safe.

Besides, if my brother's minions see him, they'll kill him. Unlike me, he's not immortal.

He swims close to my ear. "It's okay, mother. I'll keep you safe."

I shake my head. "No, please, just swim away. I can't have you hurt," I whisper back.

He smiles, and I can feel his love radiating through me like the sun's warm rays. "I have a plan."

I try to tell him again to run, but he swims right back to my stomach and wedges himself between my side and the cage. He's concealed from view, for now, but I'm still worried about him.

It's my job to protect him. Not the other way around.

I open my mouth to speak, but something subtle changes in the water. I stiffen and inhale deeply. The waters here are far warmer than my typical ones, and the scents of underwater plants and animals are stronger.

But that isn't what's changed. The animals… I inhale again. They're afraid. They're fleeing.

I know now for certain that we are in the sea dragons' territory.

To my shock, my brother's minions swim us higher and higher until my cage surfaces above the water. The rays of the afternoon sun brighten the water. They place my cage up onto the smallest island I can imagine. There's just barely enough space for my cage to rest, although the tiny mountain of land is low enough that water slides in and out of the bottom of my cage. Once the cage is stable, they leave me there.

I'm left for dead in the sea dragons' territory. Is this really how I'll die this time?

"Wait," I call out to my brother's minions, and my voice is raspy from all my screaming. "Are you really just going to leave me here? I'm an immortal goddess, an equal to my brother. Do you know nothing about the dangers of angering a god?"

The creatures look back at me, no pity in their eyes.

My teeth clench. *Assholes!*

Suddenly, one of them makes a sound, and gets pulled under the surface. A cloud of dark blood fills the water. The other creatures make sounds of panic as another is pulled under the water.

I struggle into a sitting position. *Will they still kill me if they think I'm human?* The dragons will likely know what I am, but it's the only desperate plan I can come up with.

Using my magic, I shift and my tail instantly turns into legs. Instinctually, I move Cryshon beneath my knee to conceal him. My legs shake as I stare at the clouds of blood that are filling the water around me.

One of the creatures switches directions, splashing and swimming in desperation. Suddenly, he's gone, and the sea around him is still. The dark cloud comes seconds later.

Glancing in another direction, I watch the final creature swimming. My gut clenches. A massive sea dragon explodes from the water in front of him, flings him into the air, and catches him in its mouth, swallowing him in one bite. I tremble. I hated my brother's minions, but I didn't want them to die. Not like that.

After no more than a heartbeat in time, the beast turns to me, and I realize I'm staring at the first sea dragon. The white dragon has shimmering scales and a long neck. It's Nereus. I recognize him instantly, even though I've only ever heard his description. He's the leader of his kind, the oldest of the dragons, and a powerful shapeshifter. With Nereus, *maybe* I have a chance at reasoning with him. Maybe I can—

Another dragon emerges from the sea. Okeanos has blue scales and angry golden eyes. He's a strong being, arrogant and cruel. I've heard he's capable of controlling the stars and the planets.

My heart races faster. I don't know if I can negotiate with him. I don't know if he'll even let me speak a word before he ends my life.

The water sloshes over me and my cage and drips on my head.

With my pulse filling my ears, I turn. Just behind me is a black sea dragon. His eyes are silver and his teeth are sharp. Triton is cruel simply to be cruel. He's strong and younger than his brothers, and the stories of his desire for beautiful women and beautiful things rivals that of my brother. His oceans are filled with storms and waves, all because of his temper.

I'm not surprised when a green dragon rises beside him. Pontos is never far from Triton, and seeing him gives me the smallest flicker of hope. He controls all the mindless sea creatures in his ocean, not the "monsters" like I do. I've heard that although he hates mermaids, he also has a soft spot.

Maybe it'll be enough to buy me some time.

My creature shivers beside my leg, and my stomach clenches. Even if I die today, I can't let him be hurt, not when he risked everything to keep me safe.

The dragons move closer until they surround me.

Okeanos leans forward, opening his wide jaws.

I move back, hitting the bars behind me.

His jaws grip one side of the cage and bite down.

I scream, holding my creature in one hand, and grab

Keto's Tale

the bars of the cage in the other. The cage crumples smaller and smaller. When the door pops open, I'm looking right into the throat of the creature. If he shakes me free from the bars, I'm dead!

"Wait! Wait!" I shout.

My crumpled cage drops back onto the island.

The dragons watch me with rage in their eyes.

"You know the price for entering our waters, mermaid-filth." The green dragon says, and there's no kindness in his voice.

My palms are sweaty as I hold the bars. I don't know if what I'm about to say will make things worse, or better, but I have to try. "I'm... Keto, Mother of Sea Monsters. I'm a goddess and an immortal like you. I know the rules, and I didn't seek to break them. I was trapped and taken here against my will."

The green dragon lowers its face until it's level with mine, just outside my open cage door. "And this should matter to us, why?"

I try not to flinch as I meet his gaze. "My brother is the one you want, not me. He believed that I, a princess of the ocean, would somehow tame the four of you. I knew better."

He tilts his head, studying me. "You do... smell nice."

"Pontos!" Okeanos shouts. "Why do we need to speak to our food?"

His big dragon head spins to his brother. "Smell her. Look at her."

I shift further back in the cage, clutching my sea creature to my chest as Okeanos looks at me. He inhales and exhales over and over again, his hot dragon breath almost painful against my bare skin.

Then, his head rises. "She smells... delicious. And her body and face are pleasing."

Nereus and Triton are suddenly inhaling so strongly that my hair whooshes up and down around me.

"What is it that you suggest?" Nereus asks, his tone intrigued.

"I think we should keep her," Pontos tells them, leveling me with his stare once more.

"If we allow one mermaid to live, then others will follow her." Nereus speaks, and his words seem to hover in the air.

Okeanos smiles, which is creepy as hell for a dragon. "I didn't say she'd live long, just enough to please all of us over and over again."

My stomach sinks. I want to live, but not like this. Death is better.

I feel my creature tremble against me, and I know what he's thinking. His power could save us. Could save us both. But we need others to make it work, we need—

Something moves in the sky.

I stiffen, and try not to let the dragons see my stare. But sure enough, there *is* something in the sky. No, someone. Gargoyles.

And… they're heading straight for me.

I don't even know what to think. They'll kill me if they reach me, but the plans these dragons have for me are even worse. And now, now my creature can use its magic. *If* the gargoyles get close enough.

I don't know what to think, what to do. Every choice ends in my death.

Chapter Four

MAX

Damn it all to hell. This was the last thing we needed. We already stink of failure, and we are so far behind schedule that our future is bleak.

For weeks we've searched the ocean for a monster that is legendary for her cruelty and violence, but haven't found a trace of her anywhere. We can't return without taking her prisoner, but I don't know how we're supposed to find a beast that lives beneath the sea. We have no idea what to do next.

And now? Now we see a woman in trouble, a woman who will die if we don't intervene.

"Max?" Arthur, my twin brother, is flying at my side. I can see what he's thinking without him needing to say it. He'll save this woman, with or without me.

Even though I'm our leader… my brother isn't exactly good at following orders.

I raise my voice, loud enough that it'll carry to the other two members of our Brotherhood. "I'll get her. You three distract the dragons."

Steven flies to block my path, already pulling his sword

from his back. "I'll take the black dragon. I hear he's a bastard."

Clark speaks from behind me. "Come on. You three can't really want to get involved. This isn't our battle."

I turn to look back at him. I'm not surprised he doesn't want to help some random woman, but I *am* surprised he isn't leaping at the chance to fight. Especially after how moody he's been lately.

"Go for the white one, but be careful."

He rolls his eyes, but reaches for his own sword.

The green dragon's head lowers toward the woman. My muscles tense, and using all my strength, I head for her, not bothering to fly. I just drop like the massive stone being that I am.

Air rushes around me. My teeth clench, and at the last possible second, I flap my wings to slow myself down, but not by much.

I smash into the head of the dragon and he goes down, sinking into the water. I flap my wings and pull back to avoid going down with him. Grasping the top of the cage with one hand, I reach for her with the other.

To my surprise, she hesitates, but only for a moment. In that moment, the world freezes around us. This woman is an immortal. I would bet my life on it. She has that thing that's hard to explain. She appears to be a young woman, but her eyes are filled with experience. This woman has seen emotion and heartache that few people have experienced in their youth.

And then there's the other thing…

She's beautiful, with long auburn hair, dark eyes, and a face made as if by the gods themselves. And yet, the terror in her eyes says she's not just afraid of the dragons, she's afraid of me too.

What does that mean?

Keto's Tale

I have no time to think further as the moment passes. She flings herself into my arms and I shoot up into the sky.

The roars of my battling brothers fill the air. I glance back and see their swords sinking into the flesh of the dragons. The sea dragons thrash as my brothers go flying.

My heart sinks. *They stand like flies in front of the monsters.* I've never told them to retreat before, but the command clings to my tongue.

"Drop me."

The tiny voice is not that of the woman. I look to her and see a strange golden fish in her arms. She lifts it with the greatest look of regret, and drops it into the sea below.

I don't know what I expected, but I couldn't have predicted the explosion of golden light that followed. The water itself lights up as if a million floating lights were cast on the surface. The dragons shriek and my brothers freeze in mid-air, looking to me for orders.

I'm their leader. I'm supposed to know what to do, but I have no idea. I don't know what's going on. All I can do is try to keep them safe.

"Retreat!" I shout, the word tearing from my lips.

My brothers start toward me, but the golden light leaps out of the water like an explosion. My heart stops beating. I race toward them. The golden light wraps around me for one brief second. My skin tingles and my mind goes blank.

"You're falling!" a panicked voice shouts

I can't feel my wings, but I try to fly. I feel the woman in my arms, but I can't see anything. I feel her hands on my face and my vision returns. The golden light surrounds us and all I can see is her. I see her beauty and her fear. I struggle to keep control as I realize that her warm, naked flesh against my body awakens something within me that I haven't felt in longer than I can remember.

When the light fades, nothing is left. No dragons. No gargoyles. No one but the woman and me.

I clench the woman closer to my chest and fly over the water. A hand breaks the surface and stretches upward. I grasp the wrist of whoever it might be and pull.

To my relief, it's Arthur. I tug him high enough so that he can flap his wings, and then we're both drifting above the water. I don't know if we will find sea dragons ready to take our lives or our missing brothers.

Steven pops out of the water not far from me, splashing and coughing. I go to him in an instant and pull him free. It takes him a minute to right himself, and when he starts flapping his wings, I release him.

Arthur plucks an angry Clark from the water next, and we all rise as high above the sea as we can. We hesitate, each of us searching for any signs of the dragons. I need the time to calm my emotions. Seeing my brothers fighting and then disappearing in the ocean is one of the worst moments I remember. I thought I'd lost them forever.

The woman in my arms speaks, her voice hoarse. "We should go. Quickly."

Her words shake me from my stupor.

"Let's return to camp," I tell the others, trying to sound like I know what I'm doing, like leading the team for the first time isn't as hard as it really is. "Everyone spread out and head to the camp from different directions, just in case."

Clark glares at me. "Just in case those things decide to follow us home?"

I nod.

His eyes narrow. "I told you this was a mistake." But he turns and starts flying in one direction.

Steven looks between me and the girl. "Perhaps you two should take the long way."

Because she's probably the one they want the most. For a reason we still haven't figured out. "Good idea."

"Maybe I should stay a little longer and see what happened to the dragons," Arthur suggests.

I shake my head. "They're too powerful. The more distance we can get between them and us, the better."

"But we don't want—"

"You have your orders," I say.

My brother gets that look in his eyes, the one that tells me he wants to argue. "Whatever you say, Captain."

I glare. "I'm not kidding."

He salutes me. "Yes, sir!"

I watch him as he turns and starts to fly off. If he even looks like he's turning around, I'm going to kick his ass. Gritting my teeth, I pick a direction and start flying, not taking my gaze from him.

The woman stares over my shoulder behind me. After a minute, I feel the muscles in her body tense.

"What is it?" I ask.

She shakes her head. "Nothing."

For some reason, I don't believe her. Glancing back, I see men bobbing in the water. They're perfectly ordinary looking men, except their eyes are the same as the dragons'—gold and silver and filled with anger.

Dragons can shift into humans?

"What happened to them?" I ask.

Her dark eyes are wide and innocent. "I don't know," she says, yet she was the one who had the creature in her arms.

"What was that thing? The golden creature?"

For an instant, I see her fear, and then it vanishes from her gaze. "I found it. I thought it needed help."

I don't believe her. The woman in my arms is pure trouble. I know she's more than human and I should let her go. I should drop her at the nearest beach and get my men as far from her as possible.

Despite my concerns, we pass islands dotting the ocean below us, and I don't let her go. If anything, I hold her tighter. It's not the decision a leader would make, but no matter how many logical arguments my brain presents, my heart won't let her go.

I blame it on being a gargoyle. We have a powerful instinct to protect the innocent that's hard to ignore. *Even though I'm not sure how innocent this woman is.*

After a time, I feel her relax against me. Her legs wrap around my waist, her arms around my neck.

The tension that had sung beneath my skin since I saw her and the dragons starts to fade. I hold her closer, more gently, and all at once, my body remembers that I'm a man and she's a naked woman. My body remembers the vow of celibacy all the young, male gargoyles took twenty years ago—a requirement if we wanted a chance to mate with the three female gargoyles.

Oh fuck!

My hands warm against the skin of her hips, her very soft, very feminine skin. I can picture the way I hold her in perfectly clarity, the way her legs wrap around me, spreading herself wide. Her body is open and pressing against my cock.

Despite everything, my blood rushes south, and my shaft grows hard. I'm panting as I try to think of our mission and the strangeness of meeting this woman and the dragons, but my body doesn't seem to care. Every few seconds my thoughts jump back to what it would feel like to sink into this woman, to feel the tightness of her wet body holding me.

I shudder.

Keto's Tale

She lifts her head from my shoulder, and our eyes meet. "Thank you for saving me."

I nod, my response catching on my tongue.

"Where are we going?"

It takes me a second to respond, and even I notice the arousal in my voice. "Our camp. It isn't much further. It'll be warm, and there's food."

"Why are you camping?"

Should I lie? I'm not sure it really matters. "We're hunting a sea monster… one named Keto."

She stiffens against me. "Oh."

Curiosity prickles the back of my mind. "Do you know of her?"

It takes a minute before she answers me. "Everyone knows of her."

I make a mental note to ask her about the monster later. It might actually be a huge benefit for us to have another person helping us in our search, if she's willing.

She shifts against me, and for one second my body screams in arousal, and then she winces.

For the first time I let my gaze sweep downward, and my breath catches. Her shoulders are covered in open wounds. They're no longer bleeding, but they look raw and sore. There's dried blood in her hair too, and nearly every part of her body is scraped and bruised.

There's even bruises on the sides of her breasts.

"You like my breasts?" she asks.

My gaze jerks up, and I can feel my cheeks heating. "I was noticing your injuries."

One of her hands leaves my neck, sliding slowly down my chest, and awakening every nerve beneath her touch. Then, she lifts one of her breasts and studies the bruise on one side in the most innocent way imaginable.

I swear my brain explodes like a computer that's gotten

too hot. She continues to touch her breast, her fingers sliding past the soft-looking skin and to the other breast. I tell myself to focus on her injuries, not on her hard pink nipples. Not on the fullness of her breasts.

Closing my eyes, I picture myself lifting her breasts. First, I'd kiss her bruises gently. And then I'd slide my lips across the smooth skin. I'd lift their fullness and weight in my hand, holding her like I owned her. And I'd lean down and suck those nipples, making them even harder.

"They aren't too bad," she says, and my eyes pop open. *Keep it together, Max!* "What happened to you?"

A shiver moves through her body. "The cage."

"The cage did that to you?" I'm completely confused.

"No… I… uh… did it to myself, trying to get out of the cage."

Whoa. "You really don't like cages."

A guarded look comes over her face. "No, I don't. But these injuries are… nothing. Sex leaves more marks than this."

I feel my brows rise. "Sex?"

She nods, looking earnest. "It hurts more too."

I know I'm staring. I know it, but I can't stop. "Sex should never hurt or leave bruises."

She laughs, and the sound is sad. Like the whisper of the wind through a few lonely trees. "Not for men."

Shit. Shit. Shit. I've never felt this way about anyone. Anger rushes through me as I feel this inexplicable urge to protect her. No woman should ever believe sex is meant to be painful, or leave bruises. A man somewhere has been cruel to this woman, and if I ever find him, I'm going to kill him. My grip tightens around her, and a low growl slips past my lips.

She tenses. "Are you all right?"

I take a minute to make sure my voice comes out calm.

"Any man of worth would never harm a woman, no matter what."

She tilts her head, studying me. "Nothing could bring you to hurt a woman?"

I meet her gaze, unyielding. "Nothing. I am a gargoyle. I've sworn to kill monsters and to protect the innocent. No matter what an innocent did, I would do everything in my power to keep them safe."

Her eyelids slide partially down as she stares at my chest. "I believe you."

There's something sad in her voice as she leans back down to rest her head on my shoulder.

Unable to help myself, I reach up with one arm and stroke her hair.

She sighs softly.

We continue flying toward camp. My cock is hard, my chest tight. My brain screams that whatever we do on our mission, we make certain this woman is safe first.

Damn it. My father was right. I really don't have the heart of a leader.

Chapter Five

ARTHUR

I feel weird still, like my skin won't stop tingling, and there's a headache behind my eyes. It could've been worse—those fucking dragons could've killed us all—but that's not what bothers me. I don't trust the woman we rescued.

My thoughts turn back to her as I fly lazily over the water, letting my hand skim the surface. She really is beautiful, so different from my type. She's different from *her*. I never thought I'd be into red-heads, but her hair almost glows... like magic. Her face has this strange mix of experience and innocence that intrigues me.

But how do I handle her?

The others will probably want to get rid of her as quickly as possible, and until they do, they'll be watching my every move, waiting to see me fuck up. Part of me wants to show them that I'm not the same man who threw everything away for a woman years ago, but another part of me is leaping at the idea of this woman.

I'd never say this out loud, but I'm just so sick of this gargoyle life.

Keto's Tale

I'm tired of the sanctuary. I'm tired of talking to the same people day after day. Most of all, I'm tired of waiting around like an asshole with my cock in my hands, hoping one of the three female gargoyles chooses our Brotherhood next. Who are we kidding? We don't have a shot. The women have shown absolutely no interest in our Brotherhood. That means we've pledged our chastity and have been waiting for women who will never choose us.

Which is just stupid.

I thought going hunting for monsters was just what I needed, with freedom from the sanctuary and a cause! And yet, I still don't feel satisfied. I'm still tired of this life.

No, I'll never throw everything away for a woman again, but I *will* keep searching for whatever's missing in my life, even if my Brotherhood hates me for it.

"Lost in thought?"

I almost fall into the ocean, but catch myself before I do. Looking back, I see a smirking Clark. It's nice to see him smiling, even if he's laughing at me.

"I thought we were supposed to split up?"

He shrugs. "I did. And then I saw your hopeless ass and decided to swing this way."

I grin and fly a little higher. He quickly catches up to me.

"What were you thinking about?" he asks.

I debate about lying to him. But Clark was our leader before, and he can see right through my lies. "The woman."

He scoffs. "I thought so. Planning on going rogue again?"

My jaw aches as my teeth clench together, but I force myself to sound relaxed. "She wasn't *that* beautiful."

I refuse to ever admit to anyone what a mistake it was to throw everything away for a woman. Sure, I had quickly learned she wasn't the soul mate I had imagined, but I had remained by her side for her short human life because of an illness that made her helpless. None of them could understand how honor and pride kept me caring for her until her death. I'm sure they all thought I lived out her human life happy and in love, only returning at her death because I had nowhere else to go.

I'd rather have them thinking that than knowing how badly I fucked up.

"I thought maybe you were looking for an excuse to run again." Clark's tone is neutral, but I can sense the tension underneath.

"Maybe I am," I say, shrugging.

He shakes his head. "I don't understand your obsession with happiness and being fulfilled. It's something all you *born* gargoyles struggle with. Life isn't about happiness or being fulfilled. It's about responsibility and loyalty. Gargoyles protect what we must, because it's our duty. We all share the duty to protect the sanctuary, continue the population, and do as the Elites command."

I laugh, but it comes out more of a bark. "Sounds fun."

He glares. "I didn't say it was fun."

"Well, maybe I want fun… and laughter and excitement and adventure. What's so wrong with that?"

He shakes his head. "Because, Arthur, you're chasing a fucking rainbow and dragging us all along with you. Our job is to find this Keto monster, capture her, and drag her back home. *That* should be your focus and nothing else."

We spot the island our camp is on up ahead. It's lush and beautiful, with a white sand beach, a thick forest, and a fresh water lake in the center. It's also uninhabited, which makes it the perfect place to live while we find our monster.

Not knowing what else to say to Clark, I fly faster and

head straight for the island. He easily keeps up with me, which I find irritating, but refuse to show it.

When we land, Steven's already there.

He's clearly taken a dip in the fresh water. His short, blond hair drips with water, and his white T-shirt is plastered to his skin. He looks up at us with his familiar, intense gaze as we land.

"Something's bothering me," he says, pulling his bag onto his shoulder.

"What?" Clark asks frowning.

"I don't know, but I plan to find out."

Clark raises a brow. "What the hell does that mean?"

"Have you felt strange since our encounter with the woman and the dragons?"

"Horny, if that's what you mean," I say, grinning.

Clark gives me his, *fucking shut your mouth look*. "Kind of... tingly?"

Steven nods. "And when I went into the lake... I felt even stranger. Like something across the ocean was calling to me. I can't ignore it. I need to figure out what this feeling means."

For a second I think Clark is going to tell him we need to wait for our leader. When he was in charge, he ran things like a fucking military commander.

Instead, he nods. "I'll go with you."

I tense. I'm usually not the rule follower in the group. Clark is only doing this because he's pissed Max was made our new leader over him.

Oh, hell. "Shouldn't we make sure Max approves this before you two take off?"

Clark's blue eyes darken, and he takes two steps closer to me, towering over me with his massive frame. "Since when do you ask for permission to do anything?"

I draw myself up taller. "Wouldn't it be smarter to ask the woman if she knows anything?"

"Maybe, but I think I'll go with Steven's tingly feeling instead. Since logic is just crap and all." Clark turns from me and climbs into our tent.

Steven moves toward me and rests a gentle hand on my shoulder, our eyes locking. "This trip is bringing out a lot of confusing feelings for Max and Clark. It reminds them of when you left, of when we searched for you. I don't feel the same way, my friend, but you may need to be more patient with them."

I don't know why, but Steven's kind words make me feel even worse. "You really just want to take off to pursue a feeling?"

His eyes grow sad. "I don't want to, but I feel like I need to."

What am I supposed to say to that?

"We should be back in a few days' time. And while we travel, we'll continue to look for the monster."

I nod. "Well, good luck, I guess."

Clark comes out, slipping his own backpack on. "Ready?"

Steven nods and the two of them take off. I watch them for a while, feeling lost. Things have been tense between all of us. I knew they weren't completely over what happened, but since when does being a gargoyle mean being lonely?

Turning to the lake, I strip out of my clothes and sink into the warm water. I guess I have until Max and the woman get back to figure it all out.

Chapter Six

KETO

My mind races. These men don't know who or what I am. That means that for now, I'm safe with them. As long as I stay out of the ocean and away from anything that can give me away to my brother. If he catches sight of me, he'll know I escaped the dragons, and he'll make me pay.

I stiffen in the gargoyle's arms at the realization. *As of right now,* Phorcys *probably thinks I'm dead.*

The feeling is like a light going off inside of me. He won't command me through the collar if he doesn't know I'm still living. On top of that, his sea spies might not know what happened in the battle because of what my little creature did.

He took the dragons' abilities.

I'm still in awe of its magic. I've never seen it use it at that scale before. I hoped it was possible, but I wasn't *sure*. Now I'm left with new worries. The sea dragons looked like nothing more than humans in the water after their powers were taken, but something had to absorb them, and I'm pretty sure it was the gargoyles. I have powerless enemies who can't even communicate with the sea animals, a brother who thinks I'm dead, and a gargoyle that has pledged that he'll keep me safe from anything.

Am I... am I free for a little while? My thoughts turn over each other. This mess could blow up very easily, but for now, everything is actually better than it has been for a long time.

All I need to do is make sure the gargoyles don't discover who I am.

"We're almost there," the man holding me says.

I look ahead of us to see a peaceful looking island, and then back at the man's serious face. "You never told me your name."

He glances at me and smiles. "Max."

"Max," I repeat, tasting the name on my tongue.

"And what's yours?"

Oh fuck! Of course he was going to ask my name! "I'm... I'm...Sirena."

He smiles. "Well, Sirena, let's get you dressed and fed, and you can tell us your story."

My heart races. Oh yes, I'll need a story. A convincing one. One that will make it so these men don't kill me, kidnap me, or toss me aside.

This will take some thought.

"And the other males in my Brotherhood of gargoyles are Arthur, my twin, Steven, and Clark."

I don't remember the other men well, but I'm sure I'll be able to identify them after I officially meet them. "Are they all as nice as you?"

He flashes me a smile. "Everyone thinks Arthur is funny. Steven can be very sweet. And Clark, well, he grows on you."

I'm not sure if what he's telling me is good or bad, but

Keto's Tale

after everything I've been through, I hope I can handle these four gargoyles. It can't be too hard, right?

Despite myself, I feel tense the rest of our flight.

We arrive at the island, landing gently outside of a tent and a lake with a waterfall. Immediately, I feel the pull of the water. I already know it's fresh water, and that it holds no intelligent sea animals, just some fish and tiny creatures. My brother won't know I'm there.

I'm still longing for the water when one of the gargoyles surfaces, no longer wearing clothes. His bare chest is covered in muscles and he has big, thick arms. Dark tattoos curl along his chest and one of his arms.

I'm a mermaid. Nudity means nothing to me. I've seen naked mermen, even shifted into human-form naked, and felt nothing.

But something stirs inside of me as he pushes back his dark hair and the water slides down his chest. *Am I attracted to this man?* The notion leaves me confused.

He starts walking out of the water, not yet noticing us. I can't look away, and my eyes are glued to his stomach as the water sinks lower. When his cock is suddenly exposed, I'm left staring. It's... huge! Is that what a gargoyle penis looks like?

"Arthur!" Max shouts.

The gargoyle looks up, still partially in the water. He spots us, and his cheeks grow red. He immediately crosses his hands in front of his dick.

"Sorry," Max says, his voice stern. "Apparently, my brother didn't remember we had a guest. Arthur, meet Sirena."

"It's okay," I tell him. "Can you put me down?"

He does so, very gently, like I'm something fragile, something that matters. His soft touch surprises me. For a gargoyle whose goal is to kill my kind, he's kind of sweet.

My legs shake as I walk toward his brother… this Arthur. I step into the water and move until we're just feet from each other. This gargoyle looks strikingly similar to the other one. His face has the same strong lines. His eyes are the same pale grey. But his hair is a little longer, and his lips seem permanently curled into a smile. Unfortunately, beneath his smiles, I sense sadness.

I reach down and push his hands to the side; I'm surprised when he lets his hands drop. "It's okay," I say. "My kind doesn't mind nudity."

Glancing down, my eyes widen. Has he gotten bigger? He has. His cock has risen, hardening and lengthening so much that it nearly touches me.

I study it. "You're even bigger," I say.

His hands go to cover his cock once more. "Sorry, it's been awhile since I… since I saw a woman naked."

I kneel down and push his hands aside again. "So, this is what happens when you see a woman naked?"

He lets loose a string of curses. "You've got to stand up!"

I look up at him. His eyes are wild. "Why?"

The big gargoyle glances at his brother, looking strangely helpless. "Tell her!"

I hear Max laugh behind me. "You're the one strutting around naked. You fix this mess."

Reaching up, I run my hand along his erection. "I don't understand the problem."

He throws his hands in the air and takes several steps back, stumbling through the water. "I'm taking a long dip! You… better get dressed."

I stand, frowning. "I don't like clothes."

He groans. "You need clothes."

"Why?" I ask.

His gaze goes to my breasts, then lower. Again, I feel

Keto's Tale

that unexpected warmth spreading through my body. If I truly find this man attractive, I should explore it to see if this warm feeling gets better. *Doesn't he feel the same way?*

"You just need clothes!" he says, then turns and dives into the water.

I look back at his brother. "What's wrong with him?"

Max looks like he's just won some prize, grinning ear to ear. "He's learning a lesson, that's all."

Shrugging, I sink into the water and sigh. It's warm and rushes pleasantly against my skin, easing some of the pain from my wounds.

"So, uh," Max clears his throat. "Are you taking a bath then?"

He draws closer, looking strangely nervous.

I study him. "Is your cock hard too?"

Both his brows rise. "I'm sorry?"

"Is your cock hard too?"

To my surprise, he looks even more nervous. "No."

"Then you can join me without running away like your brother."

The other brother has surfaced near the other side of the lake, near the bottom of the waterfall. "I didn't run away!"

I regard him. "Then come back here."

He doesn't answer me for a long minute. "I'd feel more comfortable over here."

I frown and look back at Max. "I don't understand."

The gargoyle sighs and shifts. I watch transfixed as his wings melt away and his skin changes from a stunning grey to a tan color. Then, standing before me, is a gargoyle who looks like a man. Like Arthur.

"Here's the thing. Our Brotherhood has taken a vow of celibacy. That means we can't have sex. So, having a beautiful naked woman running around might be a bit of a challenge for us."

Celibacy? No sex? Mermaids love sex. Well, most of them other than me. I've never really understood it, but they can fuck anywhere at any time. Usually they surface on beaches and go at it like any other animal. The women seem to prefer strong men with large cocks, so I'm shocked that these three are refraining.

"How long have you gone without sex?"

Max looks to the sky as if it might have the answers. "Twenty years."

"Wow!" I stare at him. "Is that why he got hard so easily?"

He shakes his head and laughs. "Uh, yeah, plus the whole naked woman thing."

"So does he find me attractive specifically, or would he find any woman attractive right now?"

Max stares for a long second. "Well, you're extremely beautiful, so I'm afraid it's you he finds attractive."

I nod and slip beneath the water, letting it run through my hair. I stare up at the surface, lit by the sun. In my human form, I'll need to surface for air soon. But I don't mind. I just enjoy the peace and quiet that comes in this moment.

Closing my eyes, an idea begins to form in my mind. These gargoyles find me attractive but won't have sex with me. They're looking for a "monster" in the ocean who just happens to be me. Perhaps I can offer them my help and hope they're too distracted by their attraction to see behind my lies. I'm not a deceitful siren, but I believe I can become one.

My life depends on it.

My eyes pop open, and I smile. *It's not a permanent solution to my dilemma, but it should buy me some time!*

Surfacing, I gasp in fresh air, then turn to Max.

As soon as our eyes meet, his cheeks turn red, and he turns away.

"Gargoyle?"

He glances back, looking uncomfortable. "Yes."

Be brave, Keto. You can do this.

"I think I might be able to help you find your monster."

Chapter Seven

STEVEN

I can't shake this feeling, this strange sense that the world is calling to me. The sun, the stars, and even the moon are whispering to me, and I don't understand any of it.

Except that I think it has to do with the dragons and the golden light.

"What does it feel like for you?"

I turn and look at Clark. He looks worried, and the last thing I want to do is stress him out. When the Elites called us and charged us with this task, none of us expected for them to demote Clark and make Max our new leader. The Elites made the decision, but they did it with no explanation at all. I knew Clark was worried, scared that he'd screwed up in one way or another. I felt pretty sure he was on the edge of something right now, and the last thing I want to do is push him over.

So, I try to keep the worry out of my voice. "It's sort of like the stars and sky are… calling to me."

Clark gives a curt nod. "Mine feels more like something's trying to escape beneath my skin."

Keto's Tale

We both feel it… a change.

The thing is, Clark and I were made, not born like the twins. And gargoyles who are *made* always sense things on a deeper level. We were formed from the earth, and so we're connected with the earth. Max and Arthur may have changed deep down too from our encounter with the dragons, but they just might not know it yet.

"What do you think of the woman?" Clark asks me.

Every muscle in my body tightens as I think of her. Clark, like me, always puts the needs of our people first. I can remember from the time I was carved, when I awoke in the artist's tiny shed, I felt a responsibility that weighed upon my shoulders like the weight of the world. I didn't see women for women. I didn't laugh or smile or…live.

Until my master, my builder, died.

I shake my head, trying to clear out the old memories of sadness and pain. What had Clark asked? Oh yes, about the woman.

I don't like her.

She makes me feel… different, like she matters. That is *not* something I want to feel. The only thing that should be important to me is my people and my Brotherhood, not a strange woman with deep eyes filled with pain and loneliness. I shouldn't care about a woman battered and frightened, even if a deep, painful need to protect her claws within me.

"She's just a woman," I tell Clark, staring at the horizon.

He's quiet for a long time, and I glance casually in his direction. His beard is wilder than when we were back at the gargoyle sanctuary. His skin is more tan, and his blue eyes are pale against his skin. There's something about him since we started hunting this monster—something dark and tortured that he's trying to hide.

"Arthur likes her," Clark says, his tone harsh.

I stiffen. *We can't lose him again.* "What makes you think that?"

"It wasn't what he said about her. It was what he didn't say."

I speak without thinking. "I'm sure Max has an eye on the situation."

Anger flashes in Clark's eyes. "Fuck it! Max isn't leader material. He's all about diplomacy and shit. He can't take charge when it's needed, and I know he won't take charge on this situation with the woman and his brother."

I don't want to say it, but I have to. "You were the leader when Arthur went rogue."

He turns those angry eyes onto me. "So, you're saying it was my fault?"

I shake my head. "No, I'm saying that we were all there, and none of us could stop him."

A tense silence stretches between us.

I take a deep breath. "Max didn't ask to be leader."

"I fucking know that."

"But you know he has to be. It was commanded."

"I fucking know that too."

The last thing I want is to get punched in mid-air, but I won't be able to relax until it's said. "And you also know that Max is completely out of his element and will need your guidance? Because the last thing we should do right now is make this situation harder on him."

He huffs, but I see some of the tension ease from his shoulders. "The Elites didn't seem to think he needed my guidance."

"Because they're *always* right," I say, smiling.

He turns, and the anger leaves his face. "They did welcome Medusa herself into our sanctuary."

I laugh. Medusa has grown on all of us, but it doesn't

mean any of us thought allowing her into our lands was a good idea in the first place.

Suddenly, we hear a song on the wind.

"What the fuck is that?" Clark asks, his familiar frown back in place.

"I don't know." I squint through the clouds and then down towards the ground.

"Let's check it out," he says, and before I can answer, he shoots down through the clouds.

I don't like this idea. The singing is strange. Not human. Not a creature, but something in between. The hairs on my body stand on end, but I sink lower, following my Brother.

Flying out of the clouds, the singing grows louder, almost deafeningly so. It washes over me in waves. Immediately, I spot the source of the songs. Women lounge on rocks around a small island. All of them are beautiful, and all of them are singing loudly.

Suddenly, nothing else matters, nothing but hearing more of their song. I have to be closer to them.

I dive down and land on a rock.

Five of the women crawl higher to reach me. Their song fills my ears, my brain, and my blood. They begin to pull at my clothes and strip my bag from my back.

I'm trapped, held by the song that keeps me here. Somewhere in the back of my mind I know that these women are sirens. Their faces are covered in scales as they lean over me, singing into my brain. Their eyes wild, and their scent is salty and wrong.

One of them pulls off my pants. "Oh, he's a big one!"

Her words start to tear through their song.

"What's wrong?" one of the sirens asks from above me. "Not yet ready to give us our babies?"

I think my nose is bleeding, and maybe my ears.

One of the women runs claws down my belly that slice at my flesh. "We can't enjoy you until you speak the words, but we can keep you here until you do."

I can't fight them. I can't move, can't even look to make certain that Clark is okay.

They drag me into the water, their song still coming from all around me. There are moments I think I'll drown, when I can't swim up for air, but they hold me under. Each time, just when my lungs are screaming for air, they surface, allowing a second of air before dragging me back under.

I'm pulled onto a beach. Beneath a tree a massive cage sits open. I'm dragged inside by hands that seem to be all around me. A second later, Clark is thrown inside. After binding both our hands, they close the cage and lock it. And at last. *At last*, the horrible song fades.

Outside our cage dozens of sirens cover the shore. One woman with striking blonde hair and big blue eyes smiles. "Gargoyles, welcome to our home."

"What do you want from us?" I ask.

Something drips from my ear. I look down. Sure enough, it's blood.

"We want what all sirens want from the men who are lured by our song… your seed. Once you agree to impregnate all of us, we'll release you from this cage. You can enjoy our bodies, our food, and the comfort of our island."

Clark and I exchange a glance.

His eyes narrow, and he turns back to her. "No way in hell."

Anger flashes in her eyes. "You are big, viral men, and we are beautiful sirens. What could possibly stop you?"

He doesn't flinch, even though her words are like knives in my ears. "If we wanted to 'mate' with you, you wouldn't have needed to tie us up and throw us in a cage.

Now, you should know, we're gargoyles. We're stubborn and we live forever, so understand me well, there's no chance in fucking hell we'll have sex with any of you."

She flashes her sharp teeth. "Oh, you will. Trust me. With enough time, you will."

The siren turns, and the others follow her back into the water. As soon as they're gone, we both begin trying to escape from our bindings and the cage.

Unfortunately, it quickly becomes obvious that the cage and cuffs were made by a very powerful god who is a good friend of ours. We'd know his magical work anywhere.

"I'm going to thank that asshole for this when we get back," Clark says, settling back against the bars.

I look at him and almost laugh. We're both naked and bound in a cage. Who would have thought this is how our little adventure would go?

"So, what do we do now?"

Clark shrugs. "Wait for an opportunity to escape, or hope the others find us."

He seems so casual, but then, not much ever scares him. Me, on the other hand, I'm worried. Not just because of the sirens and this cage, but because that feeling inside of me is only getting stronger.

What am I going to do?

Chapter Eight

KETO

Arthur dried and got dressed before he would speak with me further, and Max insisted I come out of the water and put on his large shirt. I don't really understand it. Against my wet skin the t-shirt he supplied is almost entirely see-through. When Max saw me in it, he simply groaned and said I was supposed to dry myself first. But how was I to know?

They're cooking something that smells good over a fire, and I've drawn as close as I feel safe to the flames. The world outside of the water feels cold and harsh, and the fire is just what I need to chase away the chill that cuts me bone-deep.

Something warm lands on my shoulders. A blanket.

I glance up to see Arthur smiling down at me. "You looked cold."

You don't know me, so why do you care? Was it a gargoyle thing? Maybe gargoyles care about everyone, even someone as unlovable as me.

At least as long as he doesn't know who I truly am.

Keto's Tale

I try to return his smile and realize that it feels nice smiling at a kind face. "I was cold. Thank you."

Max hands me a bowl of the stew, and he and Arthur seat themselves on fallen logs around the fire. I remain where I am and eat the warm food slowly. Most of what I eat is cold. Fish, sometimes coconuts, and little things I find near beaches. It's strange to eat this food, but also nice. It warms me from the inside out.

How have I gone my whole life without eating something like this?

"Do you like it?"

I look up and realize that both men are looking at with eyes darkened with desire. I swallow the bite of food in my mouth, not even tasting it.

"Yes, why do you ask?"

Arthur clears his throat, then rubs at the back of his neck, looking distinctly uncomfortable. "You were… uh… moaning."

Was I?

"Sorry," I say, blushing.

Looking down at my bowl, my thoughts turn over in my mind. As awkward as it might be, I think I'll need to find more opportunities to moan. They seemed to like it.

"You said you might be able to help us find this monster?" Max asks, changing the subject.

I take a deep breath. I don't like to lie, but I don't have a choice. "I'm a mermaid."

The men exchange a glance.

Huh, not the reaction I expected.

"Are you surprised?" I ask, trying to hide my uncertainty.

Arthur gives another smile, and something strange flutters in my belly. "We knew you weren't human."

"Why?" I ask, genuinely curious.

Max is the one who answers. "There's something in your eyes that gives you away. You look young, but you have a lifetime of pain in your eyes."

Suddenly, it's hard to breathe. He's wrong. I have many, many lifetimes of pain and suffering at the hands of my brother. It hurts to know I'm so easily read.

"And you're inhumanely beautiful." Arthur grins, but it doesn't meet his eyes.

I nod. "You're both semi-immortal. You know what it's like to not know the relief that death can bring."

Semi-immortals are beings who can only be killed in a few ways, usually by being beheaded. Unlike me, when they die, they're gone forever. So these gargoyles have likely been alive for a very long time. They must understand what I mean, and yet, they look surprised.

Maybe they don't know. Maybe it's just me.

I set my bowl of food in my lap, no longer hungry.

It takes me a minute to remember my plan. To remember my lie. "I can help you find the... the sea monster."

"Keto?" Arthur whispers as he moves closer. "Do you know her?"

I nod slowly. "She lives in the ocean. Every mermaid knows her."

"Can you bring her to us?" Max asks.

That would be too easy. "No, but I can help you find her."

Max and Arthur exchange a glance, but Max is the one to respond. "What do you want in return for your help?"

"Want?" I ask, feeling perplexed.

Just to stay with you for a little while, to be safe and free.

"Well, you aren't just doing this to help us, right?" Max is staring at me, too closely.

"Oh!" *Yes, of course, that would be suspicious. No one does anything just to be kind.* "You remember the sea dragons you

Keto's Tale

saved me from? Well, I'm no longer safe in the ocean alone. If I go back, they'll kill me."

"Why?" Max asks.

My throat tightens, and I touch my collar without thinking.

Both of their gazes move to it, and I think they've realized for the first time what it is. Not some thin necklace or piece of jewelry. No, they've realized my shame.

But perhaps for once this horrid thing can be of use. "I was their slave. When I didn't obey, they decided to end my life."

I expect many things from these gargoyles, but not the anger that comes to their eyes.

"Are they the reason you think sex hurts?" Max asks, and there's something dark in his voice that confuses me.

No, it wasn't them. My brother's second in command finds me attractive and I was forced to submit to him, but they can't know that. Even hinting at it will bring too many questions.

So, I lie. Again. "Yes."

The two men exchange a glance filled with hatred, and for some reason I feel guilty. These gargoyles really don't like the idea of a woman being hurt.

"Here's the thing," Max says, very slowly. "We can't protect you forever. We have a home we have to get back to, that we need to bring this Keto to."

Of course you do. I imagine men like these are beloved by their people. To many, many women

I nod. "I understand. Just being under your protection while you search for her would be enough. Then, maybe, you could take me to a larger body of water, but not an ocean. You can leave me there and I'll be safe from the dragons."

Arthur looks guilty. "That's all you want?"

"Yes." I hold my breath.

Max rubs his face like he's tired. "Okay. I'm sure we can find a good place for you."

"Thank you," I tell them, the words coming out in a rush.

I eat the rest of my bowl, then two more bowls. The gargoyles seem happy with my hunger. By the time I'm finished, the sky has darkened and night is almost upon us. They build up the fire, so it can offer us some warmth during the night, and then we crawl into their tent.

It's smaller than I thought. Most of their stuff is piled by the front and blankets have been laid out in the rest of the space. I don't know how the four big gargoyles fit in here, but I squeeze between the two men.

I get the sense they're uncomfortable, and I understand why. It's cold in here and I'm uncomfortable beneath the shirt. I long to strip it off and dive into the water, but I'll remain here, under their protection.

The night drags on. I don't think either of the men sleep beside me. And I shift, uncomfortable. Although it's soft, the shirt scratches against me when I move and after a while, I feel like I'm going to lose my mind. I pull off the shirt and lie back down.

Shivering, I curl closer to Max.

His breathing grows rapid. "What are you doing?"

His question is quiet in the darkness.

"I'm cold," I tell him, as if it's the most obvious thing in the world.

Reaching behind me, I tug Arthur closer. He obeys, rolling against my back.

A second later, he swears. "Are you naked again?"

I close my eyes, finally feeling warmer as their heat surrounds me. "*Mhum.*"

A shudder runs through his body. "Wouldn't clothes make you more comfortable?"

Sleep is so close. "I hate clothes." I yawn. "But I like the two of you. You're warm."

I lay a leg across Max, wrapping his waist. For the first time I realize that his cock is hard again inside of his thin shorts. My eyes open. Wiggling my ass just a bit, I discover Arthur is hard behind me too.

These celibate gargoyles are certainly quick to harden.

Again, that warmth moves through me, settling at my core. I want something from these men. I want to explore this feeling and see where it can take us, but I'm afraid it'll complicate things. I'm supposed to use their arousal against them. I'm not supposed to enjoy it.

I let my leg curl around Max's hard cock until it's nestled by my knee.

He gives a tiny groan. I want to just reach out and stroke the tip of his cock, to rub it and see how he responds, but I have to be more… casual than that. I have to be seductive.

Even though I have no idea how the hell to behave in such a way.

I move my leg, rolling him slightly.

One of his hands grasps my upper thigh. "Be still," he says.

"I'm restless," I tell him.

He's breathing hard. "Stay still."

Frowning, I close my eyes. Well, that's the least successful seduction in history. I guess even though I'm naked, and these men are hard and frustrated, I have to somehow make them want me.

Yawning, I feel sleep tugging at me. I guess I'll try again tomorrow.

Chapter Nine

MAX

I'm going to lose my fucking mind. This mermaid is squeezing my cock, her leg wrapped around me in the most possessive way imaginable, and she doesn't have a clue how turned on I am.

If she did, she'd be running the other way.

I keep rubbing my face because I don't know where the hell else to put my hands. I'm pretty sure anywhere else, and I'll touch some part of this naked woman. While that idea is appealing, it's also the exact opposite of what I should be doing.

Do not be tempted by the naked woman in your bed.

But that leg of hers keeps curling around my cock, and I'm so damn hard I think I'm going to tear right through my boxers. *Shit. This is hell. Pure and utter hell.*

Finally, I put my hands back down. One touches her thigh. I stiffen, knowing I should move it.

She sighs sleepily and places a hand on my bare chest. "That feels nice."

"Nice?" I repeat, heart hammering.

She snuggles more closely.

Keto's Tale

Very slowly, I run my hand up and down her long leg. With each small touch, she seems to curl closer against me. At last, I feel her bare breasts against my side.

Fucking hell. I need to get out of here before I do something really stupid.

I untangle myself from her and sit up.

She makes a little sound of protest, but doesn't stop me. I look to where my brother Arthur is curled against her back. He looks to be asleep. Thank goodness. I'd hate for him to see how pathetic I am right now.

Creeping out of the tent, I stumble until I come to the edge of the water. Pushing my boxers down, I pull my cock out and start to stroke. But instead of the many images that usually come to my mind when I'm masturbating, I imagine the mermaid. Sirena. She's so fucking beautiful, with her long red hair and dark eyes. Her body has curves in all the right places. Her big breasts with perfect pink nipples and her bare pussy call to me.

If this woman was made by the gods to tempt me, they succeeded. They win this round.

"Max?"

I hear her and whirl around, cock still in hand.

Sirena comes closer. She looks like a creature of fantasy beneath the moon's pale light. Every inch of her naked body is exposed to my desperate eyes. Her gaze is both curious and aroused as she stops just feet in front of me.

I should tuck my cock back in and come up with an excuse for my absence. I should lie through my teeth, even though we both know exactly what I'm doing.

But I don't.

She reaches out and pushes my hand away, and I let her. Suddenly, she wraps a hand around my shaft, and I groan in pleasure. Her grip is tight as she slowly strokes me up and down. Every nerve inside of me awakens in a completely unexpected way. Our gazes lock, and I can see an unexpected innocence in her expression.

Sex hurts. I remember her words, and everything inside of me freezes.

It'd be so easy to let her stroke me, to come against her soft skin, but I can't.

That would be all about my pleasure, not hers. This woman deserves a lifetime of soft touches and gentle kisses.

She frowns as I push her hand away and pull up my boxers. "But… I can help," she says.

Instead, I tuck the hair back from her face. Her eyes widen, and the curiosity is back in her expression. Leaning down, I kiss her neck gently. I hear her breath catch, and let my lips slide up her neck. Every so often, I stop and suck softly.

By the time I pull back, I know her heart is racing as fast as mine. She's watching me, and the arousal in her gaze makes me glad I held myself back.

Inching closer to her, I hold her gaze, wanting her to see that she can stop this at any time. And then, I lean down and kiss her.

At first, my lips are light on hers, and she kisses me back, almost experimentally. But then our kiss begins to change. Her lips grow more desperate beneath mine, and my tongue slips into her mouth.

When she moans, a shiver runs through my body, and I pull her closer, letting my hands trail lightly down her back. I want to cup her ass, feel the curves of her delicious body, but I force my hands to remain at her hips. Even when she draws closer, pressing her body against me.

And then I pull back, panting.

Her eyes slowly open, and time stands still. She looks… amazed. Surprised. And even though my cock hates me right now, I don't regret holding back my pleasure for hers.

"Are we... going to have sex now?" she asks.

"Do you want to?"

A guarded look comes to her face.

I smile and push her hair behind her ear once more. "I think a kiss was enough for tonight."

She looks relieved. "Okay."

We turn to head back to the tent. In the dark doorway, I see my brother staring at us. But a second later, he's gone. When we reach it, I push back the flap and she goes in. Arthur looks like he's sleeping, but I know better. We crawl under the blanket, and a short time later I know she's fallen asleep.

I lie awake a lot longer, confused. I'm the leader of this mission. The role brings more responsibility onto my shoulders, responsibility I thought I could handle, even if I didn't want this job. Now, seeing how easily one beautiful woman can make me forget my mission, I'm wondering if I was wrong.

If I show my brother that there's nothing wrong with touching her, I'm scared as hell I'll lose him again. I'm scared that when we catch this Keto and return to the sanctuary, he won't come with us.

I have to be a good role model and a good leader.

Even if somewhere deep inside I'm wondering if maybe this can be my time to be reckless. He had his. Don't I deserve to experience love too?

Closing my eyes, I hate myself a little, because all logic says to be a good leader, and yet, Sirena is all I can picture.

I'm screwed.

Chapter Ten

KETO

*B*reakfast is strangely awkward. I'm back in one of their t-shirts. The two gargoyles are dressed too, but they both look ragged, as if they slept as badly as I did. There's a tension between them that I don't understand.

Not that I'm helping the situation. All I can think about is *the* kiss. Even now I want to touch my lips to see if I've been permanently changed by Max's touch. Because it feels like I'm different. Like my body's hotter, softer. All I want to do is climb on top of him and see if he can make me feel that way again.

Even though I won't.

Arthur clears his throat. "So, what's the plan for today?"

At last, Max's grey eyes lock onto mine, and I swear for half a second I see the same need I'm feeling burning in his gaze before it's gone. "Where can we go to look for Keto?"

I tense. I have a plan. I just prey it isn't a mistake. "There are some sirens not far from here. I think they might have answers. We can go together, but they'll only speak to me."

Max nods. "If you think they might be able to help us, then we'll go to them."

I smile.

"What?" Arthur asks.

I turn and see him staring at me. "I'm sorry?" I say, confused.

"Why are you smiling?"

I get flustered beneath his gaze. His eyes are the same stunning grey, except these ones are filled with mischief.

For a second I debate about lying, but I see no harm in the truth. "It isn't often anyone listens to what I think."

Arthur's cheery air fades. "How old are you?"

I shrug. "Older than both of you. By a lot."

He swears softly under his breath. "Far old enough to have someone who gives a crap enough to listen to you."

His words make me uncomfortable. I finish the remainder of yesterday's stew without meeting his gaze.

Max stands and takes my bowl. "How far are the sirens from us?"

"Less than a day."

He nods and goes to wash out the bowls.

Arthur hurries around packing a couple bags, then hands one to Max when he returns.

"Do you need anything?" Max asks, not meeting my gaze.

I shake my head.

"Then let's go."

Max walks toward me, and I reach my hands up and wrap them around his neck. I jump a little to wrap my legs around his waist.

His eyes widen, and he stares at me. "*This* is how we're flying?"

Arthur's voice comes out strangely amused behind us. "What's wrong, Max?"

Max's entire face tightens. "Nothing, let's go."

Within seconds, he shifts. His skin turns the stunning color of wet stone and wings sprout on his back. His skin hardens beneath my touch, but not as much as I'd have expected. He still feels… strangely human.

"You're not as hard as yesterday."

His cheeks turn red. "What?"

I run my hands along his shoulder. "Your skin is softer."

"Oh," he says, and I hear Arthur laughing behind us. "I'm not in battle form."

"Battle form?"

He nods. "Gargoyles can shift into differently levels of stone. This is just enough to take my gargoyle form. In full battle mode, I'm as hard as stone."

That makes sense. I tighten my legs around him. "Okay, then let's go."

He swears softly, starts to flap his wings, and we shoot up into the sky. Arthur follows behind us.

"Which way?" Max asks.

I point.

Both men start forward, but Arthur quickly overtakes us.

"Show off," Max mumbles.

I smile. These men… twins, certainly like to fight, but not like my brother and I. There's love here, so deep I can sense it even when they argue.

Closing my eyes, I tilt my head back, surprised by how much I enjoy the wind blowing through my hair, and the feel of the sunlight on my skin. It feels like I'm in a dream, or in another person's life, a person who has happiness.

"You like flying?" Max asks softly.

Keto's Tale

"I love it," I say.

Shifting slightly, I feel a shudder move through his body. Suddenly, I'm very, very aware of the fact that he's hard again, and I'm not talking about his skin.

But I'm more surprised by my own reaction. I felt overdressed wearing their shirt, but now I'm intimately aware of the fact that my lower half is completely bare and only his pants separate us. My heart races, and I feel my entire body heating up.

It's hard to catch my breath. I close my eyes and rub gently against him. I feel him tense beneath my fingertips, but I continue to rub myself against him, shocked by the waves of pleasure that come from the contact. I'm practically grinding against him, but I don't care, because it feels so damn good.

"Sirena," he groans, his hands tightening on my waist. "What are you doing?"

"You're hard," I pant. "I want—"

I don't know what I want. But I know it's him. It's this feeling. I don't want it to stop.

"If you don't stop…" His words are a warning that I don't understand.

Instead, I start to bounce against him.

He swears, and I feel his entire body tense. His dick seems to swell against my wet core, and then I know he's come. I feel the front of his pants grow wet with his seed.

And for some reason, I love the fact that I made him come.

Opening my eyes, I look at him. His expression is wild.

"You came," I say.

His cheeks turn red. "Sorry, it's been awhile since… actually, I've never had a woman ride me like this."

"Did it feel good?" I ask.

His gaze locks onto mine, and he looks confused. "Of course, it felt… amazing."

I smile, glad I could make him feel good.

And then I remember his hard cock the night before. I remember my hands running along him. And I want… that. I want to see him.

"Can I do something?"

He looks like he's only half listening, but he nods.

Reaching down with one hand, I unbutton his pants and pull the zipper down.

"What are you doing?" he asks, his eyes going between us where my hand is working quickly.

I shove his boxers down and pull out his long cock, slick with his cum. Surprising even myself, I start to stroke him, and instantly, he hardens again.

"This is a bad idea, Sirena!"

I know it is, but I can't help myself. I want to watch him come this time. I want to feel him swelling in my hand.

So, I stroke him, and he doesn't stop me. Instead, he thrashes his head from side-to-side, panting.

My entire core feels like it's on fire. Every stroke of my hand, every sound he makes, arouses me beyond reason. I've never felt this way before, but damn is it amazing.

I pull closer to him, and kiss the side of his neck the way he did to me. He swears, but I know it's a sound of pleasure. Then I position him in my wet folds and wrap my other arm around his neck.

All reason is gone. I'm overwhelmed by a need to feel the pleasure that only this man can give. I rub myself against him, but this time, his pants aren't in the way. Our hot, wet bodies touch, and it's like lightning, a storm unleashed.

I don't let him enter me, but I rub against his hard

length, feeling an explosion of every nerve in my folds. I test what I like best, where I like to be touched best, and then I lose all control. Bouncing against him, I suck hard on his neck as I ride this beautiful man's cock.

When he explodes against my folds, his warm cum only adds to my own pleasure. Something happens then. I feel my nipples tighten, and pleasure shoots straight to my core. I gasp, and his name slips from my lips. My vision goes black and I continue to rub myself frantically against him until the pleasure slowly eases.

At last, I stop, breathing hard against his neck.

That was… incredible. Not sex. But so good. I've never felt anything like that before.

I'm beginning to understand why this is how mermaids spend so much of their time. It's addicting. Already I'm thinking about when and how I can feel this way again.

"Max?" I whisper his name.

He shudders. "Yes."

"That was amazing."

His hands tighten around me. "I'm… glad. I've never had a woman… do that before."

I frown. "Mermaids think of almost nothing but pleasure. Everywhere I go they fuck like wilds animals."

He's still breathing hard. "Humans and gargoyles aren't like that, unfortunately,"

The notion is strange to me. Should I try to behave like a human or a gargoyle? Is there a purpose in not exploring these feelings of pleasure? I search my mind. No, I can't think of any reason not to.

"Can we do it again?" I ask.

I feel him harden against me. "Now?"

Laughing, I shake my head and pull back from his shoulder. "Not yet."

He gives a sharp nod. "Maybe again sometimes. For now, why don't you pull up my pants?"

I frown. "I like having you out and naked. I like rubbing against you."

"Fucking hell." He looks up at the sky with such a look of desperation. "If Arthur turns around and sees us…"

"What?" I ask.

"Then I won't be able to tell him he can't touch you."

I bite my lip, thinking. "Are you not willing to share?"

"Fuck," he mutters. "No, I can share, but this isn't a good idea. We're on a mission to find the monster and return it to our people."

"We can't do… this, too?"

Our gazes cling to each other, and he leans forward and presses a soft kiss to my lips. "You're tempting… and a distraction."

I shift and he groans, his hands digging into my hips. That feeling comes back, and I'm shocked by how badly I want to rub myself against his big cock again.

If yesterday someone had told me I'd become cock-obsessed, I'd have called him a liar, but these gargoyles bring something out in me. They make me long for more than my sad, lonely life. For some reason, I want to cling to every bit of pleasure I can feel.

"I changed my mind," I tell him.

He looks down at me, his expression tortured. "About what?"

"I do want to try it again… now."

"Sirena," he mumbles.

I bounce a little against him and start to rub slowly. His eyes roll back in his head, and he groans loudly.

"Want me to stop?" I ask, surprised by how breathless I sound.

After a second he says, "Not a chance in hell."

Keto's Tale

This time when I bounce against him, he moves against me too. The friction is... even better than before. We move against each other, lost in the sensation. This time, I come just before he does, digging my nails into his shoulders, overcome by the waves moving through me. When he shoots his hot seed onto my wet folds, I find it strangely sexy.

How is it possible that I made this big, sexy gargoyle come? *Me*?

I'm definitely living in a dream, because as I collapse against him, he holds me even closer. His hand gently strokes my hair.

It's almost enough to make me forget that I'm lying to him, that he doesn't know who or what I am. He doesn't even know my real name.

I'm a liar and a fraud.

It hurts to acknowledge the truth, even though I know he'd never have touched me if I hadn't lied.

Maybe I am a monster.

Chapter Eleven

CLARK

I'm fucking hungry, hungry enough to eat Steven's awful cooking. I'd even eat it without complaining, if we weren't trapped in a cage on Siren Island, or whatever the hell this place is. I stare down at my bound wrists, straining against the metal. I've seen our metal-working god's work before, and the only way we're getting out of these is if these sirens let us out.

The blonde siren emerges from the water not far from us. I watch her shift into a human-looking woman, even though the scales continue to cover her flesh and her teeth remain sharp.

She walks toward us, completely naked.

I would've thought after twenty years of celibacy, the view of a nice pussy and breasts would be enough to harden my cock in any situation, but I feel nothing looking at her. Anger and repulsion moves through me. She smiles as she comes closer to our cage, flashing her sharpened teeth. "You men look… hungry."

"Not a bit," I say, smirking at her.

Anger flares in her eyes. "So, your plan is to starve?"

I shrug, trying to look casual. "If we have to."

She snarls. "I'm giving you something that any man would want! Dozens of beautiful women for your pleasure and your pleasure alone! What could possibly make you refuse us?"

Steven clears his throat. "Perhaps if you let us out. Perhaps if it's our choice, we would be willing. We're gargoyles, and gargoyles like to be the dominant ones in sexual situations."

I almost shout that we wouldn't fuck them under any circumstances, but he casts me a warning glance. *Uh, okay, this is all part of some plan of his.* I guess I can play along if it gets us free.

She studies us for a moment and then grins. "I don't think so. The second we let you out, you'll be gone."

"No," Steven argues, and I can tell he has a whole speech planned.

Her head suddenly jerks to the sky. "More of you?" Her smile widens. "The gods must be smiling down upon us today."

She takes off toward the water, and I slam against the cage.

"Wait!"

She just ignores me, diving back into the water.

"You think it's Max and Arthur?" Steven asks.

I scoff. "Do you know other gargoyles stupid enough to be flying around in the middle of nowhere?"

"So what do we do?"

I yank at the bars again, but they don't budge. "I guess we scoot back. I have a feeling we're all going to be crammed in here soon."

All the sirens have taken to the oceans. There's some kind of commotion in the water, but even when I squint, I can't make out what's going on.

A few tense minutes pass. I wonder if they were caught or escaped. My mind's scrambling to come up with a plan.

"When they open the door, we get out of here," I tell Steven, "and we do our best to plug our ears."

As if on cue, the sirens' horrible song begins.

"Fuck," I shout leaning down so that I can plug both my ears with my cuffed hands.

It helps a little but not enough. This time I don't feel compelled to go toward the singing, but it hurts like hell.

When the singing cuts off and I don't see my brothers, I'm even more confused. Removing my fingers from my ears, I stare off into the water. I can't see any of the sirens now.

Maybe I shouldn't worry, but I do.

And then *she* emerges from the water. The beautiful woman we rescued surfaces like every fantasy I've ever had. She's wearing one of our shirts, but it's plastered to her frame, exposing every curve of her body. My gaze roves over her hard nipples, visible through the fabric, and her long, sexy legs.

I want to give this beautiful woman a name, but I left before learning it. I guess I'll just have to call her Red. *And this Red is fucking hot.*

What the hell? Despite myself, my cock hardens.

As long as I've lived, I've never seen a more beautiful woman than this one.

Behind her, the sirens emerge from the water, shifting into their human-like forms. The blonde scrambles after the human, and I swear the siren is cowering in her presence.

Red turns angry eyes onto the siren, and the blonde points in our direction.

I sit up higher. For some reason it angers me for Red to

see us like this, naked and caged. We're gargoyles, strong, powerful protectors, not weak-ass prisoners.

Red's dark eyes lock onto mine and immediately gentle. As she walks toward us, she holds her head high like a queen. When she stops before our cage, she looks from me to Steven.

"Are you both okay?" she asks like we're old friends. Somehow I think it's important that we play along.

Steven answers. "Hungry and uncomfortable, but yes. We're okay."

The blonde siren rings her hands next to Red. "I didn't know they belonged to you. I would never—"

Red lifts a hand. "No matter, just open their cages and let them out."

The blonde doesn't move.

Red turns to the siren very slowly. "Didn't you hear me?"

The siren bows her head slightly. "I would like nothing more than to follow your orders, but you know the rules."

She looks back at us, and concern flashes in her eyes for a second before it's gone. "It'll be easy for me to prove that I own them, but you must open the doors to do so."

A tense moment stretches out, and I see the sirens closing in around us from every direction.

"Of course, but you must understand it's been a long time since my girls have lured males to them, and even longer since we found any as appetizing as these. By rights, we get to keep them. The only way they leave our lands is through their deaths."

Red levels her with a glare that makes even me tense. Power comes off the woman in waves. "They're mine, and I can prove it."

The siren bows her head in submission and touches the cage. Magic vibrates through it and the cage door opens.

We climb out slowly, aware of the dozens of sharp-toothed sirens surrounding us, capable of screaming until our brains ooze out.

"On your knees," Red commands, her tone that of a goddess.

Every instinct in me rebels against obeying her. After all, she is a woman, and a human one at that. I'm a strong male gargoyle. On the other hand, I'm no fool. Even though I want nothing more than to try to fly the hell out of here before these sirens start singing, I collapse onto my knees. Steven does the same beside me.

The siren makes an angry sound. "Already they rise for you in a way they haven't for us."

I frown and look to Steven before I realize we've both got massive erections. *I guess he* does *find Red attractive.* For a second I feel like gloating, and then I remember that I'm kneeling beside him with an equally obvious boner.

Turning back to Red, I watch her, curious for her reaction. She takes a deep breath that shakes her whole chest, and I sense nerves beneath her calm exterior. I watch as she reaches for the hem of her shirt and pulls it off.

For a minute I just gape at her nudity. I was right. gods, the woman has delicious curves in all the right places, curves I long to touch.

You're celibate, you idiot. Standing around with your cock in your hands, knowing you'll never get chosen by the female gargoyles.

She moves closer to me, grasps me on both sides of my face, and tilts me up to look at her. She gives me a pleading look before her lips descend onto mine.

She caught me off-guard. Of all the things I thought might happen, I never imagined she might kiss me. When my shock wears off, I return the kiss for all I'm worth. My mouth slants over hers, taking control, even while she's the one standing above me.

When she at last pulls back, we're both panting.

She kneels before me and runs a finger possessively along the length of my cock.

I sit up straighter, my breathing ragged. What's she going to do now? What does she want from me?

Holding my gaze, she leans down and suddenly her lips close around my cock.

I groan. "Oh fucking hell."

Her movements are uncertain as she takes me deeper and deeper into her mouth. When she pulls back, my hips jerk, wanting more, wanting her hot lips around my cock once more.

Instead, she turns to Steven. I'm jealous as she moves closer to him and begins to stroke his hard cock. My brother throws back his head and groans, rocking into her hand. She leans down to suck on his shaft, and the movement sends her ass just inches from my cock.

Unable to help myself, I shift in the sand and use my cuffed hands to press my cock into her folds. She moans around Steven's shaft. I move against her harder, wanting more than anything to fuck this beautiful woman's pussy like I own it. I start to press my tip inside her, and she jerks free from Steven's cock and looks back at me with some mix of fear and uncertainty.

Fucking. Fuck. Fuck. She doesn't want me to do this. So I can't. There's a beautiful, naked woman bent down in front of me, and she doesn't want me.

I think of her in that cage. *Was she hurt by those dragons? Or someone else?*

So, I can't fuck her. *What now?*

I glance at the sirens. They're watching us. Every. Single. One. Of. Them.

Red doesn't strike me as someone who'd want an audience while she was touched. She doesn't seem like she'd want to take advantage of our position, so I have to believe she knows what she's doing. If she is gaining our freedom with this show, who am I to question her?

But how can I keep this up and not fuck her?

The idea comes as I stare at her delicious ass and feel her wetness coating the tip of my cock. She liked it when I was just touching her. I can do more of that.

A lot more.

I wish I could say this was all about the show, but as I lie on the sand and scoot my head between her legs, staring at her wet pussy, I'm not thinking about the sirens or my freedom. I simply grab her ass and lower her down onto my mouth.

She gasps as my mouth presses into her lower lips. I flick my tongue, and she cries out. Oh yes, she likes this, and she tastes like heaven. Greedily I lick her, suck her clit, and press myself against her. I'm rewarded when she begins to grind against my lips. Her movements become more frantic.

I open my eyes to glance up and see how hard she's sucking Steven's cock. He's on his knees rocking, his hands digging into the back of her hair. She's wild between us, thrashing like she doesn't know quite what to do.

Unable to help myself, I gently press a finger inside her. She freezes for half a second, and then begins to grind against my mouth once more. Like the greedy son-of-a-bitch I am, I fuck her with my finger, and even add a second one, imagining all along that my throbbing cock is the thing sliding in and out of her.

When she orgasms above me, the sounds of her pleasure choked by the shaft buried deeply inside her mouth, I lose my fucking mind. I feel myself spew, like a rubber-band that's snapped, and my hot cum oozes down my naked cock.

Steven groans above me, and I know he's spilling his seed in her sweet lips even as she continues to ride my mouth. When she finally stills above me, I start to lick her some more. The idea that soon she'll be moving away from me, taking her tasty pussy away, makes me want to scream in rage. I could lick this woman every second of my day. I could have her for breakfast, lunch, and dinner. I could start every morning by parting her thighs and watching her turn wet under my gentle touch.

She starts to pull away from me, and a growl slips from my lips. I bring her back down, and suck that sensitive clit of hers.

"Oh, God," she gasps, and I realize she's no longer sucking Steven.

She reaches down and grasps my hair.

I look up at her and suck harder.

She thrashes, rubbing herself against me harder. "You… have to… stop."

Again, she tries to pull away from me.

I growl. "You're not taking your sweet pussy from me now."

Her eyes go wide.

Deliberately, I lick her over and over again, holding her gaze with each lick.

"The sirens," she pants.

Her words are like a crack of a whip. I forgot about the fucking sirens. I forgot about the cage and my cuffs.

I release her, and she scrambles off of me. Turning, I stare at the blonde and the dozens of sirens who surround us. Half of them are stroking themselves, and all of them look aroused.

The blonde glares, but attempts to hide her anger. "It seems you've made both males spill their seed. I would not have *wasted* their seed anywhere but my womb, but they belong to you."

She moves closer, touches my cuffs, and they fall away. Her gaze moves to my cock, covered in my cum. Her desire makes me uneasy. I rise and wipe my mouth with the back of my hand. A thousand angry retorts come to my mind, but I clench my teeth.

I just want to get off this fucking island.

Next, the siren removes Steven's cuffs and my brother stands.

Red moves between us looking uncertain. "Both of you go to the edge of the water and wait for me there."

I hesitate. There's no way I want to leave her with these blood-thirsty sirens, but Steven immediately moves to follow her orders. I have to fight every instinct to follow him, but I keep looking back.

Red moves closer to the blonde, her voice lowering. *What is it that they're talking about?*

My suspicions grow. Women are never to be trusted, especially the beautiful ones. Perhaps she had everything all planned out from the beginning. How else did she find us after our kidnapping?

When we reach the water's edge, I turn to Steven. "We should shift and get out of here."

He frowns, looking nervously at the sirens not far from us. "She got us out of our cage and out of our cuffs. I say we stay and listen to her."

Since when does Steven question what I say? Since fucking Max became the leader?

"Follow me or don't, but I'm not waiting around to see what they have planned for me next."

Within seconds, I shift and shoot into the air. I'm satisfied when Steven does the same. We're both hovering just above the water when the singing begins. This time it's

Keto's Tale

angry, almost violent. My ears scream in pain, and suddenly I'm falling. I hit the ocean like a brick wall, and for a minute, I'm choking on water, drowning and unable to see the surface.

All I want is to live, to breathe.

A strange feeling overwhelms me like nothing I've felt before. The swirling water around me glows, and I feel myself changing, stretching, growing. My chest clenches until I realize that I can breathe underwater. Then it hits me. I'm no longer myself.

I've shifted… but into what? My senses tingle. There's something delicious and alluring in the water. I shoot through the water and squint at what I'm smelling, what I'm tasting.

My heart stops when I realize it's Steven. A delicious trail of red oozes into the water from his head.

I feel uneasy but swim toward him. I don't have hands, and I'm massive, dwarfing him. Using my nose, I prod him up until he explodes from the surface of the water.

Red is swimming in front of me, her gaze murderous. "Leave him be, beast! He's mine!"

I stare at her in confusion. She points her hands out in front of her, and a wave crashes into me. Steven goes spinning from my grasp. I feel frantic until I see him in her arms.

Yet, she still glares at me. *What the hell am I?*

"Obey me or die!" she growls.

Oh fuck, I can feel her power in the water, and suddenly, it's overwhelming. It's like what I felt when I shifted times a thousand. It's as if the brightest light tugs at my very soul.

How is she this powerful?

My heart thuds wildly. If I can't change back, she's

going to kill me. I need my human-form, my gargoyle-form.

I feel the tingling again, spreading over me like a warm blanket, and then I'm back to struggling in the water. I see my hands splashing out before me. I feel my body, *mine*, not whatever the hell I was.

"It's you!" she says, but there's panic in her gaze.

I swim closer to her, torn in every way. "What the hell was that? What the hell am I? And is he okay?"

She looks down at Steven, then back at me. "You were a shark. I think he'll be okay… and I have no idea what that was."

A look comes over her face, but quickly vanishes.

Rage bubbles up inside me. Without thinking, my hand shoots out and grasps her by the throat. "You know. Tell me," I growl.

Her eyes widen as she stares at me.

"Please…" I start to squeeze. "Don't make me hurt you."

She closes her eyes, and I might be wrong, but I think tears roll from her the corners of her eyes.

My grip loosens. I don't think I'm hurting her. Right? I don't like to be lied to, but it'll be a cold day in hell before I hurt a woman.

Unless she's truly my enemy.

"I didn't think it was possible," she says, and those dark eyes of hers open again.

"What?" I ask.

She hesitates. "I think you might have the sea dragons' powers."

Behind us, I hear the distinct shrieking of the sirens.

Her eyes widen. "We need to get further from the island. Max and Arthur are waiting, but they can't get in range of their songs, we need to get out of here."

She doesn't wait to see if I obey. She drags Steven through the water and out into the open sea, only with her tail, she glides more than drags.

Wait a minute. She's got a tail? The woman we rescued is a fucking mermaid? What the hell?

After a second, I follow behind her. Logic tells me to move fast to get as far away from the sirens as possible, but her words linger. What does it mean if we absorbed these sea dragons' powers?

And won't they want them back?

Chapter Twelve

KETO

I feel like crying, like dissolving into tears and sobbing like I haven't in a long time. These lies tear at my soul and eat at my belly. And already they've put these gargoyles in danger.

I never wanted that. I wanted to be safe with them, not put them at risk.

When my little creature absorbs powers, it works in many different ways. But when the gargoyle transformed into that shark, I knew for certain.

I didn't realize that my little creature actually gave these men the power of the sea dragons. I thought they might absorb some of the dragons' powers, but never thought they would actually be able to use them.

Shifting is Nereus's power. He's the oldest of the sea dragons, and white as the sands of Calimara. So if SharkBoy has his powers, who has the other dragons' powers? One of them will control the planets and the stars, one will control the waves, and the last will control the mindless sea animals.

Keto's Tale

These are dangerous powers and even gargoyles won't be able to contain them for long.

My mind goes to the times fools have greedily tried to steal the powers of immortal gods. It has always ended in their deaths. The powers consume their fragile bodies like a parasite.

I must return their powers before it's too late. All I need to do is get them near my little creature, my tiniest "monster," but that means finding him somewhere in these endless waters…

I think back to my conversation with Parmoni, the leader of the sirens.

"The waves bring rumors, Mother of Sea Monsters," she said, *leveling me with her far too astute gaze.*

I keep my face carefully blank. "What rumors?"

"One is that you died, torn to pieces by hungry sea dragons."

My heart races. "And the other?"

She cocks her head, studying me. "That you were the one to kill them."

I don't know what to say. What is there to say? You can never trust a siren, and yet, Parmoni is the closest that a siren can be to a friend.

"Your brother had a ceremony honoring your brave death," she *continues, then swims closer. "Goddess, you have not asked for my advice—"*

"Give it freely," I rush out.

She smiles, showing her sharp teeth "Kill your brother and be free from the bastard before he learns that you yet live."

Kill him? No. As long as I wear this collar such a thing is impossible.

"I'm more interested in what you know of the god who made your cage and cuffs," I tell her.

"The same one who made your collar?" Her eyes widen. "Is that your plan then, to get him to remove it?"

"Please," I whisper. "The sea has many ears."

Her expression grows solemn. "Hephaestus is the blacksmith god, as we both know. And he disappeared long ago, after his bitch of a wife broke his heart."

"Ex-wife," I mumble. No, gods don't have traditional divorces, but he publically decreed himself done with her when he learned the Goddess of Love had been unfaithful to him over and over again.

She nods. "Ex-wife."

"So, there's nothing you can tell me?" I ask, disappointment like a pit in my belly.

She stares off for a minute before she smiles once more. "Rumors were that he spent some time on the Isle of Demons."

I laughed. Even though I avoided the island, I knew exactly where it was.

Having one lead was better than nothing.

"Thank you, sister!" I pull her into a hug.

When I release her, she grins. "Does this mean that you'll allow us to keep the gargoyles?"

I frown. "I can't do that. They belong to me." But then I think of all the places I go in my travels. "But I can see if any males might be inclined to visit your island."

She looks disappointed. "My girls will not like that, but we will see."

We head toward the island, and my gut turns. She expected me to trade the men for her information? This exchange might not go as smoothly as I thought.

"I see them!"

SharkBoy's voice shakes me from my memory, and I turn to him in the water. He's staring off into the sky. I follow his gaze. At first all I see are clouds, but then Max and Arthur shoot out of them and head straight for us.

First, Max pulls SharkBoy from the water. The big man takes a minute and then shifts into his gargoyle-form. Then Max and Arthur pull the injured gargoyle, still unconscious, from my arms. At last, SharkBoy reaches down and pulls me out of the water. Immediately I shift, making myself lighter to carry in the air.

This gargoyle is bigger than Max and Arthur. Wrapping my arms around his neck feels like hugging a tree and wrapping my legs around his waist feels even stranger. He lifts me higher into the air, avoiding the others.

"Clark!" Max shouts. "Bring her back! We can't follow you and care for Steven!"

They shout more, but he ignores them.

Why is this strange gargoyle—this Clark—taking off with me?

I suddenly become aware that we're both naked, which shouldn't matter, but for some reason it does. Against him I feel small, almost dominated by his much larger body. And I shouldn't like the feeling of this big man against me, but I do. My insides flutter with some unnamed emotion.

Does he feel it too?

My gaze moves up. He's staring down at me with the strangest fire in his eyes. Nerves tumble in my stomach. Is he angry? Or does that fire mean something else?

Shifting against him, my eyes widen as I feel his large cock harden between my thighs. My legs tighten harder around his waist, and I know that if I lower myself even just an inch, I can rub myself against him.

But I don't. Max and Arthur make me feel safe. This man? He frightens me a little.

He's tough, angry, and unpredictable, just like my brother. Oh, God, I pray he's not like my brother, but I really don't know enough about him to be sure.

His gaze tears from my face and moves to my breasts. It's suddenly hard to breathe. Does he find me attractive like the other gargoyles?

I tense. "What's wrong?"

"What's your name?" he spouts at me.

"Sirena," the lie tumbles from my lips.

His eyes meet mine once more, and his expression is enraged. "Well, Sirena, let's not play games. Did you set all of that up?"

My jaw drops and for a second I can't speak. "Set—"

"You heard me!" he shouts.

I'm lying to all of these gargoyles. I'm betraying them in every way, and yet, it hurts that he'd think I was capable of something like that. For a second I remember how he kissed me on the beach, and the way he touched me. He thought I arranged all of that?

"No," I say, the word so soft I'm worried he missed it.

His hands tighten on my waist. "I don't trust you."

"You shouldn't," the words leave my lips before I realize how stupid I was to say them. And yet, I keep talking. "None of you know me. I'm just a mermaid you rescued."

My throat tightens. I don't know how I'll reach the Isle of the Demons without them, not without being seen by my brother's minions, but perhaps the Fates have brought me into the arms of this suspicious gargoyle for a reason. To give me an opportunity to set them free, to be a good person.

Taking a shaky breath, I speak before I can lose my nerve. "You can drop me wherever you see fit and get back to your mission."

Back into the water. Where my brother will hear of me. Where I'll become a slave once more. Just the thought brings that strange pricking feeling back to my eyes. I angrily command myself not to cry.

He doesn't answer me for a long time, and I feel like he's assessing me. "So you suggest I just drop you in the sea?"

That's what I'd said, and I meant it. If he dropped me

now, the gargoyles would be safe. Far from me and the wrath of my brother and the sea dragons.

I lift my gaze to meet his. "If that's what you think is best."

He tightens one arm around my waist and reaches up with the other to push the hair back from my face. "I know better than to trust a beautiful woman."

I jerk my chin higher. "I never trust a hot man."

Why did I say that?

For a second I honestly think he's going to drop me straight into the ocean, but then the corner of his lips quirk. "So, you think I'm hot?"

I shrug, wishing I could look away from his stunning blue eyes. "I mean…I did until I saw you curled up naked in the bottom of that cage. That was… far from hot."

This time he laughs, and the sound is so delicious I wish I could eat it. "That wasn't my best moment." And then his smile falters. "What were you talking to the sirens about?"

I think back to my conversation, and then I remember he shifted into a shark. How in the world could I have forgotten? If these gargoyles have the power of the gods, they'll die without my help. The powers of the gods will consume their bodies bit by bit, day by day, until there's nothing left to consume.

Their fate is tied to mine, whether I like it or not. Any thought of leaving them behind just vanished. Even if I feel like a terrible person, it seems I'm on this path, for good or bad.

So. More lies it is, then. "She gave me a lead on Keto."

"Where?"

"The Isle of the Demons."

That strange energy arcs between us again, and I get the oddest feeling that he doesn't want to trust me. He wants to catch me in a lie, which makes absolutely no sense. Their goal is to find the woman Keto, right? They should be happy about any leads…

After a minute, he nods. "You might be useful after all."

And yet, he sounds disappointed as he says the words.

Gargoyles are confusing.

"So no dip in the sea?" I ask, trying to distract from my lie.

"For now." And his gaze gentles for the briefest moment.

Suddenly, the wind swirls around us. Max and Arthur fly in front of us, with the third gargoyle held between them. His eyes are open, but he still looks out of it.

"Clark, why the fuck did you take off?" Arthur asks.

Clark isn't amused at the reprimand. "The mermaid and I had something to discuss."

"Like how you turned into a shark?" The last gargoyle's voice sounds groggy, but Max and Arthur's heads snap back to us.

"What's Steven talking about?" Max asks, his tone light.

Max, Arthur, Clark, and Steven. All accounted for.

I feel Clark's muscles tighten under my hands. "Apparently, I've absorbed one of the sea dragon's powers."

"How's that possible?" Max looks uneasy.

And here it is. *Do I lie? Or do I tell the truth?* "I think that golden light… I think it was some kind of magic. I think it gave you their powers."

Clark's head jerks back to me. "Wait… all of us, or just me?"

I swallow hard. "I think all of you."

"Talk," he orders, all humor and gentleness gone from his face.

Suddenly, my tongue feels heavy. What more does he want me to say? "There are four of them and four of you…"

"I don't feel any different," Arthur says, shrugging. "If I have some bad ass sea dragon powers, wouldn't I feel different?"

"I don't know," I answer honestly.

"Well, fuck," Clark mutters above me.

"But I have some ideas on how we can find out, and how we might be able to reverse it," I tell them.

"How?" Max asks, looking uncertain. "Does it have something to do with that little fish you were carrying? The one that caused the golden light?"

"Yes. While we're searching for Keto, I can keep an eye out for the little creature that I suspect is responsible for this." It's nice to actually say something that's true. For once.

"She has a lead on the monster," Clark tells them, and there's an edge to his voice I don't understand.

"Well, at least that's some good news. Where do we head?" Max is studying Clark, and again I get that sense that something's going on that I don't understand.

The tension is back in Clark's voice. "The Isle of the Demons."

"That's a long flight," Arthur says.

I look between them. *Do they not want to go?* My mind goes through the possible ways I can reach the island. I really do need these gargoyles, and I hate that I do.

"Do we have a choice?" Clark asks, his tone clipped.

Something flashes in Max's eyes, and his words come out more certain. "We'll rest tonight and head out tomorrow."

Clark stiffens again. "Good idea."

I don't know what to think as we head back to the

island we already spent a night at. The gargoyles are talking, filling each other in on what they know of me, the battle with the sea dragons, and what happened on the island with the sirens. But me? My thoughts won't stop spinning.

I'm relieved they still plan to take me, but I'm also nervous. I can't remember the last time I interacted with so many people, and certainly not really sexy men. If I'm not smooth, they're going to see right through me.

They even thought that what I did in front of the sirens was some sinister plot.

I think back to the island. I've never sucked on a man's cock before. Just the idea of it has always made me feel nervous. But I had to make them come. It was the only way to prove they belonged to me. In fact, for them, I thought it might be the preferable method.

The thing is, I liked it. I liked the feel of Steven's hands digging into my hair. I liked the sounds of arousal he made, and that I felt somehow in control, even though I was on my hands and knees.

Then there was Clark. How did he know how to do that with his mouth? It felt... out of this world.

Yesterday was my first orgasm. Today was my second. *Are gargoyles some kind of orgasm-gods?* Do they have magic tongues, cocks, and hands? Do they know just how to touch a woman to please her?

Somehow I'm both aroused and scared out of my mind. My whole plan has been to keep them too distracted to see through my lies, so why do I get the feeling they're the ones distracting *me*?

I need to come up with some sexy moves, and fast.

Chapter Thirteen

STEVEN

My head aches as I lie in the warm lake near our campsite. I reach up and touch the space around my head wound, wincing. A human would've died from a wound like mine, but lucky for me, my gargoyle body is already healing. I only wish it'd heal faster.

It also doesn't help that so much happened in such a short period of time. My mind is swirling with the implications of everything that's occurred since rescuing the woman—who's a freaking mermaid— and something isn't sitting right with me.

Okay, so there's a lot that doesn't seem right. Our mission is to hunt a dangerous monster. That should be our main focus. Instead, we now have a new problem... one I'm not even sure how to handle. We possibly have the powers of sea dragons? Of gods?

That's... a complication we didn't need.

And then, of course, there's the mermaid.

Just thinking of Sirena has my dick hardening and my balls tightening. The way she sucked me off was unlike anything I've imagined. Yes, it's been twenty years since a woman sucked my cock, but unless my memories are scrambled, it was never like that before.

Closing my eyes, I picture the moment. Sirena on her knees, staring up at me with innocent eyes. When her hot mouth closed around my shaft—Fuck. I'm hard again just thinking about it.

I need to push it out of my mind. Just having her on this mission will make things harder for us. I can't be attracted to her, too. I can't spend every free moment remembering how I'd gripped the back of her head and fucked her mouth like I owned her.

Torturing myself won't help anyone.

"Steven?"

I open my eyes and inhale sharply. Sirena is in the water just a few feet from me. I never even heard her approach. I must be more out of it than I thought.

"Are you okay?" she asks, tilting her head.

It takes me a minute to find my voice. "Yeah, my head just aches a little."

She comes closer and rises out of the water. My gaze instantly goes to her breasts, which are bare yet again. My cock jerks ever-so-slightly at the sight of them. This wasn't what I needed. I'm trying not to think about her. Staring at her pale skin and pink nipples doesn't help.

Rising up higher out of the water, she gently tilts my head down until she is literally pushing her breasts into my face. I know that's not her intention, but DAMN. All I can do is stare. My mouth goes dry as I imagine myself sucking on her rosy peaks. She runs her fingers lightly around my injury, and it's strangely nice to have such a soft touch.

I've been lonely. The thought hits me like a blow. I've never imagined I was lonely. I mean, how could I be with gargoyles around me all the time? But her gentle touch?

Keto's Tale

It's almost the touch of a lover. And that I *have* missed. Even if I didn't realize it until now.

A very old memory drifts into my mind. Of the first lover I ever had. Just the memory of her makes everything inside of me tighten, old dread and heartache flaring back to life.

"I'm fine," I tell her, and my voice comes out gruffer than I wanted.

She pulls back, her eyes wide, as if frightened.

I silently curse myself. This woman was a slave, hurt and abused. She deserves kindness, not the wrath of my old injuries.

"I'm sorry," I say. "It's not you, it's my headache."

She wraps her arms around herself. "Are you sure?"

I try to smile. "Yeah, don't mind me."

She looks up at me, uncertainty in her face. "Are you upset about what happened on the island?"

My mouth goes dry. Upset she sucked my cock? Could that even be a thing? "Uh, no."

"Because… I've never done that before. If I did it wrong… if you didn't like it—"

My entire chest tightens. "Are you a virgin?"

"Virgin?" she repeats, and a darkness comes over her face. "No. I've had sex."

I don't want to pry, but every protective instinct in me flares to life. There's just something about her. Everything she says and does speaks to an innocence I don't understand, but then a dark look comes over her and I know that she's seen her share of evil. Whatever this woman has gone through, I doubt it was good.

"I'm sorry you had to do that," I tell her, watching her every movement. "I know you did it to save us."

Her arms ease from around her body. "That's okay. I liked it."

"You liked it?" I repeat, and my fucking cock gives another twitch.

She nods and slides closer to me, resting her hands on my thighs. "It was nice. You tasted… good. And I liked the way you touched me."

Fuck. Fuck. "Yeah?"

"Yeah."

I close my eyes, fighting the urge to do something reckless. I want to grab her, kiss her, and show her just how much I enjoyed what we did.

Her touch spreads warmth straight to my cock. It takes me a second to realize I'm panting. She moves closer, and one of her hands strokes my cock.

My eyes flash open. "Don't do that."

Her eyes widen.

"No," I correct, before I scare her again. "I like it… too much."

She relaxes again and continues to run her hand along the length of my cock, sending my nerves screaming in pleasure. "Then, let me touch you. You've had a long day."

"I'd rather— talk," I say, my heart racing. A groan slips from my lips. "What do you know about the sea dragons' powers?"

She slides a little closer, and her hand closes around my cock, stroking slowly in the water. "There's Nereus the shapeshifter." She presses her lips gently against my neck. "And Okeeanos who controls the planets and the stars. And—"

"The planets and the stars," I pant out. "Oh fuck," I groan. I should stop her, I really should, but I don't. "I've had this… feeling… like I can sense all the stars and planets."

She kisses higher up my neck, and unable to help

myself, I reach out and stroke the tips of her nipples. A gasp slips passed her lips. "That feels... good."

"I'm glad," she whispers. "I want to make you feel good."

"Why?" I ask, aware of every inch of her body touching me.

"You saved me. You're protecting me. And... you're nice to me."

Fucking hell. "You don't need to do this to thank me."

She draws back, those dark eyes of hers locked onto mine. "Sorry. I don't know what to do. I don't know how to act. I've been alone for so long."

Reaching out, I cup her chin and tug her closer, brushing a gentle kiss against her lips. It's like she's speaking the words deep within my soul. Until our celibacy, there were women. Any gargoyle had who we wanted. We fucked our choice of women, and I had my share, but it's been centuries since I touched a woman I truly care about.

"It's okay," I tell her. "I understand."

"Are you lonely too?"

Her question is so innocent I can't help but answer honestly. "Sometimes. I mean, I have family and friends. I have the guys, but that's different."

"There's no special woman?"

I shake my head. "Not for a long time."

She nibbles her bottom lip, her touch so incredible soft as she strokes me. "This woman you loved, who was she?"

I tense. I don't want to think about that. Those times were filled with so much death, so much loneliness and confusion. Memories of my failures are all I have left. "It doesn't matter," I tell her.

After a time, she nods and leans closer.

Wrapping my arms around her, I lean back, shocked by how comfortable it feels to hold her. She fits so damned perfectly in my arms. This tiny woman relaxes against me like she trusts me, and I want to melt inside.

And that… it warms my gargoyle heart. It makes me feel possessive of her in ways I never imagined.

"Steven!"

I stiffen, turn, and spot Clark on the shore of the lake, his arms crossed angrily over his chest.

"We're just talking," I say, too fast.

He raises a brow. "Well, when you're done *talking*, dinner's ready."

I feel strangely guilty as I move Sirena back from me.

She frowns. "Did you not like what I was doing?"

I'm shocked. "Of course I liked it! What man wouldn't?"

For a second she studies me, looking uncertain, but then she finally speaks. "What do men like?"

"Like?" I clear my throat. "What do you mean?"

She opens her mouth and then closes it. "I don't know. I just want all of you to like me."

My heart squeezes, and I move closer to her, gently placing my hands on her arms. "You don't have to… do any of that to get us to like you."

"Then what should I do?"

Who the fuck hurt her so badly that she's worried about this? "You're beautiful, smart, and interesting. You don't need to do anything to get us to like you. We already do."

She frowns and says nothing.

What's going on in her head? Why is she worried?

"Come on, let's go eat."

She nods, and we emerge from the water.

When she walks ahead of me, my gaze instantly goes to her ass. The blood in my dick pumps harder. How is that even possible? I can't believe just a minute ago I had a beautiful woman stroking my cock, and now I'm supposed to go and eat dinner with her naked.

This is not going to work.

"Uh, you want to get dressed?"

She looks back at me and shrugs. "I guess."

We both dry off, and she pulls on a grey shirt. I want to say it helps a lot. But it doesn't. She's still beautiful, wet, and not wearing pants. And I can barely zip my pants over my massive erection.

When we seat ourselves around the fire, Max dishes out stew for all of us. For a while we eat in silence, but then my thoughts start to swirl. She said one of the sea dragons could control the planets and stars. Could that be my power? Or am I imagining this strange connection?

After I get my second bowl, I clear my throat. "Did she tell you guys about the dragons' powers?"

They all nod.

Clark's spoon hits his bowl. "So, I've got the shifter's powers."

"I think I have Okeanos' powers, the blue dragon," I say.

We turn to Arthur and Max expectantly.

Arthur shrugs. "I don't feel any different."

"Me neither," Max says.

Clark and I exchange a look, but I'm the first to speak. "Could it be because you two were born? Your connection to the earth isn't as deep."

Arthur rolls his eyes. "Not this again."

I put up my hands. "I'm not starting anything!"

"Weren't you all born?" Sirena asks.

We all hesitate. She doesn't need to know gargoyle business.

"Some of us are born and some are made," Arthur explains.

Clark glares. "That's enough."

Arthur smirks in response. "Does it even matter?" Then he turns back to Sirena. "Basically, the *made* gargoyles think they're bigger and better than we are."

"That's not what we're saying," I try to explain.

But, of course, Clark's in a mood. "It's a fact that we're more in touch with the earth, so we're just fucking wondering if that's the reason why neither of you feel different, or if you didn't get their powers after all."

Arthur starts to eat again. "Who cares?"

Clark's about to go off when Max interrupts. "I guess when we find the creature Sirena thinks can help us, we can find out either way. Until then, there's no use fighting over it."

"Yes, sir!" Clark salutes him.

Max shoots Clark a dirty look, and then looks back to Sirena. When there's no response, Max clears his throat.

"Tomorrow we're sticking with the plan. We're going to the Isle of the Demons to look for Keto. Anyone have a problem with that?" His gaze goes to Clark.

Clark ignores him.

Suddenly, Sirena stands up, her expression troubled.

"Is something wrong?" I ask.

Ignoring me, she turns and starts to run.

"What's wrong?" Max calls after her, standing.

She doesn't answer, nor does she look back as she takes off through the forest.

We all exchange a look, drop our bowls, and take off after her. Something here feels wrong. And we don't have a clue what.

Away from the brightness of the fire the darkness closes in, but Sirena's path is clear. She's running for the ocean. I'm careful as I pick my way after her, watching for roots, branches, and whatever else is hidden beneath the shadows of the trees.

At last, we explode out of the underbrush and onto the white, sandy beach.

There, in the water, is a massive sea monster. We're face to face with a hydra with two heads, and it's towering over Sirena.

Oh fuck!

We race toward her, shifting into our battle mode. I pray we can reach her before it devours her. I don't have my sword, but I don't care. I'll use my stone hands to rip it limb-by-limb!

The beast roars, a sound that shakes the air around us, and Sirena whirls around with wide eyes.

"Stop!" she shouts.

We freeze, exchanging a look and then glancing at the creature towering over her. *Is she insane?*

"Get away from that thing!" I command.

She shakes her head. "Stay back!"

I see Clark and Max starting to inch closer, and I know what they're planning. They're going to attack it before it can hurt her.

Nice try beast, but get ready to die.

Chapter Fourteen

KETO

"Don't hurt him," I tell the gargoyles, then turn back to my creature.

Even from our camp on the island, I'd felt its mind reaching out for me. I'd felt its fear so deeply within my soul that it'd set me in a panic.

"What is it, Haskul?" I ask my Hydra.

In my mind I hear its answer; it's been searching for me since the battle with the mermaid-hunters. And then it heard of my death.

"It's okay," I tell him. "I'm all right."

One of its heads lean down, and Clark leaps onto its neck.

"No!" I shout.

Haskul roars and bucks Clark from his back. The hyrdra's second head darts out and it chomps down on Clark. The gargoyle dangles from my creature's mouth, and a scream tears from my throat.

"No, don't! Please!"

My creature is trying to eat him. But the stone man can't be bitten or swallowed whole. At last, my

Hydra spits him out, and he goes tumbling into the sea.

Suddenly, the other three gargoyles are on my creature. Punching, lashing out. The little hydra makes a sound, a crying that hurts me down to my soul.

I know tears are streaming down my face. None of them understand. The gargoyles think he's trying to hurt me, and he thinks they're attacking us.

If I can't stop this soon, someone's going to get seriously hurt. Or even die.

Calling the waves to me, they pull back further and further from the shore, then come crashing back, smashing into the battling males. The gargoyles go flying off my hydra and I leap forward.

The gargoyles are scattered on the beach, and Haskul is struggling against the waves.

"Stop it right this minute!" I shout.

My hydra makes a sad whine.

The gargoyles leap to their feet.

I move yet again to stand between them, my arms raised. "I'm a fucking mermaid! Do you really think there's a sea creature alive that can harm me?"

They all freeze, looking from me to my hydra.

Turning my back to them, I coo at my creature as his heads lower once more. His eyes never leave the gargoyles. I pet his heads and he purrs as I gently study his bruises from the gargoyles.

There are so many of them.

My teeth clench, and I whirl toward them. "What were you thinking?"

Clark snarls back. "It's a monster!"

Just the word enrages me, and I advance on him. "Explain to me exactly what the difference is between a monster and a sea creature?"

Anger flashes in his eyes. "I've never heard of a dolphin destroying boats and eating people, have you? But that... that's a fucking hydra!"

I roll my eyes. "He's a baby. He was scared the sea dragons had killed me. He sensed me near, but couldn't reach me on the island."

Some of the anger dims in Clark's eyes. "Maybe next time say that before you just take off."

"Well, how was I supposed to know you'd come after me?"

Max speaks, breaking into our argument. "We thought something was wrong."

My pulse starts to slow. "Just... don't ever hurt any of my creatures again. They're good, sweet beasts. I'm not scared of them. They'd never hurt me. I'm scared of men, mermaids, dragons... beings that know how to destroy without mercy."

Something changes in the air, and I turn away, ashamed to feel tears in my eyes.

My hydra bumps his head against me, and I reach out stroking his smooth scaled flesh, reassuring him. "I'm fine, my sweetie. But no one can know I still live, understand?"

He makes it clear. Many of my creatures are scared. They worry what my brother will do to them without my protection. There's something else going on, something they don't understand.

"I'll figure it out," I promise him. "And I'll keep you safe."

We remain a little longer, with me stroking both his heads, reassuring him, and trying to ease his injuries from the battle with the gargoyles.

At last, his hunger wars with his desire to be in my company. I laugh. "Go, I'm fine."

He doesn't trust the gargoyles.

Keto's Tale

"They're good," I tell him. "They thought you were dangerous."

He likes the idea that they thought he was a big, tough creature, but he hasn't quite forgiven them yet. Sliding back into the water, he gives me one last look and disappears.

At last, I turn back to the gargoyles. They're all watching me.

Fear spikes into my heart. They just saw me with a sea *monster*. Will they realize who I am?

I take a step back. Maybe I should run.

Steven sighs and rubs his head. "I think there's a story here, but I'm too damned tired to hear it right now. Anyone want to head to bed and discuss it in the morning?"

I nod, my heart still pounding. "That sounds lovely."

We head back to camp, and I watch them as subtly as I can. Are they suspicious? None of them are looking at me strangely, but maybe they're waiting for their chance to attack.

By the time we reach our tent, my nerves have started to calm. They haven't figured out the truth, but by tomorrow, I'll have to come up with a way to explain it all.

Yawning, Max opens the tent flap, and I crawl in. The guys stay outside a little longer, cleaning up dinner, and I think maybe taking a dip in the lake.

It's been a long day, and I'm tired. I strip off my shirt and snuggle beneath the covers. I know it'd be smarter to try to seduce them, but I just don't have the energy for it. Tomorrow will be good. Tomorrow I'll seduce them again.

Chapter Fifteen

KETO

The next morning the gargoyles pack some bags and leave the rest of the camp, planning on returning later. For some reason, I'm nervous. The last thing I wanted was to show them my powers. I've come up with a thousand lies; I just hope they'll buy them.

When it comes time for us to fly toward the Isle of the Demons, I'm not sure who plans to fly with me. They all seem oddly hesitant. And then, at last, Arthur comes to stand in front of me. The others are tense as he places his hands on my hips.

Strangely, I'm nervous as I wrap my arms around his neck and my legs around his back.

"You sure you got it?" Clark asks, even grumpier than yesterday.

Arthur smirks. "I can handle one little woman."

"I've heard that before," Clark mutters.

I feel every muscle in Arthur's body tense. Suddenly, he begins to flap his wings, and we take off into the sky. Looking back, I see the others squaring off. Arguing.

"What's going on?"

Arthur shrugs. "Clark's being an ass. Nothing new."

"Why?" I ask.

For a long minute, I don't think he's going to answer me, but then he does. "Gargoyles are supposed to choose a mate and share her with their Brotherhood. It's something that's been done as long as anyone can remember, probably because there's so many more male gargoyles than female gargoyles." He hesitates, and I want to touch his tense face and ease the stress I see hiding below the surface. "A long time ago, I met a woman and fell in love with her. I left behind my Brotherhood and my people to live a human life with her."

"What's wrong with that?" I ask.

His mouth pulls into a thin line. "Everything, apparently. We're gargoyles, so we're supposed to be miserable beings in charge of protecting, serving, and honoring our people. Happiness? Pleasure? Love? It's all bullshit that's out of our reach."

This time I do reach up and stroke his face. "But you didn't want that... so you chose the human woman?"

He stiffens. "Yes."

"And did she bring you all these things... happiness, pleasure, and love?"

His hazel eyes lock onto mine, and I see something crumble within him. "No, Sirena. Actually, it was the fucking biggest mistake of my life. I wanted to leave the instant I realized it."

"So why didn't you?"

"She had cancer. After that, I couldn't leave her. She didn't last long, a few human years, but I stayed at her side."

"And the others are angry with you for it?"

His frown deepened. "Yeah. They think I'm some idiot who makes awful choices, and maybe I am."

I laugh, and his gaze jerks back to me. "Wanting to be happy and loved hardly makes you an idiot."

"It did! I mean, it wasn't even love. I wasn't even happy."

I shake my head. "But you were brave enough to try and that's more than most people can say." My smile fades. "It's more than I've tried."

He looks surprised. "You've never been in love?"

I shake my head. "It's hard to even find a friend when you're… when you're like me."

We fly for a while longer before he finally talks again. "Maybe I wasn't an idiot then, but I wish they'd just forgive me for it, and stop acting like I'm going to just take off the next time I have a crush."

"Will you?" I ask.

He looks down at me, surprised.

I've said the wrong thing. "I'm sorry, I just, it sounds as if you wanted to find happiness but still haven't."

For a minute he just stares at the horizon. "I guess I don't know. Maybe they do have a reason to worry after all."

"Or maybe they're not really worried about you. Maybe they just envy you."

He laughs. "I seriously doubt that."

Sadness overwhelms me and it's almost more than I can bear. I lean closer, resting my head against his shoulder. "I envy you," I whisper.

His grip tightens around me, and I'm glad he doesn't speak. Some things shouldn't be said. I shouldn't say I'm lonely, or that I'll never find true happiness or love. Those are thoughts for when you're alone in the dark, when tears can flow unseen. Those are the thoughts that rest in our hearts and haunt us like ghosts. Speaking them aloud gives the thoughts more power.

So we say nothing. We just fly. My eyes close, and I enjoy the feel of the wind whipping around me and the morning sun kissing my flesh. More than anything, I enjoy the feeling of being held by another person.

gods and goddesses are fools. They seek power and control, when really all anyone should ever wish for is the peaceful touch of someone who they can trust.

Like the way I feel with Arthur and Max. I could let the thought disturb me, but I refuse to. I have enough worries; I won't let this be one of them.

Hours rush by before Max calls after us, pointing to an island up ahead. It's not the Isle of the Demons, so I'm guessing we're planning to rest here for a time. I'm glad. I need to use the bathroom, and I'm starving.

We all land, and I excuse myself. Searching through the woods, I find a place to relieve myself and then wander back to the beach. The sight that befalls me when I reach it, however, is completely unexpected.

Max has walked far out into the water, and yet, it's separated on both sides of him, the waves clearing a dry path for him. Freezing behind the gargoyles, I stare in shock.

The gargoyle whirls back toward us, and his eyes are wide. "Does this mean?"

Everyone looks back at me.

"Triton's powers," I conclude, "Control of the waves."

He grins and suddenly sprints in different directions in the water. The waves continue to clear his path, and it's actually kind of amazing to see. He's laughing, skimming his hands on the water on both sides of him.

I've never seen a god or goddess use their powers for something that makes them happy. I can't remember the last time *I* used my powers in such a way. Seeing him like that, it reminds me that perhaps there is more to this life than just pain and misery.

When he finally returns to us at the shore, he's grinning wildly. "I got the strangest urge to touch the water, and then I just felt this… this amazing feeling, like I was connected with the water."

I smile. I'm glad he's enjoying his powers. If everything goes according to plan, he won't have them much longer, so he might as well.

"Does this mean I have the last powers?" Arthur asks.

"Pontos's powers," I tell him. "A god who can speak to simple-minded sea creatures."

"Like you?" he asks.

I try not to bristle at the insult. "No, I speak to creatures who are intelligent, who feel, and think, and want. Pontos controls the mindless ones, like a cruel master."

Arthur's smile falters, and I feel like the lowest barnacle in the sea.

"But connecting with their minds is still an amazing thing."

That infectious smile of his returns. "Any idea how I can do it?"

I nod and walk towards him. Taking his hand, I lead him out into the water. I've never actually taught someone how to connect minds with other beings, but I imagine it can't be that hard.

When we reach the deeper waters, I tug him under the waves.

For a second I forget he can't breathe underwater, and then I see him start to struggle.

Keto, he's a land-dweller!

Pulling him into my arms, I press my lips against his and breathe a sea goddess' breath. He stiffens and tries yet again to swim for the surface. I shake my head, and he opens his mouth.

I see when he realizes he can breathe under the water. Even in the dimmer light beneath the waves, he's smiling. This Arthur... I like him.

Moving closer, I press my hands on either side of his face, and I reach out with my mind. I feel all my creatures for miles and miles around me. I feel them freeze, but I say nothing. Do nothing. I can't let them know I'm alive, not yet.

When I open my eyes, I see that Arthur has closed his. And his entire face is scrunched up, as if he's trying really hard.

After a time, his eyes open once more, and I'm sad to see the disappointment in their depths. We rise to the surface and explode into the sunshine. We're both breathing hard, and he turns to me.

"I thought I felt... something. But nothing happened."

I force a smile. "Be patient. Controlling such strong powers isn't easy."

He nods, but still looks unhappy.

We swim back to shore, and the others are eating snacks on the beach. We join them, and Max hands me a bag full of things he explains are nuts and dried berries. I eat them, frowning a bit. I haven't had such foods before, and I'm not sure I like them. They're different.

Arthur laughs. "Not good?"

I look up and realize they're all staring at me. Instantly, I feel my cheeks heat. "Human food is unusual, but I'm grateful for it."

Arthur bumps my shoulder with his. "It's okay if you don't like it; I swear we won't bite you."

My cheeks feel hotter.

"For a slave you're kind of picky," Clark says.

I stiffen.

"Clark, what the fuck?" Max glares at him.

"What?" he says, glaring right back. "You said we'd discuss the hydra and her powers today, but you chickenshits keep putting it off."

And everything seems to change at once.

They don't trust me. But why should they?

Anger flows between the men, and suddenly it's too much for me. If I thought for one second that these gargoyles could hear the truth and still trust me… still help me, I would, but that's just the thing. They'll never be able to see past what I am. No matter what. And the truth leaves me with a hollow feeling deep within my chest.

I wordlessly hand my bag of food back to Arthur and stand. My heart's hammering. I just… I need to escape. I need to be away from them.

I hurry to the edge of the water and then remember I can't just pick a direction and start swimming. It's too dangerous. There's too much of a risk that I'll be found by my brother's minions.

In fact, I never should've gotten in the water with Arthur in the first place. It was reckless and stupid. I'd gotten caught up in his excitement and forgotten every drop of common sense.

"Sirena?" Steven calls my name.

I turn back. He's standing.

"I'm fine," I say, because I can see he's worried.

"Clark didn't mean anything by that. He was just being an asshole."

Clark leaps to his feet. "Of course I meant something by it. I think she's lying to us. I don't even think she was a slave."

I stare at him. What am I supposed to say to that? But everyone's looking at me.

"Believe what you want, but I am a slave."

"Am or was?" he challenges.

My eyes prickle, and my hands curl into fists. Stomping toward him, I know I'm breathing hard. Angry and sad all at once. "You have no idea what it feels like to be owned and controlled by someone else."

He smirks unkindly. "Hate to tell you this, babe, but every *made* gargoyle has a master and creator he obeys."

"So where's yours?" I challenge.

His blue eyes darken. "Dead."

"Lucky you," I spit out. "But mine's alive and well, just waiting to control me again."

He crosses his big arms over his chest, and his face goes blank. "Are you just a mermaid?"

I stare, not knowing what to say.

"Mermaids aren't immortal or powerful. They have long lives, but that's about it. So what are you?"

Max, Arthur, and Steven look between me and him. *Now what?* I wasn't sure they knew enough about mermaids to know something was off with me, but apparently, I was wrong. Was there any point in continuing to lie?

My shoulders sag. "I'm a slave, as I said, but I'm also a goddess."

I wait for it. I wait for the moment they realize exactly which of the many sea goddesses I must be, because I'll be screwed. I'll become their prisoner, at least until my brother gets his hands on me again.

"Well, that explains it" Max says, his tone holding an edge. "So she's a goddess? That doesn't really change anything."

Clark's mouth drops open for a second before he shuts it. "It means she lied to us! She can't be trusted!"

Arthur rolls his eyes. "Mr. Damaged and Can't Trust Women is back."

In seconds Clark goes smashing into him. They roll around in the sand, and I'm shocked to see Arthur holding his own. Both men are tussling. Steven and Max jump in trying to separate them, and I'm left staring in shock.

What in the hell just happened?

Finally, Steven and Max manage to get in the middle of the two. Clark's nose is bleeding. Arthur's going to have a black eye, and both of them are panting and glaring.

"That's enough," Max says. "This mission has been—"

"Shut your fucking mouth!" Clark shouts. "I don't know why they made you a leader, but you're not leader material. You're soft! If I was in charge right now, I'd leave that lying mermaid here to rot, but you don't have the balls for it."

Max draws himself up taller. "Maybe *that's* why they chose me."

Clark's eyes blaze with anger. "Say it."

"This isn't like the old days where missions were all about killing. We're supposed to bring this Keto back *alive*. Maybe they knew, given your past, that you couldn't do it."

Tension crackles between the men, and for a second I think there's going to be another fight.

"Fuck this," Clark says.

Turning around, he grabs his bag off the sand where it had fallen.

"Where are you going?" Max demands.

"I'm going to follow my own lead, and you guys can just fuck off."

"We can't split up again." This time Max gets in his face. "This is just a stupid fight. We can—"

Clark shoves him back, shifts, and leaps into the air. Max moves as if to follow him, but Arthur catches his arm.

"Let him go cool off. He knows where we're going. He

knows where we're camping. He'll find us when he wants to."

Max shrugs his hand off. "Why did you have to piss him off?"

Arthur's brows rise. "I'm pretty sure you pissed him off too."

And then they both turn to stare at me, and suddenly, I burst into tears. All three gargoyles are around me in an instant. I try to pull away from them, to gather myself together. But they won't let me. They hold me, touch me, and murmur words of comfort.

"It's okay," I say.

But I hate myself for this. For realizing just how much their fighting and words scared me. A million moments with my brother and his second in command come back to me. They killed and hurt without thought. These gargoyles aren't the same way, so why did it scare me so badly?

"Are you okay?" Max asks.

I shake my head no, but say, "Yes."

I'm suddenly pulled into his strong arms, and I sag against him. I stay that way, shaking, with tears running down my face for far too long. At last, I look up and meet his gaze.

"That wasn't about you," he says.

"Then what was it about?"

He hesitates, then sighs. "Clark has a complicated past with his builder. It's made him mistrustful of women."

I want to pretend that's all my tears were about. "Please, don't fight again." I turn, and my gaze meets Steven's and Arthur's. "I don't like it."

They all seem to stand up taller, but it's Steven who answers. "We'll try our best."

I nod. I guess that's all I can ask for.

Chapter Sixteen

STEVEN

It's my turn to carry Sirena, and I'm so wound up I don't know what to do with myself. I honestly can't believe Max actually handled Clark like that. After everything, I can't believe that I agree with Max. He may actually be right. When the Elites made Max the leader, I couldn't figure out why. But now, it makes perfect sense.

Clark's naturally mistrustful of women, and he hates cruel women. He would've killed Keto long before we returned to the sanctuary. Too many answers are suddenly clear. If only it gave me some kind of relief.

And then there's Clark. I've never seen him lose it like that before.

"I'm sorry for everything," Sirena says.

I look down at her and find myself holding her a little more gently. Her face looks pale, and the lines from her tears still mar her cheeks. I hate that we scared her. I hate that so much of our fucked up pasts are triggering us right now, when we should have it the most together.

"It wasn't your fault."

"It was," she insists, and her expression is heartbreaking.

The last thing this woman needs is to think all our issues are because of her. She's been through enough.

"Clark is… complicated." I try to think about the best way to explain without completely betraying him. "The thing is, he and I were both made. We were created to protect our homes, lands, and humans with everything inside of us."

I swallow around the lump that's formed in my throat, for some reason. "But Clark's master was … well, she wasn't a good person. She was a woman who convinced him that she needed his help protecting her from invading armies. It wasn't until much later that he learned everything she'd told him was a lie. He holds a lot of guilt about what he did in those days, and he's never quite forgiven himself for it."

Her expression is far away for a long second, and then she gives a slight nod. "I understand. Sometimes we do things that we regret… things that haunt us. But they aren't always our fault, as much as we blame ourselves for them."

For some reason, I smile. "It's nice that you can empathize with him, even if he's a jerk."

"No, he isn't. I was lying. I'm just sorry he took off."

I push the hair back from her face, and our gazes meet. Unable to help myself, I lean forward and brush a kiss against her lips.

Her eyes widen and she leans forward and kisses me again, this time deeper.

My cock hardens and my mouth opens. Her hesitant tongue dips inside, and I feel a groan rip from my chest. My hands tense on her thighs, and I'm unbelievably aware that I could touch her right now. I could shift one of my hands just a little lower and stroke her.

Just the idea drives me wild. It's also a terrible idea, even though my brain's having trouble remembering exactly why.

I break our kiss, looking up to make sure we're not about to fly into a flock of birds or any other shit.

She clings to my shirt, panting. "Why did you stop?"

"Because if I don't, we're going to have to fuck."

Every muscle in her body tenses, and I curse myself.

"I mean, I'd want to take things further."

After a second, she nods.

I'm about to say more when something strange appears in the ocean ahead of us. At first it just looks like a floating island of mist, but as we get closer, a blood red color seems to rise through the mist. As we fly closer, I recognize the twin volcanoes that look like soulless eyes, and the red plants and trees that cover the volcanoes, disappearing down into the mist where the island is entirely hidden from view.

This is it. The Isle of the Demons.

As we draw closer, the expectant sound begins. The soft wailing, that made sailors give this place such a name, seems to crawl up my spine, leaving every hair on my body standing on end. Some instinct inside of me wants to launch forward and find the source of the sound… help whoever is making such a sad wailing, but I already know it's not a person. It's… something else. Some trick of nature.

Looking back, Max and Arthur catch up to us. Both of them have strange expressions, which makes me wonder what it was that they were talking about.

"We should land on the shore," Max says.

Arthur's nose crinkles, and he looks to the setting sun.

"We're not going to sleep at this creepy place tonight, are we?"

"Depends how long it takes us to get the information we need." Max tries to sound practical, but I can tell he doesn't want to stay here anymore than the rest of us.

We fly lower, through the heavy mist. We have to be careful. Trees and branches appear out of nowhere. I curse as my wing hits one of them, and Sirena gives a little cry of alarm. She clings to me harder, and it takes me a few minutes to break out of the branches of the tree and find a clear spot near the rocky shore. We land lightly, but my heart races faster. The wailing is even louder, and even creepier when surrounded by mist.

Slowly, Sirena lowers to the ground, but I hold onto her waist, reluctant to let her go in this place.

Max and Arthur land lightly beside us.

"So," Arthur begins. "Now what?"

Sirena seems to know. She pushes back from me and I hold her hand as she climbs over the sharp rocks, making her way closer to the forest.

"Where are we going?" I ask her.

She looks up at me, surprised. "To ask the demons about… about Keto."

"Demons?" Arthur laughs. "There's not really demons here."

She stares back at him without speaking.

"There's actually *demons* here?"

"Something like that," is all she says. She gives us a long look before she continues to climb over the rocks.

Exchanging a glance, we follow after her. When she leaps down from the rocks and stops beneath the branches of the thick trees, she turns back to us. "Stay here, I'll return with any information."

I laugh. "That's not happening."

There is no world in which I'm going to send this tiny, beautiful woman into a misty forest filled with blood-red plants, when there may be demons around. No world.

Instinctually, I shift, my wings disappearing and my human flesh appearing. I reach back and touch the hilt of my sword, reassuring myself that I'm prepared to protect her from any danger that might come our way.

"There's no need for any of you to go with me." She frowns. "I can take care of myself."

Max moves closer to her, and there's something surprising in his expression: concern. "We're not sending you in there alone."

She nibbles her lip, looking uncertain. "Someone will need to stay here. If we get lost, they can shout to lead us back to the shore. This place… it's magical. We could be trapped in the woods forever without an anchor to the outside world."

"Seriously?" Arthur asks, raising a brow.

She nods. "Hades has many wards to guard the entrances to the Underworld."

Every muscle in my body tightens. "I thought the Isle of Demons was all crap, rumors made up because of the red vegetation and strange sounds"

Indecision flickers across her stunning face, and then she speaks. "This place is dangerous. Really dangerous. As a goddess, I'll be protected from many of his little… security measures, but none of you will be. I've been here before, so I know the way."

"I'll go with her," I instantly volunteer.

Arthur and Max start to argue.

"No," I say. "I'm going."

Out of the three of us, I have the best sense of direction, and I'm the best fighter. Max and Arthur have fought monsters and creatures that threatened our sanctuary, but

Keto's Tale

I'm the only one among us old enough to have fought in wars. I'm the only one who's been charged with the protection of innocents against nearly impossible forces.

And we all know it.

Please don't make me say it. Please don't make me argue with you.

Because I won't let them be the ones to escort her. As much as I trust them to watch my back in a fight, I trust myself more than them to keep our Sirena safe. *Our Sirena? Where the hell did that come from?* I push that thought away to deal with later.

They stare at me for a minute longer, and then Max sighs. "Fine, Steven will go, and we'll stay here. Shout if you need our help, and we'll be there in an instant."

Relief washes through me. Looking back at Sirena, I'm reminded of my own builder, an old man who insisted he could go to the big city without me. Only he would be the one to learn why the church that had commissioned him to make me had failed to send someone to pick me up. I had felt this same prickling along my spine, this same instinct to go with him. I'd followed orders and stayed behind with his granddaughter and her son.

He never made it back.

Sirena looks uncertain, but she turns and I follow her beneath the shadows of the trees. Instantly the darkness swallows us. I stumble over a branch, and a second later, her much smaller hand closes around mine.

"There's a path, just a little further ahead."

I can't see her face in the dark. "How many times have you been here?"

Her hand tightens in mine. "Just a few times, to visit a friend of mine."

A friend?

I think of Clark. It's kind of strange how instantly

we've connected with this mermaid goddess, but the truth is that none of us really know her. So what's made our protective gargoyle instincts accept her so easily?

I wish I knew.

Our journey gets harder. She releases my hand as we climb up hills covered in strange red vines that remind me of veins. The trees shudder overhead, and red leaves drift down around us, catching every stray light between trees.

It also smells strangely here, damp, but also coppery. It's not quite as strong as blood… but just enough that it makes me uneasy.

"Is this place safe?" I whisper.

Sirena doesn't look back as she answers. "No."

That's… reassuring. Not.

When I see light up ahead, I have an instinct to rush straight for it, but the tangled jungle ahead of us slows me. Still, when we step out onto the pale path that winds through this thick jungle, I'm grateful.

Sirena turns as we stand on the path. "Maybe you should stay here."

I tense. *Does she feel I can't protect her? Does she think I'll be a burden to her?*

Just the thought makes my chest swell. *Of course I can take care of her!*

"I'm not leaving your side."

She frowns. "Then you must promise to listen to me when we reach our destination. I can't have you attacking without thinking, like you did with the hydra. You must believe that I'm capable of handling whatever might come my way. You must trust me."

I think of the moment I saw the hydra. Even now, my blood runs cold. It was a massive monster of legend, towering over Sirena. Its teeth were razor sharp, and its head was nearly as big as the little woman.

If another creature like that tried to harm her, could I hold myself back?

My hands curl into fists. I could try. "Okay."

"Thank you." She turns and continues down the path.

Neither of us speaks as we walk, which only further emphasizes the strangeness of this place. Around us, everything is absolutely silent. Not a bird, bug, or animal stirs in the tangled jungle of this place.

We continue walking in silence as time passes. The evening slowly fades into night, and the darkness makes me even more uneasy. In a short time, I'm sure, we'll be stumbling without anything to light our way.

"Sirena!"

She turns back to me, looking uncertain.

"Maybe we should turn back."

"Why? We're nearly there."

I move closer, looking down at her. And for the first time, I see it in her eyes. A desperation that I never imagined.

"How are we going to get back in the dark?"

She reaches up and runs her fingers through my long brown hair in a way that's tender. "Trust me, my Steven. I won't let any harm come to you."

I catch her hand and press it to my cheek. "I'm not worried about *me*."

She smiles and stands on her tippy toes to press a kiss against my lips "I can't believe anyone would be worried about me. But you're also not like anyone I've ever met in my life."

"I feel the same way," I say.

And then something changes in the air. Darkness falls like a veil around us, and my skin prickles.

I know something's watching us long before I turn to stare into the jungle on both sides of us. I see a small pair of red eyes, then another, and another, and another. They're suddenly everywhere, hundreds of red eyes in the darkness.

Moving slowly, I pull Sirena against my side and reach for the hilt of my sword.

"No," she says, catching my arm.

I look down at her, my jaw locking. "The eyes."

"Won't hurt us," she says, her voice soft. "As long as we stay on the path. Understand? No matter what, you have to stay on the path."

"I'm a gargoyle," I tell her. "Nothing can hurt me. It's you I'm worried about."

She's so tiny, so soft. Why isn't she terrified?

"Those creatures... they can hurt immortal beings. They can hurt *you*," she emphasizes. "Stay on the path. No matter if they tempt you off of it."

My hand tightens again on the hilt of my sword. Her words send blood pounding in my ears. I thought I'd be enough to keep her safe, but if I'm vulnerable to these creatures, maybe I won't be. I couldn't live with myself if she got hurt because of me.

Images from a lifetime ago flash in my mind of the first woman I loved. I see her child that felt like mine. I still remember returning from searching for my builder and finding their house burned. I still remember finding the builder's daughter and grandchild, my woman and her child, strung up outside of the burning building.

The horrors of war, brought straight to my doorstep.

Back then, I was left alone, with no purpose. I was a gargoyle who had failed in every way.

Rage and sadness rip through me and I feel a shudder through my body.

"Steven?"

My head jerks up. I realize I'm breathing hard.

Sirena takes a step back from me, fear in her eyes. "What's wrong?"

I try to shake the image away, but it lingers. I won't go through that again. Never again. I'll die before I let a woman I love be hurt again.

"Nothing," I say, but the word is almost a growl.

She's shaking, wrapping her arms around herself. "Don't pull out your sword. They'll see it as a threat. It gives them permission to step onto the path."

Her words shake me from whatever the hell had pulled me under. I release the sword and take a step closer to her. She takes a step back.

"I'm sorry," I say.

"What happened to you?" she asks, and there's fear in her voice.

"I was just remembering," I consider lying, but the words come tumbling out. "The first woman I loved. She… she died. I just never want—"

The words won't come. I stand, feeling lost. Why can't I just say it? Why can't I tell her that I don't want to lose her too?

She's suddenly in my arms, holding me like she's trying to pull me together. "I'm so sorry."

I stare down at the tiny woman who's trying to comfort *me*. "I shouldn't have gotten angry. When I think of it, everything inside me just goes crazy. All logic goes out the window."

She pulls back from me. "It's like that with me when I think about sex. I know it's uncomfortable, painful at times, but it isn't the worst thing I've been through. Not even close. All of you have been so gentle with me. You've all made me feel things I never have before. But still, whenever it gets brought up I just—"

"Feel scared?"

She nods.

If I thought I was enraged before, that was nothing compared to what I feel like now. My fists are clenched. Blood races through my veins and my muscles tighten. When I meet the man who made her feel this way about sex, I'm going to kill him.

"That's not how it's supposed to be," I tell her, forcing my voice to remain calm. "When a man makes love to a woman, he wants her to feel pleasure. He wants her pleasure more than his own. And he would never, ever hurt her. He should only do what she asks for."

She frowns. "I never told him no."

"Did you ever tell him yes?"

She shakes her head.

I have to swallow to keep from roaring. "Then he deserves nothing but death and pain. He took you when you didn't want him. He knew you weren't enjoying what he did, and he still did it. There is nothing worse a man can do."

I swear there are tears in her eyes. "Do you really believe that?"

"I do," I say.

She's quiet for a long minute. "I'm never going to let him touch me again."

"I'm never going to let him touch you again," I say to her, echoing her words. My voice is harsh as I make the promise to her. To me.

She takes my hand. "We need to keep going."

I nod, and my gaze slides back to all the eyes in the jungle on both sides of us. She said we were safe on the path, but she's right. We shouldn't linger in this dark, creepy place any longer than we have to. All the things I want to say to her, they can wait until I know she's safe.

We continue down the path. Her steps are nearly silent, while mine are louder.

Up ahead, I see light. Red and orange and flickering like a nightmare. At first I'm not sure what it is. The mist plays around it, and the wailing seems to grow louder, more miserable.

I think we might be heading straight for the source of the sound.

And then, I realize what I'm looking at. Torches. Lots and lots of torches.

They line the path, and we step between them. The fire light plays against our flesh in the strangest way, in a way that screams of magic.

When I look at Sirena, my stomach clenches. It's like her skin is on fire. The light dances in an eerie way, illuminating her.

She turns back to me. "Remember, say nothing. Trust me."

Up ahead, torches encircle a large open space. At first I'm not sure why, and then the mouth of a massive dark cave comes into view in the center of the circle. The wailing grows in volume, swelling out of the cave. The sound sends goose bumps rising on my flesh.

"Stay," she whispers to me.

I freeze, my instinct and my promise warring within me. If she tries to go into the cave, I swear I'll come after her. I'll break my word and destroy my honor. I'll do anything if it means keeping her safe.

She walks the twenty feet to the mouth of the cave before she stops in front of it.

I hold my breath.

"Cerberus!" she calls.

My muscles tense. *Cerberus?* We've come here to see the three-headed dog that works for Hades?

I crouch, my hand going to the hilt of my sword. I won't draw it yet. I'll wait and trust her. But if the beast should try to attack her, I'll kill it. No matter how powerful it is.

"Cerberus!" she calls again.

A sound echoes through the cave, and the wailing seems to grow quieter. The sound is strange… like the clanging of metal. Like metal being dragged.

My instincts are screaming to pull her back, to keep her safe.

And then, something emerges from the darkness… a dog. Not a three-headed dog, but a beast with flaming fur. Red, yellow, and orange flames dance from its back, and its eyes glow red. It's also big, not as big as I imagined it would be, but easily the size of a person on all fours.

It growls low, the sound vibrating through the air.

I tense, ready to attack if it should show the slightest sign that it plans to hurt my mermaid.

But instead, it dips its head and its entire body shudders. Its fur slowly fades into its body, and smooth flesh appears. The flames continue to dance, but after a long moment it's no longer a hellhound, but a woman on her hands and knees.

She's naked, but still covered in flames.

When she looks back up, her pupils are red, and a curtain of dark hair covers most of her naked body. And yet, her flesh is covered in raised, painful looking scars. Bruises and wounds cover the rest of her skin, and a massive, thick collar lines her neck. It's attached to a thick chain that leads back into the darkness.

"Cerberus!" My mermaid races to the shifter's side and kneels down.

She tries to touch her, but the shifter jerks back. "I'm fine." Her voice comes out rough and scratchy.

Keto's Tale

The shifter rises to her feet, struggling with every movement beneath the weight of the collar. And all along, Sirena is there, hands out as if to catch her if she falls.

When this woman… Cerberus, finally manages to fully stand, her back is straight, her shoulders back. And there's an unexpected pride to her eyes.

At last… the fire that seems to consume her fades, and then she's just a woman. She's a woman who looks like she's been to hell and back.

"What has he done to you now?" Sirena has tears in her voice.

"The same as always," Cerberus says, and her voice is flat, emotionless.

Sirena nods, and I can see she's shaking. "We need to talk."

The shifter looks at her and slowly nods.

"But not here." Sirena looks back at me.

For the first time, the shifter seems to see me. Rage flashes into her eyes, and the red returns, bleeding into her pupils. "Who is that?"

"He's okay. A friend," Sirena rushes out.

"A friend," Cerberus spits the words out. "Our kind doesn't have friends, only people who seek to use us."

"Please," Sirena whispers. "He's good. Kind."

Cerberus' eyes seem to bore into my soul. I can't look away. I can't breathe. And then whatever power holds me seems to snap, and I stumble back.

"He stays where he is. Unless he wants to die." She turns her back to me and disappears into the darkness.

My mermaid looks back at me. "Stay here. On the path. Let nothing remove you from it. And don't come after me, no matter what. Stepping into the cave for anyone but a god means instant death."

And then she disappears into the darkness.

I take a step forward. *Do I really just let her go? Can I let her go?*

A sound in the jungle makes me jump. Looking back into the darkness I see the eyes everywhere. And then I hear a blood-curdling scream. A voice I recognize.

Arthur?

It's coming from the jungle. My heart races. She said not to leave the path. She said these creatures could hurt me. But I can't just leave Arthur if he's in trouble.

The screaming starts again. The muscles in my legs bunch, but I hesitate.

Stay or go?

Chapter Seventeen

KETO

We go further into the entrance to the Underworld until we are deep enough that we reach a tiny cave off the main tunnel. Two miserable torches light the space that looks like little more than a jail cell. Cerberus leads me inside and seats herself on the edge of the stone bed. Ignoring me, she picks up a bone from a metal plate and begins to chew on it.

"I've come for your help."

She laughs. "I don't know what help I can be to you." Her voice raises, and she throws her arms out. "Look around you! I'm no help to anyone in this fucking place!"

I tremble. Not because I'm afraid, but because I forgot just how bad Cerberus lives.

My gaze goes to her collar. *Perhaps?* An idea blossoms in my mind.

"Hephaestus made your collar too, right?"

She smirks. "Got to love the fucking gods, right? Making our lives miserable since the beginning of time!"

I ignore her anger. I'm used to it, and I don't blame her for it. "I was told he was here for a time."

She nods. "Yeah, when I was a child. Dear old dad, Hades the fucker himself, said he was here to make me a birthday gift." She tugs at the collar. "Nice gift, huh? Probably should've had some kind of registry."

My stomach clenches. Cerberus is younger than I am. I didn't know her as a child, but I can only imagine the day she realized that she was going to be Hades tool, not his child. Not beloved by anyone.

"I'm so sorry."

She shrugs and goes back to chewing on her bone. "Not your fault. But if you ever see him, do me a favor and punch him right in his godly face."

"About that," I clear my throat. "I'm looking for him."

She freezes and regards me with suspicion. "Why?"

I move a little closer, look towards the entrance to her home, and lower my voice. "I want him to remove my collar."

She drops the bone and something unexpected flares to light in her eyes. "Won't your brother stop you before you can?"

"He thinks I'm dead."

She studies me for a long minute. "I know where he went after this."

I tense. "Where?"

She looks down at her collar, then to the huge chain that's connected to it. I don't understand why she won't tell me. Why she's holding back.

"I'll tell you, but only if you promise me something."

"What?" I ask, confused.

"That you find a way to get me free too."

I stiffen. *Free her from Hades?* I can't imagine that's possible.

She looks up and meets my gaze. "I've heard Hephaestus is different now. He regrets a lot of what he did for the gods and feels terrible for being tricked by his ex-wife into doing so many terrible things. If you speak to him, I think you could get him to come back and release me."

My word is everything. If I give it, I have to fulfill my promise. "I don't know if it's possible to free you."

Sadness fills her eyes. "Then… just promise that you'll try."

Of course I'll try. I can't believe I didn't think about it before. "I give you my word as The Mother of All Sea Monsters, as a Goddess of the Sea."

My promise holds power that we can both feel, like the heat from a fire.

It takes a long minute before I take a shaky breath.

"Okay," she says. "Hades doesn't know this, but I overheard Hephaestus talking." She looks around, lowering her voice to no louder than a whisper. "There's a sanctuary, a hidden place of magic that not even the gods know about."

"A sanctuary?" I can't believe it. "Do you have any idea where I can find it?"

She shook her head. "But if you can find a gargoyle, I think you could find it."

I stiffen. "Why?"

She raises a brow, staring at me as I'm completely clueless. "Because that's where they live."

Sitting back, I'm stunned. So all I need to do to get free is have the gargoyles take me to their home? That can't be too hard.

Can it?

Chapter Eighteen

STEVEN

Arthur's still screaming, begging for me to save him, begging for my help.

I can't decide if this is a trick by these creatures, or actually him, but I'm losing my mind. Looking back at the cave, I still see no signs of Sirena. What if by the time she comes out he's dead?

I have no one here to tell me what to do.

"Steven, please," he cries out. "We went looking for you. And… they attacked. We need you."

My hand closes around the hilt of my sword, and I slowly withdraw it. In an instant, every torch goes out. The lighted path dims, no longer a golden trail in the darkness. Shadows creep in, but so does the scarlet color, washing over the path like blood.

I take a step back, holding my sword out in front of me. The mist grows thicker, swallowing the path, swallowing the blood-red that moves every step closer and closer to me.

Backing up, I keep the cave behind me, trying to stay

Keto's Tale

out of the mist. Trying to avoid the red that I know is hidden beneath the cloak. But it's coming for me.

All of it's coming for me.

A beast emerges from the shadows and steps onto the path lightly, as if testing it. It looks like a tiny hellhound. The thing is no bigger than a small dog, but there's something wrong with it. Its flesh is… all wrong. It is strung together muscle and bone, but there's no skin. Its eyes glow red and he has long, sharp talons for feet.

It draws back its lips and growls, flashing jagged teeth. *Oh fucking hell!*

More and more of the creatures step onto the path, and I get the distinct impression that they can't yet come where I am, although the leaking blood and mist moves closer to me with every second. I continue to step backwards, inching closer and closer to the cave.

Arthur's cries are now silent, and I can't decide if that means he's dead or if this was all just a trick.

I've reached the entrance to the cave. And instantly, I know something is wrong. The air is cold. Not just chilly, but a bone-deep cold. It claws at me in a way that feels strange. The cold reaches so deep that it digs into my very soul.

My breath puffs out in front of me and a chill moves down my spine.

She was right about this cave. I shouldn't go in. I feel it deep in my bones.

And yet, the mist is continuing to creep forward. Dozens of the fleshless dogs have come out of the jungle, all staring at me, lips drawn back, teeth flashing.

Shifting, I go into battle-mode as my skin turns grey. My wings sprout on my back. I can't leave Sirena here, but I also don't plan to remain and see what these creatures are capable of.

When the mist is nearly touching the tips of my shoes, I launch into the air. I make it about ten feet before it's like slamming into a brick wall. I tumble back to the ground, smashing into it, my head spinning.

Instantly, the dogs are on me. When the first one sinks its teeth into my flesh, I scream in shock. Rolling onto my back and leaping to my feet, I stare at my arm. A chunk of my stone is gone, and beneath it, I bleed like any human.

Heart in my throat, I hold my sword out in front of me. These creatures *can* hurt me. They can *really* hurt me, but Sirena will be out soon. If I can't fly her to safety, then the only path out of here is the way we came.

A dog leaps at me. I slice it in two, the pieces falling at my feet.

Breathing hard, I stiffen as the dog's pieces slide back towards each other and then begin to knit back together.

Oh fuck! I'm in trouble.

More of the creatures leap at me, but no matter how quickly I cut them down, there's always more. One bites onto my other arm. I shake myself free and try to ignore the sting of its bite. It's fucking cold, the same chill that was in the cave.

That scares me in a way I never imagined.

The fight is a whirl of pain and fighting. I slice the bastards, kick them, punch them, but they keep coming back, knitting themselves back together, and more and more emerge from the shadows.

Things are only getting more dangerous by the second.

"Sirena!" I shout.

It's time we get the fuck out of here. There's a voice in my head that says I won't survive this, but I'll be damned if Sirena doesn't.

I hear someone gasp behind me. I turn, and six of the dogs jump onto my chest. Stumbling back, I tumble over

Keto's Tale

something, and then they're all covering me. Biting, tearing at my flesh.

Sirena is above me in an instant, tossing the dogs off.

And then I hear a roar that shakes the very air.

A massive hellhound leaps onto me, sending the little dogs flying. They whimper, but the massive hellhound continues to attack, crushing the dogs in her teeth, and eating them like they're nothing at all.

Sirena helps me to my feet. My head's spinning, and blood runs all over me.

She takes the sword from my hand. "We need to run now, understand?"

I nod.

She puts her shoulder under my arm and half carries me as we stumble forward. Some dogs try to leap at me, but she swings the sword and takes them down. Her movements are awkward, inexperienced, but sure.

More growls and sounds come from behind us. I see the hellhound. Dozens of the little dogs are attacking her, but she can't go after us. The chain holds her there.

"She needs... to get to safety," I bubble out.

"She'll go back into the cave. She's trying to distract them so we can escape."

My head continues to spin. My thoughts are foggy, and yet, I'm shocked. I can picture in perfect clarity the blood that runs down the hellhound's back and legs. Why is she helping us? All I know of Cerberus is that it's a cruel three-headed beast that works for Hades, guarding the gates of the Underworld.

Nothing about the stories of the three-headed beast connect with the lone woman fighting for our sake. *I guess she isn't the monster I thought she was.* The thought is oddly troubling.

We're moving faster down the path, her dragging me with a strength that no mortal woman could have.

"I feel... weird," I gargle.

And I do. My head's spinning. My limbs don't seem to be obeying me.

It's like I'm drunker than I've ever been in my life and in mind-numbing pain, all at once.

She makes an angry sound. "Of course you feel weird! Those beasts devour the pieces of you that make you immortal, killing not only your body but your soul."

Huh? "I didn't leave the path."

She *tisks*, sounding out of breath. "Did you... try to... attack them?"

"Maybe."

I'm surprised when she swears.

We reach the end of the path, and she drags me out into the jungle. We're falling, stumbling over roots and tangles of plants.

"Arthur! Max!" she shouts.

We hear nothing.

She continues to drag us forward, sliding down uneven hills and getting back up to keep dragging me forward.

"Arthur! Max!" she shouts again.

We hear something somewhere in front of us.

She adjusts our direction and drags me along a little longer, then shouts again.

A sound comes again, and this time I know it's Max and Arthur.

We keep going, and their shouting grows louder and louder with every step. More of the fucking beasts attack us in the darkness, but Sirena is shockingly focused as she cuts them down.

When we at last explode out onto the shore, we practically tumble into Arthur and Max's arms. She shoves me at

Keto's Tale

them and whirls around, my sword in hand. For the first time I realize she's coated in blood, mine or hers, I don't know. She backs up slowly, over the uneven rocks, keeping the sword held out in front of her.

Red eyes glow in the darkness, but none of them leap forward.

After a long, tense moment, she lowers the sword. "They can't come out here."

"What the fuck are they? And what happened to Steven?" Max demands.

She doesn't turn around. "You don't want to know, but we need to get the hell out of here."

"I… agree," I mumble, sounding strange even to my own ears.

She finally looks back at me. "We need to go someplace close. And then we need to take care of him."

Saying nothing more, she wraps her arms around Max's neck.

Arthur holds me tighter and shifts, launching us into the air. I watch, my head spinning as the misty, red island fades below us. The Isle of the Demons, *ha*! I can't believe I thought it was just some stupid human fairytale.

My eyes start to close. *It was fucking hell.*

Chapter Nineteen

CLARK

I hate everything about this situation. I'm supposed to be the leader of our Brotherhood. They're supposed to look to me for advice and guidance, just like they've always done, and yet that mermaid seems to have completely clouded their judgment.

Until our fight, I'd seen Max as our leader in name only. We all knew I was our real one. He was like a child, walking around in his father's shoes.

But now?

I toss a stick in the water, glaring out at the waves. Now, Max challenged me. He actually said that he was the better leader on this mission… and no one disagreed with him.

The worst part is I know I'm right. As much as the mermaid makes me feel things I never expected, I don't trust her.

Just the thought makes me stiffen. Fucking Arthur said it was because of my past. It's not! At least, I don't think it is. I can't help but think back to Catherine. I awoke to her tears. A beautiful woman on her hands and knees, begging for a miracle. For protection.

I'd come to life and knelt down beside her, lifting her chin. Seeing tears in her bright blue eyes had made me feel more human than I thought a gargoyle had ever felt. She'd told me an army of invaders were coming, and that she and her guards had no chance of surviving them.

There was no hesitation before I declared myself to her. I vowed to protect her against anything and everything.

She'd pulled me down onto that cold stone floor and made love to me, something I never thought a gargoyle could do with one of his masters. It awakened something in me, a thirst for more than just my life of stone.

Each time an army advanced, I killed them with efficiency. I was an impossible foe against their human bodies. Each time afterwards, she pulled me close to her and made love to me again with a beautiful smile on her face.

Then I decided to end the war once and for all. I chased the enemies to their base only to learn the truth. They were not the invaders. She was. She had stolen their castle, slaughtered their people, and used me to protect her position.

The people I had been fighting? They were my real masters. I could feel it deep down to my soul. Even if they could never accept me or forgive me for what I'd done.

I'd returned to where she waited for me in her bed and I'd killed her.

Squeezing my eyes shut, I fought the pain the old memories brought rushing back to me. She'd betrayed me. Lied to me, and yet, I'd loved her.

I'd never loved again since then. And I never would..

This Sirena? I... my heart begged me to love her too, but something felt off. I couldn't name it, but I felt it. *Maybe the fact that she's a liar too.* The thought should have reassured me, but it only made me feel worse. Perhaps I was only destined to love bad women.

A disturbance made my eyes fly open and my entire body stiffened. Looking around the little island I'd come to, I searched for the source of the prickling at the back of my neck. There was nothing but the wind, carrying the saltiness of the sea, and the waves crashing softly against the shore.

As I watched, a man emerged from the water.

His hair was the same bright auburn color as Sirena's, and his eyes the same dark shade of brown. His skin was pale, but muscled and strong, and I knew without question that he was another immortal.

Without speaking, I drew my sword from my back.

He smiled. "No need to fear, gargoyle, I've only come to talk."

What could he possibly want from me? "So talk."

He remained partially in the waves, regarding me in a way that made my skin crawl.

"Do you know who I am, gargoyle?"

"Nope, and I don't really care."

His smile spread. "I am Phorcys, god of the sea."

That uneasy feeling grew. I know who he is... Phorcys, god of hidden dangers of the deep, and brother to the very monster we're hunting.

"Congrats," I tell him, but my hand tightens on the hilt of my sword.

He looks at my sword, then back at my face, clearly amused. "Alright then. I see you're not much for small talk or manners. That's fine. Let's get straight to it then. I've recently made the acquaintance of some *friends* of yours."

I wait, not taking his bait.

"I met some Sea Dragons…" he continues, "Who want their powers back."

Everything inside of me tenses, but I just stare, waiting.

He raises a brow. "I can see you're reluctant to give back the power of a god, although I doubt you've even had time to truly explore your new gifts. I don't blame you. Everyone wants powers like ours. Few are willing to except the consequences of stealing them…"

Fine, I'll take the bait. "First, we didn't steal their powers, they were forced onto us. Second, we don't want them. Third, what fucking consequences?"

His eyes seem to glitter beneath the moonlight. "Your bodies can't contain the power of the gods. Soon the powers will feed on your bodies and souls, destroying you, and then return to their owners."

I stare. *Is he lying?* I can't tell with this guy, because I kind of get the sense he's lying about everything.

But information is power. "So, how do we get rid of these *powers*?"

He lifts his hand. Clenched in his grip is a small cage with a little golden creature in the bottom of it. The fish-thing looks… wrong, unhealthy somehow. Maybe it's even hurt, but it's *exactly like the one Max described.*

"The only thing that can restore the balance is this little monster."

And of course this creepy, destructive god just wants to give him to us. "What do you want for it?"

Even though I don't even know if it can do what he says it can, I can't help but ask.

"What do I want?" he repeats. "Nothing. Just return the powers to the sea dragons. See, I've worked out a deal with them, and I'll be greatly rewarded for making this little arrangement."

My mind spins. "And I'm sure you'll allow us to walk away from this meeting unharmed."

"You have the word of a god."

And a god can't break their word. I guess that's something.

"Fine, where should we meet you?"

"The Lonely Island will do just fine."

I nod, knowing the isolated place.

He's lips curl. "And one more thing—"

"The mermaid." *Of course they want her back. But should we give her up?* Just the idea made my stomach turn.

His smile fades. "Mermaid?"

"Yes, the mermaid they planned to eat."

He slides closer to the shore, and something dark appears in his eyes. "Does this mermaid have red hair?"

Suddenly, I feel uneasy. I don't want to talk to him about Sirena. Even if I think she's a liar.

So, I shrug.

His eyes flash. "I thought Keto was dead."

"Keto?" I repeat. "No, not Keto. A different mermaid."

"A beautiful mermaid with the powers of a goddess?"

Every single muscle in my body tenses.

He laughs. "Keto always did know how to fool men, but I never thought gargoyles would fall for her lies."

I'm shaking with rage. She was lying to us! All along she was the person we were looking for!

"Angry?" he asks, enjoyment in his every word. "Why be angry when you can have revenge, gargoyle? Bring her back to me, and I'll make certain she pays for her lies."

If only I could, but our mission…

"We need her," I grit out.

He shrugs. "Then you can have her… when I'm done. I simply need to have a little word with my sweet sister. But tick tock, gargoyle, my offer won't last for long."

The bastard slides back below the waves and vanishes, and I'm left on the beach, sword in hand, enraged, with no one around to punish.

Keto's Tale

I hate myself right now. I hate myself because as much as I felt I couldn't trust the mermaid, I liked her. I was compelled by her sad eyes. My body wanted nothing more than hers. She made me feel things… things I hadn't felt for a long time.

All along, every word out of her mouth was a lie. A complete and utter lie.

I thought I had grown and changed so much since my first mistake, since Catherine. It cut me deeply to realize I hadn't. Just show me a woman with a lovely face, and I was lost.

Re-sheathing my sword, I stand. It didn't matter. What mattered was finding… this Keto, and luring her to the meeting place. I'll have to find a way to deal with the others. I had a feeling they wouldn't be able to do what needed to be done.

Fortunately for them, they had me.

Now to find them. Stretching my wings, I head off toward the Isle of the Demons, anger churning in my gut with each flap of my wings.

Chapter Twenty

KETO

I'm shaking as we land on the little island not far from the Isle of the Demons. Max instantly goes to work, setting up a tarp on the ground, laying out blankets and supplies. Arthur cleans Steven's wounds as he lies unconscious, but it's obvious he doesn't know exactly what he's doing.

I doubt many gargoyles have been this injured before.

If we don't do something soon, I'm actually afraid Steven might die. These are wounds a god would hurt from. A simple semi-immortal? It's tearing at his soul and pulling him step-by-step closer to mortality.

He'll die if I don't get help.

I have to go into the sea, no matter how much it puts me at risk of losing everything. Steven came there for me. I lured him there for my own selfish reasons. He can't die for me. I won't allow it!

My gaze goes to him, and my heart clenches. I want to stroke his long, brown hair. I want to touch the strong lines of his face. I even want to see the way his dark eyes sparkle when he looks at me, but I won't be able to do any of those things if I don't go soon.

"I think I can help him," I say.

Max and Arthur look up at me.

"How?" Max asks.

"I'll find someone who can heal him."

Arthur looks worried. "Is it safe for you?"

I try to keep my face blank. "If I don't go, he could die."

That's the moment I realize that they had no idea how serious this is. Both men turned pale, their eyes widening. Their concern bleeds through every inch of their flesh.

"I'll be back," I promise.

Turning my back to all of them, I walk into the sea.

Instantly, the water washes over me and almost feels strange on my flesh. I've been away from the water more the last few days than any other time in my life. Shifting, my tail sprouts. Parts of my body sting and burn in the salty water, but I ignore it, dipping below the waves. Whatever injuries I sustained on the isle is nothing compared to Steven's. I can endure them.

Reaching out with my mind, I search and search. I sense my creatures stiffening. They feel my mind brushing theirs like an instinct they can't quite identify, but I don't stop to speak to any of them. Not until I find the creature I need.

I swim deeper and deeper into the dark depths of the ocean. My eyes adjust, but my nerves feel on edge. As if I'm waiting for my brother to sense me. As if I'm waiting for his minions to come for me.

I continue to swim as time passes, until at last I sense my creature. She's a beautiful being filled with absolute goodness, and when I call to her she comes, barreling through the sea.

I head back to the island, sensing her following me with every mile that swims past.

And then something crashes into me in the water.

I struggle, trying to escape. Trying to fight even as I tumble through the water.

Arms are suddenly around me, and then a familiar voice comes, as clear as if on the surface. "Keto, I missed you."

My heart twists. "Aphros."

I feel his smile against my hair. "And I'd worried you'd forgotten about me."

He turns me slowly around, and I have to fight every instinct not to flee from him. My brother's second-in-command is a merman with long golden hair and eyes the color of seaweed. He's also a big man, and a god. He's not nearly as powerful a god as my brother and I, but he's a god all the same.

And I hate him with every ounce of my being.

"When I heard the sea dragons killed you, I was heartbroken."

My mind senses my sea monster. She draws closer, but I should have time. I have to escape this bastard before he can see her and hurt her.

"Well, now you know," I tell him.

He smiles and starts to draw me closer.

I jerk free of him, panting in fear. "Don't touch me!"

His smile vanishes. "What's come over you?"

I don't know what's come over me. Never before would I defy this man, but now I know so many things that I didn't understand before, things the gargoyles have taught me.

Aphros was always a bad man. Just like my brother. But I'd always felt that what he did to me didn't matter. Now I knew differently.

"You are never to touch me again," I tell him.

Anger flashes in his eyes. "And who are you to command me to do anything?"

"A goddess of the sea," I emphasize each word.

He laughs. "Has your time away made you forget your place? Then, let me remind you."

He jerks me closer, and his mouth crushes mine.

I strike out, clawing his face and shoving back.

The smell of his blood lingers in the water. He touches his face and then narrows his eyes in that evil stare that I've feared for way too long. "That was a mistake, Keto. When I tell your brother that you still live, he will tighten your fucking collar until your head is nearly severed. And then I'll watch as you suffer, slowly knitting your immortal flesh back together."

He's a coward. The thought makes me freeze. This low-god, he has no real power over me, just the power he steals from my brother. How is it that I never realized that before?

"Do what you have to," I say, my voice strong and sure. "But you will never touch me again."

His lips curl. "The pain you'll feel—"

And then my creature barrels out of the water and chomps down on him in one bite.

I'm in shock as I watch the cloud of blood that fills the water, and my creature throws back its head to fully swallow him.

The massive creature comes closer, rubbing its large head against me. I can hear it in my thoughts. She didn't like the way the merman spoke to me. She could sense my anger and fear, so she helped.

I'm speechless. What is there to say?

He's a god. Eating him won't kill him. But he will have

a rather awful next few days as he passes through my creature's system and out the other end.

Rising to the surface of the water, I explode in the moonlight. My creature drifts under me and lifts me higher until I'm riding on her back. Laughing, I stretch out my arms.

That bastard who hurt me? He's going to be shitted out by one of my creatures!

I can't stop laughing. My creature makes a pleasant sound beneath me as she heads toward the island, and my gargoyles waiting for me. She's glad she made me happy. She likes to make me happy.

"He's going to want to hurt you for that," I tell her.

She's not afraid. She has places she likes to go that the stupid merman and my brother won't find her. She's never liked either of them.

"I feel the same way," I say, still laughing, tears of joy running down my face.

They say immortals can't change. But the thing is… I am changing. There were so many things I thought were outside of my control, but they aren't. I know where to go to get this collar off. One of the men who hurt me is getting a very fitting kind of revenge, and I have gargoyles I care about.

Life could actually be a little good.

As soon as Steven has healed.

Minutes pass. I close my eyes, feeling the wind against my face and tasting the salt on the air. Even the moon glows brighter, a beautiful blue unlike anything I can remember in my long life.

Or maybe everything's exactly the same, and I'm just different. The thought makes me smile.

And then there's something else, a strange knowledge.

Keto's Tale

Tonight, if my gargoyles are up for it, I'm going to let them make love to me. I'm going to make love to them.

Because I'm not afraid anymore of being hurt. I'm afraid of wasting more days being lonely and unhappy.

Why have forever if I never do anything with it?

Chapter Twenty-One

ARTHUR

There's so much blood and so many wounds. I'm trying to help Steven, but I don't have a clue how to. Max has created a place to rest for the night. He's built a fire, and caught fish that he grills over the fire. I've bound all Steven's wounds, and yet, it isn't enough. We know it's not.

I just keep staring, feeling useless. Max just races around, as if keeping himself busy will keep Steven alive.

Nothing we do can save him. I feel it in the pit of my gut.

"Fuck," I mutter and rise, feeling agitated.

Stripping off my clothes, I toss them onto the shore and walk out into the ocean. I try to wash Steven's blood from my body. I try to clear my head before I completely lose my mind.

And then, there beneath the waters, I see them. Little fish with lights on their bodies seem to come from every direction. They fill the water around me, creating a stunning glow.

Breath held in wonder, I reach out. They allow me to run my fingers along their soft bodies. Like cats. For a

Keto's Tale

minute none of it makes sense, and then I remember my power, *control over the mindless sea creatures*. Is that what this is?

Closing my eyes, I'm shocked at what happens. Inside of me, I suddenly sense the oceans spreading across the world, covering nearly every surface of our world. And within them, I sense billions of little lives. They move about their business, strangely innocent, content in their lives.

I stumble a little on the sand as the waves pull at me. My eyes open, and I continue to stare out at the water. This power? I like it.

And then I hurl straight into the water.

"Fuck!" I grip my head as pain tears through it.

"What is it?" Max comes to stand on the shore not far from me. "Are you okay?"

I'm breathing hard as the pain slowly subsides. "I don't know…"

Suddenly, we hear Steven. He's shouting words that make no sense.

I wipe my mouth and dive beneath the waters, trying to calm myself. When I surface again, Max is at Steven's side. I hurry toward them and kneel down.

Steven is tossing his head from side to side. His face is pale and sweat rolls down his face.

"*Nuh, no, na,*" he mutters, sounds that make no sense.

"What do we do?" Max asks, his voice shaking.

"Wait for Sirena," is all I can say.

And then I feel something. A change in the air. Power. Magic.

I look to Max. His eyes are wide.

"You feel that?" I ask.

He nods.

The moon seems to grow brighter. Our gazes slowly

move up, and sure enough, the moon seems to be growing brighter… bigger. Closer?

"What was Steven's power again?"

Max answers without hesitation. "Power over the stars and planets."

"This isn't good, right? Screwing with this stuff can cause… issues?"

"Yeah." His expression is troubled. "Especially with the waves." He shudders. "Actually, he's causing a lot of problems with the waves. Fucking shit!"

"What?" My heart's racing.

"Massive waves are growing, racing for land. It's going to… it's going to kill a lot of people. It's going to cause a lot of destruction. I can feel them in my mind, growing, becoming more and more powerful."

I stand. "You can control the waves, right? You can stop it?"

He looks pale. "I don't know."

Suddenly, a massive creature comes into view. My glowing fish move as it heads straight toward us. But this being, it's unlike anything I've seen before. It has one massive neck and head, but also strange arms that seem to move like tentacles in the breeze. It has the almost translucent quality of a jellyfish, only with a little more substance.

Whatever the hell it is, I doubt it's good. And I doubt we're going to like whatever it has planned for us.

Heart in my throat, I scramble for where my clothes and weapons are tossed on the shore. Gripping the hilt of my sword, I pull it free.

This is just what we need. Another fight.

And then I spot Sirena on its back. And she's… smiling a big, happy smile.

Relief makes my tense muscles relax ever so slightly. Is

Keto's Tale

this the creature she sought out to help Steven? Why the hell can't she have any furry, cute little sea animals?

Like mine. I think with a smile.

When she reaches the shore, she slides from the beast's back and into the water. Her tail vanishes and she walks out of the water, heading right for us.

"Is that the beast that can save Steven?" Max asks.

Her smile falters. "She's a creature that can help him, yes." Kneeling at his side, she looks between him and the moon. "We need to get him into the water. Near my creature. She can help heal him."

"There's another problem," Max says. "The waves—"

"He's affected them," she says. "That's okay. You can fix it before too much damage is done."

Max shakes his head. "I can't. I don't know how."

She gazes up at him, and her sweet expression takes my breath away. "Yes, you can. I know you can. Just go into the water. Think of the waves, reassure them, like a living creature, and tell them to calm."

"I—"

"Trust me, Max, you can do this. I know you can."

He draws himself up taller and begins to undress.

Then she turns to me. "Help me get him in the water, and leave your sword. My creature frightens easily. You'll need to move slowly and calmly."

"I can do that."

Steven tosses and thrashes in my arms as I pick him up and carry him into the water. Each step I take I feel more and more nervous. The massive white creature looks terrifying with its huge teeth and creepy tentacles moving about it.

Sirena leads me to stand just in front of it. Then she takes Steven from my arms and presents him to the creature. Very slowly, its tentacles move toward my wounded Brother.

I shudder when the tentacles lock onto him. The sucking sound sends a chill down my spine.

When all four of its tentacles are on him, the creature begins to tremble. It opens its mouth and a strange sound comes out. It reminds me of the song of a whale, beautiful and powerful, full of an emotion that calls to my soul. The creature begins to glow with different colored lights underneath its surface. It's like an alien, a beautiful alien.

Then I feel an echo that travels through me. My glowing fish glow brighter, swimming around the creature as it sings its sad song.

I'm overwhelmed. Emotions I never imagined claw deeply inside me. And I feel something… a connection to the ocean. Not just through my powers, but through my soul. It's a mysterious, but beautiful, part of our world, one I never truly respected or understood until now.

My gaze moves to Steven. I can't see most of his wounds, but he doesn't look any different to me. What if this doesn't work? My stomach clenches, and I look to Max.

He's standing in the water, his arms spread out, his eyes closed. Will he be able to stop the waves in time? Can he save lives with a power he has yet to understand?

This mission of ours… it seemed so simple when it began. But now? Now it feels like something else, like an awakening.

And then the creature's singing stops. My fish continue their strange dance around the towering creature. But it draws its tentacles back from Steven. Sirena is there, catching him in her arms.

She stares down at him with tenderness, then back at her creature. "Thank you," she whispers.

Keto's Tale

The creature uses one tentacle to stroke her face in a gentle way, and then it slips beneath the water and its lights dull. Within seconds, its disappeared.

Sirena slowly removes Steven's bandages. Underneath them, his skin is smooth.

She turns back to me with a smile. "He's going to be okay."

I move closer, and I'm shocked when Steven's eyes open.

"What?" He blinks. "What happened?"

She leans down and kisses him lightly on his forehead. "You saved me."

For a minute I can't stop staring at them. She's holding him so gently, so lovingly, and he seems so content in her arms.

Is this love? This connection we feel to her?

Because if it's not, then I don't know what love is. This bond… I don't just like how it makes me feel. I like the impact it has on my Brothers.

Except Clark. But I had no doubt that he could come around to her too.

We weren't going to get a female gargoyle. Being celibate was pointless. If our people couldn't accept Sirena, maybe we didn't need them either.

Even though it'd be hard to walk away from everyone and everything we loved. It'd be worth it for her.

Steven struggles to sit up, and I move to him and help. It takes him a minute to steady himself. And when I look at him, he's got bright red marks where the creature latched onto him. But it's clear every one of his wounds are gone.

"That was… weird," he says.

I laugh. "You have no idea."

We go to Max. His eyes are open, but as we draw closer, we see they're silver and spinning slowly. I freeze, staring. He radiates power, just the way Steven did. And I can feel it, flowing through him, and flowing into the water.

I swear I can even see the bright blue glow radiating out from him and into every drop of water. At last he drops his hands, and the silver fades from his eyes. He's breathing hard as he turns to us.

"I stopped the waves."

Sirena smiles. "I knew you could do it!"

He turns and hurls into the water.

I wince, remembering that same feeling.

Sirena's at his side in a moment, rubbing his back. Her happiness has faded and concern fills her face. Again, I think of how nice having her around is, how wonderful it is to have a gentle touch when we need it.

"I don't know what the fuck is wrong with me," he mumbles.

"It's the powers," she tells him.

"So that's just what happens when we use it?" I ask.

She looks up at me and shakes her head. "I—I didn't want to scare you guys."

I stiffen. "What?"

She hesitates before she lets out a rushed breath. "You're semi-immortals. Meaning, it's possible to kill you. You can be beheaded. You can be killed by a powerful god's powers. You're simply... not as strong as a god or goddess. You know that. With me, no one can kill me. If I'm beheaded, it'll hurt. I'll feel the mind-numbing pain of it all, and I'll wake up in the Underworld. It'll take time to regain my body for this plane and to resurface, but I won't ever die permanently. But that kind of power... only a god can contain it. The four of you have the power of gods, but you aren't meant to. If we can't remove it from you soon, it'll kill you."

Keto's Tale

My breath rushes out of me. "So we really need to find that friend of yours."

She nods. "But we have time, so don't worry too much."

All of us take a minute in the water to wash ourselves, and then we return to shore to eat our very cold meal of overcooked fish. It's strange. The more we eat, the better all of us seem to feel. Even Steven seems like his old self, only better.

He snorts as I tell him about how he was healed. We laugh as I talk about my cool little fish. And Max insists my powers are far better than his.

All in all, it's a nice night. *If only Clark was here.*

We finish our meal and clean up, throwing more driftwood on the fire. And then we lie down beneath the stars on our little tarp with our little blankets.

This time, all of us are naked. Our wet clothes are spread out on rocks near us. As strange as I thought it'd be, it's actually kind of nice, almost relaxing.

"I'd like to have sex tonight."

Every muscle in my body tenses, and I sit up. Sirena's staring up at the sky, her tone casual, but my heart's suddenly racing.

Max clears his throat. "With who?"

"Well, all of you. Would that be okay?"

My treacherous cock hardens. I meet Steven's and Max's gazes, and I know we're all thinking the same thing. Is there any reason not to?

A thought rings through my mind. *Not a single one.*

Chapter Twenty-Two

KETO

I thought I'd be nervous about tonight, about saying what I wanted aloud, but something's changed. These gargoyles have met some of my monsters… and even though there were some bad moments, they were able to get around what they were and see who they are. It gives me hope. I have hope that maybe when they find out who I am, they can forgive me. Just maybe they can even love me.

And what's more, Aphros is gone. He'll return, like all the fucking gods, but I finally told him no. I stood up for myself and saw that the world wouldn't end because I did so.

My brother thinks I'm dead.

The sea dragons are without power.

When I get this collar off my throat and find my little creature to return the gargoyles to normal, everything will be good in a way it's never been before. I want to celebrate. I want to be like Arthur. I want to enjoy this life.

I can think of no better way than to make this final connection with my gargoyles.

Keto's Tale

"Do you... do you want to have sex with me?" I ask, because the gargoyles have been quiet for far too long.

Arthur's gaze meets mine. "Of course we do. But are you sure?"

I hesitate for just a moment, and then decide to go for it. "The only man I've ever had sex with was a man named Aphros. He... works with... the sea dragons. Tonight I saw him. He touched me and—"

"What?" Max sits up, and his eyes are filled with rage. "He touched you?"

Steven and Arthur rise, and there's something deadly in their gazes.

"Where is he?" Steven asks, his voice deathly calm.

Angry men scare me, but somehow, I don't feel afraid. I feel loved.

"It's okay," I say, speaking around the lump in my throat. "I told him no. For the first time. And... my creature ate him."

Something changes in the air.

"He's dead?" Max asks, sounding far too relieved.

I shake my head. "He's a god, he can't die. But he'll be inside my creature until—"

"Wait," Arthur interrupts. "He's going to be shit out?"

I nod.

He starts to laugh, and the harder he laughs, the more the anger fades from the other men. They sit back down beside me, and Max pulls me into his lap.

"I still wish we could kill him," Max says, stroking my hair.

I smile at him. "Me too."

"But being shit out is a pretty close second," Steven says, grinning.

Max continues to stroke my hair. "Did he hurt you?"

Steven and Arthur's humor fades away.

I shake my head. "No. Not tonight."

For a while he just holds me, and as time passes I become more and more aware of the fact that we're all naked. And that his very hard cock is pressing against my ass.

Lifting my head off his shoulder, I meet his gaze. "You're big again."

The moonlight makes it hard to be sure, but I think he might be blushing. "Sorry, having a naked woman in my lap…" He trails off.

Arthur grins. "He means, we're trying to be gentlemen."

I glance at him. He's hard too. When my gaze sweeps to Steven, I'm satisfied to see the same. "If being gentleman means having small, soft cocks, you're all failing."

Arthur chucks, but the sound is husky. "You did mention you wanted to have sex."

I nod, and my stomach flutters. That is what I want.

Turning to Max, I whisper, "Will you kiss me?"

His gaze goes to my mouth, and without speaking, he leans forward, his lips crushing mine. At first his touch is soft, and then his mouth grows harder, more demanding. I part my lips, and his tongue sweeps inside.

I groan and press myself against him, my nipples growing hard as they brush his chest. My hands grip the back of his head and my fingers dig into his hair. My entire body seems to awaken. His kiss sends ripples of pleasure straight to my core.

When he draws back, he's panting hard.

"What now?" I ask.

"Fucking hell," he mutters.

Steven and Arthur draw closer.

Keto's Tale

Steven's voice is husky as he answers. "We could touch you, if you'll let us."

This time, I don't hesitate. "I trust you."

Max's mouth descends back onto mine, but it's his turn to bury his fingers in my hair. Slowly, oh so slowly, he tilts me back, his tongue tangling with my own. My pleasure awakens with each flick of his tongue.

And then, someone brushes my core.

I gasp and pull back.

Steven strokes me very slowly, watching my every move.

I shift my legs, spreading myself for him.

He swears softly and then parts me. When his fingers brush my wet folds, I cry out, digging my nails into Max's shoulders. His cock seems to grow harder beneath my ass, a reminder of what he wants.

When Steven continues to touch me, Arthur reaches forward. His fingertips brush my nipples.

My breathing comes in ragged.

"Like that?" he asks, watching me.

I nod, speechless.

He moves closer and leans down, his lips locking around one of my nipples. Pleasure explodes through me, and I can't catch my breath. I can't even think.

I lean back further, feeling as if my gargoyles are everywhere, touching me like I'm something beautiful and fragile. I'm not afraid. I'm excited. It's like a dream come true.

The collar around my neck might still be there, but I don't feel like a slave anymore... I feel *free*.

Just as that thought enters my head, I feel someone's mouth on my hot core. My eyes open, and I gasp. Steven's between my thighs, gently licking my folds in a slow, leisurely pace.

The sight of him turns me into jelly. My muscles jerk,

and I dig one hand into the back of his hair, my body moving with each stroke of his tongue. I'm overwhelmed, lost to these men and their touch.

Arthur grips my other breast and begins to roll it between his thumb and finger. I swear I leave my body for a minute. I'm overwhelmed, overflowing with arousal.

Max trails kisses down my neck, then stops to suck.

I hold onto them, so turned on that I know I'm bucking against Max's ass beneath me, rubbing against Steven's lips.

A shudder moves through my body.

I don't know how much more I can take.

When Steven sucks on my clit, I cry out, and my body shakes. I'm so close, on the edge of that beautiful pleasure that I need so badly.

As if sensing how close I am, they adjust. Max leans back, spreading his legs straight out in front of him. I'm still resting on his cock, but now we're aligned so it'd take nothing at all to take him deep inside of me.

Steven leans over me. Holding my gaze, he grabs Max's cock in a matter-of-fact way and starts to slide it in my wet folds. My nails dig into his back. I'm pretty sure I say one of their names, but pleasure overwhelms me, stealing all logic.

When he takes the head of his cock and places it at my ass, I watch him, wondering. These men won't hurt me. I trust them. But I never really considered the logistics of having them all inside of me. Is this how they'll fit?

Steven eases me inch by inch down onto the other man's cock until we're all breathing hard. Max is buried deeply inside of me, almost uncomfortably so. But I'm so wet, so ready, that his presence is tight, but not painful. How could I have gone without this for so long?

And then Steven rises over me, positions his cock at my

core, and holds himself there. At first I'm not sure what he's doing, and then I wiggle on him, taking him deeper. He swears, and I feel an overwhelming desire to have him inside of me.

I start to take him deeper, but he holds himself still, reaching between us and starting to stroke me again. The combination is like a strike of lightning. There's a big cock in my ass. There's a cock easing into my pussy, and now this man is stroking my clit like I need more pleasure.

It's all too much.

Arthur leans forward, and suddenly, he's kissing me. His kiss is harsh, demanding, desperate. He grasps my hand and curls it around his cock. I grasp him, feeling powerful and sexy all at once. Each stroke of my hand has a string of curses exploding from his lips. And then he goes right back to kissing me, to claiming my lips like a man on the edge of madness.

Steven eases deeper and deeper inside of me, filling me entirely and completely, until I know he's reached his hilt.

That's the moment. Lying there on the sand, beneath the stars, with the water rushing in my ears, I know true happiness. I feel… loved. I feel like I belong.

When they start to make love to me, that feeling only increases. They move together in a rhythm that feels familiar and new all at once. My body is open to them, ready for them. And nothing has ever been better than this.

Steven and Max increase their rhythm inside of me. Their cocks working together to build my pleasure higher and higher. With one hand, I dig my nails into Steven's shoulder, and with the other, I stroke him.

When I look up, Arthur is kneeling at my side, his eyes closed. I know what I want, what I need. I turn my head and close my lips around him.

His eyes fly open, he growls my name, and his hands dig into the back of my hair as he pushes himself deeper into my mouth. My tongue curls around him. He swears again as I suck with all my might.

The men thrust in and out of me. My mind is gone. The stars spin overhead, and my pleasure builds with each second. I feel a shudder move through my body. My inner-muscles clench the cocks inside me harder, as if wanting nothing more than to milk them of their seed, and then I fall over the edge.

Crying out around the cock in my mouth, I move between the men, riding them like a wild creature. Thrashing. Taking them deep. Squeezing them harder, and riding the waves of my pleasure.

Arthur explodes in my mouth with a guttural sound, his cum filling my mouth. My own arousal builds as I continue to thrash.

Max comes next, his seed hot in my ass, warm and wet and so unbelievably satisfying.

As my orgasm begins to fade, Steven groans and comes, filling my pussy in a deliciously perfect way. He continues to move above me, thrusting in and out for several long seconds before he finally collapses above me.

Arthur pulls his cock free from my mouth and falls onto his knees. We're all breathing hard, in complete peace.

I've never felt like this before, so unbelievably complete.

And yet, I find myself wishing Clark was here. If he was, maybe he could learn to care for me too. Maybe he could see the goodness in me, before he learns of my lies and deceit.

The men reluctantly pull out of me, and we lie together on the tarp beneath the stars, feeling content. My eyelids feel heavy, but my body hums with pleasure. I want

Keto's Tale

to hold onto this moment forever. But I also want this to be *real*.

"I need to tell you all something," I whisper.

Steven strokes my hair. "*Hum?*"

"Cerberus told me how to end this all. To finally be free."

No one asks, and the only sound is the crashing of the waves.

"There's a god, Hephaestus. He's the only one who can help."

"Hephaestus?" Max sounds confused.

"Cerberus says he's in a sanctuary that only gargoyles know about."

Max sighs. "I feel like there's more to this story."

"There is," I take a deep breath, prepared to spill it all. "He can also help me remove my collar. He can—"

"Sirena?" Arthur asks.

I freeze. "Yes?"

"I know we have a lot to talk about, but all I can think about right now is burying myself deep inside your pussy."

My body responds to his words in an instant. My muscles tighten and my breathing increases. "But tomorrow we'll talk?"

Arthur reaches down and starts to stroke my wet core. "Yeah, tomorrow."

I close my eyes, already leaning into his touch.

As much as I want to tell them the truth, I guess one more night can't hurt, right?

Chapter Twenty-Three

CLARK

It's nearly morning before I spot the little island with the dying fire. Before I even see them, I know that it's them. These desolate, miserable islands aren't exactly a tourist destination.

Landing quietly near them, I stiffen. They're all naked. Curled around the lying sea witch like lovers. And then, I know it. They *are* lovers.

I drop my sword and bag on the shore, my anger churning.

If they've fucked her, they're already too far gone. They won't have the balls to do what needs to be done. Yet again I'm glad that I'm here. I'm their protector, whether they know it or not.

Creeping toward them, I shake Keto's shoulder softly. Her dark eyes open sleepily, and for a minute I'm struck by her beauty. Before I remember she's been lying to us from the start. She's no slave, no innocent woman in need of our protection. She's nothing more than a lying bitch.

My jaw clenches, and I motion for her to follow me.

She untangles herself from my Brothers. I hold my

Keto's Tale

breath as I watch, afraid she'll wake them, but they simply frown and remain sleeping. We step further from them, and I scratch the name of the Lonely Island into the sand, before leading her further down the shore. *Just in case.*

When we're out of ear-shot, I turn to her and try to mask my rage. "We need to go."

She looks confused. "Go? Where?"

I say the words I practiced. "I know how to get what you want."

"You know where Hephaestus is?"

Hephaestus? The blacksmith god? Why would she want him?

I keep my face blank. "Yes, if we leave now, we can reach him."

She smiles, and I hate that her happiness tugs at something in my chest. "Where is he?"

"On the Lonely Island."

A flicker of doubt comes and goes from her face. "That isn't far from here. If we leave now, we can be there before midday."

I'm relieved that she believes me so easily. Yes, only relieved, not guilty.

"It'll be faster to reach if we swim," she says.

I tense. "Not the way I do it."

She smiles. "But you can shift. Why don't you shift into a merman?"

I stiffen. "I don't know,,,"

"You want to get there quickly, right?"

That's exactly what I want. "Okay, show me what to do."

She nods, and then frowns. "But the others—"

"It'll be a quick trip," I reassure her. "There's no reason to wake them."

"And they'll be safe here?" She looks back down the beach.

My gods, she's an amazing actress. I almost believe the concern in her face. Unfortunately for her, I see right through her.

"Of course," I say.

She nods after a second and reaches out for my hand.

I reluctantly slip it into hers.

"I know you're still angry with me," she says. "And you have every right to be, but I promise, I'll make it up to you."

Like hell. "It's okay. I've already forgiven you."

She surprises me with the most incredible smile, then leans up and brushes a kiss against my lips that has my heart racing. "Time to take off your clothes."

My cock hardens. "My clothes?"

"You don't want to destroy them shifting."

Oh. "Okay."

As I remove my clothes, she watches me, her gaze lustful. I hate that I feel a spike of pride that she likes how I look naked. I'm proud until I remember that it's only an act.

Once I'm naked, she walks up to me. Her gaze slides down to where I'm hard-as-fuck. I grit my teeth as she reaches down and strokes me slowly. If I could just forget what her brother said, I could close my eyes and let this beautiful woman stroke me to completion, but I can't forget.

A betrayal is a betrayal. There's no coming back from that.

"We should hurry," I state, swallow, "and get there as soon as possible."

She looks a little sad as her hand drops from my cock, but she still holds my hand as she leads me to the water. We go deeper and deeper until we can disappear beneath the waves. Her hair is damp. Her smile's bright.

"Just imagine becoming a merman. Imagine what it'll feel like. Imagine how your body will feel."

And then she tugs me beneath the water. For one second I panic and want to shoot to the surface, but instead, I remind myself that this is all necessary to deliver her to her brother and get the little creature that can save our lives.

As those thoughts fill my mind, I also remember what she said. I imagine being a merman, what it would feel like. What—I feel my body shifting and changing again. For a second, it's hard to breathe, and then the world seems to explode into color.

Not only can I see more clearly beneath the water, but I'm also breathing under water. I take a deep breath, just to be sure, and then smile. Looking down at myself, I see that I have a blue tail, colorful and bright in a way I never expected. I notice for the first time the stunning pinks and purples of her tail. The colors feel powerful and significant somehow, in a way I don't understand.

"Come on," she says, and her voice rings clearly in my ears.

Still holding my hand, she leads me deeper and deeper beneath the ocean. She points out amazing plants and animals I never imagined, their colors bright and stunning with my new eyes. Then she takes me deeper still. The sea animals grow stranger, and yet just as beautiful in their own way.

I want to ask her where she's taking me, but I'm overwhelmed by it all. I'm experiencing something I know I'll never experience again.

And then as time passes, I see bright lights in the very depths of the ocean. As we swim closer, I'm stunned to see a small city beneath the sea. It looks just the way I imagined some kind of mermaid Atlantis to be.

There are towering rock structures that enclose more of the coral buildings in a strange kind of safety. Bright coral covers every inch of the structures, weaving with blue flowers that light up the darkness. It's beautiful and strange.

Mermaids play in the streets, they swim, they chase one another, they eat and laugh. Many, many of them fuck.

It's almost a shock. No wonder she thinks nothing of nudity. Everyone is naked, and apparently sex is as normal as eating here.

She leads me past it all until we reach a very strange place. It's a place that looks like a necklace of underground volcanoes, only the substance that flows out of it is a stunning pink.

Lovers fuck all along the necklace. And I'm not sure what it is, staring at them or seeing all the nudity, but I feel my arousal increasing with each moment that passes. She takes me further and further, and then tugs me beneath one of the strange pink volcanoes. In the tiny cave, bright flowers illuminate every inch, and moss softens the rock.

"Just shift your tail," she whispers.

And I watch in fascination as her tail fades away, replaced by her legs.

Closing my eyes, I try to imagine doing the same thing, and I'm unbelievably proud when I feel my legs return.

She smiles at me and pushes me back into the glowing moss. Before I can speak, her lips find mine, and she steals my breath with a kiss so powerful that it sends my thoughts spinning away. I feel her pussy come to rest above my cock as she straddles me, and something primitive awakens within me. I must possess this beautiful creature.

Rolling so that I'm on top of her, I capture her wrists and hold them above her head. To my surprise, she wraps her legs around my back. Gripping her ass with my free hand, I angle her, then press my tip into her folds, seeking her entrance.

She leans closer to me, and unable to help myself, I lean closer and kiss her, capturing her lips in a crushing kiss. It's a possessive kiss. I have the unbelievable instinct to claim this woman as my own. I want to make her shout my name and swear that she's mine.

Plunging my shaft deeply inside of her, a shudder runs through my body when she cries out against my lips. I fuck her then, hard and fast, loving her sounds of pleasure, watching her breasts as they bounce with each of my thrusts. I need to hear my name from her sweet lips.

When my balls tighten and my shaft throbs, I force myself to continue to fuck her until she shudders and comes, finally shouting my name. Then, and only then, do I fill her with my seed. I pump in and out, claiming her as my own.

We continue moving against each other for several long seconds until I collapse above her.

"Oh, Clark," she whispers. "I love you."

Her words make every muscle in my body tense. Without answering her, I turn her around. Positioning myself at her ass, I thrust deeply inside. She cries out again. I hold her in place, my hands still around her wrists, and my other hand reaching around to stroke her clit while I fuck her ass.

I don't know what I'm doing. Punishing her for destroying me? For saying the words I long to hear, even while I know they're a lie.

Pretending for a little while longer that I'm not about to betray her, to return her to her people, and call her out for her lies.

I don't know what I'm doing.

I continue to fuck her beautiful tight ass, enjoying her

every sound of pleasure. I enjoy the way her inner-muscles tighten around my shaft and I love it when she comes again and I fill her with my hot cum.

When we're done, I don't pull out of her.

She tries to turn around, but I hold her in place. The second this is done, reality is going to capture us. This will fade away, and we'll be back to enemies.

Even if she doesn't know it yet.

So I kiss her shoulders and her back. I close my eyes and let myself feel my cock still buried deep inside her, and I memorize the feel of it all.

I imagine it'll be years before I touch another woman again.

And I imagine it might be forever before I trust another woman enough to feel this way about one again.

Angrily, I feel myself harden again. Pulling my cock out of her ass, I growl, "turn around and open that pretty little mouth of yours."

I release her lips, and her eyes are wide when she turns around. "Again?"

I don't answer her. I position my cock over her mouth, and my mouth over her sweet pussy. I grasp her ass, and I begin my slow licking of her folds. In the water, I can't quite taste her, but this isn't about tasting her.

This is about something else. Something I don't understand.

I'm lost in touching her. Time has no meaning. The strangeness of making love underneath the water means nothing. It's just me and her in this magical place.

I stroke her legs as I lick her, as I kiss her core. I want my hands on every inch of her, memorizing every line like she's the last thing I'll ever touch. When she orgasms, her hands are buried in my hair. It takes nothing at all to come into her sweet, warm mouth.

Keto's Tale

Then, and only then, do I pull away from her. I go to the mouth of our little cave and stare out into the fantastical mermaid city.

She's at my side in an instant. "Clark?" Her hand touches my shoulder.

I want to shake her off, but I don't. "We need to go. We've wasted too much time already."

"Okay," she says, and she sounds hurt.

But I don't care. I don't know why the hell I fucked her. I don't know why the hell every moment of it seems to be carved into my heart like a scar I can't forget. I do know one thing. I don't plan to waste any more time thinking about it. It's time to deliver this liar to her family... and to save my own.

"To the Lonely Island then," she says.

I don't respond.

She hesitates only a moment. "Remember to shift your tail back."

I nod and concentrate again. The shifting comes easier this time, but my head also pounds horribly. I hiss, holding it in my hands, waiting for the headache to ease.

She's there in an instant, her soft touch moving over my head. "It's okay. It's the effect of the sea dragons' powers on you."

Wincing, I look up at her. "What do you mean?"

"Your semi-immortal body can't handle it long. That's why I need to find my friend and rid you of these powers, before they really hurt you."

For a minute I'm stunned. She's actually telling me? I thought she planned to hide this information from us. She had until now, so what had caused her to finally tell the truth?

"Who's this friend of yours?"

She looks uncertain for a minute. "It's actually a little creature… the golden creature Max told all of you about."

"Why didn't you tell us that before?"

Her dark gaze meets mine. "I was scared. I never intended this to happen, not really. I just wanted to get free from the dragons."

I hate that I believe her. But the little creature was the same one her brother held. And yet, does her one confession negate all her lies?

My mouth curls into an angry line. No. She's still a liar. She's a *monster*.

Her brother wishes to speak to her, so he can. When he's done, we'll get her back, and we'll take the little monster to our Elites and be done with this mission. They'll hear the details, and they'll know for certain that they made a mistake making Max the leader. They'll reinstate me, and there will be no question who was meant to lead our Brotherhood.

We just need to get through the exchange.

"Let's just go," I say.

"You're sure you'll be okay?"

"I will be," I tell her, and I mean it.

I'll be fine when I get rid of this Keto. I'll be able to go back to my other life and just forget her. Forget her face. Forget her touch. Forget the feelings that seem to have awakened inside of me.

I just need to get free from her.

Chapter Twenty-Four

KETO

We've nearly reached the Lonely Island. I'm filled with both elation and confusion. Soon I'll meet Hephaestus, and he'll be able to free me from my collar. My brother will never again be able to make me hurt anyone or anything.

I'll become the second most powerful god of the ocean, second only to the queen of the ocean herself, Amphitrite. My creatures will obey me and only me, and my brother will return to the bottom of the sea… to the place of hidden dangers, where he belongs.

I won't be a slave to anyone, and I'll be able to tell my gargoyles the truth, and see if they can love a monster.

My belly flips, and my gaze goes to Clark, who swims beside me. Sex with him was different. It was still good, but different. His touch was almost angry, demanding, and possessive. It aroused me in a completely unexpected way.

And yet, he feels far away. Like I touched him, but I can't actually touch him. There's an air around him, like he's put up his same wall between us, and I'll never be able to crack through it.

The others might be able to accept who and what I am, but can he?

I pray to any god who might care that he can.

Up ahead, I sense the island. Despite my nerves about what's happened between me and Clark, and what will happen when I tell the gargoyles the truth, I speed up. When we reach the island, I instantly transform into my human form once more. It takes Clark a little longer, but he emerges from the water too, back to his old self.

We step out of the sea and onto the shore, and my gaze sweeps over the tiny place. It hardly seems like a sanctuary, but then, perhaps there's magic I don't feel. I stretch my senses out until I feel a cloaking magic not far ahead of us.

"He's here, isn't he?" I ask.

Clark takes a long minute to answer. "Yes."

"I can feel him," I say. "He's hiding."

I start to move forward. Clark catches my wrist.

I look between his face and my destination. "What is it?"

"You're Keto."

His words drop between us like bombs. I tense, unable to look away from him.

"Yes, I am."

Rage flashes across his face. "You lied to us. You led us on a fake mission to find *you*, tricking us about bullshit men who hurt you and being a slave."

I feel tears prick the corners of my eyes. "You don't understand."

"I understand all I need to."

"No," I say, tears swelling my chest. "I was scared to tell you the truth, but I am a slave. I am my brother's slave, and the man who hurt me was his second-in-command."

"And the sea dragons?" His voice is dry. He doesn't believe me.

Keto's Tale

"They planned to hurt me and eat me. My brother gave me to them in order to have access to their waters."

The rage in his face doesn't dissipate. Instead, he leans forward, his words just a hiss. "I don't believe you."

"Please," I beg.

I want to say more, but suddenly I can't. My collar—it begins to tighten. I claw at it, but it only tightens further and further.

"Keto?" I hear Clark's confused voice, but he feels far away.

My vision goes black, and I hear the sound of my bones breaking. Warm blood leaks from the collar, spilling down my chest.

Someone is suddenly holding me. "Stop! Stop!" Clark's shouting.

And then, the pain subsides.

I'm rasping in breaths. Pain clouds my vision, echoing through me. I'm limp, unable to move, and blood continues to drip down over my flesh.

"What the fuck is this?"

I know that he's here before he speaks. *My brother.* He smiles as he comes closer, filling my cloudy vision.

"I said I'd want time with my dear old sister before I gave her to you… or at least what is left of her." His stare seems to tear through me. "Now, where are your brothers?"

"My brothers?" Clark repeats. "You're supposed to give us the fish! You're supposed to help us get rid of these powers!"

My brother's smile fades. "Are you a fool? We need them here to do it. To pull the powers from them and put it into the dragons."

Suddenly, I see them. Four naked men with the swirling eyes of the dragons.

"Where are our powers, gargoyle?" One of them hisses.

Clark sounds utterly confused. "I thought—"

"Well, you were wrong," my brother says. "We have a deal, and as of now, you've failed to uphold your end of the bargain."

"I—" Clark begins.

"At least he brought my powers." A different dragon-man steps forward.

My brother's eyes flash with rage, but he smiles. "That he did."

He motions with his hand, and one of his minions climbs out of the sea, clutching a small cage with my creature in it. My heart aches at the sight of him. My sweet baby is pale, his color dull. I can't imagine what they've been doing to him… actually, I can, and that only makes it worse.

"Work your powers," my brother commands my creature.

"Wait!" Clark shouts.

But the golden light explodes from the fish and Clark sinks to the ground, dropping me in the sand. I'm still bleeding and gasping around my broken throat when my brother comes closer. He grabs me by the wrist and starts to drag me toward the water.

Clark reaches out to me, winces and curls over his stomach.

"When you bring us your brothers, we will take care of their powers and save your miserable lives," my brother says angrily over his shoulder.

"Keto!" Clark shouts my name.

I hear the enjoyment in my brother's voice. "You can have what's left of her, when we're done."

As we sink beneath the waves, I feel tears rolling down

Keto's Tale

my cheeks. I'm brought back to the time before the gargoyles, when I'd give anything to die, to not suffer anymore at my brother's hands.

I'm sure before this day is over, I'll remember why I felt that way.

Chapter Twenty-Five

MAX

We fly with all our might toward the Lonely Island. My heart's in my throat. For some reason, waking with no sign of Sirena and evidence that Clark had been there scares the hell out of me. I want to think he won't hurt her, but when it comes to his irrational mistrust of women, I'm not really sure what he's capable of.

"There it is!" Arthur shouts, pointing just ahead.

We fly harder.

Steven's at my side in an instant. "What do you think we'll find there?"

I'm the leader. I'm supposed to know everything. But I don't have a clue what to expect. Every single possibility is running through my head, but none of them are good.

When we reach the island, we spot Clark, and instantly know something's wrong. He's kneeling in the water. His hands are dropped at his sides. His face looks bleak, and Sirena is nowhere to be found.

We swoop down, landing near him. My hand itches to reach for my sword, but instead I rush to his side.

Keto's Tale

"Are you okay?"

Clark doesn't look at me.

I grab his face and jerk him to look at me. His eyes are vacant.

"Are you okay?"

His face crumbles. "I think… I think I fucked up."

Ice moves through my veins. "How? Where's Sirena?"

"Not Sirena," he corrects me. "Keto."

"Keto?" *What the hell is he talking about? Has he lost it?*

"Sirena was lying. She was Keto the whole time."

It takes a minute to remember to breathe. "Are you sure?"

He nods, his gaze wild.

My mind goes over everything that we'd experienced since meeting her. My confusion slowly fades. It actually makes perfect sense. She's a goddess, and her creatures? They do seem to be more like monsters than fluffy little bunnies.

I glance up and lock eyes with Steven and Arthur. This can't be why Clark seems like he's been completely destroyed.

"Where is she?"

He stares into the sea. "They took her."

What? "Who took her?" My voice is shaking.

"I fucked up," he says again.

I'm starting to feel scared. "Who took her, Clark? Fuck, talk to us."

I shake him a little, but his expression only becomes more wretched.

"Her brother came to me. He said that the sea dragons needed to take our powers back, or the powers would kill us. He had a little… fish thing. He said it could help reverse it. I had to agree to bring Keto to him in order for him to make the deal."

375

"What did you do?" I feel like I've swallowed a knife.

"They took their powers from me. And they said until I brought the three of you, they would… they would do what they wanted to her."

"Fucking shit!" Arthur shouted, pacing. "Where is she?"

"They took her somewhere under the water. I've been trying to reach her, but… but I can't." He takes a shaky breath. "And she was a slave… but to her brother. I saw him use some kind of magic to tighten her collar around her throat. It… broke her bones. She was bleeding. I think they plan to kill her, even if she'll be able to come back. It's… I can't let them do this. I shouldn't have brought her here. I shouldn't have—"

I rise. "It doesn't matter now. All that matters is getting her back."

"But we can't." He sounds on the edge of something dark.

Arthur rushes to the edge of the water. "I'll try to see if I can get any little creatures to get them to come here." He closes his eyes, spreading his arms out.

But hell if I think that will be enough.

Steven withdraws his sword. "And I'll be ready for them when they come."

"What if they kill her?" Clark asks, sounding broken.

I hit him. Hard. He hits the sand and water, his eyes widening in shock.

"Pull your fucking self together! Find something useful to do!"

He reaches up and touches his mouth, where blood leaks from the corner of his mouth. "Okay."

"Okay," I say, then reach down and help him up.

We stand at the edge of the sea, staring out.

"You said they want their powers back."

Keto's Tale

He nods.

"Then we'll give them back, but only if they give us her."

"They're powerful, Max. They're gods."

I reach for my sword and slowly pull it free from my sheath. "I don't give a fuck."

Arthur turns and drops his arms. "I think… I think they're coming."

He moves to stand beside us, and we all stare out at the water. Long moments pass, moments when I can think of nothing but what they're doing to Keto. It tears at my soul, killing me slowly. She's ours to protect now, Keto or Sirena, I don't really care. It's her I love, despite what they call her.

And then the water seems to pull back.

A man emerges first. I instantly know him as Sirena's—Keto's brother. Their hair is the same auburn color, their eyes the same dark brown. Both of them have the same inhuman beauty. When he smiles, it's one creepy as fuck smile. "You've returned!"

"We're here," I say. "But I don't give a fuck what deal my soldier man and you agreed upon, I'm the leader."

His eyes narrow. "Is that so?"

"Yes."

"And so what, fragile gargoyle, do you demand from a god?" His voice drips of passive-aggressive anger.

"I want Keto."

His entire body stiffens. "I'm afraid we're not quite done with her."

"I want her *now*."

He regards me for a long minute, then shrugs. "If I give her to you now, I have your word that you'll give up the sea dragons' powers without incident?"

"Yes," I agree with ease.

He motions to someone I can't see.

A minute later a beast emerges from the water. Its face is that of a lion, but it has the arms of a man. And he's clutching Keto. A beaten, bloody Keto.

I swear I see red. I leap toward the god, and the waves smack me back against the shore.

The god laughs. "None of that now, gargoyle. I never promised what condition I'd bring her back in."

Steven growls low in his throat. "We're going to kill you for this."

He tilts his head, that creepy grin of his widening. "Oh, if only such a thing was so easy."

The creature approaches the shore, and Arthur is there in an instant, taking Keto from his arms. Blood still runs from the gashes around the collar on her neck. And she doesn't move, other than the unsteady rising and falling of her chest.

"You have what you want now," the god says. "Now the dragons' powers…"

I give a sharp nod, clenching the hilt of my sword harder.

Three naked men emerge from the water, and I'd know the dragons anywhere. Rage swells from their flesh, and their eyes spin both silver and gold.

The god lifts a little cage with a golden fish creature inside, and gold sweeps across us. It tears within my chest and it feels as if they're pulling an organ straight from my body. I can't catch my breath. The pain is excruciating.

And then it ends, and I crumble to my knees.

I don't even have the strength to lift my sword. And as I watch, the men change, shifting and growing until three dragons lift their heads above the water.

My gaze swims as I turn toward my Brothers. We're all on our knees. Keto has tumbled from Arthur's grip, partially in the water, partially hanging out of it. Her eyes are open now, but her mouth remains open, as if in a silent scream.

I want to reach out to her. I want to touch her. But when I try to move, I only tumble over, unable to move.

Clark is beside me in an instant, lifting me beneath his shoulder and righting me. Then, he takes my sword.

"Now, go!" he commands the god and his dragons. "You have your powers back!"

Keto's brother ignores us, turning instead to the dragons. "I have done what was asked of me."

The white dragon growls, a sound that vibrates through my chest. "You are now allowed in our seas." His gaze swings back to us. "And now we will have our revenge."

The god laughs. "As was our deal."

"No, our deal—" Clark begins.

"Was that I wouldn't harm you or your gargoyle friends," the god says. "I never said a word about what the dragons could do to you."

"I'm going to kill you!" Clark shouts.

The god laughs. "I think one of us is going to die today, but it won't be me."

Clark's skin shifts to grey and wings sprout on his back. He moves as if he plans to fight the bastard, but a dragon's head shoots towards him.

His sword darts out, slashing the white dragon's muzzle. It rears back

"That was a mistake, gargoyle!" he roars, and the ground beneath us shakes.

I try again to rise, but my knees buckle before I can. Beside me, I see Steven and Max struggling, but neither one of them can lift their sword arm.

I can't even shift into my stone-form.

For the first time in my life, I think I'm actually going to die.

There's no way out of this situation. It's one gargoyle against four sea dragons. The rest of us lie here useless.

In that moment, I make a decision. Falling to my side, I reach out and touch Keto's face. She's shaking, her entire body wracked with the uncontrollable movements of a person in more pain than their body can process. Tears leak from her eyes. She doesn't speak, but I can still sense something beneath her surface.

She wants to fight. She wants to live.

I admire her for that.

If I'm going to die, I want it to be looking at her, touching her. The waves wash over us as we lie on the shore. I can hear Clark shouting. I can hear his blade striking. I can hear his cries of pain. But I don't want to watch. There's nothing I can do now.

And then, something changes in the air.

Something I don't understand.

Turning my head slightly, I look toward the water.

Around the sea dragons, one monster after another emerges from the waves. I watch as they come forward. First the baby hydra, then the glowing beast who healed Steven. One that looks like something sharp and poisonous. One with a dozen dark heads. More and more of the creatures emerge from the depths of the waters until they spread out in every direction.

The white dragon's head jerks toward Keto's brother. "Tell them to stop."

Her brother's eyes are wide. "I can't. They're under her control."

"Make her stop them, then."

A sound like a powerful hissing comes. It's from a massive creature who rises higher and higher, its long neck large enough to circle all the dragons and yank them from the waters. It stares down at all of them, dripping water. "Our Mother can tell us to stop, but we won't obey. She is a goddess. She is a queen. And she has bowed to unworthy wretches like you for far too long."

I can sense the dragons are afraid. Hell, I'm afraid.

"We'll leave," the white dragon whispers.

"I was already done," Keto's brother said, backing to hide behind his lion-headed minion.

The giant snake creature flashes its teeth. "Too late."

I've never imagined the sound of dragons screaming, but I hear the sound now. As the beasts launch themselves at them and Keto's brother, there is no escape. There's only a pool of blood that darkens the sea. There's only the sound of screaming, bones cracking, and then silence.

Utter silence.

When I look at Keto, she's smiling.

The many monstrous beings move toward the shore. They touch her, nudge her, and then move back so that the glowing beast can place its tentacles on her.

Her lips are cracked and bleeding, her cheeks covered in deep slashes, but her raspy voice comes. "I called them. And I knew they'd come." Her gaze connects with mine. "I needed to protect all of you. This was all… my fault."

Her head lolls to the side and her breathing stops.

Chapter Twenty-Six

KETO

My eyes open. I don't know where I am. I'm not in the water and not on an island. The sky above me is a crisscrossing of wood that makes no sense.

And my throat hurts. It's so painfully dry that I suddenly want nothing more than a drink.

I struggle to sit up and someone is instantly at my side. *Clark.* He lifts my back and presses a water cup to my lips. I drink and drink, not stopping until the cup is empty.

When he draws it back, I can't stop taking in deep breaths. Had it just been my imagination, or did I die?

"Wh—?"

"You're in the gargoyle sanctuary," he explains, his voice soft.

I'm… where? Oh no, the sanctuary!

"Am I a prisoner?" I ask, my heart racing.

Clark shakes his head. "No, we've spoken to the Elites. They don't want you as a prisoner anymore. They understand that you were only doing what you had to. You're here because we brought you to Hephaestus."

The blacksmith god?

I see movement out of the corner of my eye and turn slightly. A massive man rises from a bench. Metal of every kind lies scattered about the table, and not far from him is a raging fire in a metal container of some kind.

"Good morning," he says.

The god's voice is deep, a rumbling that comes from his chest like the voice of an ancient tree. Like most immortals, he appears to be a young man. His dark beard is long and tangled. His arms are bigger than my head. He screams of power.

This… this is the man that made my collar for me. Who made Cerebrus' collar for her.

Rage uncoils inside of me. As he leans over my bed, I react without thinking, punching him square in the face. He stumbles back, and I know it's more because of surprise than that I actually harmed this mountain of a man.

"Keto!" Clark shouts.

"You bastard!" I try to scream, but my voice comes out nothing more than an angry whisper. "You did that to me. To all of us."

I see the moment he understands. His face falls, and a misery comes over him. "I'm sorry."

"That's not enough!"

He turns his back to me and goes to the table. Turning back, he holds one item up… a broken circle. And then another item, a tool of some kind.

"I removed your collar."

My hands fly to my neck. My bare neck. Beneath my fingertips are a sea of scars… but the metal, it's gone.

"We brought you here right away," Clark says, and there's nervousness in his voice. "We were afraid that your brother would hurt you again when he was reborn in the Underworld."

I nod, shocked, still stroking my bare neck. "You did the right thing."

He looks relieved.

I'm amazed. *Am I… really free? Free forever?*

"I can't believe it," I say, and tears form in my eyes. "He made me do so many things. He controlled me for so many years."

Clark shushes me. "We know. It's okay."

I slowly rise, and Clark helps me, his touch gentle.

"I'm alive," I say.

He gives a ghost of a smile. "You are."

"And free."

His gaze runs lovingly over my face. "You are."

I throw my arms around his neck. "It's… a miracle."

Maybe I cry a little. Maybe I cry a lot. But Clark holds me all along, stroking my back and murmuring words of reassurance.

At last, I pull back, feeling silly. "I'm sorry, I just can't believe it."

He touches my face hesitantly. "It's okay. You deserve it."

I try to stretch, but my muscles feel strange. "How long was I out?"

He doesn't answer me for a long minute.

Nervousness blossoms in my belly. "How long?"

"A month."

My jaw drops. "A *month*."

He nods. "You were almost dead. If it wasn't for your creature—"

I can't believe it. My body must have undergone a lot of trauma to need that much time to heal.

Keto's Tale

A shiver moves through me. Flashes of my beating roll through my mind.

I don't want to think about that. I don't want to remember that.

"Well, I'm alive now." I sit up straighter. "And I have something important to do."

"There's, uh, more," Clark says.

I shake my head. "I don't care." Turning to the blacksmith god, I level him with my most serious stare. "Will that tool remove any collar?"

He nods. "Yes."

"Even Cerberus's?"

His entire body stiffens, and his eyes fill with regret. "Yes," he says, his voice no louder than a whisper.

"Then I'm going to her and we're going to free her too."

I straighten my back and push away from Clark, standing fully on my own two feet.

"Keto—"

"No, she's suffering. Like I was. I won't be able to rest until she's free."

I stumble toward the god and take the tool from his hand without a word. It takes me a second to figure out the way out of the building, but then I continue stumbling out the door, looking for a body of water.

Outside, the other gargoyles are walking up the path. I freeze. They all look as much of a mess as Clark. Thinner. Paler. Their hair a disaster.

"Guys—"

They take off toward me. Arthur pulls me in his arms, squeezing me gently, and then the men are holding me, and talking all at once.

I laugh. "I'm fine. I promise."

"You're awake!" Arthur exclaims.

I laugh again. "Yes, and I have something to take care of."

They all freeze. Max speaks slowly like I've lost my mind. "You need to lie down and rest."

"No." I shake my head. "I need to help Cerebus."

All eyes go to Clark. "Didn't you tell her?"

He's slow to answer. "I didn't have a chance yet."

My muscles tighten. "Whatever it is, is it more important than helping someone?"

Everyone is silent. Steven brushes my hair back from my face and tucks it behind one ear. "You're pregnant."

What? Slowly I look down at my belly. I'm wearing a little white dress. But I don't have a belly. In fact, there's no evidence at all that what they say is true.

I glance back at them in confusion.

"You're not very far along," Steven continues. "But the healer confirmed it. You're carrying our child."

Pregnant? Me? With a child of my own? I touch my belly in wonder, imagining the little child growing within me.

It's a miracle. More than I ever imagined.

But this news doesn't change what I need to do.

"Okay. But I still need to help Cerberus."

Max shakes his head. "I don't think you understand. Gargoyle babies are rare. It's almost impossible to get pregnant, and even harder to stay that way. You can't just take off into danger, not when you're carrying our child."

I have this strange feeling I can't explain. Like my collar is closing around my neck once more.

"I'm free," I say, and then realize that doesn't truly explain anything. "You can't make me stay here."

"I don't think you're explaining it right," Steven says to Max, then looks at me. Very gently, he touches my belly. "We've spent a month watching over you, making sure you were safe, hoping and praying that you'd be safe. When the

Keto's Tale

healer told us you were pregnant, we feared for you even more. We can't just have you wake up and leave… we can't."

"And I won't be your prisoner!" I tell them.

Silence stretches between us.

"Keto," Max begins.

I draw myself up. "Yes, that's who I am. And I'm not ashamed. You might think I'm a monster. You might think I'm dangerous." My gaze slides to Clark. "And you might think I'm a liar. But I don't care. I won't be ashamed of who I am anymore, or the things I've had to do to survive."

"We don't want you to be ashamed," Steven says.

Arthur gives an uncertain smile. "We know who you are, and we don't care."

"You're *gargoyles*!" I say.

No matter how much I care for them. No matter how much I want to be with them. I won't allow all my happiness to depend on them. I'm free now, and I can have a real future.

Pregnant or not.

"We don't care," Arthur begins again. "We love you for you."

I shake my head. "No, you can't."

"We do!" Steven emphasizes. "And we can't be happy without you. We have *nothing* without you."

Max's voice sounds broken. "I know we couldn't protect you when you really needed us, but we won't ever let that happen again. We'll care for you and our child in every way."

Their words are like everything I want to hear and more, but somehow I can't seem to believe them. Something's missing.

Slowly, I turn to Clark.

Our gazes meet, and his expression crumbles. "I'm so

sorry. They were right. I let my fucking messed up past cloud my logic and I almost got us all killed. My mistake got you hurt—" His voice cracks. "So hurt." His entire body shakes. "And it was all because of me. I understand if you hate me. I understand if you can never forgive me."

Time seems to stand still. I go over the events since meeting these gargoyles. I told so many lies, I hid so many things. Clark made some mistakes, but did I blame him? I searched my soul and the answer came with ease: no.

I blamed my brother.

I blamed his second-in-command.

I blamed the sea dragons.

But I didn't blame him. "Do you feel the same way about me that they do?"

I hold my breath.

"Yes." The word tears from his lips. "Even if I don't deserve to."

There it is. A feeling inside of me. The one that says this is where I was always meant to be. That these men were the ones I was always meant to be with. Only, this time, it feels right. There's nothing missing, because I have the love of all my men.

Taking a step towards him, I pull him into my arms. "It's okay. It wasn't your fault."

His voice is filled with misery. "It was."

I shake my head and draw back from him, touching his face. "It was their fault not yours. They're expert liars, Clark. You can't blame yourself for falling for it."

"I do," he says, drawing himself up taller.

Leaning forward, I brush a light kiss on his lips. "You'll forgive yourself one day. Trust me."

His eyes shimmer. "I do…. trust you. With all my heart."

I turn back and look at all my men.

Max clears his throat. "So, you'll stay with us?"

"No," I say.

Panic unfolds in their gazes.

I rush the rest of my words out quickly. "At least not until I help Cerberus."

They all have the same mirrored look of relief.

I laugh. "When I've done that, I'll stay with you. As long as I have water."

"You do," Arthur interrupts.

"And *freedom*," I emphasize.

"As much as we can give," Max rushes out.

Then I smile. "Well, let's go help my friend and get on with our long, *happy* lives."

They grin, and I'm suddenly kissed and spun between them. I laugh. The world looks brighter. The air smells sweeter. The pregnancy and my freedom haven't quite settled in yet, but hope for the future has.

And it's the best feeling in this world.

Chapter Twenty-Seven

KETO

I linger by the mouth of the cave. The torches light the space around me, flickering in the darkness. And the mist curls around my feet, as if beckoning me further, but no matter how many times I shout for my friend, she fails to emerge.

She's probably a bleeding, broken mess somewhere along the tunnel to the Underworld.

The thought makes my gut clench. I wish it was just a stray bad idea, but the truth is that I'm probably right. And that I can't go searching for her.

So I select a dark rock and scribble my note into the side of the cave, careful not to say anything that could have the wrong person learning what I've planned. And then, very carefully, I place the bundle containing Hephaestus's tool. I tuck it against the wall of the cave and wedge a rock on top of it.

Rising, I frown. I wish I could have given it to her. But at least it's here when she returns.

Sending a prayer to the gods, I hope that it falls into her hands.

Keto's Tale

Then, turning, I leave the Isle of the Demons behind, promising that one day I'll return.

But I'm not yet done. I have another stop to make. To my dear friend Lamia. I can't imagine what she's felt since killing those men on the beach to protect me, but I'll ensure she knows that she has nothing to feel sorry for.

And I'll tell her what I know now for the first time, there is hope for us. There are people who can love us monsters.

We just need to find the right ones.

Chapter Twenty-Eight

KETO

*O*ur home beside the long river that runs through the gargoyle sanctuary is beautiful. It's nestled so close to the water I can take two steps out and dive into the warm and welcoming river. And what's even better, it connects with the ocean, just beyond the invisible shield that protects the sanctuary from the outside world. I still have my freedom, my creatures, and so much more.

Stretching my feet out, I kick the water gently, sitting on the shore and watching the sun sink below the horizon. My belly has gotten bigger. The child inside is still healthy and a source of pride for us all.

I'd be completely happy if only I'd found Lamia and Cerberus. And yet, I'd left them both messages, as well as, the tools to perhaps find love and freedom of their own one day.

Arthur plops down beside me. He rests his big hand on my belly, almost absentmindedly. "Did the little one like his dinner?"

I laugh. "Yes, and so did I."

He leans forward and kisses me, taking my breath away. "You know I live but to serve you."

I grasp his shirt and pull him back. "Then serve me again."

His mouth descends on mine, and his tongue slides inside. Every stroke of his tongue against mine has my thoughts spinning. Without breaking our kiss, I move to straddle him.

He groans, and I fumble with the button on his jeans. At last I pop it open and slide down his zipper, gripping his cock and pulling it free.

I'm pushing his tip into my core when Max steps out the door and swears. "Fucking hell, couldn't you guys at least make it inside?"

I break our kiss. "Stop complaining and put your dick in my ass."

He drops the little towel in his hands and reaches for his shirt, yanking it off. He's struggling out of his clothes. When he finally makes it behind me, his big hands press me forward, and I feel his tip touch my back entrance.

Moaning, I sink lower onto Arthur and Max slowly plunges inside.

We start to fuck, loudly and with abandon.

Steven and Clark appear in the doorway a second later. Neither says a word as they struggle out of their clothes, and then I have two big dicks in my hands.

I ride my big gargoyles and stroke them. I'm no longer uncertain, no longer nervous. I touch them like a woman who knows just what to do to make them come, which I do.

Only, it's me who goes rushing off the edge, shouting and moving between them as my orgasm consumes me. I barely feel the cum that slides down my hands. But I sure as hell feel the hot seed that fills my ass and pussy.

At last, slowly, we all collapse.

"The other gargoyles—are going to—complain again," Steven pants.

"It's their fault for always thinking we're in trouble," I say as a shudder moves through me.

"Or maybe you shouldn't scream so loudly they all come running," Clark teases, grinning.

I swat at him. "You like me loud."

I hear movement not far from our house.

Max sighs and reaches for his boxers. "I'll meet them outside and tell him no one was murdered. Again."

I laugh and slide from my men and into the water. It's warm and just about the perfect ending to my long day. Okay, maybe all the cock was a perfect ending, but the warm river certainly helped.

"You coming inside soon?" Arthur asks.

"Soon," I promise him, then dive beneath the waters.

It still feels like a dream to me. I have men who love me. A home. A child on the way. And my freedom.

I always thought the things I'd done in my past made me unworthy of happiness or love.

Being wrong has never felt so good.

And then I think of Cerberus and my other monster-sister. *I hope they'll find love too.*

Because now I know the truth: even monsters can be loved. There's hope for us all.

Celaeno's Fate

Chapter One

CELAENO

I am described quite simply as *the darkness* by those who fear to anger me. And by the others? A creature of nightmares. A horrifying being with cruelty to spare.

But the truth? The truth is that I'm none of those things.

I'm just... a woman. A shifter. Caught in a lie that was told so many times that it became the truth to all but me. Sometimes late at night, I even whisper to myself, "You're not a monster," because I fear that hearing it so many times might make it true.

All the many lifetimes that I've lived have been filled with heartache and loneliness that eat at my very core. And yet, I still hope that this time things will be different. It feels as if I've finally found a place I belong.

"Cel, you daydreaming again?" Ashley says from behind me.

I startle, raising my head from where it'd fallen on my palm. I'd been so lost in thought, staring out at the busy city and enjoying our quiet little coffee shop, that I hadn't heard her come in through the back entrance.

Turning, I face Ashley. She's late again, but I don't mind. She's the closest thing I've had to a sister since my sisters abandoned me. She's different from the few beings I've grown close to in the past. For one, she's a human, a very pretty human with long legs, blonde hair, and a heart-shaped face. For two, she's young, fun, and social.

Not at all like the grumpy witches who I've been grateful to talk to in the past.

"I was just enjoying the silence."

She looks at her reflection in the metal surface of the display case and rubs some lipstick off of her teeth. "I hate the silence. Give me a busy day with hot business men coming in and out, and I don't need anything else."

I laugh. Ashley loves men, and she's good with them. Something I envy about her.

"Don't worry, I'm sure your latest guy will be here any minute. It's almost his coffee break, right?"

She grins. Leaning down to look at her very low cut shirt, she unbuttons yet another button to show off her lacy pink bra underneath. "Yeah, and it's been almost two weeks of flirting. This guy is definitely making me work for it."

I grab my rag off the counter and start to wipe everything down again. "You really think he's the one making *you* work for it?"

She saunters up to me and holds her arm out. A little gold bracelet hangs from it. "He slipped me this last time."

I touch one of the little links. "It's beautiful."

"It really is." Sighing, she drops it. "Would it be okay if you covered me for a while after he comes in?"

I know what that means. *More loud sex in the back.* The thought almost makes me laugh. Listening to her has got to be one of the most uncomfortable things I've had to do in my long lives.

But I don't *really* mind. Nothing about her bothers me. Not even that she's usually late and takes a lot of breaks, because she talks to me. She makes me feel normal and included. She calls me when she's sad and crying about whatever has gone wrong in her life. She even trusts me enough to ask for favors.

She really does make me feel like a sister.

I look up, meeting her gaze. "Of course, whatever you need."

"Awesome! Thanks!"

I go to the sink and wash the rag out. "Just, this time try not to knock flour all over everything."

Her laugh makes me smile. "That guy was like a rabbit with a carrot." Then she winks. "A very *big* carrot."

Man, it feels nice to act as young as I look. "I'm glad it wasn't a mini one."

"Oh no, it was big and hard and quite the perfect snack."

We're both laughing like fools when her latest find strides in. This time, he doesn't even glance at me or pretend to buy one of our drinks or specialty desserts. His gaze is solely focused on her.

"Damn, you look beautiful," he says.

She gives her fake, flirty little laugh. "Thanks. And I'm even wearing your gift."

He crosses the room and smirks. "Glad you like it. Any ideas on how you'll thank me?"

I almost roll my eyes. Does he want some wine with that *cheese*? But, of course, Ashley doesn't seem to mind his cheesy line. Or that he sounds like some asshole in a bad movie.

Grabbing his tie, she leads him into the back. "How about you help me with some… cleaning?"

Why doesn't she just pretend he's a plumber and tell him she needs her pipes cleaned? It'd be more subtle. I grin like an idiot at my own joke and turn up the store's music when her shouts and their pounding against the counter gets to be too much. A couple of customers come in, glance curiously at the back, and order their drinks and donuts to go. I don't blame them. If they're half as horny and lonely as I am, that's the last thing they want to hear.

A few minutes later, her new guy comes out of the back. He adjusts his tie and dusts off the powdered sugar covering the front of his suit. He doesn't say a word to me before leaving. I feel a little flip in my stomach. I doubt he'll be back. That's one thing about being as old as I am. You get a sense for people, and I think he's gotten what he wants.

Going toward the back, I knock on the little swinging door. "You decent?"

"Come in!" she calls, sounding satisfied with herself.

When I come back, she's sitting on our metal countertop against the wall, buttoning her shirt. Dozens of donuts are on their wire racks next to her, covered in powdered sugar. And now her clothes are covered in it too.

"So how was Mr. Gold Bracelet?"

She shrugs. "Good enough, but I don't think I'll be going for round two."

Then I listen as she tells me about a new bouncer at her favorite club and how he said she'd look beautiful in diamonds. I love listening to people talk to me like I matter, but I also feel this itch to get back to the front. Papa Rye pays us to run his shop. He might treat me like his granddaughter, but Ashley *is* his real granddaughter. I'm here to work, and I always want to do the best job I can to thank him.

When she's just about to launch into another story about a bitch she met in the club the other night, I open my mouth to tell her we should talk at the front of the store, but then my gaze falls on something.

"Comet!"

She freezes. "What?"

"The comet," I repeat, running over to the donuts.

There, leaning over in the middle of the donuts, is Ashley's favorite cleaning product. I've told her time and time again to put it away in the back when she's done with it. Chemicals are the last thing you want just sitting around with food, but she never listens. Now, the powder has covered the donuts, along with the powdered sugar. I can't tell looking at everything what's safe and what's not.

"We have to throw it all out," I say, frowning.

We'll have to tell Papa Rye about this. Otherwise he'll wonder why this month's numbers aren't adding up. I don't want to, but he's going to ask.

Ashley scrambles off the counter and picks up the can of cleaning supplies. "I don't think we really need to throw *all* of it away. Maybe just the couple next to it?"

I shake my head. "That has bleach in it. If anybody eats any, they could be really sick. It's just not worth the risk."

She throws out the couple of donuts that were directly next to the comet with loud plunks straight into the massive trashcan. "You're just being a worrywart. Look, all better."

My stomach flips. I've never had to stand up against Ashley before, but I just can't do it. Kids and older people come in here, customers I've grown to care about. If there's even a tiny chance…

"Would you eat them?" I ask, hoping to get her to change her mind without directly confronting her.

Her nose wrinkles. "I'm not throwing these out. Papa will get mad."

I try to gentle my voice. "We'll tell him together, okay?"

For the first time, she looks at me the way she looks at other women. Her eyes narrow, her mouth pulls into a thin line, and something flashes in her gaze.

I wring my hands together. I don't want to fight with her. I really, really don't.

"Please," I say.

Out front, I hear the bell on the door jingle.

Glad for the temporary distraction, I run for the front. Maybe with enough time, Ashley will realize that what I'm saying makes sense.

Mrs. Andrew and her sweet son are here. She smiles at me when I race over to the counter. "Hi dear, can we get the usual? Your strongest coffee for me, a strawberry shake for the little guy, and two powdered donuts."

I nod, ringing it up on the cash register. But then I look in the case and freeze.

"Uh, sorry, we're out of donuts."

The door to the back hits the wall as it swings open. "Actually," Ashley says, in her sweetest voice. "I just made some fresh ones."

No…

I turn slowly, my stomach dropping as she carries the wire rack of contaminated donuts out.

The little boy squeals in delight, and Ashley reaches for a plate.

"No!" I say, the seriousness of my tone surprising even me.

Ashley freezes and turns to me with innocent eyes. "Why not?"

Celaeno's Fate

I look back at Mrs. Andrews and her son. "Sorry, those aren't for sale."

She looks confused. "Why not?"

"They... they just aren't."

The door of the shop chimes again, and I look up in horror, spotting Papa Rye. He's trimmed his white beard, and he has his finest gold cane, the one with a little donut on top. He's smiling too, and I swear I'm going to puke.

"How's it going, girls?"

Ashley pipes up first. "This customer just wants her usual, drinks and donuts."

"But she said I can't have the donuts..." Mrs. Andrew says, trailing off.

Papa Rye's clouded eyes turn to me. "Why not?"

"Uh..."

What do I do? What do I say?

"Oh, my gosh!" Ashley suddenly shouts, emphasizing each word. "Are these the ones you got cleaning chemicals on? I told you to throw those out!"

My mouth drops open. "N—no..."

Mrs. Andrews grabs her son's hand. "Chemicals? Cel, are you serious? You were going to feed us something that'd make us sick? I'd never expect something like that from you."

I shake my head. *This can't be happening.*

Suddenly, the woman is dragging her son out the door, glaring at me. "You should be ashamed of yourself."

My head feels light, and I swear I must be trapped in a nightmare. This can't actually be happening. Mrs. Andrews was my first customer, a little over a year ago. She's never looked at me like that before, and I feel like from this moment on she'll only have that look for me.

"Celaeno?" Papa Rye says my full name in complete disbelief. "Is what Ashley said true?"

I open my mouth, and then Ashley breaks into tears and runs to her grandfather. He holds her as she sobs on his shoulder, and I feel the knot in my belly slowly untangling. She's going to tell him the truth. She's going to fix this thing.

"She told me if I tried to stop her, she'd blame it on me!" she wails.

I swear I sink into the ground, my bones melting. My mind is blown. I can't believe her fake tears and pointing fingers. It feels like something children would be involved in, not an immortal being. And yet, I'm trapped in this unbelievable situation, and I don't know how to get out of it.

Papa Rye looks up at me really slowly, and our eyes meet. I think a part of me hoped he wouldn't believe her. I mean, I've never seen someone cry as convincingly as Ashley, but I really thought he'd see through it. I've never given him a reason to think I'm that kind of person. Now he is looking at me with complete disgust.

I'm pretty sure my heart turns to dust.

"I didn't," I whisper, trying to talk around the tears gathering in my throat. "I wouldn't."

He closes his eyes, and suddenly he looks older. "Give me your apron."

I shake my head, tears blurring my vision. "Please don't."

"Your apron," he says, simply.

My legs are shaking as I move around the counter and toward him, my fingers struggling to untie the knot at my waist. At last, it comes undone, and I pull the apron off from around my neck.

Standing just feet in front of him, I see one of my tears hit the polished floor. "I would never give someone something that would make them sick. I'd never say that to Ashley. I'm your family."

After a long moment, he reaches out for the apron. "*We're* family. I'm afraid we were mistaken to treat you the same."

My fingers are numb as they let go of the blue apron I wore with such pride. He pulls it away and holds it against his granddaughter's back. She peeks up at me, her makeup smeared by tears. Her expression is one of interest, as if she's evaluating my reaction.

"Time to go, Celaeno," he says, his voice uncharacteristically gruff.

I stumble toward the door. And for the first time, I realize how powerful my emotions are. I freeze, fingers curled around the handle. I can't be this out of control. It's dangerous.

Pull yourself together. You've experienced real heartache. This is nothing…

But in my mind, I sense a storm brewing. And I know this isn't nothing. This is something powerful on the verge of unleashing.

And I can't let it.

Chapter Two

CELAENO

Swiping at my tears, I pull on the tattered shreds of my control and force my sadness down. I cannot let myself feel. I need to walk away and get as far from this city as possible before I lose it.

Opening the door, my chest aches at the familiar jingle of the bell, but I don't look back. I step out into the city. A cool, crisp wind slams into me, the air charged with nature's power. Autumn's perfect wind and grey clouds whisper of rain. I try to focus on that, not the people walking on the sidewalk, bundled up and hurrying along. Not my birds.

But despite my best intentions, my gaze moves up. Birds of every kind line the rooftops, staring down at me. I see the pigeons, loyal and relentless. They're flanked by songbirds, who bring their powerful voices and sharp claws. The hawks ignore their usual prey and focus on me, their mother. The mother of all birds.

The door behind me jingles again. I whirl, not sure what to expect.

Ashley is standing in the doorway. She just stares at me. "Listen…"

What's left of my heart lifts, waiting for her apology, waiting for any kindness that can let me forgive her, my only friend.

"I could still really use your help moving next week, and you said you'd put the moving truck on your card."

You have got to be kidding me. I'm staring. I know I am. My thoughts honestly can't make sense of her words. No one is this awful. Right?

Rage heats within my chest, turning the ashes of my heart into glowing embers of fire.

"*You*," I begin, and then I take a deep breath. "You lied. *You* blamed me for something you did. *You* made Mrs. Andrews think I was a *monster*. *You* made Papa hate me. *You* made him fire me!"

She puts one hand on her hip. "I did not! You blamed me for those chemicals when we both know it was you! I don't make mistakes like that. You're the klutz! You're the one who's there all the time, not me! So don't blame me for your mistake!"

People have stopped to stare at us, but I don't care.

"I don't use comet! I don't put fucking cleaning products out with food, because I'm not a complete dumbass, like you! There's no way in hell I did it, and we both know it. So own your shit!"

My finger is flying, jabbing closer and closer to her chest with each word.

For one brief second I see it on her face. She knows she did it. She knows everything is her fault. She knows she can't win.

To close the deal, she bursts out crying like someone who has been struck across the face.

A man steps forward. "Are you okay?"

More people crowd around us.

"She," Ashley sobs, pointing at me. "Tried to poison our customers. When I tried to stop her, she started shouting at me! She's blaming me for getting her fired, just because I told the truth."

"That's not what happened, you bitch!" The embers in my chest have grown to flames. I'm not crazy. Everyone might be falling for her act, but I'm not.

I replay everything that's happened, breathing hard. None of this was my fault. I didn't do anything. Right? I think I'm losing my mind.

"Why don't you just leave her alone?" the man growls, glaring in my direction.

Leave *her* alone?

"You've got to be freaking kidding me! She's a bitch! She's a selfish user who doesn't care about anyone but herself!"

She clutches her chest. "You were my best friend," she wails.

Two men step in front of her and one of them draws himself up in a threatening pose. "Leave her alone."

"No!" I shout at him. "Because I'm right! She's the liar!"

The crowd closes in around me and everyone shouts at once, calling me names. Someone is holding Ashley as she leans against the man, snuggling into his suit.

My head spins. They're comforting *her*. My world has fallen down around me, and they're comforting *her*.

"Apologize to your friend!" a woman demands, her face suddenly inches from mine.

Her face swims in my vision. "No."

"Your words were venomous, awful," she spits out at

Celaeno's Fate

me. "I've never heard someone talk like that about someone else."

I stare her down. "She's the problem, not me."

"Get out of here, bitch!" I hear a shout and suddenly, a drink hits my shoulder.

I turn and look at the soda dripping from the sleeve of my grey shirt. That fire inside of me? It explodes.

The screeching of birds fills my ears as their wings flap all around us.

Screams tear through the air. Birds start pecking everyone in sight, descending upon them like a plague. They're clawing at Ashley's hair and face, leaving bloody gouges from their talons. The humans are scattering, running away as fast as they can. *They always run.*

"No," I whisper, trying to calm the fire inside of me, but it won't calm.

"Stop," I command my birds, but they don't hear me. Instead, they *feel* me. They don't hear me when they feel my emotions so powerfully.

When I'm out of control, they're out of control. *I need to calm myself.*

But I can't. I'm angry. I'm heartbroken. I'm lost.

I run around the building, slipping into an alley. I transform within seconds, my bones breaking and shifting.

I know the moment I've become a raven. My wings spread, and I launch into the sky. I circle the street once, seeing that some people have taken refuge in shops. But others are still being chased by my birds. Ashley lies on the ground, and my birds cover her like a blanket of feathers. Her screams fill the air.

If I could stop them now, I would. But if I remain here, my emotions won't calm. Instead, I fly as far and as fast as I can to my safe place. The air whips around me, cool and filled with the scents of a city. I'm aware of all of it, but underneath I'm in a web of turmoil.

When I land on my roof I shift once more, my knees hitting the ground roughly. My palms press against the cool concrete as I get my balance. I'm so angry. I can't believe that one lying woman—a person I considered my best friend—has destroyed everything. My family. My job. My whole life is gone and I have nothing to show for it. I'm so angry...

The anger leaves me like a flash of wind and I'm sobbing, my entire body shaking. The fire in my heart cools into nothing.

I cry until there are no tears left, and then, I cry more. The sobs come from my belly and explode through me.

It doesn't take long before I feel feathers against me. Tiny heads press alongside my body, rubbing against me, trying to bring me comfort. I open my eyes and stare into the wise face of a hawk. He lowers his head and our foreheads press together.

"Thank you," I whisper to them all.

Their presence makes me feel less alone, but more than that, having them here with me means that they're no longer hurting the humans.

The myths might say I'm a monster, a cruel harpy with the body of a bird and the face of a woman, a grotesque thing without kindness or empathy.

But like I said, I'm none of those things.

As much as I want to pretend that Ashley crying in pain is satisfying, it's not. I don't want to hurt anyone just because I'm hurting. I just wish I could feel my own feelings without my birds sensing it. If I could, there wouldn't even be an ounce of truth to the rumors.

I'd just be me.

My birds warm me with their bodies, and more tears

fall. I'm no longer out of control, but the tears keep coming. I've lost so much. In the next few weeks, Ashley will have comfort. She'll have Papa and people to lean on. They'll tell her I'm awful. They'll tell her the angry birds were a freakish problem outside of her control.

But me? I'll be alone with my birds. With nothing.

There's no point in me remaining here, but I don't know where else to go. I've seen the world. And there's no place in it for me.

So I keep crying.

I think this is one of the lowest moments in all my lives. I have hit rock bottom.

A disturbance among the birds causes me to open my eyes.

I'm startled when I see the most beautiful man imaginable leaning over me. His hair is the color of the deepest night. His eyes are dark, not brown, but an impossibly deep black that seems to go on forever. His face is chiseled as if by a loving hand, and his body is massive, like a titan of old.

"I—"

Out of nowhere, his big fist punches me in the face.

My head snaps back as my vision goes black.

I come to with the sensation that I can't breathe. Something cold is being tightened around my throat. I hear my birds shrieking, their comforting feathers gone.

I blink as my vision returns, but I still can't move. He's on top of me, holding my arms above my head. Fear seizes my heart. My instincts tells me to shift, to escape whatever he has planned.

I reach for my other form—and nothing. It's just not there.

"That's right," he whispers above me, his mouth

curling into a cruel smile. "You can't shift. There'll be no escape for you, monster."

For one terrible moment I struggle with all my might, and then something inside of me twists. I really can't fight against someone this much stronger than me. Not like this. *So what can I do?*

Chapter Three

ENDER

We're supposed to stay hidden in this fucking alley, but I can't seem to relax. My instincts are going crazy. We were sent here to find a monster, and we damn well found one. Over and over I can picture those birds attacking the humans. We'd watched from the building, wanting more than anything to intervene, but Grey made it clear. The Elites had sent us here to collect the monster. If we gave away the fact that we were near, we'd never figure out which of the people below was the harpy.

So we'd stood. And watched. And witnessed the tiny woman race into the alley and shift.

My heartbeat speeds up as I imagine her. *I can't believe she's a harpy!*

Old tales of the harpies filter through my thoughts. They're supposed to be monstrous creatures. Beings with the faces of women, with wings and sharp claws. They were creatures who abducted people and tortured them. Guardians of the Underworld.

This woman… she was none of these things, so far. Except for violent.

She was tiny. So tiny that I can't imagine her small frame containing all the power that she's supposedly capable of. And instead of holding herself with confidence, or even anger, she just seemed… lost. Almost sad.

"Was this what you expected?" Journey asked, his tone troubled.

I try to sound casual. "No, I kind of thought we'd find a monster in a cave filled with human bones."

He doesn't laugh. He just continues to stare off toward the busy road. "I'm glad we'd prepared for the possibility of her being a shifter. And that the rumors about her controlling birds was true." Journey doesn't sound happy.

"Then everything is going well, right?" I ask, studying him.

The big guy is leaning against the other side of the alley, arms crossed over his chest. His blond hair is a little tousled from the wind, and his skin is a little darker from all the sunshine we got on our flight here. But his expression… he's worried about something. *But what?*

"I don't know. It's nothing," he says.

"Come on," I press. "It's got to be *something*."

He sighs and runs his fingers through his tangled hair. "I guess I just don't like the idea of harming a woman… even if she's a monster."

"Neither do I." I shrug. "But I think we'll never be sent on another mission if we fail this one."

Journey's quiet for a long second. "I just keep thinking about killing her when we're done…"

I think back to the tiny woman. Hopefully she'll attack us. Hopefully it'll be the kind of epic fight we used to have. Because yeah, I couldn't just kill her either. Not in cold blood at least.

But Grey could. When he hears about a monster, he sees red.

I picture the tiny woman, and my stomach twists. I don't even think he'll keep her alive long enough to finish our mission, not if he gets to her without us close enough to stop him.

Again, I think about the scene we witnessed. I see the people gathered around her. She was too far away to hear, but she looked out of control. Not evil

And we're sitting here like assholes while Grey hunts her alone…

"Okay, I'm done waiting to regroup." I stretch my massive grey wings out behind me. "I say we go looking for this Celaeno."

"Grey said—"

"I don't care; I'm not missing out on all the action!"

Shooting into the air, I make sure my glamour is in place. No use scaring all the humans. And then I go soaring over the buildings, searching for the dark-haired woman. She can't have gotten far, right?

For some reason, I already suspect this mission won't be going the way we expect. Not at all. And that should bother me, but it doesn't.

The unexpected is exactly what I've been craving.

And hunting a harpy seems like the perfect way to insert some excitement into our lives.

Chapter Four

CELAENO

"You hit me!" I shout at my attacker, glaring. My face throbs and I try to catch him by surprise and twist free, but I get nowhere. I can't move against him and he knows it.

The man lowers that face… the one I thought was beautiful just seconds ago, so that his mouth almost touches mine. He hums with strength, with something masculine and powerful. A shudder moves through my body that I don't understand.

He doesn't answer, just hovers above me, glaring.

I stop fighting and submit to his hold.

"What do you want?" I ask, my voice wavering.

"Grey!" someone shouts behind us.

His head spins toward the source of the noise, his nostrils flaring. The muscles in his jaw clench so hard I think he's going to break his teeth.

Another man moves closer to us and into my vision. I'm immediately struck by his size. Like the man on top of me, he's as big as a god. His hair is lighter, if only by a little. And it's shaggy, pushed back from his face like he runs his fingers through it far too much. His face is gentler than the man above me, and yet, he's angry. His brows drawn together in frustration.

"You've got the collar on her. Get off of her."

The man above me growls low in his throat like a beast whose been challenged.

I remember the coolness at my throat. Did they really put a collar on me? I wondered about my inability to shift. Does it have anything to do with the collar? Or is it something these men are doing to me?

"You heard him," I say, steadying my voice. "Get off of me."

The man doesn't move, and his body feels heavier and heavier.

"Now!" I shout.

"Grey…" the man begins again.

At last, he rolls off of me.

Before either of them can react, I leap to my feet and start running. The edge of the building comes faster and faster. I can sense them behind me, feel their breath as they draw closer. The only sound I hear is their feet pounding the concrete.

I reach the edge of the roof.

"Don't!" the second man shouts. "You can't shift!"

My lips curl into a smile, and I leap. Crossing the impossible distance, I land on the other building. Then, looking back, I grin.

"Sorry, boys, not today,"

I continue running, leaping from one building to the next. I have to put as much distance between them and myself as possible. I don't know why I can't shift, but I'll figure out a way to get this collar off and see if that fixes it.

Either way, I'm not sticking around to see what the two hot assholes want.

I reach the edge of the next building and jump for the next. In mid-air, I'm caught by something—someone—and a shout of shock explodes from my lips. I'm held tight, in an unbreakable hold, and we're rising into the sky.

This is a third man, different from the other two. His dirty blond hair covers one of his eyes and his thin sweater is stretched across broad shoulders. And yet… it's his skin that draws my attention. It's… grey. Behind him, big, grey wings take us higher and higher.

"Gargoyle," I whisper in complete terror.

He glances at me, his eyes unreadable. "Celaeno?"

No. No. This can't be happening! Gargoyles used to crowd the skies, the only predators who hunt my kind. They were known to kill anything that threatened mankind.

And yet, as the years have passed, their numbers have faded. I can't remember the last time I saw one. They've become more myth than reality.

I'd even forgotten to fear them.

"You have the wrong person," I say, even though the words come out too high.

He's holding me tightly, but not cruelly. I'm trying to figure out what he's thinking. Does he believe me? Or does he know who I am and plan to kill me? He tilts his head, studying me without a word.

And then I feel the air shift. Beside us, two more gargoyles appear. I recognize the men who attacked me earlier.

I've just had the worst day of my life, and now three gargoyles have come to kill me.

"We know who you are," he says, after a long minute. "We saw what you did to those humans."

There are so many things I could do right now. I could

call for my birds' help. I could try to escape, and yet, I've lived such a long, lonely life.

Maybe death is the only way to truly escape.

I lean my head against his chest, and despite everything, I start to cry again.

We fly for a long time before we stop in a clearing in the middle of thick woods. He sets me down, and I collapse onto my knees. Before I can rethink my choice, I bow my head.

"Just do it."

My request is met with silence.

Squeezing my eyes shut, I clench my hands in front of me, waiting for the sword that will take my head. All gargoyles know that beheading is the only way to kill my kind. Sweat trickles down my back. Birds sing sad songs in the trees around me. Still, I don't move.

This is it.

I hear the slightest sound. And I know without looking up that the cruel gargoyle with black eyes has come to stand in front of me.

Inhaling, I hold my breath and wait.

Of all the ways I imagined how today would go, I never thought it would end like this.

Chapter Five

JOURNEY

As the harpy bows her head, time seems to stand still. I've never before kept a secret from my Brotherhood, but I'm keeping a secret now. And it twists within me, making my entire body ache.

Medusa and Keto live within our sanctuary. As uneasy as it made all of us at first, we've come to accept that they're exceptions from everything we've ever known about monsters. Only, the others don't know the truth: they aren't exceptions at all.

I am the assistant to the Keeper of Knowledge. A man who relinquished his title of an Elite and works in the labyrinth beneath the sanctuary, the one filled with ancient books, magical weapons, and powers beyond the understanding of most beings, immortal and semi-immortal alike.

After Medusa and Keto joined our town, the Keeper of Knowledge was brought before the Elites. He asked of me a task that was difficult to follow—wear an ancient ring that conceals me from sight and follow him into the great meeting hall. I did as asked, as I always do.

They questioned him about what he knew about female monsters.

What he said next left me in shock.

And then, not long after, I was sent on this mission. I'm troubled by the information I know that I can never tell, and also because of the harpy. She could be evil. Or she could be good.

Because that's part of the secret... not all monsters are bad.

If word got out, that truly Medusa and Keto are not the only exemptions to everything we've been taught, it would have a dire impact on gargoyle society. I think it could be for the best. But who am I to question the decisions of the Elites?

Only... what if I'm exactly the kind of person who *should* question them?

Is that why the Keeper had me follow him?

My thoughts slide back to the present, to the woman kneeling before me. Is she one of the bad ones or the good ones? It's a question I need to have the answer to before I can kill her.

And if Grey should try to hurt her again, I'll have to stop him.

My best friend. My brother. It'd change our relationship forever. But I'll do it.

My gaze slides to Ender. He's staring at the bowing woman, looking troubled. Maybe even intrigued. He probably thinks the same thing I do: does she actually want us to kill her, or is this all part of some sinister plot?

But Grey... his face is twisted in rage. His hand is wrapped around the hilt of his sword. Anyone else would think he was truly about to kill this woman, but they don't know him like we do. Behind his anger, his eyes are uncertain.

And I'm sure that only makes him angrier.

So for now nothing has truly changed. I'm concealing a dangerous secret. I've been sent to kill the woman kneeling before us. And I don't yet know if she's good or bad.

No, nothing has changed. And yet, it feels like everything has.

How can I be a warrior when I know too much? How can I ever again hunt monsters if my blade can't swing without hesitation?

Knowledge truly is power.

And this knowledge may just end in my death.

But will it be at the hands of the tiny woman with the sad eyes?

Chapter Six

CELAENO

I wait and wait for my death, but nothing happens.

One of them sighs roughly. "What are you doing?"

Is this a trick? I squeeze my eyes closed even tighter. "I'm waiting for you to kill me."

There's another sigh, one that sounds strangely annoyed. "Open your eyes. We're not going to kill you."

I shake my head. "Please. Don't drag it out. Just do it."

A second later, something hits the ground beside me.

Heart in my throat, my eyes snap open. The man with shaggy brown hair is kneeling in front of me in his human form. His green eyes are strangely amused as he gazes upon me.

"I said, we're not going to kill you. At least not right now."

My mouth curls, and I snap. "Then, what's this about? You're just kidnapping women for fun?"

He raises a brow. "You did attack a group of humans."

"Not on purpose!" I protest.

"I'm sure the harpy did it by mistake!" The man standing, arms crossed in front of us, is glaring as if he can make my head pop off just with his angry gaze.

I glare right back at him. "Harpy is an offensive term, I'll have you know, made up by a man who couldn't handle me dumping him and decided to paint a *very* different picture of who I am."

His mouth turns into a thin line. "You mean, you don't use birds to hurt people?"

He's got me there, but I'm not going to admit it. I've had a long-ass day, and I'm just too tired to deal with one more asshole. Being nice got me nowhere. Maybe I'm sick of being nice. I'm sick of being a doormat. And lucky for me, this temperamental gargoyle is the perfect target for my bad mood.

"Gargoyles aren't exactly known for their patience and diplomacy either. Aren't you guys ugly statues that attack anyone who crosses your master's land?"

I swear, his eyes widen and fire blazes in his pupils. "We don't have masters. We—"

"Oh, did I strike a nerve? Sucks when people just assume the rumors about you are true, right?"

His mouth closes, and he's back to glaring.

The guy in front of me watches us like it's his favorite new show. The only thing missing is popcorn.

When he realizes we're done, he pouts for a second in a way I refuse to find cute. "Well, Grey, looks like she won that one. One point for the harp—" he catches my thunderous expression and trails off.

And then, something occurs to me. "You're a gargoyle named Grey? What, did your parents hate you or something?"

The guy in front of me starts to laugh. And it isn't a

little chuckle either. He's laughing like I just said the funniest thing in the world.

I try to hold onto my anger. I try to remember these guys are shitty gargoyles who abducted me on the worst day of my life, but his laugh is infectious. My lip quivers as I fight my need to join him.

He's grabbing his stomach now, and tears roll down his face.

Grey starts to stalk towards him.

The third gargoyle jumps into the middle of them. "Whoa, whoa, let's just stay calm," he says.

"Get out of my way, Journey," he orders through gritted teeth.

I turn and look at the blond, my gaze traveling up the tattoos on his very yummy arm. "Journey? Oh geez, don't any of you have normal names?"

He looks back at me, raising a brow. "Says the girl named Celaeno."

"Touché," I admit begrudgingly. "But it's classic."

Blond guy—Journey—smirks and says nothing more, but the fight has left his big, angry friend.

The guy in front of me finally stops laughing, wiping the last of the tears off his face. "I can't remember the last time someone challenged the big guy."

I look at… freaking Grey. Yeah, I have to imagine not many people want to get on his bad side. "What? Is everyone scared of his stink-eye, because guess what *Grey*, I'm not."

His gaze narrows, and his arms cross in front of his big chest.

"That might work on your sidekicks here, but I'm afraid you'll have to think of something better with me." As if in answer, my face starts to sting. Frowning, I reach up and touch my eye, wincing. "Oh, right, you're the asshole who hit me, a woman, crying on the ground. Big man, aren't yah?"

The guy in front of me rubs at his face and looks to the heavens, as if they might have the answer to all of this.

Journey glances at the guy in front of me. "Ender, will you just explain the situation to her?"

Ender? Geez. Who named these guys?

"Yeah, Ender, why don't you explain why you and your friends kidnapped me? I mean, do you guys usually attack women you find crying? Or was this something special?"

He looks at me like he can't decide what the hell I am, and I don't blame him. I'm a mess. One minute I was ready for death, and now I'm fired up like a demon. I'm just so tired of everything. Was it too much to ask for that I had a friend, a job, and a life? I mean, was I asking for the fucking moon?

"Okay, where to start?" Ender begins, running a hand through that shaggy hair of his.

His hair looks soft. My fingers itch to touch it. Maybe before I escape these clowns I'll have to ask what conditioner he uses, because my dull, brown hair looks nothing like his flowing locks. Freaking jackass. And, of course, he has long eyelashes too, ones that should be on some gorgeous woman.

Ones I wish I had.

"So," he starts, "we need your help with a problem."

"My help?" I repeat, staring at him as if he's grown an extra head. "You guys hit me, put a collar on me like some kind of animal, and kidnapped me, all because you needed my help? I mean, why not just kick me in the stomach and ask for directions, while you're at it?"

He smiles, and when he does, his whole face changes. "You have got to be the strangest woman I've ever met."

"She's a monster, not a woman," Grey growls behind me.

"And since you're carved from stone, and probably weren't given dicks, am I even allowed to call you men? Or should I just refer to you as the no-dicks?" I ask, trying to look sincere.

Grey launches himself at me and Journey has to hold him back.

"I've got a dick for you!" he shouts. "Want to see it?"

"Sure!" I challenge his bluff. "But don't be disappointed when I'm not impressed with the sad little hotdog you're hiding."

"Fuck!" Ender shouts in front of me, grabbing my shoulders. "Shut up, you hilarious idiot! He's going to kill you!"

At that moment, I do the most immature thing imaginable— I stick my tongue out at Grey.

He freezes. "We should've cut her head off when we had the chance."

"Too late now." The minute I say the words, I realize that the time for wishing for death is over. I didn't really want to die. I was just feeling hopeless. And now, for some reason, I'm feeling different. Like I'm ready to take on the world again. Starting with these three.

"It's never too late," Grey says, quietly, with a darkness that gives me goose bumps.

Ender releases my shoulders. "Okay, well, like I said, we came here to ask for your help."

I raise a brow. "Sure, since you all have been so charming and sweet."

He shakes his head again, as if he can't believe the things coming out of my mouth.

Frankly, neither can I. Maybe I had a little fire in my belly in my younger days, before my ex ruined my reputation and turned me into some kind of monster. My confidence has gone to shit since then. So, the woman who's all fired up right now? She's like an outfit from my past that I haven't been able to fit into for years, except right now, it's fitting like a glove.

"Have you ever heard of the town of Cherish?" Ender asks me, trying to sound as if everything's normal.

I shake my head. "No. Why? Should I have?"

He glances behind him, and he and the others exchange a look I can't quite process.

"How do your powers work exactly?" he asks.

I shift, moving so that my legs are crossed in front of me. "You first."

Ender stares and stares. "This isn't a game. We need to know about your powers. How close do you have to be to control birds, and how do you give them orders?"

"You're kidding right?"

Silence descends between us.

"Celaeno…"

"What?" I challenge him. "You think I'm going to fork over my secrets to three assholes who kill my kind and who, so far, have been nothing but unpleasant to me?"

He rubs his forehead.

Journey clears his throat and moves away from Grey. He sits down beside his friend, just a couple of feet in front of me. I ignore the way the sunlight clings to his blond hair, and how the dark strands weave with the blond to create a strangely beautiful head of hair for a man.

How do they do that? Is it their conditioner? I mean, geez, men aren't supposed have freakishly beautiful hair.

"So…" Journey begins, trailing off.

I lower my eyes to meet his and stare into those deep blue eyes, so damn beautiful that for a moment I can't breathe. I tear my gaze away, and my glance hits his massive shoulders. The dark blue sweater strains across his chest and arms, and his bigger-than-my-head arms, covered in sexy-ass tattoos, are exposed by the sleeves he's pushed up.

Damn it. What does it say about me that these three guys are the most appealing men I've met in years, maybe even my whole life, and they've literally beat me up and taken me captive? For what, I still don't know. I need counseling… some kind of counseling for screwed up immortals.

"There's a town called Cherish that's having a bird problem."

I immediately perk up. "What do you mean?"

There isn't much I care about in life, but I do love birds. They're sweet, gentle souls who aren't given the credit they deserve.

"They… aren't acting right."

I frown. "What does that mean? Are they hurt or suffering?"

Journey stares at me for a long time, as if evaluating me. "No, they're attacking people. Much like your birds attacked those humans on the street."

My stomach twists. "Birds don't just attack people. They hunt to survive, but they're really just gentle souls."

Grey snorts. "Yeah, they looked really gentle earlier."

I leapt to my feet. "Shut your damn mouth! That wasn't their fault! It was mine! I couldn't control my emotions. I was too caught up in…," I trail off, feeling my eyes sting. "I was hurting and let my emotions take over. It's not their fault I was having a bad day."

My eyes lower to the ground and some of the fight goes out of me. I remember the way I felt, and I'm ashamed. It was like I was trapped in an abyss of my own suffering. I'm too old to be forgetting that I can't let myself feel too much.

Suddenly, a robin lands lightly on my shoulder. It's a beautiful, graceful bird who looks at me with sad eyes.

I smile and stroke the top of his head. "It's okay. I'm all right."

The bird rubs against my finger, as if his touch can take away the sting of heartache that still lingers.

"Admit it. You're commanding the birds to attack in Cherish."

I stiffen and look down at Ender in disbelief. The robin on my shoulder takes flight. "First of all, I can't command birds that far away. And second of all, I wouldn't do that. I don't just attack humans for no reason, nor would I put my birds at risk like that."

"Excuse us if we find that hard to believe," Grey says, his words cutting.

I want to tear chunks of hair out of his beard and see if he has a weak chin under all that hair. Just the thought makes me calm a little, and I realize my fists are clenched.

Slowly loosening them, I try to keep my voice level. "So, what do you want from me?"

"Can you stop them?" Journey asks.

If I tell them no, will they just kill me? Is that the only reason they're keeping me alive? My mind moves a thousand miles a minute. I'll help those birds no matter what, because something is happening in that town. Something that's upsetting the birds. Besides, I have a strong feeling that if I tell these gargoyles no right now, I'll end up dead.

Helping the birds is sort of a win-win.

But the gargoyles don't need to know that.

"I don't know. I'll have to go there and see them to find out what's wrong."

Journey looks relieved. "We can do that."

"But if I help you, I want your word as gargoyles that you will remove this collar and leave me alone afterwards."

"Fuck that. Not happening," Grey mutters.

I shrug. "Then no deal."

He pulls his damned sword off his back. The metal scrapes as it pulls through the scabbard.

"Well, maybe we'll just kill you now then."

My heart races, but I don't back down. "That won't help you with your bird problem."

He's back to glaring.

"Her deal seems fair," Journey hedges.

"But the Elites…" Ender doesn't say more, but the effect of his words is instantaneous. Tension hangs so heavily between the three of them that I could reach out and touch it.

Ender rises. "We'll give you a twenty-four hour head start."

"Two weeks," I negotiate.

"Two days."

"A week," I say, holding out my hand.

Everyone stares at me, and watches until Ender takes my hand. "Deal."

The tension eases and Grey mutters something under his breath before re-sheathing his sword.

I lift my arms. "Who's taking me?"

All the men exchange a wide-eyed look, and then Grey moves awkwardly forward, shifting before my eyes into a gargoyle once more.

"No talking," he commands as he leans down, and I wrap my arms around his neck.

For a second our gazes meet, and the anger drains from his expression. Time stands still, and I forget to breathe. My stomach drops as we shoot into the air.

I scream and tighten my legs around his waist. He swears again, but I don't care. Flying with a gargoyle is nothing like flying as a bird.

I can't wait until this is over and I can shift once more.

If *they hold up their end of our deal and I don't end up dead.*

Chapter Seven

GREY

My entire body is so hard I'm having trouble breathing. I have a fucking thing for tiny women. It's been twenty years since the last time I fucked a woman, and I can still picture in perfect clarity the many different ways I can spin a tiny woman on my dick.

It's so easy to position them against a wall, their legs over my shoulders and my cock plunging in deep. And they can ride me in any direction on the bed.

Fuck. I need to stop thinking like this.

But it's impossible not to. The woman has her arms around my neck and her legs wrapped around my back. My dick is hard as a rod, begging me to plunge deeply inside of her.

If she wasn't a monster, it'd take nothing at all. I'd dive down into the trees far below. Pick a spot, and ask her how she wants it. She'd be on her knees sucking me off before I could finish the question.

But she is a monster, which means she's off limits.
Which means I shouldn't want her… I don't want her.

I'm just so fucking horny.

"How much longer?" she asks, her voice soft, almost shy.

"As long as it takes," I grit out.

She looks up at me and for a minute I'm lost in her auburn eyes. I've never seen a shade of eyes like hers before. It gives her an inhuman quality that should make me uneasy, but only makes me feel like I'm looking deep inside of her.

"You don't have to be a total dick."

I stiffen. Is that a dig? She's got to feel how hard I am, right?

"Talk as sweetly as you want. Act as innocent as you please." I lean in. "But I know what your kind is capable of, so don't think I'll believe you for one second."

"Oh, and what am I capable of?"

The words come out before I can stop them. "One of your little monster-bitches killed my best friend."

Her eyes widen. "Who?"

"That slithering bitch, Lamia."

Something strange comes over her face. "Oh, Lamia." She says the beast's name with such pity.

Why? Why does she pity the creature?

In my mind, I can still picture it all. My brother and I had just awakened atop a castle—one that was being torn down brick-by-brick. We rose from our perches and set out into the woods. Later that night, we split up, looking for firewood.

I came into a clearing to find a half-snake, half-woman creature on top of my brother. She had drained his blood, her face and chest covered in it. He lay dead, and his entire chest was painted in his blood.

It was my first time seeing someone I loved dead. I'd been in so much shock that when she slithered away into the woods, I'd simply rushed to my brother and tried to save him. As a gargoyle, the only thing that should've been able to kill him was to be beheaded.

To this day, I don't know how she was able to do it. I didn't know why either.

All I knew is that I couldn't save him, and I couldn't find her.

So, I knew first-hand what monsters were capable of. And I wouldn't lose one of my brothers again… never again.

"I'm so sorry you lost someone to Lamia, but she isn't some heartless beast… she's just complicated."

Anger awakens within me. "Killing an innocent doesn't make someone complicated."

Her gaze meets mine, and I can feel she's evaluating me. "Have you ever read about vampires? How they drink blood to survive? Well, Lamia needs blood to survive. I've met her many times before. She hates what she is, but she doesn't have a choice. And she does everything in her power not to kill."

I hear my teeth clench together. "If you're trying to make me feel sorry for that murderous piece of shit, then you're barking up the wrong tree."

She tenses in my arms. "Is that anger doing you a lot of good?"

I stare in confusion. "What are you talking about?"

"Does being angry help you deal with his death? Does it give you peace?"

"Who said I want fucking peace?"

How dare she question anything when she's a dangerous killer too?

"I'm just saying that it's a hell of a lot easier to hate someone than to try to put yourself in their shoes."

"You some kind of psychologist, *harpy*? Huh?"

She tries to slap me.

I catch her arm, releasing my grip on her thigh in the process, and her leg slides.

She cries out, grabbing my shoulder more tightly with her one free arm. As if she really thinks I'd let her fall. But then again, maybe she needs to learn a lesson.

Unable to help myself, I release her other leg.

She gasps, her legs frantically trying to hold on as she slips.

"Don't forget your place, monster. I could so easily send you slamming into the ground. Healing after that would hurt like hell."

Letting go of her arm, she immediately clings harder to my neck, and I reach down and pull her legs back around my waist. I hate that the friction has me even more frustrated.

When I'm done, she's panting against my neck.

Something I refuse to find sexy.

"You are such an asshole!" she yells at me.

I try to hide my grin. "Maybe next time don't try to hit me."

"I'll hit you whenever I want to!" she shouts.

"Keep it up, and I might have to spank you." The moment I say the words, I wish I could take them back. *Spank you? Who says spank you to a woman?*

A horny idiot is who.

She looks up at me very slowly. "I think you'd like that a little too much."

I picture her naked, bent over my lap. A groan nearly tears from my lips. Yes, I'd like that. Way too much. *God damn it, I'm dropping this woman the first chance I get.*

"You know I think you're lying, right?" I say, changing the subject.

"Big surprise," she mumbles, then louder. "About what?"

"I think you're causing the bird problem in Cherish."

She rolls her eyes. "And I think you need to get a life."

"No defending yourself then?"

She licks her lips, and I'm glued to the small movement. "I have a feeling no matter what I say, you won't believe me, so what's the point?"

For some reason, I can't remember what we're talking about. She shifts against me again, and I swear my balls tighten. Oh fuck, I think I'm going to spill my seed right here against her.

I will not embarrass myself like that.

Adjusting my direction, I head down toward the trees.

"What are we doing?" she asks, sounding panicked.

"We're going to make a short stop."

Her gaze goes far ahead, where I can see the specks that are my brothers. Probably flying together and talking about me. Annoying assholes.

"Won't they wonder what's happened to us?"

Her legs hold me tighter, and I swear out loud before I can stop myself. "We'll catch up to them," I answer, panting.

We lower through a slight opening between trees. When we reach the ground, I instantly drop her on the ground.

She falls like a sack of potatoes.

Glaring at me from the ground, she climbs to her knees and comes level with my hard erection.

Time seems to stand still as I stare at her. I think of how easy it'd be to plunge right into her sweet lips. To close my eyes and feel the warmth of a woman.

Only, she's not a woman. She's a monster.

Springing back from her, I can feel my heart beating in my ears. "Stay here for one minute. Don't run. I'll be right back."

I don't watch to make sure she obeys. Without her ability to shift, even if she runs, I'll be able to catch her with ease. But it'd be easier if she just listened.

When I find a stream, I open my pants and pull my hard length free. It takes nothing at all to wrap my fist around myself and start pumping. I try to think of the female gargoyles. Of every human woman I've ever fucked. But it isn't them that makes my cock swell. It's the image of what Celaeno would look like naked. It's the thought of how tight the tiny woman must be. In my ears, I even hear her moaning my name.

Every muscle in my body tenses and I explode, my seed decorating the forest.

I continue to pump myself for another long minute, until I'm sure every drop has come free. Taking a deep breath, I know this was the right course of action. The tension that's been under my skin since meeting the woman has eased… at least a little.

Using the river, I clean myself off, then zip my pants back up.

Now to handle the harpy with a clear mind!

Going back through the forest, I come to where I left her. Only, she's gone.

Of course she's fucking gone.

Enraged, I shift back into my gargoyle form and launch myself into the sky. I circle around until I spot movement, and I fly lower, just above the treetops. Celaeno is running with all her might through the woods, and I smirk. Did she really think she could escape me?

When I see an opening between the trees up ahead, I shoot toward it and drop down. I come exploding through the leaves and branches just feet in front of her.

Those stunning auburn eyes of hers widen, and she turns around.

I race toward her and catch her around the waist. She goes down like a brick wall.

As she struggles under me, her ass rubbing against my cock, I'm shocked when I harden once more. *Is this a fucking joke? I just stroked myself off.*

But looking down at her, my arousal only deepens. She's so fiery. So filled with passion as she swears at me and tries to struggle out from under me.

"Stop," I order her, more angered by my own reaction that her.

She turns and looks back at me. "You're an asshole!"

"You've said that before," I say, hauling her to her feet.

When I yank her against me, she looks up at me, and there's a little sadness there that pulls me in. "Even if I escaped, I'd help the people and the birds."

I hate that a small part of me believes her. That some place deep inside of me thinks maybe this monster is different than the others I've faced. Because it makes me an idiot. All monsters are the same.

"Of course you'd still help the humans if I let you go," I say, my voice filled with mockery. "What do I look like, a sucker?"

She takes a long second to answer. "No, you look like someone who's been hurt and can't trust again. It's sad."

Sad. The word echoes through me. No one has ever called me sad before.

And I don't like the way I can't seem to let go of the word.

"Let me clear something up for you, harpy. Don't look at me like someone sad and hurt. Look at me like a soldier, and you and I are enemies. Got it?"

She nods, but her gaze remains strangely gentle. Like I didn't just insult her and declare us enemies. She actually looks like she feels bad for me.

Which again, I hate.

"Shall we go?" she asks, reaching her arms up.

I lean down, place my hands on her waist, and her legs wrap around me. But instead of instantly flying away, I seem to be frozen. Holding this woman who calls me sad and looks at me with gentleness in her eyes.

I need to stop this. Now. Before it becomes something more than it is.

For some reason, my thoughts and emotions are all over the place as we launch back into the sky. *I'm not sad, am I?* I think of my life at the gargoyle sanctuary. I think of my time with my Brotherhood of Gargoyles, Ender and Journey.

People would call me angry. But somehow as I repeat the word in my mind, it doesn't quite feel right. And I hate that I can't seem to shake off what she said. *Sad* just rolls over and over in my mind.

My castle was destroyed. My lands taken from beneath my protection. And my brother murdered.

I've been so angry… or is *anger* what I've been feeling?

Fucking hell. I can't wait until we reach the town. Then I won't be left alone with my thoughts. I'll be focused again. On our mission. On helping humans and obeying the Elites.

Which is what I should be thinking about. Not that Celaeno might have seen something in myself that I've never seen.

And that I think she might be right. Because for some reason, that idea shakes me to my core.

The sooner we reach our destination, the better.

Chapter Eight
———————

JOURNEY

We stop for the night in a clearing in the middle of nowhere. Grey goes to gather firewood, in one of the worst moods I've ever seen him in, and Ender follows him. I can't decide if Ender going will make things better or worse, but I can't do anything about it. I've been tasked with guarding the woman. I mean, the monster.

"Hungry?" I ask her, swinging my backpack into my lap and opening the top.

She gives a strangely shy smile. "Starving."

I pull out a couple of granola bars and hand her one. She thanks me and opens it up carefully. But when she takes a bite, she winces.

Opening mine, I smile. "No good?"

A blush darkens her cheeks. "It's fine. Really. I just spend so much time cooking I don't really eat things like this often."

"You're a cook?" I ask, surprised.

She nods. "Well, when you're semi-immortal, you learn how to do a lot of things. I don't have to tell you that. But my last job was at this little coffee shop." Her smile freezes and slowly fades, the happiness and excitement drains from her voice. "I baked a lot there. Mostly desserts. Donuts, cookies, cakes. And I loved it so much that I started baking even more at home. Every time I got together with our… with our group of… friends, I brought treats."

Every word she speaks seems to drain her face and her happiness. By the end, I think she might start crying.

I can't help myself. I move closer to her on the ground. "Are you okay?"

She blinks rapidly, and I see the tears in her eyes. Lowering her head, she holds the bar in her lap. "Yeah, I'm fine. It's just… I can never go back there again."

"Because of the birds?" I prod.

She shakes her head and wipes a stray tear from her cheek. "No."

"Did something happen?"

Slowly, she draws her shoulders back and sits up straighter. "It doesn't matter. A friend screwed me over is all. It's not like that hasn't happened before. My ex. My sisters. That's just life. You trust someone, and they make you regret it."

Fucking hell. I want to take this woman in my arms and hold her tight. I want to tell her that not everyone takes friendship and love so lightly. But I also have to be careful, she's my prisoner, not an innocent I'm charged with protecting. *So I'll keep it short.*

"Not everyone is like that." I strive to sound casual, but I think I fail miserably.

She gives a sad laugh. "Yeah, right."

As I stare at her, my chest squeezes. I look towards the trees where Ender and Grey disappeared. There's nothing wrong with making her feel better. That doesn't make me a bad monster hunter.

Right?

"It's true." I don't know why it's important that she believes me, but it is. "The last time I awoke from my stone-form, the other gargoyles in my manor had been smashed. We'd awoken together every time our manor was in trouble for hundreds of years. I'd never before awoken alone. So, I felt lost. I left, but I had no idea where I was going or what my purpose was.

When I found the other gargoyles, most of them had created Brotherhoods with the gargoyles that served with them. I was alone. And I thought I would always be. But somehow, Ender and Grey were alone too. We came together and knew instantly that there was a bond between us. We became a family. We served together. And one day, we'll take a mate together and raise a family together. I trust them with every ounce of my being."

She's stared silently from the first moment I started talking, and when I finished, she gave a forced smile. "But you don't have my reputation…"

"As a harpy?" I ask.

"As a monster," she says.

What am I supposed to say to that? I am here, after all, to catch her. A monster. Someone we consider a danger to humanity. Someone I've been told to kill after her use to us is gone.

I can't exactly argue that her label—her reputation—doesn't matter.

"Celaeno—"

Suddenly Ender comes barreling through the woods with his arms loaded with wood, and the moment shatters between us. He drops the wood into the center of stones we've created for a fire.

Grinning, he plops himself down. "Grey says he'll be back when he's back. So, what are we talking about?"

I clear my throat, wondering if Celaeno will mind my questions. She looks a little lost in thought, eating her bar slowly as she stares at the pile of wood. The truth is, she intrigues me. I know Grey will think I'm stupid for believing anything she says. But for some reason, I want to know more about her. And this feels like the perfect opportunity to do just that.

"We were discussing how she got her harpy reputation."

Her expression freezes, and she looks between the two of us.

What's she thinking? Grey would say she's coming up with a lie, but I get the feeling she's just deciding if she's going to tell us anything.

Ender clears his throat. "Haven't harpies always been known as being monstrous creatures who—"

"No!" she cuts him off, the words springing from her lips like she can't stop it. "Just because I've lived so long that my reputation is just accepted as the truth doesn't make it so." Her mouth pulls into a thin line. "Word of advice, boys: never date a god. They're assholes."

"Your ex was a god?" Ender says, sounding taken aback.

She nods. "I was actually in a pretty serious relationship with Hades, before he met Persephone."

I can't help looking shocked. I am shocked! The old gods used to run things with the air of arrogant, attention-loving celebrities. But over the years, they pulled back. They let most of the world see them as nothing but myths, I think largely so they could do what they wanted without being blamed for it. But I've never actually met a god. And the idea that she dated one? It's kind of crazy. But it also has a strange ring of truth.

"I thought you just worked for him, dragging souls off

to the Underworld," Ender says, and I can tell he's as intrigued as I am.

She snorts. "No."

Then she sighs. "You guys really want to hear this?"

"Yes!" we both say at once.

She laughs and shakes her head. "Okay, but be careful who you tell this story to. Hades is a dangerous man, and he doesn't like the truth getting out."

"Got it," Ender says, drawing closer.

She leans back, looking unsure.

I stand, hoping to make her less uncomfortable, and gather dried pine needles and smaller twigs from around us. With quick movements, I begin to build the fire so that when it catches, the flame will stay.

After a quiet minute, her voice comes, soft and musical. "Elektra was our mother, a nymph of the clouds. She bore triplet daughters, my two sisters and I. We were raised on the surface of this world, filled with sunshine, clouds, and happiness. But some of the gods grew angry at our freedom, and so they handed down our job—to be guardians of the Underworld and their punishers to the guilty. We weren't happy in the Underworld. It's as dark and dreary as you can imagine. But then there was a beam of hope: Hades. At least I thought that's what he was."

"Yeah, I heard he's a real ray of sunshine," Ender interrupts.

I cast him an irritated glance. *Doesn't he want to know what happened?*

She sighs and adjusts, pulling her knees up to her chest. "I was young. He was a handsome god. When he said he loved me, I believed him. And then I learned he was secretly courting my sisters too. So I confronted him about it. He cast me out of the Underworld, promising that no one would ever love me again. That's when the rumors began. That I was a monster. That I'm dangerous and evil…"

When she stops talking, her gaze is faraway. Lost as if remembering.

"I can't believe rumors would be that bad," Ender says, his tone light.

I've known him long enough that I know he's just trying to break the tension in the room, but his words make me wince. Rumors can be as dangerous as any sharpened blade.

Her gaze locks onto him. "You believed them."

Ender's smile fades. "We—"

"And no matter what I say or do, you'll continue to believe them. Even now, you're probably wondering if I made my story up. Right? That's the power of rumors. They don't have to be true. They just have to be believable. And the worst people are the ones that build their lies on a grain of truth. You saw what I can do, I *am* dangerous. I'm just not evil."

I return to building the fire. Drawing my flint from my bag and coaxing sparks that grow into little licks of fire. All the while, Ender and Celaeno watch me, saying nothing. And I'm surprised, because it's not a tense silence… it's almost comfortable.

At last, I'm confident that the fire will continue to grow. Sitting back, I watch as night begins to descend over us. One side of the sky is grey, and the other is black, with stars beginning to shine. Birds began to sing their songs, the ones that mean the day is done.

Suddenly, Celaeno grins. "Want to see something?"

Uh-oh. That doesn't sound good…

"Sure!" Ender says, before I can stop him.

She smiles wider, but nothing happens. As my nerves start to relax, I hear the flutter of birds' wings. My hand instinctually reaches back for the hilt of my sword, and I see Ender do the same.

Birds of every shape and size land around the clearing. Several of them land lightly on Celaeno's shoulders and arms. As the minutes trickle passed, there has to be a hundred birds around us. I'm tempted to shift into my gargoyle-form, but I also don't think the danger these birds pose isn't worth potentially insulting Celaeno before we know what she has planned. So I hesitate, waiting.

But I don't have to wait long. She begins to whistle a happy, little melody.

When she stops, the birds sing the melody back to her, and the sound is unexpectedly beautiful. I don't think I've ever noticed before the different sounds birds are capable of, but together they're like an orchestra, the instruments of their voices coming out in perfect harmony.

She whistles another tune, this one faster. They repeat it back to her.

And then her smile falters. She whistles a different kind of song. It's sad and slow. I've never thought a whistle could capture emotion, but hers does.

We're transfixed by her. The flames from the fire bathe her in a soft glow, making her unusual auburn eyes seem brighter, and illuminating her dark strands of hair. It all frames that beautiful face of hers. Gentle and innocent.

The birds join in with her melody, and for one minute it's like we're in a fairy tale.

"What the fuck is going on?"

The song stops.

I whirl around and spot Grey. He drops his armful of massive pieces of wood. In an instant, his skin turns grey and his wings unfold.

"Don't!" I shout at him.

He ignores me, reaching for his sword.

The birds leap into the air, a flurry of wings. He withdraws his sword, and I swear he's going to cut down every single bird he can reach. But then there's Celaeno, standing before them, her arms wide, facing down Grey. The thunderous anger in her expression dares him to challenge her.

"Get out of the way," he says.

"Or what?" she taunts. "You'll hurt tiny birds?"

"I've seen what your *birds* are capable of. Now, get out of the way."

They're both breathing hard. Neither backing down. All the birds are gone from the clearing, taken to the sky or trees nearby. Ender and I remain where we are, watching, waiting, unwilling to make this situation worse.

She draws herself up taller. "If you think you're the first big man to think that you can hurt me and I'll just back down, you're wrong."

I see it in his eyes, a question. His gaze goes to mine. We don't hurt women. We value them above all else. But he's thinking of Lamia. Of the monster that killed his best friend. I'm sure coming upon this scene in the woods brought him back to that dark place.

"She was just singing with her birds," I tell him, keeping my voice as light as possible. "And even if she wasn't, it takes us a minute to shift. We'd be fine."

"Unless she knows how to kill a gargoyle," he says, his whole chest rising and falling rapidly, and I know he's spiraling.

"I don't," she says. "Lamia is special."

"Special!" he shouts, and his eyes are wild. "That *thing* is not special."

The fire goes out of Celaeno's gaze, and her hands slowly drop. I can see it now. That she knows exactly what's going on.

Celaeno's Fate

"I know we're enemies, and nothing I say will change that. But don't confuse me with someone else. I'm not Lamia. I'm just me."

His sword slowly lowers, but I can feel his tension from across the clearing.

"Dinner anyone?" Ender asks, but even he can't feign cheer in this situation.

Grey huffs and resheaths his sword, lightly knocking Celaeno's shoulder as he walks past her. She turns back to us and glares as he retreats.

That night, Ender, Celaeno, and I lay down beside the fire. Underneath the stars.

Grey refuses to sleep. He simply sits, back against a trunk, and pretends to have a heart as hard as his hard-stone flesh. He says he'll guard over our prisoner and make sure she doesn't escape.

I'm pretty sure he's actually trying to make sense of his reaction to her.

The night grows deeper, and the stars begin to shoot across the sky.

Celaeno gasps. "A meteor shower!" Then, very softly, "Make a wish."

But I don't look to the stars, I look at her. Her eyes closed. A smile pulling at the corners of her lips.

My chest tightens. The Elite's secret comes back to me. *Not all monsters are evil.*

And then there's the other thing. The thing I can never say allowed: they think the only chance our kind has to survive is by breeding with the female monsters.

But after they have our children, they might kill them anyway.

I think of Keto and Medusa. *Will their time soon be up?* And why were we commanded to kill Celaeno, not kidnap her?

Is there something that makes her even more dangerous than The Mother of all Sea Monsters and a woman whose gaze turns people to stone?

My stomach twists. There's something I don't understand going on here. But one thing I do know, I like Celaeno. And if I were to bet, I'd think the Elites might be a hell of a lot more evil than she is.

And that thought alone makes certain I won't be sleeping any time soon.

Even though I know I need sleep. Soon, after all, we're going to Cherish. The place we'll learn, once and for all, the truth about this beautiful monster.

Chapter Nine

GREY

I jerk awake. Fucking hell, I must be struggling more than I thought if I fell asleep while on duty. Gargoyles, after all, are the best guards imaginable. It's probably because I've never been this mentally exhausted before.

The fucking harpy is doing all kinds of things to my brain.

And, of course, now I need to take a piss.

Rising, I put another log on the dying fire, then glance at the harpy. There's no way in hell she's awake. Her head is lolled to the side, and I swear there's a little drool in the corner of her mouth.

I smile. She's cute when she sleeps.

Cute? Oh fuck, this woman is *not* good for me.

I step around my snoring brothers and head out to find a good tree to relieve myself. The moon is bright tonight, and the stars seem brighter than I've ever seen them before. Most people might think it's all kinds of beautiful and peaceful, but not me. Until I fell asleep, all I could think about as how much this place reminds me of the place my brother, William, was killed.

It makes me feel wound up. Like every muscle in my body is begging me to do some serious harm. So I don't have a clue how I feel asleep, except that I'm blaming it on our irritating prisoner.

I piss and go to the river to wash my hands. Running the cold water over my face and hair helps to make me feel more alert. But when I straighten, my face and hair damp, something feels different in these woods. The darkness around me seems to have deepened. I know it's probably just my imagination, but I'm feeling uneasy.

Rising, I head back toward camp. My protective instincts are alive. In tune to each crush of leaves beneath my feet. The scent of greenery and life. The way the wind moves through the trees in a lazy way that barely stirs the air.

All things I sense on a deeper level, and yet, there's nothing that should alarm me. *Fuck.* It probably is just my old memories teasing me. Haunting me.

I need to snap out of this.

Suddenly, a movement catches my eye. At first all I see are shadows in the leaves, and then a shape comes into focus. A black crow rests on a branch, watching me intently.

The hairs on the back of my neck stand on end. I continue moving forward, past it, my pulse racing.

It's just a bird, and nothing more. Unless the "innocent" Celaeno has sent one of her foul creatures after me. And yet, one bird isn't exactly a danger to me. So… maybe it's just a bird.

"Where you going, big boy?"

I whirl around. Where the crow just stood, a woman now sits on a branch. She has dark hair, but it's cut short above her ears. And her eyes, they're the same unusual auburn color as Celaeno's.

Another fucking harpy?

"What do you want?"

She smirks, and there's something evil in her little smile. "What do you think I want?"

"Celaeno?"

Her nose wrinkles. "Not a chance. You can have that spineless, pathetic creature. The second she abandoned her post in the Underworld, she was dead to me."

Interesting. "Then what do you want?"

She laughs, but the sound is unpleasant, and she leaps down from the branch in one graceful movement. When she soundlessly rises, she moves until she's close enough to touch me.

A growl slips from my lips, and this time I do reach for my sword.

Her gaze goes to my weapon, but she looks amused more than frightened. "What I want is to ask why Celaeno's still alive. Are you gargoyles so bad at your job that you can't kill one little harpy?"

I scowl at her. "That's none of your business."

She giggles and reaches forward to trail a hand along my arm. "Want to hear something interesting, little stone-man? My mother, the goddess of the clouds herself, forbade us sisters from killing each other when we were just small children at her knee. She even made us promise it, putting her power as a goddess into the promise, and so we'd have no choice but to obey her. Literally."

"That's completely normal," I say, imagining a mother telling her kids they can't kill each other.

"Among the gods it is," she says, rolling her eyes. "Haven't you ever read *anything* about them? But that's not my point. My point is that I *want* her dead. I want to break my promise and kill Hades's ex and punish her for abandoning him. But as I said, I can't."

"How unfortunate," I say, dryly.

She cocks her head, and her hand comes to rest on my forearm. "There have been so many times that I set the wheel of fortune spinning, hoping to finally bring an end to my dear sister. But each time, she somehow manages to survive."

I wonder if Celaeno knows this is happening. "Why are you telling me all this?"

"Because, stupid gargoyle, I'm here to discover whether you're finally going to rid me of her once and for all."

I stare at her for a long minute in silence. "That's our business."

Her smile falters. "Drop the attitude. This is important to me. I've fallen out of favor with Hades, and I need my sister's head as a gift. Will you bring it to me?"

"No," I answer, without hesitation.

I don't know if I'll kill the harpy, but I won't do it for this creature, no matter what.

Her auburn-colored eyes turn a shade brighter. "Unfortunate choice."

It's like a gong rings through my body. I can't feel my limbs. My vision seems to get both bigger and smaller, fluctuating around me. My heartbeat fills my ears.

Everything's moving in my vision, like reality is spinning away. I finally come to realize that my arm hurts, but I can't pull it away. Looking down, I see black veins blossoming beneath the harpy's touch.

She leans in closer, and I can't pull away. Her lips brush my ear. "You thought I was like my weak sister. Shifting. Controlling birds. Absolutely useless powers. But the great, sexy god of the Underworld bestowed upon me the ability to take lives, and guess what? I'm taking yours."

I crumble to my knees. Her face hovers over mine.

My blood pounds louder in my ears, and I feel liquid sliding from my eyes and my mouth. Images flash back to me. Of William dying in woods just like these ones. Of learning that no life is guaranteed.

What a fool I was to think I was any stronger than him.

"Aello!"

The harpy is knocked back, her grip on me disappearing. And then I'm on the ground, breathing hard, my limbs shaking.

Celaeno comes to stand in front of me. Her hands are curled into fists. "Leave him alone!"

Her sister laughs and a wild gust of wind slams through the woods, lifting her from the ground. She floats there, her hair flying around her, and I instantly know Celaeno will be no match for her. I try to shout, to get my brother's attention, but even my throat won't work.

Aello's eyes go brighter, almost glowing. "You're actually going to protect a gargoyle that kidnapped you?"

Celaeno's head raises just an inch. "Leave. Now."

"Come on, I know you. You're not going to fight me. You're going to run away with your tail between your legs, just like you always do. Face it, Celaeno, you're just not the kind of person to really fight for what she wants. And you haven't been for a very long time."

Celaeno's hands remain curled as she stands in front of me, but she says nothing for a long minute. Has she already lost this battle?

"In the Underworld you all made me feel like I was a fool for thinking Hades was unfaithful. My own sisters convinced me that I was insecure and crazy. You broke down my self-esteem day-after-day until I thought I didn't deserve more than what I had." Her tone softens. "I'm not perfect, but I've grown since then. I know I deserve better."

Her sister laughs and the speed of the wind increases. "No, the only thing that you deserve is what we have planned for you. And today I'm going to kill that gargoyle, and you're not going to stop me."

Celaeno's voice is soft, but strong. "You can bring your angry winds, but they mean nothing, dear sister. Because I might be his prisoner, but at least I'm not Hades' slave. Like you are. Still."

The harpy points her hands toward Celaeno, thunder in her gaze. But nothing happens. After a minute, she screams in outrage.

"You can't kill me." Celaeno walks slowly towards her. "So just stop this nonsense."

"No!" Aello shouts. "You don't understand… you don't—"

Celaeno moves closer to her, closing the space between them. "You're no longer favored by Hades." It's not a question, it's a statement.

The other harpy's anger falls away. "Don't speak of him."

"I know what it feels like. It's as if someone has reached inside your chest and ripped out your beating heart, but it'll get better. I promise. And if you need my help—"

"Your help? You can help me by giving me your head!" her sister shouts, but the words feel forced.

Celaeno shrugs. "I'm here if you need me, but Hades doesn't care enough about me—one way or another. My death will mean nothing to him."

Her sister rattles off a string of colorful curses. "This was my last chance!"

"No." Celaeno reaches out and touches the other woman, and the winds calms. "This was never really a chance. Once you fall out of favor with Hades, there's no coming back. And certainly not with the head of someone he doesn't care about. He wouldn't even acknowledge you. So it's time to just accept a life without him. To make a new life on your own."

And then, Aello is crying on her sister's shoulder. Celaeno whispers words I know must be meant to soothe. They remain like that for a time, while I'm lying useless.

At last, Aello pulls back and dries her eyes. "I can't do this. I'm just not ready yet. I'm going to return to the Underworld and beg Hades to forgive me."

"Don't." And all the gentleness is gone from Celaeno. "You're strong enough to walk away from him and the Underworld. I promise."

Aello backs away from her, shaking her head. "I'm sorry. Sorry about what I said before. Sorry about everything. But I'm not as strong as you, Celaeno. I never have been."

Celaeno reaches out for her sister, but Aello vanishes.

The forest is quiet once more, strangely still after the violent winds and fighting.

Celaeno turns slowly around and walks toward me. When she kneels down, I can see tears rolling down her face. "Are you okay?"

Reaching out, she takes my arms. A few stray black lines remain, but otherwise, I look normal. If only I felt normal. She traces the lines and then presses her hand against them, closing her eyes.

Tingles run through my body. But it isn't magic. It's her touch. It's having her this close to me, in the darkness, touching me.

When her eyes open, her gaze locks with mine. "You'll be okay. The marks will be gone by morning."

My mouth feels funny when I try to speak. "Thanks."

She moves and struggles for a ridiculously long time to

help me sit up. I'm almost laughing by the time she gets me up and wraps my arm around her shoulder.

"Maybe call the guys," I mumble out, amused.

She raises a brow at me. "Do you think I'm a moron? I tried to get them over here when I woke up and realized something was wrong. Aello wasn't working alone; she cast some kind of sleep spell. Luckily for you, spells don't work as well on me."

So that's why they weren't here. I'm just now realizing that with all the wind and the shouting, they should've been here in an instant.

"So," she continues, "we're going to have to work together to drag your heavy self back to camp."

I look at the tiny woman, still huffing and puffing from helping me sit up. "I don't think that's going to work."

Again, she raises a brow. "I'm stronger than I look."

"I'm heavier than I look."

Her annoyance melts away, and a smile teases her lips. "Then what's your suggestion, genius?"

"Stay here."

She studies me. "I guess my sister won't be back... so it should be safe."

I say nothing, just continue to stare at her.

"Do you... do you want me to leave you here and go back with the others?"

No. Why in the hell would I want that? "I'm vulnerable like this."

"Of course!" she says, shaking her head. "You need me here. Okay, I'll stay. I just didn't think you'd want me—but yeah, you need me."

As she lays me back down, I'm kind of surprised by how I feel. It hurts that after saving my life she still felt like I wouldn't want her here.

Celaeno's Fate

I mean, I don't, right? She's still a monster. Nothing's changed. *Has it?*

Despite my thoughts, she lays down beside me, my arm under her head. Overhead, the stars shine brightly down on us.

"Thanks for saving me. You didn't have to."

I don't know why I say it, but I feel like it needs to be said.

She shrugs against me. "I wasn't going to let her just kill you, for your sake and hers."

"Hers?" I ask, shocked.

She nods. "Aello isn't bad. She's just... lost."

What is it with this woman and seeing the good in everyone? Is it because of who she is, or what she is?

Either way, I can't decide if it's a trait I'm starting to find endearing rather than annoying. Actually, I kind of do think it's endearing. How can a being who has lived as long as she has and been through as much as she has still be able to see the good in everyone?

I feel like I'm the opposite. Which is the logical way to be.

"You think your crazy sister is just lost? She wanted me to kill you."

She laughs. "She has threatened to kill me since we were kids. But you know what? She's powerful, and she has a lot of powerful friends. If she actually wanted me dead, I would be. I think she more so lashes out, trying to make everyone as miserable as she is."

"And yet you still wanted to help her..."

She's silent for a long time, but then shifts, resting her hand on my chest. "Do you know what the Underworld is like?" She shivers against me, and I wish I could wrap my arms around her. "There's so much darkness, so much hatred and anger. Do you know what a Shade is?"

"No."

"A creature born from something violent. The gods use these creatures to get revenge on murderers. That's just one of the creatures that haunt the Underworld." She takes a shaky breath. "And there's Cerberus—"

"The three-headed hell hound?"

She leans up over me and grins. I hate how just looking at her makes my heart race. "Cerberus isn't a three-headed hell hound. *She's* just a woman."

Anger flashes inside of me. "Like Lamia."

Her smile falters. "Cerberus was a child. The daughter of Hades. On her birthday, he dragged her out of bed, stood her in front of the gate, and put a collar around her throat with a massive chain attached to it." She tugs at her own collar, and I wince. "A collar like this one, probably made by that asshole Hephaestus."

"It was," I say, surprised when I feel an unexpected wave of guilt.

"Well," she continues. "Imagine being a child, running downstairs for your birthday gift, and becoming your dad's prisoner. Tasked with keeping all the Undead in the Underworld." She stares at me, as if waiting.

"Well, maybe he thought a hellhound was too dangerous—"

"No," she interrupts. "I was there. Cerberus was just a sweet, little shifter. She didn't deserve that. And now, now she's talked about by people like you like she's a monster."

"So, she's not the least bit dangerous?" I ask, unable to stop myself from challenging her.

Her gaze locks with mine. "We all have a little monster in us when we have to fight that hard to survive."

I hate that what she says rings true, because it challenges everything I've ever been taught. In my mind, I go through the monsters I've killed in my lifetime. I remember the battles. The blood. And my injuries.

Monsters *are* dangerous. Anything capable of that kind of destruction is. So why do I keep picturing a little girl chained to the Underworld? Why do I imagine Celaeno defending me against her sister?

"So you saved me to protect your sister?"

"No, I stopped her because you don't deserve to die, even though you want me dead. And I didn't hurt her because she doesn't deserve to die for trying to kill you. We're all powerful semi-immortals. Unless someone cuts off our heads, we'll live forever. We're also all dangerous in our own ways, so I don't think it's my responsibility to determine who lives and who dies. All I can do is try to keep the people I care about safe. And keep them from doing anything I think they'll regret one day."

The people she cares about? Is she talking about me or her sister? Either way, neither of us deserves her loyalty.

"You're a strange woman."

She laughs and lies back down beside me. "I know. A lot of people think my perspective makes me weak. Or a doormat. And maybe sometimes I don't know the right moments to speak up, or when to stay silent. But I have a long life to learn. Hopefully."

"I'm always ready for a fight."

"I noticed," she says, but her voice is kind. "But we all deal with sadness and loss differently."

There's that word again. Sad. But was she talking about me or herself? "Are you sad? Did you lose something?"

She shivers and curls closer to my body. "Yes."

What did she lose? What's she sad about? But I don't ask. All of this has been too much. I'm not supposed to get to know this harpy. I'm not supposed to feel any empathy for her or the other monsters.

And I don't.

So knowing the truth about her history shouldn't matter.

Should it?

Then, after the briefest pause, she continues. "But I'm doing better, because I forgave them. And forgiving someone doesn't mean you forget what they did. Forgiving them doesn't even have to be for them, it can be for you."

I won't forgive Lamia. Never. And this monster doesn't have the right to even suggest it.

"I'm tired," I tell her gruffly.

She tenses against me. "Okay, good night then."

Turning, she faces the other direction, away from me. I tell myself I don't care if I hurt her feelings. I don't care that she feels warm and soft beside me, or that I long to wrap myself around her as she shivers in the chill of the night.

Because it doesn't matter. None of this does. I'm a soldier. A warrior. And I have a job to do. A town to save from a bunch of crazed birds, and a harpy to kill when I'm finished with her.

Yet I stay awake for a long time staring at the stars and feeling smaller than I ever imagined possible.

Chapter Ten

ELITE EDGAR

The gargoyle sanctuary is quiet tonight. I walk through it with soundless steps, staring up at the sky. From down here I can just barely make out the shimmering magical barrier that protects and keeps us hidden from the outside world, at least to everyone except those that know it exists. This place is my legacy. My pride and joy.

When it seemed the days of gargoyles had ended, I had to call in every favor I'd gathered in my immortal life to create it. And it was a challenge to bring so many of our kind here, but it was worth it.

Not only will gargoyles continue to survive, but we'lll thrive. And one day, rule. Because I have secrets. Delicious secrets. And with them, and an army of gargoyles behind me, I'll be unstoppable.

But the female monsters are a complication. The thought makes me frown. Yes, they have given us hope. Medusa's twins. Keto's healthy pregnancy. Through them, we will have a future.

And yet, our future doesn't include them. Eventually,

their use to us will be gone, and it'll take some creativity to exterminate them without riling the anger of their mates. Already I have a plan on how it can be done to further my cause.

Reaching the largest building in our small town of perhaps a dozen buildings nestled between trees and surrounded by a forest, I push open the large doors. Inside, my feet sound loud on the stone as I pass the colorful window that depicts a gargoyle crouching on top of a building, overlooking the city he protects. Going to my throne at the end of the room, I grit my teeth and yank it back. Behind it is a dark passageway.

I light a torch and step into the darkness, pulling the throne back into its place before I keep going. Stairs wind down further and further, and minutes tick by. At last, I step out into a library lit by glowing balls of magic.

Legacy already waits for me. He's an old gargoyle, older perhaps than me, with long blond hair, a youthful face, and a stern expression. I hate that he's taller than me, because it further adds to my feeling that he's always looking down on me.

"We need to talk," I tell him.

He raises an arrogant brow. "I assumed that's why you were here."

My teeth clench together. "You know I sent a brotherhood to kill the harpy, Celaeno."

He frowns. "And here I thought you planned to use the female monsters for breeding purposes."

I hate that he knows my thoughts. "Some of the monsters will help create the future I imagine, and some will not."

It has been seen—Celaeno will take gargoyles from our flock, not add to them. And so, she's not only useless to me, she is dangerous to my plans. Which is something I can't allow.

"So what is it that you need from me?" Legacy asks, crossing his arms.

"What I always need." My voice takes on an edge. "More information."

He stares at me for a long minute where the room filled with shelves of books seems darker and quieter. His hazel eyes have locked onto mine, and I know that he wants to refuse me. He must, by now, know what kind of future I imagine, and I don't think he likes it.

But as a Keeper of Knowledge he's sworn his allegiance to the Elites, and so, he must obey me.

"What information do you need?"

I keep my face carefully blank. "I want to know the best way to exterminate the female monsters and still keep peace amongst the gargoyles."

His brow rises. "The babes need their mothers."

"For now."

His mouth pulls into a thin line. "There is also information about these women who have been labeled monsters. We have their true histories. We have hidden accounts of moments where they were blamed as being cruel. We have—"

I hold up a hand. "I don't need any of that. I need what I came here for."

Legacy gives a curt nod. "Then I'll do what you've asked. I'll consult the books and bring you answers."

"Very good."

I turn and start back up the steps, grinning. If I find a good solution, then I can send more and more gargoyles to capture female monsters. I can continue to use Galena's Sight, her ability to see the future, to determine the Brotherhoods best suited for the female in question.

Never before had I imagined I would play matchmaker between gargoyles and monsters, but knowing the future has its benefits.

The children from these couplings will be special. If I can exterminate their mothers at the right time, and keep their fathers occupied with an enemy, I can shape their young minds. I can turn them into the perfect army.

But only if I know this last piece of the puzzle.

I can't risk bringing in more female monsters if I also don't know how to rid us of them when their use is done. Already, I suspect we need a powerful enemy to blame their murders on. But who?

The Phoenixes are a natural choice, but the monsters could be as well. Or even the gods.

There are so many possibilities, and Galena will not use her Sight in any way that involves hurting the female monsters. I can lie to get some information, but not what I need now. So I must rely on information and my own intelligence in this matter.

And if history is any indicator, this will be yet another thing that I succeed in.

No matter how many lives have to be sacrificed for the greater good.

Chapter Eleven

CELAENO

*I*t's still morning when we leave camp. We fly along the coast, and I find myself missing my wings more and more. Being a shifter, a bird, it's in my soul. There have been times in my life—dark times—when I was a bird more than I was a human. And right now, I'm missing that part of myself like an aching in my heart.

But I'm also not alone.

Glancing at Ender, who carries me as we fly, I notice that his gaze is on the horizon. Because he doesn't notice my stare, I greedily drink him in. Right now, his skin has the grey tint that always comes when he takes on his gargoyle-form. His hair is even messier than usual, and the wind plays with it in a way my fingers itch to replicate. His green eyes are distant, lost in thought. And for some reason, seeing him without his usual merriment adds a depth to the man that I didn't expect.

Or perhaps I'm just reading into him.

Because it's true, as much as I miss being a bird, I love having the company of the gargoyles. And I know that what I'm thinking might make me absolutely insane, but I also like knowing their angle. They've made it clear they want to hunt and kill me. They're keeping me alive because they need my help.

When was the last time that anyone I associated with was so translucent?

Everyone who's ever hurt me, who has ever tried to take my life, I considered them my friends. My family. I trusted them.

Thinking of my sister brings a familiar pang deep inside me. All semi-immortals age differently, in a sense, because experience shapes us more than years. Aello is just… so young. It still hurts that she betrayed me, sleeping with the man I loved behind my back, but I don't blame her anymore. We were all looking for a light in that dark place, and Hades was the light we needed.

I just wish she knew that she was strong enough to leave. And that she trusted me enough to let me help her.

My gaze slips back to Ender. I *am* glad to not have to help her right now. Because I'm enjoying my kidnapping in the most ridiculous way imaginable. I shift slightly, and I'm intimately aware of every hard inch of Ender. He has the most delicious muscles. Big strong arms. A narrow, muscled stomach. And a chest that feels rock hard. I wonder if I could take just a little nibble of him without him noticing.

Probably not. I almost sigh aloud.

It should be enough that I'm being carried by this big, hot man, but apparently I'm a greedy shifter who wants more. *Bad, greedy shifter. Wondering if you can rip his shirt open and lick every inch of him.* This time, I do sigh aloud. That would be *so* nice.

Ender tenses beneath my touch, and my instincts sharpen.

"What's wrong?"

Celaeno's Fate

"Nothing." His gaze slips to me. "They're pointing up ahead, just saying we can land and rest for a little while."

Oh, good! For some reason, I feel like I'm just waiting for the next big disaster in my life. Which I have a feeling has more to do with my anxiety than any kind of pessimism.

We fly lower until we land on a white sandy beach devoid of all human-life.

Ender holds me as I slide my legs from around his waist. When my feet touch the ground, it takes another long minute before my legs stop shaking enough for me to feel steady.

"You good?" he asks.

I smile. "Yes."

He releases me and steps back.

I watch him turn and stride to where the other gargoyles have landed. They talk amongst themselves, and I'm so happy I don't even mind. Down here, I can smell the salty sea. I can even taste it on the breeze. And hear the sound of the waves crashing on the shore.

This is the kind of place I wish I could live forever. *If only.*

Knowing that the future isn't a guarantee, I decide the hell with it. I'm going to enjoy today. This moment. In a way I haven't in a long time. Pulling off my shoes, I walk across the sand. When my feet press into the wet, sandy shore, I'm overwhelmed for a moment. How many times in my semi-immortal life have I stood upon a beautiful beach? Or walked through a busy city? Or lay alone awake at night?

So many times. So many times that the days have blended together.

Which means it's absolutely foolish that today feels different. But it does. And that's kind of nice.

Out in the water I see something. A flash of color.

I freeze. *What was that?*

The thing rises out of the water again, but this time my eyes pick out what it is. A siren.

Uh oh. I have no beef with sirens, but I can only imagine that if the gargoyles and sirens cross paths, there's going to be trouble.

Stripping off my shirt and pants, I toss them on the sand. Glancing back at the shore, I see that the gargoyles are still engaged in a deep conversation. *I better stop this before it becomes a real problem.* Taking a deep breath, I dive into the water.

I swim about halfway to where I saw the siren, when I nearly run straight into her. Breathing hard, I surface. As her eyes meet mine, I nearly gasp. I know this siren, because she's like no other. She's someone I care deeply for. Aglaope is a hybrid. The result of a reckless night a god spent with a siren.

Her hair is pale brown with light blue weaved among the strands. Her skin has only a light dusting of scales, that look more like shimmering glitter, and she has a softness about her that reminds me of the young girl I met many years before.

"Aglaope," I greet her, a smile in my voice.

Her gaze meets mine, and the innocence there wars with a nervousness I don't understand. "Celaeno." My name is a whisper on her lips. "I've missed you."

My smile widens. "I didn't know if you remembered our days together. You were so young. A girl fascinated by my books and stories."

She shakes her head. "Your weeks on my tribe's island were the only good days in my life."

I feel my smile fade. "I'm so sorry, but Aglaope… you know you don't have to stay. You're not a full-siren. You're different. If you—"

"I only came to you to give a warning."

The hairs at the back of my neck prickle. "About what?"

"My tribe is angry. They lost gargoyles that they wished to use for breeding, and our queen has become obsessed with finding new ones. She saw you and your gargoyles flying. The whole tribe will be here soon, and they'll begin their song…"

She doesn't have to say more. Their song doesn't work on me. But I can't protect the gargoyles from it.

"Thank you," I tell her.

She reaches out a hand and touches the collar at my throat. "Are you a prisoner?"

I hesitate, looking between the shore and her. "In a sense."

"Keto was a prisoner too." She looks at me. "Does a person need to have metal shackles to be a prisoner?"

My heart twists. "Anyone who isn't free, who is scared to leave, can be a prisoner."

Her brows lower, and her gaze is thoughtful. "Thank you, wise one. Now, you should go. They're getting closer."

"Thank you," I repeat again.

Turning, I swim as fast as I can. When I reach the shore, all three gargoyles are waiting for me.

"Were you swimming?" Grey asks, sounding shocked.

I grab my clothes and start to haul them on, not caring that I'm dripping wet. "We need to leave. Now."

"We need to rest and eat," Grey says.

"You don't understand—"

"You're the one that doesn't understand. What you did for me yesterday—saving my life—I appreciate it, but it doesn't change anything between us. You're the prisoner! You don't tell us what to do! You don't give demands!"

I look to Ender and Journey. Both have their mouths

hanging open, staring at my breasts. I yank my shirt over them and both gargoyles seem to snap back to reality, their gazes moving to my face.

"We need to go!"

Grey takes a step forward, and I know he means to appear menacing. "Sit down."

Anger uncurls inside of me. "Fine. There'll be a few dozen sirens here soon, who will sing until your ears bleed, and then they'll drag you off to their island and demand you spend your life fucking them. And then when they're done with you, they'll kill you. But what does little old me know? Nothing, I guess. I'll just stay here and then walk away perfectly free when they have you under their spell."

Grey's eyes are wide. He looks to the sea, then back at me. "How do you know that?"

"I have a friend who's a siren. She warned me."

He scoffs. "You can't trust a siren."

I raise a brow. "I guess if you're willing to gamble all your lives on it…"

Ender clears his throat and shifts uneasily. "Actually, a siren once sort of helped me, so it might not be the worst idea to—"

"A siren helped you?" Grey says, sounding incredulous.

Ender shrugs. "Well, she was sort of a hybrid."

"Aglaope?" I ask.

His eyes widen. "Yeah, how did you know?"

"She's my friend too."

Journey clears his throat. "Uh, maybe we can continue this conversation elsewhere? That whole ears bleeding and becoming sex-slaves thing is something I'd rather avoid."

Grey huffs, which I take as a yes.

Ender grabs me, and we launch into the sky.

"Higher!" I tell them, glancing down.

There's definitely motion in the water, like a group of

dolphins swimming rapidly for shore. If we're close enough for the gargoyles to hear their song, we're in trouble.

We fly higher and higher, until I'm sure we're safe. And then we pause.

"Why don't we go?" I ask.

After a moment Grey says, "I just want to see how honest your little friend was."

Seconds later, sirens come pouring onto the shore. They look toward us. I'm sure they're singing, but we can't even catch the smallest sound on the wind.

Everything changes at once. There's a commotion, and then Aglaope is dragged from the water and thrown into the center of the sirens.

"They know she helped us!" I say, horror in my voice.

"How could they know?" Journey asks, but there's something in his voice that says it doesn't matter.

More and more sirens surround her. "They're going to kill her!" I look to the gargoyles.

None of them react.

"If she's hurt, it's because she helped us. Doesn't that matter to you?"

"Is there any way we can go down there without being caught by their song?" Journey asks.

We all know the answer, without it having to be said.

"You don't even want to try." I can hear the words in my voice. "Because she's a monster. Because her life doesn't have value to you."

"No," Ender's voice is soft. "We'd help if we could."

I never heard their song, but I do hear Aglaope's scream, caught on the wind like the cry of a ghost. Tears sting my eyes. The gargoyles could put me down—somewhere where they can't hear the sirens—and I could run back.

But even I know I won't make it in time. Sirens have

sharp teeth. And sharper claws. They'll tear her to shreds, like knives cutting apart fish.

One of my birds lands lightly on my shoulder. I look at the seagull. She felt my sorrow. She came to offer her protection.

Suddenly I can feel my seagulls all around me, gathering closer, flying from different directions. Pulled to me by my emotions before I even recognized my turmoil.

And there it is. My chance to save her.

I look to the gargoyles. "I have to do this."

Journey gives a slow nod, and I can feel it in the air. Seeing my powers will remind them yet again of why I'm a monster. Of why I'm dangerous. I hate that I'm losing any traction we've made, but I have to help the young siren.

Closing my eyes, I call to my birds. I picture the scene with the sirens, and I send what I want to happen. The image of them attacking clear in my mind.

The birds switch directions, moving to obey.

I watch with bated breath. I hear another scream rising on the wind, and I swear I smell the scent of blood. And then, the birds descend. From up here, the battle is strange. The sirens don't understand. They throw their hands at my birds. They move about, clumsy on human legs, trying to stop my birds' attack.

And I see Aglaope. Forgotten for one brief moment. I want to scream at her to run. But I can't. Even if she heard me, so would the others.

She drags herself to the water. And my heart races with her weak movements. Each moment that passes seems like a lifetime.

Just keep going. Just keep going.

The sirens don't see her. But she's so slow. *How injured is she?* Even if she makes it to the water, will she survive?

And then she disappears beneath the waves.

Celaeno's Fate

A siren catches one of my birds. She tears off his head with her teeth.

I cry out, the bird's pain radiating through my soul.

Tears slide down my cheeks. The bird's death was quick. But not painless. It's rare for death to truly be painless. And I hate that he died at my command.

I see no more signs of Aglaope, but I know she needs as much of a head start as possible. Every second gives her a greater chance at survival.

Minutes tick by. Some of the sirens start to throw rocks at my birds. A rock hits one of my birds, and I feel its pain echo through me. More of the sirens start to pick up rocks. My heart races.

They're going to get seriously hurt.

Heartbroken, I order them back. They've done what I asked them to and more. They distracted the sirens long enough for Aglaope to get free. I can't ask them to do more.

And yet, did I give the young siren enough time?

My birds fly past me, one of them unsteady with each flap of his wings. I thank them each, sending them my love. Sending healing thoughts to my injured one. They circle around us, one, two, three times, then shoot away.

Down below us, it only takes a few moments for the sirens to realize that they've lost their prey. They race for the water, shift, and fade beneath the waves.

"I think she got away," Ender says, his voice rough.

I look to him. "You don't understand. Even if she did, by betraying her tribe she'd become an enemy to every siren. She was already an outsider because of her parentage. Now, now she won't be safe anywhere she goes. And she'll be alone. She gave up the only type of family and friends she's ever known to protect us."

My words seem to linger between us.

"Why would she do that?" Grey asks, and he truly looks confused.

I stare. "She wanted to save your lives."

"She's a *siren*," he repeats to me, like I'm slow.

I laugh unkindly. "And you're an asshole."

After a minute, his voice comes out quietly. "Maybe I am."

They begin to fly again, and I'm ashamed to say that I rest my head on Ender's shoulder and cry. Even when I'm free, I'll never be able to find one terrified siren beneath the sea. All I can do is hope that she can find a place to be safe. Maybe even loved.

But for some reason, I don't feel much hope. And that makes me cry even harder.

Chapter Twelve

CELAENO

None of the gargoyles speak much the rest of the day. We stop for a couple of breaks, and then when evening sets in, we see the lights of a big city. Grey steers us away from it, circling around until we find a massive, sprawling manor a short flight from the city. It's surrounded by a tall, strong wall of white stone, and the castle is made with the same stone. The tiny forest and garden within the wall looks to be newly tended, and there's a "for sale" sign posted out front.

The lights are turned on, but there aren't any cars outside. And there's a general sense that no one has lived there for a long time.

We land in the front yard. Ender goes to the front door and pulls out a small set of tools. Kneeling down before the handle, I realize he plans to break in. I want to ask them if this is a good idea. Aren't we risking getting caught? I want a soft bed and bath more than anyone could imagine, but I'm not sure it's worth breaking into a house.

But I'm still mad at all of them for not seeming to care

about Aglaope just because she's a *monster*, so instead of asking my questions, I walk away, heading for the back. For a while I don't really pay attention to the garden, other than a passing thought that it's kind of lovely. And a ridiculous display of wealth.

My mind is just consumed with thoughts of Aglaope. She's little more than a child. A semi-immortal who has already had a hard life. Unwanted and unloved by the other sirens, she was miserable when I briefly stayed on her tribe's island.

Through my time there, I saw her for what she was: a fighter. A smart child with a will to survive at any cost. And now? She had gone against her people, destroyed everything she'd worked for, just to protect me and my gargoyles.

We owe her so much.

Certainly more than to disdainfully act as if being a siren meant her sacrifice meant nothing.

Moving down a path, I look up to see a statue. I continue on until I'm in front of it, and then I stare in shock. It's a gargoyle. One still in its stone-form. It's also… a woman.

I rack my brains. I've seen a lot of art in my long life. And many gargoyles perched on the tops of buildings. In fact, in my bird-form I've slept beneath the comfort of stone gargoyles more times than I can count, taking refuge from the rain.

Because I never really knew that the monster-hunters and statues were the same. I bet few monsters know that, because if they did, we'd likely have gone around smashing all the statues before they could shift into creatures capable of killing us.

And yet, as I stare at this statue, I'm distracted by my sadness, my curiosity aroused. What made this statue remain when the others transformed? And what artist created a female one, and for what purpose?

"Holy shit!"

I spin around to see Grey and Ender staring up at the statue.

They rush toward me.

Ender reaches up as if to touch the statue, then curls his fingers back. "Do you think the Elites know about her?"

Grey shakes his head, his gaze distant. "We'll have to tell them so they can purchase this place while it's available."

"They buy places with gargoyle statues?" I ask.

Ender answers without thinking. "Not all statues awaken. Some statues take a great deal of time. But our leaders try to buy places like this, to protect our kind as much as possible."

"And especially because she's a female," Grey's voice is soft.

I hate that I feel a ping of jealousy. "Why does that matter?"

"They're rare," Ender answers, and Grey shoots him a dirty look.

Rare? Why? I open my mouth to ask questions.

Grey cuts me off. "That's more than you need to know."

I glare at him. "Remember this the next time you have any questions."

He raised a brow. "Noted."

Journey comes hurrying down the path. "We have a problem, guys."

"Stay here," Grey orders me.

Ender and Grey rush after Journey, and they all head for the house.

I feel annoyed as I stand in the garden. These gargoyles

owe me nothing, not really, but this song and dance is getting old. I don't expect them to treat me like a friend, or even someone they care about, but I'd be nice to not be treated like shit for a little while.

"Who are you?"

I whirl around at the sound of the strange man's voice, my heart racing.

Three men stand behind me. All have nothing more than a band of cloth tied around their waists. All three have long hair and wild expressions. And they're massive. As massive as my gargoyles.

Something about them makes me uneasy, like I'm facing three wild animals rather than men.

"I—I was going to stay the night. Do you live here?"

The men exchange a glance.

One of them steps toward me, his eyes almost golden in color. "We live here. It's our home. It has been for as long as we can remember."

"I'm sorry," I tell them. "I'll go."

"No," he says, and his tone is tender. "It's been so long since we've seen a female. And you—you're a beautiful female."

I know I should be scared by these three. There really is something dangerous about them, but I also get the feeling that they won't hurt me. It's the same way I feel about my gargoyles.

Taking a deep breath, I take a chance. "You guys aren't human, are you?"

The golden-eyed one shakes his head. "No, we're gargoyles." He moves closer and reaches out, his fingers stretching out until he brushes my cheek. "Does that frighten you?"

For a minute, I'm torn. Moments flash in my mind, of Ender, Journey, and Grey looking at me like this. The times

Celaeno's Fate

when their touch was gentle. I don't want this gargoyle the way I want them, but there's something strangely precious about this moment.

It's like a reminder that without my label of "monster," I can be seen as a woman. As attractive.

"Who the fuck are you?" Grey's voice comes from far behind me, and he sounds enraged.

The gargoyle before me stiffens, but he continues to touch the skin of my cheek like he can't stop. His gaze pulls from mine and goes to Grey.

"You're the gargoyles that were born here, aren't you?" Grey asks, but he still sounds angry.

The man who touches me nods. "And you are gargoyles too. Is this your female?"

"No," Grey rushes out.

It stings how much the one word hurts.

The man cocks his head. "Then, can we have her?"

"No fucking way!" Ender shouts, and I realize Grey isn't alone. "Get away from her!"

I turn just slightly to see all three of my gargoyles at the top of the path that leads down to where we stand. And I'm shocked, because they look angrier than I've ever seen them before. Do gargoyles not like each other?

"She's not yours…" the gargoyle continues.

"But she does belong to us," Journey says, the words holding a possessive tone.

"Which is it?" The gargoyle asks. "Is she yours or not?"

I wait, holding my breath. Will they make some kind of claim to me to keep these strange gargoyles from wanting to take me? Or do they hate me so much that they can't even pretend to make this situation easier?

"She's our prisoner," Grey says, his words dropping like ice.

"Prisoner?" The gargoyle looks at my collar. "Since

when do gargoyles imprison females?" He snarls. His hand drops from my cheek, and he pulls his sword free. "We have been asleep for a long time, but not so long as to have forgotten that we are protectors! Defenders of the innocent! And I swear, gargoyle or not, you will die by my sword if you try to harm a female."

My heart beat races in my ears. The two gargoyles behind this one withdraw their swords, but my gargoyles remain standing. Ender and Journey look to Grey, and I can see them waiting for the slightest signal showing what they should do.

A woman's voice whispers in my ear. "Be careful."

I shiver, glancing around. Cold fingers seem to trail up my spine. *A ghost?* It's been awhile since a ghost reached out to me. Fewer and fewer since my time in the Underworld.

"She isn't a female, not really." Grey pauses.

Don't say it. Don't say it. If he says it—

"She's a monster."

His words drop between all of us like stones. The wild gargoyle looks to me.

"Duck before you lose your head," the ghost whispers into my ear.

And sure enough, the gargoyle pulls back his sword. I leap out of the way, almost losing my head.

On the ground, I spin so that I'm on my back. The wild gargoyle roars and leaps toward me.

Grey is there in an instant. Their swords clang together.

"Brother, why do you fight me?" the gargoyle shouts.

Grey's voice comes out strained. "Her use isn't over yet."

The gargoyle makes a sound of disgust. "No monster has a use!"

I scoot back and see that Ender and Journey are

squaring off with the other two gargoyles. My heart races. I don't see how this can possibly end with all of us alive.

"You've been asleep for a long time," Grey continues. "There's a lot you don't understand, but all your questions can be answered in the gargoyle sanctuary."

The wild gargoyle glances between me and Grey. "Sanctuary?"

"The place most gargoyles live now. Where we're given missions. Monsters to kill. Things we must do in order to receive a mate."

"Mate?" one of the other gargoyles asks, lowering his sword. "If we go to this place, we may be given a mate?"

"Yes," Grey tells them.

Another tense moment passes. The wild gargoyle looks to me. "And what will become of her?"

Grey answered without hesitation. "She'll die."

The way he says it. I hate that it breaks my heart.

The wild gargoyle nods and resheaths his sword. His two companions do the same.

"Tell us where to find this sanctuary."

Grey nods and gestures for them to follow him across the well-manicured lawn.

When they're far enough away, Journey walks towards me and holds out a hand. I ignore him and rise to my feet. My skin still feels irritated from the sea water. My clothes have dried, but they feel stiff and uncomfortable. I'm covered in twigs and leaves. And these gargoyles just spoke about killing me as if it was inevitable.

The last thing I want is for any of them to touch me.

Journey sweeps a hand through his tangled blond hair and his blue eyes look at me with guilt. "We've found your room for the night."

I give him a sharp nod and walk up the white path

leading back up to the manor. But each step I take, my heart breaks a little.

Why do I keep doing this to myself? Did I really think it was a good thing that they're upfront about their plans to eventually kill me?

I'm a complete idiot. It's not. It just means I've surrounded myself with assholes again.

New day. Same old stupid Celaeno.

Chapter Thirteen

ENDER

I keep picturing the gargoyle touching Celaeno, and I feel absolutely enraged. Isn't it enough that the chances of us ever having a female of our own is pretty much zero? Now these newly awakened gargoyles immediately start hounding in on her.

It's stupid that I'm mad. But I am.

And what's worse? Then he tried to fucking kill her.

My hands bunch into fists. I'm not an idiot. I know why we were sent here. But it doesn't matter. If Celaeno had been a second too slow, she'd be gone forever. Her life snuffed out like a candle forever. No more of her shy smiles. No more of her stories that keep me fascinated.

No more laughter.

Because as much as Grey is making these idiot "baby gargoyles" all kinds of promises about the sanctuary, it isn't like that at all. It's a place with only three females around our ages. These females choose the males they want with each pregnancy, and the rest of us are left alone, wishing for even a ghost of a chance at love.

Celaeno can't be our chance at love. She can't be our female.

But for a little while, I can pretend. There's nothing wrong with pretending that when I touch her she could be mine. There's nothing wrong with thinking that sparkle in her eyes is because of us. Right?

"You like her." One of the newly awakened gargoyles looks at me.

His long hair is dark and tangled, hanging over his face. His eyes are strange, such a pale blue they're almost white.

"I don't know what you mean."

He cocks his head. "You like the monster. I can see it in your eyes. I can see that you see her as yours."

I smirk at him unkindly. "You don't know anything, baby gargoyle."

He prickles at the insult and takes a step toward me.

Grey's conversation dies with the man before him.

"They're going to head to the sanctuary now," Grey tells me, his every word measured.

I look back at the baby gargoyle and dare him to keep talking. Dare him to keep walking towards me and see how much a lifetime of fighting has sharpened my skills.

His mouth draws into a thin line, and he takes another step closer.

The blond-haired gargoyle places a hand on his shoulder. "We will not waste energy fighting against our own kind. We head toward this place—the one where we will be given monsters to kill and women to fuck."

My gaze slides to Grey, but his expression gives nothing away.

"And what of the female gargoyle?" the blond asks.

The gargoyle shrugs and looks to Grey. "She has not

woken in our past few battles. Perhaps she has gone too deeply into her slumber and can no longer be reached."

"We can't just abandon her!"

Grey speaks before the strange gargoyle can. "We will let our leaders know. They can purchase this property and keep her safe."

A long minute passes, and then the blond relaxes. "You say this sanctuary has women for fucking and monsters for killing?"

His companion laughs and pets our shoulder. "We should go before all the good females are gone."

"Good bye, Draven, Kage, and Soren. We'll see you soon, when we're done with this mission."

The dark-haired one clasps his arm. "Thank you, Brother."

We watch them leave, saying nothing. I don't care what Grey had to say to get them to leave. I don't want them anywhere near Celaeno.

"Think they'll be mad when they get there?"

Grey shrugs. "We're all mad."

I hesitate. "They could have killed her."

"I know."

"You shouldn't have told them what she was."

He turns to me with anger in his eyes. "And what? Let them take her into the woods and fuck her like animals?"

"Like you want to do to her?"

He grabs the front of my shirt and hauls me closer.

I keep my hands curled into fists.

"Just because that's what you want doesn't mean that's what I want." He releases me, but I don't move away from him.

"Do me a favor, oh perfect leader, lie to me all you want, but don't waste your time lying to yourself." Turning, I start back toward the manor.

487

"None of it matters, Ender. We have a mission. And there's only one way it'll end."

I keep walking. Not just because I want to escape him, but because I want to escape the truth.

Chapter Fourteen

CELAENO

I'm lying in a tub filled with hot water, which feels like absolute heaven on my sore muscles. So unbelievably good that I swear my brain has melted into a pile of happy goop.

Did I find this place creepy at first? This isn't creepy, it's amazing!

Yeah, it's filled with antique furniture… and the closets are full. And there's personal touches everywhere, as if the owners simply vanished a long time ago, and nothing was touched. But that's just eccentric, not weird.

Nothing really matters as long as I'm soaking in a giant tub filled with hot water.

Someone recently seems to have dusted, washed the bedding, and turned the water and electricity back on. If I were to bet, I'd say it was done to help sell this place. Which is totally normal.

Maybe not totally *normal.*

And yet, I wouldn't have a hot bath or clothes to change into if this place wasn't so strange, so that makes it worth it. Anything if I can just stay in this bath and forget my troubles for a little while. Forget that the three guys I've been feeling a strange connection to don't feel the same way about me. Even though I imagined maybe they did. At least a little.

A light shimmers at the end of the tub, and a ghost slowly comes into focus. It's that of a young woman with a kind smile. She's wearing a nightgown from another era, and her hair is loose about her shoulders. All in all—she looks to be a nice ghost. Which I'm grateful for.

They're not always nice.

She smiles at me. "Hello."

I hear her familiar voice and smile back. "Thanks for the warning in the garden."

She laughs, and the sound is a little sad. "No, thank you. You are only the second being that could see me. It was nice to be heard, if only to save your life."

After my time spent in the Underworld, and likely because of the job I was responsible for, I can often see ghosts. Sometimes the experience is good, and sometimes not so much. But the reason the ghosts remain on this plane is always the same: they have unfinished business.

"What's your name?"

"Catherine," she answers easily.

"Catherine," I repeat. "And why are you still here, Catherine?"

Her easy smile fades. "I was the loser."

"Loser?" I repeat, generally curious.

She nods and seats herself lightly at the end of the tub, the light growing dimmer around her. "Our family has secrets. Secrets that need to stay hidden. One of us had to remain behind to ensure it. And I was the loser."

"Makes sense." I already know this family didn't die from violent means. If they did, she'd be one angry ghost, but I still ask. "And what killed your family, if you don't mind me asking."

She shrugs. "An illness. It swept through the house, killing our family and all those serving in our household."

"I'm sorry."

"It was a long time ago."

I take a little fancy soap I found in one of the bathrooms and start to scrub my skin and hair. Some people might feel weird having a ghost watching them take a bath, but anything becomes normal with enough time. And I've had ghosts pop up at far stranger times than this.

"I know you are the prisoner of those gargoyles," she says, after a time. "But do you think you could help us hide our secrets?"

I freeze. "Would you be able to leave this place then?"

She nods.

"Am I going to be hiding anything creepy? Bones and that kind of stuff?"

I'm not sure, but I swear she blushes. "Just one set of bones. Some journals. A couple paintings."

Even though that's the last thing I want to do right now, I can't imagine walking away and leaving her here to spend eternity trapped within these walls. There really isn't a choice. I have to help her.

"Alright."

She clasps her hands together in excitement. "Thank you!"

I dip beneath the water, washing the soap from my body and hair. Beneath the bubbles, images of the gargoyles come back to me. I try to push them away, but they linger. I hate how much my treacherous heart likes those three.

They don't deserve the tiniest sliver of my heart.

When I resurface, the ghost begins to tell me her plan.

I listen halfheartedly, trying not to think about the three jerks. When she'd done speaking, I get out, dry off, and put on one of the old gowns in the closet. I hand washed my clothes, which are currently still drying by the window, so this is all I have right now.

Following the ghost into the cellar, I help to undig the tiny skeleton. It's the bones of her father's child out of wedlock. And I'm thankful that rather than hiding these bones again, all she wants is to give them a proper place in the family cemetery. I wrap them in a blanket, carry them out to the overgrown cemetery in the very back of the estate, and bury them beside the others. Taking a piece of wood, I etch her name into it, *Eveline Winters, beloved daughter.* Then I collect the items on her list from their secret locations and burn them near the cemetery.

When I'm done, I turn to the ghost. The look of relief that washes over her face warms my heart.

"Thank you," she whispers.

I smile. "You can go now. Your reason for being linked to this earthly plane is gone."

She has the most stunning look of happiness as she glows brighter and vanishes.

On to some place better than this.

Using the little shovel, I cover the smoldering remains in the tiny hole. I'm suddenly so tired, and yet, I need to take another bath. Without looking back, I toss the shovel on the ground and return to my room, where I take another bath and put on another gown.

When I'm done, someone knocks at my door.

Opening it, I come face-to-face with Journey. Relief flashes over his face when he sees me.

"We couldn't find you!"

I shrug. "I had something to take care of."

He takes a deep breath that seems to shake his whole chest and nods.

"Is that all?"

He hesitates. "I'm sorry about earlier."

"What about?"

His gaze locks onto mine, and I hate how my heart flutters under his stare.

"You know."

"No, I don't," I press.

"We didn't mean to put you in that situation."

"Grey did. He told them what I am, and he didn't have to."

He shakes his head. "He told them because he was afraid they were going to take off with you."

"So he would've rather had me dead?"

He shifts a little closer to me, his voice lowering. "You have to know he never thought that was going to happen."

I stare back at him. "If he was sorry about it, wouldn't *he* be the one here rather than you?"

"It's complicated…"

"Because of his hatred for monsters? I know. I know about his Brother. I know about it all."

He reached forward and very slowly brushes my wet hair back from my face. Everywhere he touches seems to awaken. For a minute, I'm actually foolish enough to think he might kiss me. The tension that sings between us seems to scream it. The distance between us seems to grow smaller, and I can't quite catch my breath.

And then he drops his hand. "Get some sleep, Celaeno. I'll be right across the hall if you need anything."

I nod. "And better hurry off and tell the others I didn't make a break for it."

He looks sad, but he turns, and I know he's doing exactly that.

I close the door. My legs are shaking. Tomorrow we'll finally reach our destination. I'll see what's wrong with the birds in this town of Cherish, and I'll try to help.

And once I do, I'll have a week's head start. I'll have time to scramble and get as far from these men as possible. If they keep their word. But either way, that will be the last time I see them. The last time where we have this weird agreement between us.

After that, the rules of war will apply. Which means there will be no rules. It'll be kill or be killed.

So I'll stay away from them. And any memories of them will fade from my mind.

As I climb into the bed, I hate that I feel strangely sad about that. Because one thing is clear: I feel something for them. But no matter what they feel for me, it isn't enough for them to see me as anything but a monster.

I brush away the foolish tear that slips down my cheek. There's no reason to cry. I don't have anything, so I'm not really losing anything.

Chapter Fifteen

ELITE GALENA

The moon's bright tonight, and the sanctuary is silent. Tiny fairies flutter around me in the clearing, dancing from flower to flower. I wish I was at peace enough in this moment, enjoying the simplicity of this moment, but the future darkens my mood.

Being Seer, a healer, and an Elite is complicated. I see the future, but only in pieces. And the pieces I've seen… they've left me even more confused.

Before Medusa, life was simple. Monsters were bad. We were good.

But things have changed. Some of the Elites act as if this change occurred over night, but it didn't. Like a wheel of fortune, our fate has been spinning and changing for a long time.

It began when our numbers started to dwindle. Gargoyles were soldiers going out into the world. Dying for our cause. At first their deaths seemed to mean little, but then fewer new soldiers were born. Artists were no longer creating our kind with the love and care that's required to give them a soul. There were some statues still made, yes, but mostly manufactured somewhere without artists or souls—like empty bags of flesh. Stone objects never to awaken.

Edgar had made this sanctuary and we'd all worked together to search out as many gargoyles as possible and bring them here. This was the only way we could see to preserve our numbers. We no longer allowed the gargoyles to go out into the world, battling monsters without thought. There simply wasn't enough of them for that.

We sent Brotherhoods on carefully calculated tasks, the purpose of which was mostly to distract them. A town of warriors who can't fight and don't have women creates a volatile situation. So when we felt them becoming too restless, we sent them out.

With Medusa, collecting her had been a mixture of a favor and a necessity. When a human in charge of keeping the paranormal world secret from the humans contacted us about her existence, we saw it as Fate. The future showed me that she was a key to continuing our kind.

I thought it would be because of her ability to turn us back into gargoyles, being capable of shifting from a human-like form to stone, and being immortal. There was no way to predict she might save us all because of daughters she would give birth to.

Being her midwife, caring for her, it was impossible for me to continue to hate her. It was impossible to see her as just a monster, and not a woman. And then there was Keto.

Sighing, I turn and stare at a flower.

The fairy queen stares back at me.

Her voice comes soft and musical. "What is it that you see that has you here again?"

She settles down on the petal of a red flower, spreading her skirt made of lavender out around her. Her skin shimmers, as if dusted with glitter, and her eyes are a piercing gold.

"Your majesty," I greet. We've grown to be friends over the years, but the fairies like formality.

She inclines her head in acknowledgement. "Speak freely."

I smile, glad for her wisdom. I can't speak to any of my own people about what's on my mind.

"Our role is to hunt monsters."

She nods, saying nothing.

"There is honor in killing a dangerous beast and protecting mankind." I hesitate. "But are all monsters truly monsters?"

The questions hangs between us like something powerful. Like a storm that's been building.

Her wise eyes gaze into mine. "No. Your entire society is founded on a lie. You created a common enemy and foolishly decided the world was black-and-white. Now you're seeing the grey, and you're afraid. And you should be."

My heart races. "Edgar says that to acknowledge that possibility will destroy our society."

"It might." She raises a delicate brow. "But now that you know the truth, can you really pretend you don't?"

I swallow hard. "Edgar finds the names of female monsters. He asks me to look into the future and see if they'll add to our society or take away from it. Depending on what I see, he dispatches a Brotherhood with the goal to either capture the women or kill them. Those that are captured he hopes will fall in love with the Brotherhood I See as being a possible match for them. And those that are killed he sees as a proper distraction for the men… to keep them occupied so they don't see what's happening."

"And this bothers you?" the queen asks, studying me.

I stare down at my hands, feeling strangely young and confused. "I don't want to help with this mission, but I'm scared that if I don't, we'll lose everything."

The fairy doesn't answer me for a long time before she rises slowly to her feet. "You must decide, gargoyle, if you will continue to help this man in a task you know is wrong, simply because you fear the destruction of the society you hold so dear."

"I know," I say, frustrated. She hasn't helped me at all. "But what should I do?"

She smiles. "That's for you to decide."

I incline my head out of respect when she flutters away, but my thoughts continue to turn. If I keep helping Edgar to kill the women and kidnap them, am I really doing anything wrong? We've always killed monsters. This is no different.

Right?

I think of Medusa and her babies. I think of Keto and her big pregnant belly.

Damn it. Since when did gargoyles start feeling like monsters?

Chapter Sixteen

JOURNEY

The three of us stand at the top of the building. We'd had one moment of panic, when we went into Celaeno's room and couldn't find her. But now we knew she was safe.

And I think our response to not finding her had scared all of us.

I don't think a single one of us was worried she'd ran away. I think we'd been scared the gargoyles had come back and taken her from us. None of us had said it, but our terror was clear.

"She's our enemy," Grey says, his voice lacking its usual harshness.

I gave my word to keep my secrets to myself. But it seems my secret grow more significant with each moment that passes. A gargoyle's word is his pride. If I don't keep mine, then what kind of man am I? But then, how can I look at my Brotherhood and lie?

"What if she isn't?" My voice is soft, but I know they both heard me.

Grey looks at me, his expression unreadable. "The line

between monsters and the rest of us is clear. There's no grey area. It's black and white. It's always been that way, and it'll always be that way."

"How do you know that?" I press him.

His gaze narrows. "Is there something you know that you aren't telling us?"

I take a deep breath. Time seems to stand still. "No. But surely we've lived long enough to know that nothing is that simple?"

Ender runs his hands through his hair in an agitated way. "Fuck it. I'm saying it. I've run into Aglaope before. And she helped me then. It made me question this whole them and us thing. And now with Celaeno… well, I have to say, I'm not sure everything is all that cut and dry after all."

"We were given a task." Grey has the slightest note of pleading in his voice. "We can't question the Elites. This was the mission we were given. And if we don't do it, someone else will. Someone that might not be as gentle with her."

"So we just keep going, knowing we'll kill her?" I ask.

He gives a sharp nod. "Nothing has changed."

Anger races through me. I shift into my gargoyle-form and leap into the air. Ender calls after me, but I ignore him. How can I possibly keep my word and get them to understand?

Is there even a way?

I search my thoughts, but no solution comes. And so, I fly. I fly over the city. I fly over the coastline. I fly until exhaustion tugs at my thoughts, and then and only then do I return.

But instead of going to my room, I land lightly on Celaeno's balcony.

Soundlessly I shift back into my human-form and walk

through her balcony doors. A slight breeze tugs at her white curtains. I enter the room like a ghost, moving to her as if this moment has always been inevitable.

Standing over her, I'm both disappointed and relieved to find her asleep. Her dark eyelashes dusting her pale flesh. A trail of tears just barely illuminated beneath the moon's light.

I swear that no matter how long I live I'll never see a female as beautiful as this one. Somehow this tiny woman has made her way into my heart, and I can't see a way of getting myself free of her.

There's a strange kind of misery that comes with seeing a woman I could love, that I could have a future with, and knowing that it'll never be. That my knowledge about the female monsters can't overcome my Brother's prejudice against her. And that the only woman we can be with is a woman we can all love.

But still, I lean closer. If she opened her eyes right now, I know what would happen. I know that we'd make love, and that every promise and every bit of loyalty I have in this world would fade away beneath her loving touch. That I'd give up everything, even my Brothers, for the kind of love I know this woman can give me.

Yet, she doesn't open her eyes. She sleeps peacefully. And when I go to leave, I can't help but look back, wondering what could have been. And wondering if perhaps in the morning our futures will be a little less bleak.

Chapter Seventeen

CELAENO

*T*he gargoyles weren't kidding when they said something was wrong in this town. The second I arrived, I felt a dark presence that was almost suffocating. It's like being trapped beneath a blanket of suffering and grief that chills my very soul.

In all my life, I've only been to a few places that felt like this. *All* of them were cursed.

We're standing on a hill, overlooking a small town surrounded by woods and mountainous hills. The sky overhead is a deep, sleet grey, and the clouds are heavy with the promise of rain. All and all, this is exactly the kind of place I'd expect weird shit to happen.

I shiver, looking down at my jeans and t-shirt. I'm definitely not dressed for this weather. Not the chill or the icy winds clawing at my flesh.

"Cold?" Journey asks behind me.

"N—o—pe," I stammer through chattering teeth.

He gives a soft smile and grasps the bottom of his sweater. I swear my heart skips a beat as he peels it off, leaving behind a thin t-shirt.

"Want it?"

"Uh-huh," I say.

Boy do I want it. I want it against a tree. I want it on the ground. I want this big man to keep shedding his clothes until I get to see if they carved his package as nicely as they carved the rest of him.

Calm down! I order myself. But that's the thing, I'm starting to realize that half of the reasons I find these gargoyles so frustrating is because I find them so hot.

"Celaeno?"

My head jerks up, and my cheeks burn. He's holding the sweater out in front of him, and there's no chance he didn't see me eye-balling his junk. So much for playing it cool.

I was playing it cool up until now, right?

"Thanks," I mumble, grabbing his sweater and putting it on to hide my embarrassment.

With his sweater around me, I'm wrapped in his scent. I swear I have to hold back a groan of pleasure. It smells that good, so rich and manly that my inner muscles squeeze in the mostly pathetically lonely way.

Man, I hate myself right now. It's like spending half the day riding Journey in the air has turned me into a desperate, horny woman. The worst part is that I've been getting the same sense from the guys. Ever since the strange gargoyles tried to take off with me, I've been catching them staring. And maybe I'm delusional, but they look as sexually frustrated as I feel.

"Better?" he asks staring at his sweater on my much smaller frame, his voice tinged with a huskiness I'm digging.

I pat my small breasts and run my hands down my stomach, caressing the soft material. "Much."

When I look up, all three men are staring at my chest.

Ender's mouth is hanging open, Journey's eyes are bugging out of his head, and Grey looks like he's about to do something bad—something I might enjoy. *Where did that thought come from? I can't be considering Grey romantically, not after he called me a monster and swore he'd be killing me soon.*

But then I think of what he said about his brother dying at the hands of Lamia, and my heart aches a little. I understand loss. I understand how angry it can make us, and how that anger can tear at our souls.

I'm still mad at Grey. I still think he's a jerk. But I also know that his anger and bravo is all in an effort to hide the way he truly feels: sad. And that somehow makes me feel closer to him.

Even though I hate it.

Looking at the gargoyles, they continue to stare at my breasts. It's almost comical.

"What? Have none of you seen breasts before?" The second the words slip from my lips I wince.

Grey adjusts the front of his jeans and storms away.

Journey gives me a guilty look. "Sorry, being celibate has its disadvantages."

I think my brain just stopped working. "I'm sorry, but did you say *celibate*?"

He nods, looking pained.

"So… none of you have sex at all?" *How has this not come up until now?*

Ender exhales noisily. "No."

Wow. The mere idea that they're celibate makes me feel all kinds of things I didn't expect. For the first time since meeting them, I'm grateful. It's nice to know they're probably as horny and miserable as I am. It's even nicer to know that when this is all over they won't be going home to bang a bunch of gorgeous women.

That idea makes me scowl. Of course their type would be big busty blondes with long legs.

"I bet there's a pack of tall models just counting the days until they can take you guys for a spin again."

Oh fuck, I can't believe I said that out loud.

Ender laughs, and Journey is grinning like a fool. "Afraid there's no 'pack' of models anywhere."

"Nope, we *always* share one woman…" For one second I picture a Celaeno sandwich with these gargoyles, but Ender has to ruin my fantasy by continuing to talk. "So, there's only going to be one gorgeous model somewhere."

I cross my arms over my tiny boobs. Maybe I'm barely five foot two inches, and maybe my figure is as flat as a board. So what? Tiny-boobed women need love too.

And here I thought they weren't attracted to me because of the monster thing. And then I imagined they were attracted to me. Turns out I'm just not their type.

"So, you guys wanted to show me these birds, or what?" I know I sound a little grumpy, but I don't care.

Grey perks up from where he's been kicking dirt by a tree. "Finally, something that isn't a waste of time."

He hurries up before I can respond. I trail after him, annoyed that I'm a little hurt.

Ender's suddenly at my side, walking slower to match my stride with his long legs. "There's another thing wrong with what you said."

"Surprise, surprise," I mutter.

He lowers his voice. "We're not so much into models as we are into smart-mouthed brunettes." My hearts races as he leans closer, his hot breath ticking my ear. "And we've got this thing—where we really want some tiny girl we can fit perfectly between us."

I'm pretty sure the spot between my thighs melts. We keep walking, but I'm lost in horny thoughts.

When thunder rolls in the distance, my head jerks up. Frowning, I stare up at the sky. Inhaling slowly, I get that feeling again, but this time it's worse. Every step we take toward the town deepens that feeling of dread.

I catch the sour scent of a curse on the air. Something's wrong here. Really wrong.

I stretch my awareness out and feel my birds, but that's not right either. I dig a little deeper, frowning.

"Shit," I stumble, clutching my head. I go down on my knees, trying to stop the pain.

Ender's kneeling in front of me in a second. "What's wrong?"

Tears sting my eyes. "My birds—"

My words get caught in my throat. Touching their minds was like touching a hot poker. Anger burns within them, and behind that fear, sadness, and confusion. Their emotions were so intense that for a second I was lost in them. I've never felt anger that strong before.

It's scary… and dangerous.

"Celaeno," Ender says my name softly, and then, he's caressing my neck.

I stiffen. His fingers are like magic, drawing me back from the pain, drawing me out of their minds.

My head falls to rest against his chest, and my hands rest on my thighs.

He continues to rub my neck and shoulders, erasing the tension that I've allowed to build up for years. "What's wrong with her?" Grey asks, and there's an edge of something in his voice.

I sigh. "This feels so good. You have no idea."

"Really?" Ender whispers.

"Yeah. I can't remember the last time someone touched me like this."

"Fuck," he mumbles.

Journey speaks from above us. "Better stop talking like that, small fry, or Ender's not going to be able to handle himself."

I laugh, surprised yet again by the change in these three. What has come over them? Or was it something that has come over *me*?

We'd had a good night's sleep. But that wasn't it exactly. This morning they'd been… different. Almost openly kind to me. Was it really just because of the strange gargoyles trying to kill me?

Or maybe it's because we've reached our destination, so our time together is almost over? That actually has a strange ring of truth to it.

When I look up, all three gargoyles are staring at me. What were we talking about again? *Oh yeah…* "How long have you three been celibate?"

My question's met with silence.

I snuggle closer to Ender as his hands move down my back. "Don't everybody answer all at once."

Man, this feels nice. Too damn nice.

"A little over twenty years," Journey says, very slowly.

My head shoots off Ender's chest. "*Twenty* years? Fuck! You three must be going nuts."

Grey glares. "That's exactly why some hot little monster shouldn't be rubbing her breasts, moaning, and getting massages. We're here to do a job, not to do *you*."

I stare at him. "I didn't *rub* my breasts!"

His eyes flash with anger. "When you put on his damn sweater! Don't act all innocent here. I know exactly what you're doing. You know how hot you are, and you know just how to work the three of us into a frenzy."

"I was not…!" I freeze. "Wait, you think I'm hot?"

Grey rolls his eyes to the sky. "Did we piss off some

asshole god somewhere to have to deal with this shit? Let's go."

Ender is grinning again as he stands and offers me his hand. I take it, still staring at the gargoyles. Do they really think I'm hot? The concept is so damn weird to me I don't even know what to say.

We keep walking toward the town, but this time in a group.

"So what exactly happened back there?" Ender asks.

I stiffen, remembering the wrongness of my birds.

When I glance around the trees, the feeling deepens yet again. Why are there no birds in this area? I sense that all of them are concentrated in one area ahead, but that goes against the natural instincts of birds.

"Whatever this curse is, it's powerful."

They all freeze.

"How do you know there's a curse?" Grey asks, and for once he's not scowling.

I stare at him in shock. "Didn't you all feel it the second we landed?"

They shake their heads.

Maybe I can sense it because of what I am. "There's a powerful curse across these lands and my birds are being affected by it."

That seems to silence them. For several minutes we continue forward, and with each step my belly twists tighter and tighter. I fight the urge to run, clenching my fists. I'm ready to fight whatever is causing such pain to my babies.

When we leave the forest and reach the town, my jaw drops. Every single roof is lined with birds of every sort. I spot a few cars on the roads, but no one is outside.

"Fucking creepy," Ender whispers beside me.

I can't help but agree.

"Are we safe to walk through the town?" Journey asks, and all eyes turn to me.

Hesitation makes my pulse race. "If we walk slowly and talk softly, we should be okay. They won't attack unless something frightens them."

"Are you sure?" Grey's dark eyes are glued to the rooftops.

"No," I say. "But the only way we'll stop whatever's happening here is to find out the cause of it."

Moving forward, I follow my own advice and head slowly toward the center of town. After several seconds, I feel the gargoyles following.

The birds' heads turn and follow us as we move, and a tingling sensation moves down my spine. They're wound so tightly that the smallest thing can set them off. Poor things.

When we come to the first shop with an open sign, I cautiously pull the door open. The little bell on the handle gives one lonely chime before I clench it in my fist and tear it free. Turning, several of the birds have spread their wings, but none of them take flight.

The men follow me into the little shop filled with candles and bath products. Behind the counter a young woman looks up, her eyes widening. She can't be much older than a teenager, with dirty-blonde hair and pale eyes.

When I hear the door whoosh shut behind us, I speak without looking back. "You guys do some shopping."

Grey makes a sound of protest, but I plaster on a smile and ignore him. The girl watches us curiously, and her cheeks heat when her gaze lands on the sexy gargoyles behind her. I want to laugh—*girl, I don't blame you one bit*!

"Hey," I say.

She gives a shy smile. "Hi."

"We're just passing through," I tell her.

She nods. "Yeah, I figured. I've lived here all my life, so I know pretty much everyone in Cherish."

I go to the front and start smelling the candles lined along her counter. Something drops loudly behind me. I look back and see Ender sheepishly picking up a metal candleholder from the ground. All the guys are holding things, staring at them as if they're alien products.

I laugh out loud. I can't help it.

"What?" the girl asks, but the word holds a smile.

"Nothing, it's just like seeing bulls in a China shop." Her smile widens as I turn back to her. "Hey, I don't mean to be insulting or anything, but what's with all the birds?"

Her eyes widen and her smile vanishes. "I don't know."

"Has it always been like this?"

She shakes her head. "It started a few weeks ago and seems to get worse every day."

Interesting. "Anybody know why?"

"The town brought in some bird experts. They even… even tried to… exterminate some of them, but that made things worse. A lot worse."

I have to push down my rage at just the thought of someone hurting my birds. "What did the bird experts think?"

She nervously starts to arrange some things by her register, spending way too much attention on a tree with earrings. "They couldn't find a reason for it."

"So what, everyone's just going to live like this?"

Her gaze meets mine, and she looks worried. "No, on Friday they're going hunting. They plan to kill all the birds. All of us are supposed to stay inside away from our windows, so we don't have a repeat of last time."

"Last time?"

I see her visibly swallow. "The birds killed some of the hunters. Including my brother."

Celaeno's Fate

Shit. "I'm so sorry."

Her eyes fill with unshed tears. "Some people think it's some kind of virus, like rabies, but I just know it's because of—"

She drops the little tree of earrings on the ground and kneels down behind the counter.

I circle around and help her pick them up. "Why do you think they're like this?"

She shakes her head. "It's stupid."

I smile. "I like stupid."

We just keep picking up the earrings in silence, and I can tell she's turning something over in her mind.

"Do you believe in... weird stuff?"

A little tingle moves down my spine. "Yes."

"Because no one in this town does. My dad says if we can't see something, it doesn't exist."

"No offense, but your dad sounds like he's one of those annoying logical types."

She frowns. "Yeah, Mr. Police Chief is all about the logical."

I pick my words with care. "But I'm not at all. I think the world is full of things we can't understand or explain. Paranormal things."

Her head jerks up. "Like ghosts?"

I nod. "Yeah, I believe in ghosts. Do you?"

She stands and puts the earring tree back on the counter. I stand too, but don't move away. Instead, I wait and look back at the guys. All of them have moved on to other things. Ender's sniffing a candle. Grey swears when he accidentally spills some body glitter on his shirt. He wipes at it with his hands, but it's absolutely hopeless. I bite my lip to keep from laughing.

"Around the time the birds came, someone disappeared."

My attention snaps back to the girl. "Who?"

"A woman I was friends with. She used to come here a lot. People… they didn't think much of her, but she was always nice to me. She was a dancer down at the club on Marlene Street. She just vanished. They looked for her, but not very hard." Her hands are wringing together. "I think maybe the birds and her disappearance are connected."

Her eyes fill with tears again, and I see she's trembling. My heart gives a squeeze.

Reaching out, I touch her bare shoulder. A tingle moves through me and I freeze. This girl has witch-blood in her. No wonder she's got her theories. No wonder she can't just pretend this has an easy explanation. She senses something is wrong.

"Can I be honest with you?" I ask her.

She turns those tear-filled eyes onto me. "Yes."

"My friends and I are ghost hunters and we came here just to figure out the solution to the bird issue."

Her gaze snaps between us. "Are you serious?"

I nod.

"Are you guys any good?"

Smiling, I can't help myself. "*I* am. They're mostly here to look good."

She gives a small laugh and wipes the tears from her eyes. "So you think you'll be able to stop this before the hunt? Because, well, my dad is leading it. He's angry about my brother. He doesn't seem to realize that if things go wrong I'll—I'll have no one."

My heart goes out to her. I know what it feels like to be alone. "We'll take care of it, but anything else you can tell us about this woman would help."

The gargoyles have stopped pretending to shop. Instead, they move closer and stare at her, waiting for her to answer.

She sweeps a nervous hand through her hair. "Her name was Candy Spring. And… and she had a few boyfriends. Craig Olsen and Jack Calwin. She also had a regular at the club who made her uncomfortable… a Richard something. She lived on Drop Off Avenue, at the end. There's a really broken down house there."

"Did she live alone?" I ask.

She shook her head. "She had a daughter… Angel… she's in foster care with the Jensens now, until they can find her a permanent home."

"Well, thank you. We'll look into it. We might come back if we have any more questions."

"Of course," she says.

We tell her goodbye and head back out into the street.

Walking shoulder to shoulder down the quiet street, Grey leans closer. "So what now? What's the plan?"

"We break the curse," I tell him simply. "And if it wasn't created by this woman's disappearance, we keep looking."

"This town definitely needs our help," Ender says, glancing again at the birds.

"Before Friday," I tell them. "That's when they plan to kill the birds."

Just four days.

"Celeano—" Journey begins.

I whirl on him. "I know you guys don't care about them, but I do. Every life is precious. We can't let them be hurt because of something that's not even in their control."

All three men are looking at me in the strangest way, but I don't care. They couldn't possibly understand what it's like to have seen as much death as I have.

I'll do anything I can to keep more blood from staining this world.

Chapter Eighteen

GREY

I don't understand Celaeno. She was supposed to be a monster, a creature that feeds on pain and misery. When I saw her outside the shop, attacking the humans, I was certain that all we'd been told by the Elites was true.

But what if they were wrong?

Ever since she was nearly killed by the other gargoyles, and then disappeared, I feel like I'm fighting to hold onto the things I've been told. I speak the words I know I'm supposed to say to my Brothers, but I don't feel them anymore.

I stare at her as she strides down the street. She's gorgeous, and somehow even sexier while wearing Journey's sweater. It's massive on her tiny frame and reaches all the way to her knees. It makes her look fragile, and the image calls to me, like a woman who belongs to us.

And yet, she's a monster…

Gargoyles are built to protect the innocent. So why do my instincts cry out to protect *her*? She's the enemy, right? I think about the moment I hit her and it makes me sick. All

I saw was a monster attacking innocent humans. I think of the moment I saw her birds gathered around my Brothers. It terrified me, even though somewhere in the back of my head I knew she wasn't dangerous. And then I think of the way she defended me against her own sister.

Each time I told myself that she had to be the monster we were sent to kill. But now? I see a beautiful woman who has been put in danger because of me. It turns my stomach to think about it.

Now I'm even angrier. I shouldn't be having these complicated emotions. This task should be cut and dry. Instead, meeting her, the real her, has me swamped with emotions that I don't understand. I wanted to think the way she gentled when I talked about losing my brother was all an act, but is her concern for her birds and the people in this town an act too? Maybe. Maybe not.

I blame her, this intriguing creature that is nothing like we were told.

"We'll check her house first," she tells us softly over her shoulder.

Her voice is musical, light. Sometimes she sounds like a being who has lived for thousands of years, and sometimes she sounds young and innocent. That's probably why my instincts are screaming to wrap her in my arms and take her out of here.

And the worst part of it all?

Journey and Ender are completely smitten with her. We've kept our vow of celibacy, hoping against hope for a chance at one of the female gargoyles as a mate. When their current mating sequence finishes, they will be allowed to pick another harem of males to father their next children. That has always been the tradition—they pick from chaste mates.

Unfortunately, we think we know who they'll pick next,

and it's not us. Chances are we'll never be fathers, which is making it hard for us to feel like our celibacy is anything but a pointless torture.

Until we can get our heads on straight, we shouldn't be anywhere near an attractive woman, certainly not a woman who has captured the attention of all three of us. Which was why we volunteered to take care of this problem in the first place. Capturing and killing a heartless monster seemed like just the thing to make us forget about our constant hard-ons.

How were we supposed to know that the monster we'd be catching would be hot as fuck?

Celaeno freezes in front of us. "I'm thinking Candy's house is pretty far down this road. Maybe you guys should just fly us there?"

I stiffen. Just the idea of her wrapping those little legs around my waist again has me hard as fuck. There's no way I'll be able to hide my attraction for her.

Ender turns to me. "Actually, it might be dangerous. Why don't Journey and I have a thirty second head start and check it out?"

I glare at him. He knows perfectly well I don't want to touch her again.

"Sounds perfect!" she says, looking back at me with a challenge in her eyes.

"Fine," I huff, even though I'd much rather sneak off to the woods and masturbate until this tension eases.

We slip into an alley, eying the birds that watch us closely. Silently, we shift into our gargoyle forms, and Ender and Journey fly into the distance with slow, even sweeps of their wings. I'm still watching them when she leans against me and wraps her arms around my neck. I lean down further to give her better access and our eyes meet.

She tilts her head and a sadness stills over her face that takes my breath away. "It's okay, you know, about what happened with those other gargoyles. It hurts when people call me a monster, but I get it."

My brain reaches for anything to put distance between us. "You still blame us for how we see you after what you did to those humans?"

To my surprise, the hurt on her face becomes heartbreaking. "I didn't mean to." Her words are almost a whisper.

"Then why did you do it?" I don't know why I asked. I guess because something in me needs to know.

Her hands drop from around my neck and slide absently down my chest. Every muscle in my body tenses at her sweet touch, but her expression is far away. "It's stupid."

I wait.

And then, a story pours out of her lips. Rage builds inside me with every word she speaks, but to my surprise, it isn't at her. It's toward the bitch who hurt her. Who lied about her poisoning customers and got her fired from a place that actually felt like home to her. When she finishes, she looks like she is doing everything in her power to keep from bawling.

Again, I feel an overwhelming need to protect her. I want to wrap her in my arms and tell her I understand. That I think the bitch deserved to have her eyes pecked out.

But I say nothing.

Because the second I hold her, the second I reassure her that I'm on her side, everything will change between us. Even if it already feels like it has.

I'm not sure I'm ready for that.

She takes a deep breath that rattles her whole chest. "Sorry, that was more than you probably wanted to know."

I shrug and wince at the hurt in her expression. I didn't know what to say, but maybe saying nothing was worse.

"Let's just go," she says, and there's an edge to her voice.

I pick her up carefully, as if I'm carrying something precious and fragile, which I am.

We fly above the road the missing woman lived on until we reach the shambled house at the edge. My brothers have just emerged from the doorway, and they glance up at us as we approach. Ender waves a hand, and I shoot straight for them. Settling down in the grass, Celaeno immediately shoves away from me.

That should have no impact on me, but I have to admit it hurts a little.

"It's safe inside," Ender says.

She hurries past him and Journey and goes into the house.

My brothers come slowly out to where I'm standing.

"Why does she seem upset?" Journey asks, his question an accusation.

I'm quiet for a minute, trying to decide what to say. "She told me why she attacked those people."

They stare at me. Waiting.

"And I think they deserved it."

Ender's eyes widen. "I kind of thought something was up. So what does this mean?"

It means that the only proof we have that she's actually a dangerous monster is now gone.

They're looking at me, waiting for my answer to a decision I haven't yet made. "It means right now I want to fuck her more than I want to kill her."

Celaeno's Fate

Journey looks back at the house. "Fuck her? Or keep her for ourselves?"

That's the problem. I'm thinking it might be both. I want to fuck her *and* keep her for ourselves.

"But," Ender says really slowly. "If we don't kill her, won't the Elites just send someone else to do the job?"

I thought of that too. "Let's just focus on solving the bird problem. Then we'll decide what to do with her."

Because none of this was simple. Seeing Celaeno as an innocent woman changed everything. Not just how to handle her, but also our purpose in this world.

Our kind hunt and kill monsters. It's true we haven't done it much since our numbers dwindled to almost nothing. Since breeding with humans has been a fail, and breeding with our own kind is so slow, the Elites haven't been willing to risk gargoyle lives. It wasn't until recently that they seemed to have changed their minds. I think because they realized that tensions were growing higher between all the males who had nothing to do but think about how horny and lonely they were.

So what else are we supposed to do if our purpose is taken? Hunting monsters is as natural to us as breathing. If we don't kill Celaeno, we'll lose the faith of our people. Letting her live goes against everything we are. How can we fail at something so simple? Yet how can we go through with it?

Despite everything, I can't picture us hurting this woman when the time comes. Which is—

A woman's scream rips through the air, jerking me out of my thoughts and into action. We race across the grass and into the house in a panic.

That was Celaeno's scream.

Why the fuck did we leave her alone?

Chapter Nineteen

CELAENO

A ghost stands just feet away after popping out in front of me. Her expression is thunderous.

This spirit is angry and dangerous. Everything around her tiny living room floats, waiting to attack.

"What's wrong?" Grey whispers. "What is this?"

"The ghost…" I manage to say, my voice trembling.

"Ghost? All I see is a bunch of floating crap," Grey mutters, but his words are tense.

"Can you really not see her?" I ask.

My eyes meet hers. She's pale with golden hair that floats around her face. A glowing white light circles her. She's beautiful and young, which makes her death even more tragic. And if her spirit is angry, she didn't die in a peaceful way. The clash of beauty and danger that happens with ghosts always rips my heart out. Every spirit deserves a peaceful afterlife.

Even if she wasn't affecting my birds, I wouldn't abandon her now.

"We're here to help," I tell her.

Indecision flickers in her eyes. *Oh, Candy, who hurt you?*

"We know something happened, and we know your spirit isn't at rest. Show me why. Once I know, you can pass on." My teeth grit together. "And the person who did this can pay."

All of the floating objects in the room drop in an instant, and she turns, disappearing through the wall.

I race back to the front door and go around to where she faded. She's in the woods in the backyard, waiting expectantly for us.

A shiver moves down my spine. The woods here are old with red, gold, and orange leaves that have just begun to fall. Beneath the trees, the shadows are deep. I can't tell if it's my instincts, my fears, or my sense of magic, but something tells me that it's not safe there.

"Is this a joke?" Grey growls angrily into my ear, startling me.

I stiffen, but don't take my eyes off the woman. "No, Candy's ghost was in the house. And she's definitely the reason for whatever's happening in this town."

"I don't see anything," Journey says.

"Me neither." Ender steps forward, squinting at the woods.

"Just… trust me," I tell them.

The ghost turns and disappears into the shadows. My muscles tense. *If we're not fast, we'll lose her!*

Hurrying after the ghost, I fully expect one of the gargoyles to stop me, to argue that I'm lying. From Grey's response to my story about my friend, I realized something that turned my stomach. No matter how I justify my actions, these three will never see me as anything but a monster.

Which means, once this issue is solved, they're going to kill me.

They're gargoyles, and killing my kind is what they do. It doesn't matter that I feel attracted to them, or that there's something that intrigues me about them. I can enjoy them for now, as long as I never forget that the second this job is done, I need to get as far from them as I possibly can.

Maybe I'm a fool, but I think I might be able to have my cake and eat it too.

There's just one more problem with my plan.

I tug at the cold metal at my throat, but it doesn't budge. I have to find an excuse to get them to remove my collar. That will be tricky, but I'll never escape if I can't shift.

I'll figure something out…

We continue through the woods. Just up ahead, the ghost of the woman is a pale light the shape of a person. She stays as far from us as possible, just close enough that I can see her in the shadows between trees.

When she suddenly disappears, I pick up my pace and start racing. Her anger is building and building. I can feel it all around me like a storm.

Exploding out of a tangle of branches, I start tumbling, falling, with nothing but air beneath me. I scream and try to shift as I go over the edge of a cliff, but the collar keeps me in my human form. There's a lake, ringed by sharp rocks that come closer with each passing second. I struggle in midair, trying to save myself, but gravity pulls me to my doom.

And then, just before impact, something grabs my ankle and I freeze, dangling inches from the sharp rocks. Breathing hard, I look up. Journey's holding my ankle, his expression terrified.

He lowers us to a strip of sand away from the rocks and pulls me into his lap.

For a long time he just holds me, stroking my hair. My

head rests on his chest, and the pounding of his heart matches my own.

"Don't ever do something like that again," he growls at last.

I look up at him, and his deep blue eyes hold a wealth of emotion that makes me feel things I shouldn't.

"I was just following the—"

He silences me with a kiss.

For one second I'm too shocked to react, and then I moan and wrap my arms around his neck, pulling him closer. His lips are warm and demanding, pressing harder against mine, coaxing my lips to part. Once I obey, his tongue dives inside, claiming my mouth as his own. My tongue tangles with his, and I swear I'm melting in his arms. It feels so damn good to be kissed like this.

I don't think anyone has ever kissed me like they *need* to in my life.

"Journey!"

His mouth yanks away from mine.

I look up at him. His eyes are darkened with desire, and his gaze runs slowly across my face.

"Journey," Grey repeats, his tone a threat.

At last, the gargoyle who holds me so tightly looks away, breaking the spell. "She was nearly hurt."

My kind wouldn't die from a fall like this, but it'd take weeks just to be able to walk without a limp. And the pain would be… mind-numbing.

"We're not here to kiss monsters," Grey says, aggression in his voice.

For one second, I think Journey will disagree, but then his grip loosens around me. I feel strangely disappointed.

"It looks like that ghost was trying to get you killed." Ender picks up a rock and tosses it into the lake. "I'm not sure we can trust it."

I open my mouth and freeze.

Climbing from Journey's lap, I see the ghost again. She's halfway between the bottom of the cliff and the top, near the rock wall, on a little overhang near the mouth of a small cave.

"I don't think she was trying to hurt me. I think she wants to show me something."

"What?" Grey sounds irritated. "If she died here, we'd see her body, right?"

"I'm not sure she died from falling." I start walking, climbing up the rocks. It's going to be tough to reach the cave without getting hurt. I just wish I had my wings.

"Where are you going?" Journey asks, and I sense him behind me.

I point. "She's standing near the cave."

Suddenly, someone sweeps me into their arms. I turn, and I'm staring into Ender's face. Something inside of me twists, and I hate that every nerve in my body feels alive and aware of every inch of him. He cradles me gently without moving for one long minute, his gaze running over my face, and then lifts me into the air.

"Are you sure we can trust her?" he asks softly, as if he doesn't want the others to hear.

I almost smile at the concern in his voice. "Ghosts aren't usually cruel. They just want someone to end their suffering. To help them get justice… and peace."

We reach the tiny landing outside the cave, and the ghost disappears into the dark hole.

"Have you spent a lot of time with ghosts?" Ender asks, not yet putting me down.

I shrug. "When you've lived as long as I have, you're bound to run into them. And when I do, I help however I can. No one should be trapped in their suffering like that. This time though, I'm surprised by the power of her spirit.

Something isn't adding up. She should be able to torture the person who hurt her… but not an entire town."

He holds me for a minute longer, studying me. "I wouldn't have thought one of your kind would get involved with ghosts and human problems."

I feel a rush of anger. "Because my kind are so awful, huh? Put me down!"

He hesitates.

"Now!"

He does, and the other gargoyles squeeze in next to him on the landing. I feel the weight of their stares. Do they still not believe me? I don't want to look at any of them. I'm angry, at myself more than them. I know what they are. I know why they're here. I shouldn't feel confused just because I'm lonely. I should expect them to treat me like their monstrous prisoner… and nothing more.

"Listen, Celaeno—"

I cut Ender off. "She went down here. I'm guessing that's where her body is."

I start forward, but Grey catches my arm. "We can't fit down there."

Looking back at the hole, I realize it'll be a tight fit for me too. "That's okay. You guys stay here, I'll go."

His grip on my arm tightens. "Not a chance. That ghost already tried to kill you once. We'll figure out another way inside."

I turn and look at him. His dark eyes are angry. His square jaw clenched.

"Don't worry, gargoyle. I'm a monster. I'm expendable, right? Worse case, she cuts off my head and saves you the trouble." I yank my arm from his grip and enjoy the look of surprise on his face before I duck and step into the cave.

Immediately, he hauls me back. "We'll find another way inside," Grey says. "Even if she doesn't have something bad planned for you, that space is too small. You'll get stuck."

"Then take off my collar. It'd be easy for my raven to get inside."

He hesitates.

I let my gaze slide over each of them, and that fire inside of me builds. "Fuck all of you, pretending you give a crap about me. Admit it. You don't like my kind, and you don't trust me. You three just stay out here and be assholes together. I'm going to help this woman find peace."

Spinning, I start for the cave again.

I'm yanked back against a hard body for a second time.

Glaring, my gaze meets Grey's.

He leans down so our lips are inches from each other. "You really think you can get in and out safely?"

I nod, hating that I'm transfixed by him.

His hands reach up and wrap softly around my throat. My heart races, and I lick my lips. There's something so damn possessive about the way he looks at me, the way he touches me.

It's no wonder I'm so freaking confused.

And then he yanks on the collar, and it snaps off in his hands.

My eyes widen and I touch my bare throat, suddenly feeling the weight lift off both my body and my heart. *Does he actually trust me enough not to just take off?*

"We'll look for another way in and stay close. You be careful."

I nod again, feeling the heat of his body along my back.

"Is this a good idea?" Journey asks.

My gaze shoots to him.

He blushes. "I mean, sending her in alone, not the collar."

Grey shrugs. "I guess we just have to trust that she can do what she says."

I feel a strange thrill at his faith in me. As I walk to the entrance of the cave, I look back at them. All of them seem worried, but none of them are moving to stop me.

Was I wrong about them?

Shifting, I feel my bones crack and my shape change. In seconds, I'm in my raven-form once more. Stretching my wings out, I internally sigh. It feels good to tap into this part of myself once more.

It's strangely freeing.

Pumping my wings, I lift off of the rock and fly into the darkness. My heightened senses help me steer clear of sharp rocks and the twisting in the tunnel. Up ahead, I see the ghost's light once more and fly faster.

When I explode out of the tunnel, I find myself in a big cavern. Natural light drifts in from far above. The ghost stands in the middle of the smooth dirt floor.

My heart races as I fly closer and stop on the ground.

A witch's symbol has been made on the ground, written in blood. The coppery scent fills the air, and the sweeping lines of the symbol are more black than red now.

Candy's body lies in the center of it. Laid almost peacefully. Her hands folded on her chest. If not for her slit throat, wrists, and ankles, and the blood that splatters her body, she could be a woman laid to rest by her loving family.

It all makes sense now. Candy hasn't cursed this town. A witch sacrificed her to create this powerful spell. How many witches could there be in this town?

I shift back into my human-form, wincing and rolling my neck. I usually don't shift back and forth so quickly. It makes me remember that I'm not young anymore.

Standing, I look from the ghost to the woman. My

heart squeezes, and I swallow around the lump at the back of my throat. I can't imagine what this human experienced. She probably felt lost in these tunnels, away from the sunlight, afraid for her life. The witch would have fed on that fear before she drained the girl's life blood. No wonder Candy was angry.

"You were sacrificed?"

She nods.

"By your jealous ex?"

She shakes her head, and I feel her anger building.

"A man from the club?"

The sand from the ground begins to lift around me. Again, she shakes her head.

I know she's growing impatient and frustrated. She wants me to solve her death. She wants me to lay her to rest. But what am I missing? Who would want to do this to her?

"An enemy?"

The cavern overhead shakes, and tiny rocks and debris fall.

I cover my head, my heart racing as I look above me and back to the ghost. If I keep making the wrong guesses, she might just bring the roof down on me. And the idea of being buried alive… now that's a nightmare I wouldn't want to experience. An immortality trapped beneath rocks.

I shiver. *Stay focused.*

"Not an enemy then…" Every muscle in my body tenses. "A friend?"

The shaking stops. The falling of the sand slows. And she crumbles to her knees, her face in her hands.

I watch, my heart aching, as this ghost cries over her dead body.

Unable to help myself, I move toward her and kneel at

Celaeno's Fate

her side. Placing a hand softly above her translucent back, I whisper, "I understand."

She looks up at me, and our eyes meet. Tears gather in the back of my throat.

There are few things sadder in this world than seeing a ghost cry. Their tears glisten down glowing cheeks. Their suffering fills every inch of them, keeping them bound to this world. Slaves to their worst moment.

They have no one to hold them, to tell them it'll all be okay. They have no one to wipe away their tears or even to hear their story.

I know what that feels like.

My vision blurs with my own tears. "We're going to solve this problem."

She reaches out and touches the pocket of her body with fingers that pass through it.

"You have something you want me to see?"

She nods.

I don't relish the idea of touching her dead body, but I take a deep breath and reach inside her pocket. She has a tiny wallet with her phone attached. And the picture in her little wallet? It's of her with a little blonde haired girl. They're holding each other so tightly. Matching smiles on their faces.

I choke out my words. "You want to keep your daughter safe?"

She nods.

Setting her wallet carefully down, I look at the picture one more time. "We'll keep her safe. I promise."

I press the picture between her chest and her clenched hands. "So that she's always with you," I tell her.

The ghost reaches up and touches my face. All I feel is the slightest chill.

"So, your killer is a friend. And a witch? Can you lead me to her?"

Her hand drops, and she shakes her head and points at her body.

I immediately understand. "You can't go far from it."

She nods again, then points to the wallet again and fades from my sight.

For a while I remain kneeling there, head bowed, reciting an old prayer for her peace. When I rise, her wallet and phone clenched in one hand, I realize I'm not alone. Several feet from me, a dark, shadowy figure looms over the bloody scene. Evil comes off it in waves, filling the air with the scent of death, rotting bodies, and blood.

A guardian of the witch's sacrifice. So no one can weaken her curse.

Heart racing, I inch slowly back from it, knowing it's here for me. Reaching down, I scoop Candy's body into my arms, trying not to wince at how stiff she is. I stand with careful movements and take a step back toward the direction I came from. I have no idea how I'm going to escape and take Candy's body to put it to rest, but I have to try.

The skeletal arm of the creature rises and points upwards. The top of the cavern begins to shake, harder and harder with every passing second. My throat closes and dust fills the air as I head for the exit. I would run, but I'm carrying what's left of Candy.

My feet slip in the dirt, but I keep moving. Seconds before I reach the exit, rocks crumble down, sealing me inside. I step back, coughing and choking on the cloud of dust the collapsed tunnel creates. Panic claws at my spine.

Now which way do I go?

The shadowy figure remains, its hand still raised. Power rolls from it in waves.

Squinting through the dust, I look for another exit, anywhere I can escape from. But I see nothing. I know there are exits high above me, but I refuse to leave this woman's body down here. I tighten my hold around her. *I won't do it.*

Moving back toward the shadowy figure, I gently set Candy down. Taking a deep breath, I charge at the creature. It vanishes, and for a moment the cavern goes still. Then the creature reappears across the room and the shaking begins again.

Gritting my teeth, I hate how helpless I feel. I could destroy it by calling my birds to me, but I refuse to bring them into danger. So I attack it over and over again, kicking, punching, anything I can think of. I only manage to slow it down.

I'm sticky, covered in sweat and grime, and my knees are shaking. Every time more rocks and dust crumble onto me, I replay the image of myself buried here forever, but I can't bring myself to abandon this woman's body. If I leave now, I have no doubt this thing will bury all evidence of her death from sight.

There's a loud crack above me and I look up to see large rocks falling. I have to roll to avoid being crushed. A second later, Journey is there, between me and the creature. His wings beat back the dust, and he floats there for a moment like the gargoyle of legend, strangely beautiful and powerful.

Then, he spots me in the corner. "Come to me!" he shouts.

I point at Candy's body. "We need to take her too."

His brows rise, but he grasps her body and reaches out for me. I fling my arms around his neck, and he lifts us into the air and out the larger hole he's created above us. We shoot out into the light of day, and the other two gargoyles are there in an instant. Grey snatches me from his brother's arms, and we fly higher. Down below, the entire side of the cliff crumbles into itself, leaving behind a mess of boulders and debris.

They take us to the other side of the lake. Journey lays Candy's body down, and suddenly all three gargoyles are around me.

"Are you okay?" Journey asks.

"Were you hurt?" Ender says, his hands running over my arms.

I'm sure I look horrible. I feel exhausted, and I'm shaking. But I'm okay. "I'm fine."

Grey says nothing, he just holds me for a while. Somehow, that's nicer than anything I would've expected from him.

"So you found her?" Ender looks between her body and me, his expression unreadable.

I nod. "A witch performed a ritual using her body... which is why this curse is so powerful."

"Fuck," Ender mutters shaking his head. "So what do we do?"

I close my eyes, thinking. "We leave her body at the bottom of the cliffs to be discovered by the locals. And then we find who did this to her."

"And we get you cleaned up and checked over," Grey adds, a little too gruffly.

Ender arranges Candy's body at the bottom of the cliffs. The gargoyles say their own little prayer, and then we're off. By the time we reach the little motel, evening has settled in. Journey goes into the office in his human-form, gets a little room, and we all go in. They give me the shower first, promising to return with food and clean clothes.

I'm bone-tired. The events of the day have eaten at me

like termites. And now, it takes everything in me to run the cheap motel shampoo and conditioner through my hair, and to scrub the layers of dirt off my body. I don't even care when I leave the bathroom to find the room empty. I dry off and slip under the sheets.

I toy with the idea of leaving, escaping the three gargoyles, but I sense something has changed with them. I'll help this town and then see where we are. At that point, I'll be able to slip away.

If *I have to leave them*, I think, with a foolish smile.

Chapter Twenty

JOURNEY

We've killed monsters. Rescued humans. Protected entire societies from the darkness that threatened to consume them.

But apparently, we can't pick out clothes for one tiny woman.

We argued about the size. About the color. And about the style. After each choosing an outfit for her from the only clothing store still open in the tiny town… maybe the only clothing store *in* the town, we're heading back to the motel with four large pizzas and three women's outfits.

Hopefully *something* we bought will make her happy.

Opening the motel room, the same tiny lamp we turned on is still illuminating the desk in one corner, but the room is strangely silent. For a minute I panic. *Is she gone? Did something take her?*

And then my gaze slides to one of the beds, and I freeze.

She's there.

Holy fuck.

She's lying on her back, the sheets tangled around her

Celaeno's Fate

waist... completely naked. The sight of her bare breasts, small and perfect, begging to be touched and tasted, has melted my brain and hardened my dick. All I can do is stare and stare, like a man starved.

I'm shoved from behind.

"What's the hold up?" Grey growls. "I've got a mountain of pizza."

I don't even care.

I'm finally shoved out of the way. The two men pile in behind me. Grey is mumbling to himself when he sets the pizza down, but I know the instant both men see her.

We're all absolutely silent.

Staring in shock.

We have a beautiful, naked woman in one of our beds, and we don't have a clue what to do about it.

"Is she waiting for us?" Ender asks.

"You wish," Grey says, but his response is breathless.

Swallowing hard, I move to the edge of her bed. My fingers curl into my palms as I stare at her hard nipples, her smooth stomach, and her skin that looks soft as hell. If she was here waiting for us but fell asleep before her seduction, I should wake her with a kiss. But if I do, and that wasn't what she planned at all, I'll feel like an ass.

It's almost painful to lean down and whisper her name. "Celaeno." My voice comes out rough with need. "We brought food... and clothes."

She moans in her sleep and arches her back, shifting her position.

My cock twitches uncomfortably in my pants, begging me to free it. Her lips part slightly, and I imagine her sweet mouth wrapped around my shaft. Once the image fills my mind, there's nothing else.

The Fates must be laughing their asses off imagining

three celibate gargoyles spending a night in a room with this naked vixen.

The mattress suddenly shifts, and Grey sits on the other side of the bed. "Celaeno," he growls, "wake up!"

She wrinkles her nose in the cutest damn way. "What? You grouchy old gargoyle!"

"Get up!" he says.

Without opening her eyes, she sits up. The blankets slide further down her body, and I swear, one more inch and we'll see every inch of her. "What?" she mutters. "What's so damn important?"

Grey pulls her into his lap, and her eyes finally flash open. They look at each other, and Grey may appear mad, but I know better. He's so aroused he's about to snap.

"Do you know what you're doing to us?"

She looks confused. "Yes."

His mouth draws into a line. "And you want this?"

Again, she looks confused. "Yes."

"Fuck," he groans, and then his mouth is on hers.

I think Ender and I are too shocked to move for an instant. If Grey's kissing her, that's the green light for us both to lose control. And we're more than happy to… if she actually wants us.

As their kiss deepens, she shifts in his lap, her hand digging into the back of his hair and pulling him closer. When his hand raises and curls around one of her breasts, she pulls back from his kiss and makes a squeak of protest.

"I'm naked!"

Grey flicks her nipple. "Yes, you are."

Her gaze sweeps from Ender to me. "So, you all want to…"

"Yes," I answer, too quickly.

"Then what are you waiting for?"

I know I should play it cool, but I'm struggling out of

my clothes like a teenage boy. I lose my balance while trying to get my damn pants and shoes off, but then I'm on the bed next to a naked goddess, and I don't give a fuck about anything.

Grey's kissing her again, stroking one of her mouth-watering breasts like he owns the damn thing.

I yank her out of his grip and pull her sweet, naked body into my lap. The friction of her ass on my hard dick makes me want to come right there.

Grey looks like he's about to punch me.

"Take your clothes off first, asshole," I tell him.

And then I'm burying my face between her breasts, licking the soft skin. She moves across my lap to straddle me. I groan and clench my teeth. Oh, fuck. If I knew we were going to break our twenty-year run of no sex, I would have masturbated beforehand. A lot.

But since I didn't, this will take every drop of control I have.

When she starts to moan and slide on top of me, my thoughts snap back to the naked woman. My mouth trails to her nipples, and I suck and play with them. I am such a breast man, and everyone knows it. Large or small, I could spend my day buried between them.

I'm going to enjoy every second of this.

The bed shifts, and I see Ender rise up behind her. He reaches between us and strokes her between her thighs.

She cries out and wraps her hands around my head, drawing me closer. I don't mind a damn bit. She's also bouncing against me, which is doing all kinds of things to my control. My hands go to her hips and I adjust her so I'm sliding just where I want to be.

Every muscle in my body is tense.

She's bucking against Ender's hand, which causes her to rub against my erection. I can't be sure, but I think she might be trying to drive me insane. My hands tense on her hips and I'm breathing hard, but I just keep sucking on her beautiful breasts, loving how she shoves my head against her as she thrashes.

And then Grey is lying beside us. I turn to look at him and see that he's stroking himself. His expression is entirely focused on the action, his eyes dark. He's waiting, biding his time for her sweet mouth.

It's been a long time since we shared a woman in our bed, but we haven't forgotten. You never forget. When Grey moves closer and captures her neck, pulling her into a kiss, I continue to lavish her breasts. I hear Ender swearing softly under his breath, and then her entire body tenses.

I glance at him. He's easing himself into her from behind.

"Do you want me to stop?" he pants.

She shakes her head. "Just… I want… both of you."

My head feels light. She wants me inside of her?

I adjust her, pressing my tip at just the right spot. I'm repeating the names of every type of stone I know in my head as I ease myself into her tight body. Inch by inch she squeezes me harder. Her nails dig into my shoulders, and I know Ender is sliding into her from behind.

When I can go no further, I look up and meet her hooded gaze. Our woman looks overwhelmed but satisfied. My stone heart warms.

Grey rises up beside us and guides her head to the side. She takes him into her mouth, and the sight of her greedily sucking him only deepens my arousal.

I lift her by her hips and plunge her right back down. She cries out around the dick in her mouth, but I don't slow. Ender and I find a rhythm, thrusting in and out of her tight body as it squeezes and clenches around us.

I'm back to listing every type of stone I know. Back to trying to keep myself from spilling my seed before I've satisfied my female. She starts to spasm around my cock. Her nails drag down my shoulders, slicing into my flesh, and she's coming. She rides us in a frenzy and takes Grey even deeper into her throat.

I stop listing stone. I grip her tight as my thrusts grow even faster, racing toward the edge, and I'm coming, filling her sweet, tight body with my seed.

Every nerve in my body is awake, in tune to every twitch of the woman on top of me. Ender shouts, and then he's coming too. I lay back and watch her face as she's filled by both of us. Grey growls and grasps the back of her head. His expression is one of complete ecstasy as he finishes into her mouth.

For several long seconds, we're all just surrounding her, filling her.

She connects us in a way we haven't been in a long time.

Grey and Ender pull out of her and lay on the bed. It's a tight squeeze, but we manage it. She stays on me, my dick still buried inside of her. I like that her head rests over my heart. I run my fingers through her long, beautiful dark hair, and my thoughts circle.

If this was just about sex, I'd be showering now. But I'm not. I'm lying here, enjoying every second in this woman's arms, and that scares me. I like her. I like the way she challenges Grey and the way she makes Ender laugh.

When we return home, we'll be with the other gargoyles, watching the three females, swollen with their pregnancies, watching the fathers doting over them.

And us? We'll be lonely. We'll be dreaming of… this.

But we've had sex before. We've dated before, both humans and non-humans, and it was never like this.

I thought it was because we knew there was almost no hope of children with them. With Celaeno? I don't know… I guess if we had to give up our dream of fatherhood, she's the woman I'd give it up for. The slim chance that a female gargoyle will one day choose us to impregnate her seems less important than a lifetime with just this woman.

And yet she's a monster.

I stiffen. There's that too. If we brought her home, they'd kill her. If we don't come home to report her death, they'll send other gargoyles after her.

Is there any hope this could work?

I lean down and kiss the top of her head. She looks up and her dark eyes catch mine. We're staring at each other. My heart wants to imagine she's thinking the same thing I am—that she wishes this moment would never end.

Because when it does, we're going to have to truly decide if we will betray our people, or if we're still going to kill her.

Either choice claws at my heart.

So I'm just going to pray this moment stretches on without limit, and that we never have to decide.

Because even if people claim gargoyles have hearts of stone, we don't.

Chapter Twenty-One

CELAENO

After eating a ridiculous amount of pizza, the three gargoyles fell asleep… naked. Did I mention they were naked? They shoved the two queen beds together, and now they're in a pile of naked, rock-hard goodness. And I'm just curled up in a weird sundress one of them bought for me, with little song birds all over it, watching them and slowly eating cold pizza.

I seriously can't look away. I want to lick every freakin' inch of them. I want to run my hands along their tattoos. And the idea of sliding my hand down their naked chests and gripping those giant cocks of theirs… well, I guess I'm hungry for more than just food.

But I can't bring myself to wake them up for more sex. Or fall asleep next to so much hotness.

What happened—it still confuses me. Do these gargoyles actually care about me? Or was this about finally 'getting some' after being celibate for so long?

The truth is, I don't know. I should be figuring out the bird problem and getting the hell out of here. So why does the idea of leaving make my stomach turn?

I toss my cold pizza down in the box and pad quietly to the bathroom and wash my hands. Glancing up at the mirror, I look away, then back up in shock.

Is that… me?

My hair is long and tangled. My face looks pale inside a face with too-big eyes. Despite all that, I've never looked prettier. Which is saying a lot, because I'm pretty sure I've never thought I was pretty. Ever.

But in the mirror? I look kind of… sexy. Or maybe feeling wanted by the three hottest men I've ever met has changed something inside of me. Either way, I like the change.

Smiling, I go back to my chair, but freeze. Near my clothes, Candy's little wallet had fallen out of my pocket.

Heart racing, I kneel down. The phone isn't working, but I find a courtesy charger in the end table and plug it in. While I wait for it to have enough battery to turn on, I go through the rest of her wallet. It doesn't have much: a couple of credit cards, a folded twenty, and a business card. For the candle shop we'd visited earlier.

I frown and stare down at it, flipping it over.

I feel bad, but for some reason I can't imagine Candy in that place. Everything was overpriced and super girly, not at all like anything I saw in her place.

Maybe I'm wrong though. I didn't know her. I didn't explore her whole house or anything. Maybe her bathroom was covered in candles.

Or maybe my instincts are screaming at me because there's something weird about her carrying around this card. I rub my forehead and exhale deeply. I'm getting tired. That's probably all this is.

I'm about to stand up when I look back at her phone. Shrugging, I hit the power button and watch it turn on. The background is of her and her daughter again. It makes my heart hurt. What must that girl be going through, losing her mother at such a young age?

I open her messages and see dozens and dozens of unanswered texts. People searching for her. Scared for her. Asking if she's okay. And then, I get to her old messages.

All of them are from men. Reading them makes me feel… slimy. Candy's responses were always oddly professional. But their messages to her? Geez. What the fuck did they think? That because she was a stripper they somehow owned her body? That they could talk to her however they pleased?

Any one of these guys could have killed her for not returning their interest, but she said it was a friend.

Frowning, I keep searching until I see a woman's name. Sarah.

I hit the message thread. I hate that my pulse starts racing and that sweat trickles down my back. This woman was indeed her friend. They messaged multiple times a day. And yet, Sarah didn't text her after she'd disappeared.

People who had barely sent her a single message before had filled her inbox with their concern. But not her friend?

Maybe I'm overthinking it. Maybe I'm wrong. But I'm pretty sure this Sarah is the killer.

But who is she?

It's still dark out, although morning is just a few hours away. I'm exhausted, but I won't be able to sleep until I know.

Leaving the phone still plugged in on the floor, I smooth the fabric on the weird bird-sundress and slip back into my shoes. Grabbing the key card to the door, I look back at the sleeping gargoyles. I don't need to wake them. I'll be back in just a minute.

Still, I have the unexplainable urge to kiss them before I go, which is silly.

Turning, I slip out the door and shut it softly behind me.

Instantly, I'm overwhelmed by the cold. It's the kind that bites right into your flesh. And that feeling of wrongness I felt during the day? It's about a million times stronger in the darkness. Even the horrible sour smell is so strong I'm trying not to gag.

I stare out across the quiet, empty parking lot, searching the shadows for any signs of danger. I see none. But that sense of wrongness? It's only growing stronger.

Looking up at my birds, they still line the rooftops. Every edge is just them, standing like silent sentries. It hurts my heart. How much longer can they remain like that?

I long to touch my mind to theirs, to bring them some kind of peace or reassurance, but I remember the feeling last time. Gritting my teeth, I turn and head toward the office of the motel. I move slowly, aware how tense my birds are.

Reaching the office, I open the door and am thankful for the warmth of the heater. Behind the desk, a woman sets down her phone and regards me suspiciously.

"Can I help you?"

Shit, I should have planned this out better.

"Uh, yeah."

I move closer to the front desk with its ancient computer and meet her gaze. She's young, probably in her twenties, with dark brown hair and light brown eyes. Her attitude oozes off of every inch of her, and I have to remember that she probably thinks we're roughly the same age. So, I should, uh, act like it.

"So, I heard about that stripper who got killed. Candy, was it?"

Her brows rise. "Yeah."

"That's got me freaked out a little. I can't seem to sleep."

She shakes her head and looks back to her phone, speaking under her breath. "I wouldn't be *sleeping* in a hotel with those hot guys you showed up with either."

I feel my cheeks heat and try to push back my embarrassment. "I just wondered. Aren't you worried there's a killer on the loose?"

She looks annoyed as she glances up from her phone. "Candy was a *stripper*. I doubt someone's going around killing just anyone. She probably had it coming in one way or another."

I have to curl my hands into fists to keep from smacking this bitch. "So, you aren't worried."

"Nope," she says, eyes back on her phone.

"So all she did was hang around with low-life guys?"

"Pretty much," she says, not looking up from her phone.

"And Sarah."

Her nose wrinkles. "I wouldn't say they had a relationship, even though I think Candy wanted one... because of their connection. But Sarah tried to stay away from her, as if that'd make us all forget. Like *that's* possible. Sarah might be the Sherriff's daughter now, but she's just as trashy as her mom, and even weirder. She's just better at hiding it." She gives an unkind laugh. "Working at the candle shop. Getting good grades. *Always* obeying all the rules. Basically, just trying too hard to seem sweet and not at all a freak. It's pathetic."

The girl from the candle shop is Sarah?

I sort through my memories of the sweet, blushing witch. There's no way that's Sarah, the woman I suspect of being the killer. It just doesn't add up.

"What do you mean?" I lean in, as if exchanging gossip.

She raises a brow and sets down her phone down. "Sarah's Candy's daughter."

What? "I thought her daughter was really young."

After not being interested in talking to me at all, the other woman is suddenly excited to be able to tell someone new the story. "Candy had Sarah when she was like thirteen, and Candy's dad went to jail for impregnating her. Candy gave Sarah up to be adopted by the sheriff. No matter how hard Sarah tried to act like the perfect daughter, like her mom wasn't a whore and her dad wasn't her fucking grandfather, no one forgot it. No one *lets* her forget it."

I'm blown the fuck away. A parent got his daughter pregnant and no one has any kindness or understanding for her and her child? People blame them? What the hell is wrong with this town?

And then there's the other thing. Never would I have thought that girl was Candy's daughter.

"Sarah must have been really upset when her mom went missing."

She shrugs. "Not really. From what I heard, she was pretty mad that her mom gave her up but kept Elizabeth. I think she was kind of glad to see the girl getting her mom ripped away too."

I feel sick to my stomach.

Could Sarah really have done this?

I think back to my meeting with her. I knew she was a witch. I just thought she didn't know it. If she was powerful enough, she could do the ritual and create this curse over the town.

"Uh, well, thanks for telling me. I guess I can sleep easy knowing I won't be murdered in my sleep."

The excitement goes out of her eyes. "Yeah, but if I was you, I'd be gone by tomorrow."

"Why?"

"Because the birds attacked another person today... so they've decided to kill them all tomorrow. The whole thing creeps me out. I don't know what those things will do when people start shooting them, but if I were just passing through, I'd make a point to be gone by noon."

My throat closes. "Thanks."

I practically run out the door. Outside, gasping in the cold air, I am completely overwhelmed. I'm pretty sure Sarah killed her mom. But what do I do with the information in less than twelve hours? I don't want to kill some confused, young woman.

But I also have to end this thing.

I have to give Candy justice. I have to let her soul rest.

But how?

I start back to my motel room. My steps sound loud on the pavement. Overhead, a light goes out.

Okay... that's not creepy.

I keep walking, a little faster now. The lights above me keep going out, one after another.

My heart's racing. Something's out here with me. Something's wrong, but I'm so close to my room, I try to make it.

My fingers are sweaty on my key card, despite the cold. I reach my door, slide it, and get a red light. I try again, hand shaking.

Something hits me from behind.

I feel myself falling. And then? Nothing.

Chapter Twenty-Two

ENDER

There's nothing better than waking up next to a beautiful woman. Opening my eyes, I find myself staring face-to-face at Grey's ugly face. Scowling, I roll to my other side and find Journey snoring beside me.

Fuck.

Are we all naked in bed together?

Uh, pretty sure we're missing the jam in our little bread sandwich. Where's Celaeno?

I sit up, scratching the back of my head and frowning. My gaze runs over our room, but the tiny woman is nowhere to be found. Crawling out of bed, I head for the bathroom. She's not there either.

"Guys?"

They don't move an inch.

"Guys!" I go back to the bed and yank the covers back. Grey sits up, and as soon as his feet hit the floor, he's swearing up a storm.

Journey's eyes flash open, annoyance coloring his expression. "Is there a reason we're staring at your naked junk in our face this early in the morning?"

Celaeno's Fate

"She's gone."

Grey stops swearing. "What are you talking about?" But he knows.

Ender gets up and it's the three of us, scrambling around naked, looking for a woman who's not here.

Grey finally comes to stand in the center of the room. I sit on the edge of the bed, watching him. Waiting for him to snap.

"She left." I open my mouth to speak, but he continues. "We are the biggest fucking morons in the world. We took off her collar. We let her seduce us into a sex-coma, and then she just strutted out of here."

"No," I tell him, shaking my head. "She wouldn't do that."

He whirls on me. "Why? Because she's beautiful? Because she makes you hard?"

"She makes all of us hard!" I shout at him. "But that's not why. I don't see her doing that. She cares. About people and her birds. She wouldn't just abandon all of them."

"She could be pursuing the case without us," Journey says, his words soft.

"No," I tell them both. "Something must have happened to her."

Saying the words aloud makes me realize that they're probably true. There's no doubt in my mind that she didn't leave of her own free will, which means she was taken, but by who?

"Just because you don't want to believe that the little monster took off to protect her own ass doesn't mean it's not true." Grey starts dressing, his movements jerky and angry.

Journey and I dress too. More slowly.

"So what do we do?" Journey says.

"We hunt her down, that's what we do!" Grey says. "And then we don't take our eyes off her again… until it's time to take care of her in a more permanent way."

"You've got to be fucking kidding me!" I shout back at him. "You can't still be planning on killing her. Not after—"

"Sleeping with her?" His eyes are cold. "You bet I plan on killing that manipulative monster the first chance I get."

He storms out of the motel room, and I'm left staring after him. I challenge Grey a lot, but it's mostly to get a reaction out of him. The thing is, if he tries to hurt Celaeno, I won't let him.

Even if it rips us all apart.

I follow him out of the motel room even more slowly, but freeze when I see the key outside our door. Kneeling down, I pick it up and swipe it in our door. It works.

Celaeno's key. But why would she toss it on the ground?

The sense that something's wrong intensifies.

Journey shoves open the door a second later, nearly smacking me in the face. "You guys need to see this!"

We hurry back inside. He shows us a phone plugged into the corner. On the floor near it, Candy's wallet, with her ID still inside, and a business card from the candle shop lay.

"What does this mean?" I ask.

Grey grabs the card and crumbles it in his hand. "It means we might know where to find our little runaway."

I follow after him, heart hammering. I want to find her.

I just don't want Grey to find her.

So what do I do?

Chapter Twenty-Three

CELAENO

I wake up and wince. My head feels like hell. My hair practically prickles around the massive bump on the back of my head.

Groaning, I blink open my eyes. I'm staring directly at the sun.

"Fuck," I moan, and turn my head to the side.

Which is how I see that I'm lying in the center of a massive symbol painted in blood. I struggle, but I'm bound to the ground. My wrists and ankles are tied to God only knows what, but I feel the kiss of metal against my flesh.

Sarah's young face suddenly fills my vision. "Oh, good, you're awake."

My mouth feels dry as I struggle to speak. "What are you doing?"

She smirks. "You know, when you and those three hotties showed up in my shop, I didn't think you'd be a problem. Just more humans sniffing around, trying to figure out something that was beyond their understanding. But then, something animated my creature in the caves. And guess what? They came across Candy's body near the lake… meaning someone pulled her body free. It didn't take me long to put two and two together and realize that you were going to complicate my plan more than I thought." She shrugs, pulls out a long, narrow knife with symbols on it, and starts sharpening it. "I realized two things then. That I'd need to get rid of you, and that I'd need another body to have enough power to extract my revenge."

I stare for a long minute. She sounds so casual as she talks about killing her mom, about killing me, and destroying this town. It's… creepy. It's like she has no soul.

"You killed your own mom."

She freezes in her movements, the knife and sharpener bright in the morning sun. "Do you know my grandpa is my dad? She actually let me become some freak born as my grandpa's kid."

Bile rises in the back of my throat. "You can't seriously think anyone would want that. I mean, she was a fucking child when she got pregnant with you. She was the victim—"

Her eyes narrow. "She wasn't the victim, I was. And then she didn't even bother to keep me, to try to protect me from this town. She just… gave me away, like I was nothing."

"She was a child. How could she take care of a baby? She gave you to a family who could give you what she couldn't."

I'm surprised by the coldness that comes over her face. "She was the reason I was suffering, so I planned to use her for my revenge, but she fucked that up too. So now, today, when most of the town attacks those birds—they're all going to pay. This place will be littered with bodies."

My thoughts are scrambling. "Like what happened to your brother?"

She stares at me, and I expect to see regret, but her eyes lack all emotion. "He wasn't my brother. At least not by blood. I had to kill him, to rile the Sheriff up."

I feel sick. People might call me a monster, but that's because they haven't seen true evil like I have. This woman, she's pure evil. Her eyes are dead, with no empathy or feeling whatsoever. I can't believe I didn't see it before.

"You don't have to do this. I know the town wasn't nice to you. I know—"

Her knife moves in a flash, slicing one of my wrists.

A scream explodes from my lips as I feel hot blood leaking from my veins.

"Enough talk," she says, calmly. "It's almost noon, and my power demands a sacrifice."

I shake my head. "Sarah—"

She slashes my other wrist. Mind-numbing pain tears through me, and it takes me a second to breathe. My vision blackens, and my head falls to the side as I stare out at the dark forest that surrounds us.

"You don't know what you're doing," I force out.

And she doesn't. She has no idea how dangerous this is.

She ignores me, picking up an ancient book. The words of her spell come, murmured to the trees, while she holds up her knife, covered in my blood. The dark liquid runs down the handle and slides across her flesh, staining it.

I struggle against the metal that binds me, thrashing, using the little strength I have left, but they hold.

Closing my eyes, I try to shift into my raven form, but the magic of this witch's circle keeps me where I am. I reach for it over and over again as my raven tries to save us both, but she can't. My eyes open, and I stare at the grey sky. A cloud passes over the sun, and the shadows darken around us. A cool wind blows, raising the goose bumps on my arms.

It's hard to admit, but I'm going to die today.

I feel movement near my feet and she slashes my ankle. I arch against the chains that bind me, screaming.

"Let me go!" I shout, my voice heavy with pain. "I'm not what you think I am."

But she just keeps reciting the spell, ignoring me. The power of her curse grows with each drop of blood that leaves my body. I have to stop this. I have to protect my birds and this town.

An image flashes of my gargoyles. Their stone flesh will protect them. Right? I hope so. I hope they don't die because of me.

She slashes my other ankle, and I bite down on a curse. I try to say more, but nothing comes. There's a moment, like the instant before a storm unleashes, when she looms over me. Her chant comes faster and faster, and her eyes grow black. I try to warn her, to tell her, but she slashes my throat.

I'm choking on blood. I taste it, filling my mouth. My head lolls to the side as blood soaks the symbol beneath me.

The curse explodes across the land around me, sour and heavy with warning.

Sarah smirks above me. "Thanks, ghost hunter. Now the second those idiots attack, everyone is going to pay for how they've treated me."

Death clutches me in its grip, and my vision fades to blackness.

How is dying always so painful?

Chapter Twenty-Four

GREY

The little candle shop is closed when we get there. But I don't give a fuck. I punch through the glass door, watching as it shatters. The birds on the rooftops rise, filling the air with their beating wings. But we're in our stone forms, unafraid.

Birds scratch and claw at our stone-flesh, but I move forward into the building. We search every inch of it, looking for a clue, but there's no sign of Celaeno, or suggestions of where she went if she'd been here.

My anger and frustration rise. The woman completely had me. I was ready to give her everything that she wanted, anything she asked for. I had started dreaming of the life we could have together. I'd accepted we'd have to turn our backs on our people and keep her safe from more attacks from our kind.

And I didn't care. Anything was worth the price to keep her as our own.

Realizing that she'd used us and betrayed us hurt in a way I wasn't prepared for. I don't trust easily, but she'd gotten her little fingers in the cracks of my stone heart and made me forget all logic.

I hated her for that.

I hated her because I knew my feelings for her were more than just attraction, and I was determined to punish her for my broken heart.

Breaking the door to the back of the shop, I squeeze my huge frame inside. I start to tear everything apart but freeze as one of the drawers spills onto the floor. Kneeling down, I see several ancient books. Spell books.

My heart races. Shifting through them, I spot a letter. Pulling it out of the torn envelope, I read the words of a mother begging her daughter for forgiveness. It's addressed to Sarah. Signed by Candy.

Pieces of this puzzle start to slip into place. I look at the envelope again, memorizing Sarah's address. Then, I stand.

Maybe Sarah was powerful enough to create that curse alone. Maybe she had help. Either way, she has something to do with all of this, and I'm going to find out what.

Out in the shop, Ender and Journey are still searching, trying to push away the agitated birds without hurting them. I hate that Celaeno has changed us. Because as easy as it would be just to kill these rats with wings, not even I can do it, not after seeing how much she loves them.

"Come on," I tell them. "I think I know what to do."

Ender stops waving the birds away. "What did you find?"

"The girl who works in this shop is Candy's daughter… and a practicing witch. And it seems they didn't get along."

Ender stiffens. "Do you think she took Celaeno?"

How are you this naïve? "No, I don't think a shifter who can control birds was taken by some little girl."

"She could be in trouble," he says, a little more gruffly.

I smirk, even though my chest hurts. "She's not. Get it through your head; she took off the first chance she got. We just need to focus on finding this girl and stopping the curse. Without Celaeno's help."

He shakes his head. "You're wrong."

"I guess we'll see," I say, waving away birds as I head for the door.

How can my brothers not see that Celaeno betrayed us? Because I know she did, and I've also accepted that eventually I'll have to kill her. Even if it'll destroy me to do it.

We hurry out of the building and storm down the road. On the end of the next street, dozens of humans are crowded together with guns. I stiffen for a moment. I know our glamour makes us look human, but no paranormal creature likes to see a mob of armed humans.

"They're going to kill the birds," Journey says, sounding worried. "I thought we had until Friday."

"Something must have changed." Ender can't hide the concern in his voice. "A lot of people are going to get hurt."

The protective gargoyle inside me rears its head. Stopping the curse is the best way to help this town, but it'd be nice to try to solve this issue with all the humans safely tucked inside. If they are out here pissing off the birds, it's going to make this more complicated.

"Journey, go try to reason with them. If you can't stop them, at least try to buy us some time."

He nods and starts off down the street.

I turn to Ender. "Let's fly to Sarah's house."

We slip into an alley and use our glamour to completely conceal ourselves from the humans' sight. Then we take to the air and fly just above the roads until we spot Sarah's street. We follow the numbers until the houses start to spread out on larger and larger lots of land. When we find her house, we go higher, searching for any sign of Sarah.

Something catches my eye in the woods behind her house. Flying lower and lower, I squint, trying to figure out what I'm seeing. My heart lurches.

The same symbol that was in the cave is on the ground, and someone is lying bloody in the center of it. I shoot lower and only have seconds to realize that I know that dress… it's Celaeno.

I crash into the ground, and the earth beneath me splits. I can't breathe. I can't see anything but her. Lying, without breathing, covered in her own blood. Ender lands beside me and snaps the chains around her feet and hands.

Without thinking, I pull her into my lap and cradle her against my chest.

Ender was right. Fuck, why did I think she'd betrayed us? And here she is, dead because of our stupidity. Dead because my pride made me doubt her, made me not search for her before this happened. I'll never forgive myself for this.

She suddenly gasps in my arms, and her eyes fly open. Her instincts make her struggle as she comes back into her body and back into the world. But I hold her tightly, murmuring things—I don't even know what. I stroke her dark hair, matted with blood, and I don't let her go until she calms and relaxes against me.

The loss of blood has made her even paler. There are dark shadows under her eyes. Her lips move as she tries to tell us something, but her slit throat means the words don't come out.

"It's okay," Ender says. "We know Sarah made the curse."

She reaches out and grasps the back of my head in her

Celaeno's Fate

weak grip and pulls me down. Our eyes meet, and I feel some kind of power wash over me. All I can smell is a terrible sourness, and something that whispers of death. The air feels heavy, dark, and dangerous.

With each second the feeling intensifies, and then I realize what she's doing. "That's the curse," I whisper.

She nods, and her hand drops. Her head lolls to the side, but her eyes still stare, almost vacantly.

I look at Ender. "We need to get back to the town. Those humans are in serious trouble."

"You take her to safety," Ender begins.

But Celaeno jerks in my arms, her eyes wide. Her movements frantic.

Fuck. I'd do anything to calm her.

"You want to come with us?"

She slumps back and nods slowly.

I look at Ender. "I'll keep her on the rooftop. Journey's with the humans, but I have a feeling Sarah will be somewhere she can see the destruction of her curse. Find her and kill her."

He nods.

We fly straight for the town center. I land on a rooftop, tear off my shirt, and cover Celaeno. She shivers uncontrollably in my arms, but she's still alert. Her gaze searches all around us.

At last, she points, and I follow her finger. Sarah's standing, almost entirely concealed, on another rooftop. Birds line the edge of the building, and she leans over it, grinning at the humans.

Journey stands in front of the humans in the street, and I can tell they're getting agitated. The sheriff steps forward and shoves Journey out of the way, and the humans start walking, guns pointed at the rooftops.

I see Ender not far from us and wave my free arm to

get his attention, to point out Sarah, but he's not looking at me. The witch raises her hands in the air, and I know she's saying the spell to finally destroy these people. I want to keep Celaeno safe, but I have to stop this!

Still carrying Celaeno, I lift off the rooftop, fly over Sarah, and land behind her. Removing my glamour, I hear her murmuring the words to the curse.

Celaeno struggles out of my arms.

Heart in my throat, I let her go down. She sits on her knees, breathing hard.

"Sarah," she whispers.

The girl whirls around. She has a vial of blood in one hand, and she looks between us with wide eyes.

Celaeno pants to get the words out. "You killed me, but you don't want to use my blood for this curse."

"How are you still alive…? It doesn't matter." She looks terrified, but strangely determined. "Nothing matters but my revenge."

"No—" Celaeno lifts a hand.

But it's too late, the woman drinks the vial of blood in one quick movement.

The clouds overhead darken. Lightning splits the sky and thunder roars around us. Every single bird stiffens on the rooftops, and Celaeno's head falls onto her chest.

The birds lift into the sky and the beating of their wings fills the air. They block the sun, darkness covering the town like a cloud. Guns go off in the distance. Birds fall, but the mass remains as one, hovering. I clench my hands, ready to defend Celaeno from their claws and beaks. I pray Ender and Journey will be powerful enough to keep the humans safe.

The storm of birds unleashes… and heads straight for us.

Celaeno's Fate

Wrapping my body around Celaeno, I pull her to my chest, heart pounding.

And then I hear screaming. But it isn't the screaming of the humans in the streets below, it's Sarah. Lifting my head, I stare in shock as the thousands of birds descend upon her, covering every inch of her flesh. Hovering in the air above her like the smoke from a fire.

More shots ring out, but they have no effect on the birds. The screaming is like nothing I've heard in my life, blood-curdling. Filled with death's pain.

And then the screaming stops. The air changes. The clouds part, letting forth a stream of glowing light. The gunshots stop as the birds withdraw. Where Sarah was standing? There's nothing.

Some of the birds fly off into the woods, but some of them remain. They land near Celaeno.

I tense, ready for anything, but they crowd around her, rubbing her with the tops of their heads.

A sigh escapes her lips, and she pushes lightly from my arms. She lies on her back on the rooftop, stroking the birds' heads, wearing a blanket of her creatures.

I don't have a clue what just happened, but I have a feeling… I think the curse is gone.

Chapter Twenty-Five

CELAENO

One week later

We spent a week in the hotel while I healed, a week of me not speaking and the gargoyles staring at me with big frightened eyes. They wouldn't let me walk on my own. They carried me to the bathroom, they bathed me in the shower, and they held me closely at night, as if scared I might disappear again.

It was a strange experience. Never in my life had people treated me like this before… as if I was something fragile and important.

On the eighth day, I awoke and touched my throat. Scars are all that remain from my death, and I know they'll soon fade too. I swallow hard, slip from the sheets, and get a glass of water. My gargoyles must be exhausted, because for once they don't spring into action with my movement.

It's nice to be walking around again, even though my legs and arms tremble at the exertion. After a quick trip to the bathroom, I come back and sit on the little chair by the table and drink the water slowly. I clear my throat and speak. To my surprise, after a few creaky words, I sound almost normal.

I'm better… at least enough. Enough to leave.

My heart aches. I should go. They'd promised to give me a head start, but would they? Would they even remember that promise, back when they were desperate to break the curse? I wasn't sure they would keep their bargain.

A powerful part of me had hoped they could forget what I was, hoped they were taking care of me because they felt something for me. But the truth was, they were probably caring for me until my voice worked again, until I could explain what happened with Sarah. Then they would kill me as they had intended all along.

Pulling off Grey's big shirt, I slip into another one of the ridiculous outfits they'd given me. This one was a big white shirt and gray sweat pants. The clothes swallow me whole, but it's better than nothing.

Lingering in the doorway, I look at them one last time and head into the coldness of the town. Unable to help myself, I walk through the streets. It's early morning, but people are still out living their lives. Some are driving and a few hardy souls are jogging. The air smells of pine needles instead of the curse.

I'd heard Candy's body had been found and put to rest. Her daughter had found a permanent family, people who had been wanting a child for many, many years. Too many of my birds died that day, but I tried to focus on all the ones we'd saved and the humans that got away unharmed.

I heard the sheriff was looking for his daughter. I wanted to tell him the truth, but that was the one thing I couldn't do. No parent needed to know their child was a monster.

Or dead.

Sliding into an alley, I shift and fly to the rooftop. Shifting again into my human-form, I stare out, watching the sun rise. This town is beautiful. Maybe someday I'd come back to it.

I think of all the places I'd lived in my life. None of them appeal to me now. I'll just have to pick a direction and start flying, and maybe I'd find someplace new where I can be happy.

Behind me, something large hits the roof. Spinning, I'm shocked to see Grey. He grabs my arm, rough as always. For a second I think about shifting, but then he yanks me against his chest.

For a long time he just holds me, and all I can hear is the racing of his heart.

It feels good, but I'm still scared. He was sent here to kill me. I know he has feelings for me, but can his feelings trump his duty?

Two more heavy gargoyles land on the roof with identical thuds.

"You found her!" Ender cries out, and then I'm in his arms.

He squeezes me gently, then holds me out in front of him. "What the hell?"

I look at Journey. His gaze connects with mine.

"We thought someone had taken you again," Journey explains, his voice filled with misery.

I clear my throat and reluctantly pull back from Ender's hold. "I know you want to know what happened with Sarah. She made the mistake of thinking that her curse was more powerful than my connection with my birds. The second she used my blood to command them, they instinctually attacked the person who had killed me. I tried to warn her… it's happened every time someone has killed me. Their need to avenge me broke the curse."

Grey just stares at me. "You think we give a fuck about that mess?"

I stiffen. "I don't understand."

"We care about *you*. About you being safe."

I wrap my arms around myself, feeling strangely vulnerable. "But I'm a monster."

Journey moves closer and cups my chin. "That woman was a monster. Anyone who tries to hurt you is a monster. You, you're a woman. *Our* woman."

Staring in shock, I try to process his words. "But you were sent to kill me."

"And Grey will return to our home and inform them that you died. Which you did."

All I can do is stare. How is this even possible?

Journey continues in the most logical voice I've ever heard. "He'll then inform them that we have decided to live in a human city for a while. They won't like it, but they won't stop us. He'll come back, and we'll create a life together, wherever you want."

There's silence for a moment before Ender adds. "If you want."

The words rush out of me. "Fuck, yes!"

And then they're hugging me in their massive arms, their huge bodies making me feel warm and safe.

I smile. My life starts to unfold in front of me, and now, there's so much possibility.

Grey whispers above me, "But if you ever try to escape again, we'll renege on our deal. There's no way we'll give you a week head start."

I pull back from them and laugh. "Deal!"

Chapter Twenty-Six

CELAENO

We go to my old town and collect some of my important things from my apartment. It's been four months since we started traveling together, the best four months of my life.

But my lease is up and I need to move my stuff out or get it thrown out.

So my boys each carry a bag on their shoulders of the special things I didn't want to leave behind, and I'm giving them a quick tour before we leave. People move out of my way as I walk, in a way they never have before.

Well, they get out of our *way.*

Not a single person jostles my small frame. Instead, they move around the massive men who surround me. They must be scared to get their asses kicked.

Which is a very real possibility if they hurt me in any way.

I smile. These guys treat me like I'm made of glass… I can't wait to see how they react when I tell them my news.

I'm lost in thought for a minute, and then I look up.

Freezing, I stare, wide-eyed, as Ashley and Papa Rye

head straight for us. They don't see me until it's too late, and then we're all staring at each other, blocking the sidewalk. Papa Rye won't even look at me.

"Cel," Ashley greets, in a rude little voice.

I try not to feel satisfied about the little scars all over her face.

"Ashley," I acknowledge her, but give them nothing more than that.

"Wait, this is Ashley?" Ender asks, and his gaze snaps back to her.

I nod slowly.

Ender moves in front of me and directs his attention to Papa.

"You must be Papa Rye then," he says with a sneer.

I peek around his massive frame and see Papa nod. That single cold movement makes my heart lurch.

"Are you aware that your granddaughter is constantly late, takes long breaks, and fucks men in the back of the store? That's how the comet cleaner got on the donuts. She was fucking the guy who gave her that gold bracelet and knocked it over. She blamed it on Celaeno."

The air whooshes out of my chest and I stare in shock. No one speaks for an awkwardly long minute.

Papa Rye taps his cane on the ground and sighs. "Since I fired Celaeno, I've been getting a lot of complaints. The store opens late, closes often, and the food and drinks are subpar. Ashley's given me a lot of excuses, but I suspect she hasn't been doing her job. In fact, she hasn't been doing her job since I hired her."

"Papa!" Ashley exclaims.

"Shut up," he says, his voice gruff. "Cel, I'm sorry. I should've believed you. If you want to come back and work for me, you're welcome any time."

My brain freezes at the question. It's all I wanted since this drama started and for a minute I can't respond.

Ender draws back and my guys stare at me, waiting.

Ashley bursts into tears, but to my satisfaction, no one gives her the least bit of attention.

"Thanks for the offer," I say, "and the apology. But I won't be coming back to the shop again."

He and I ignore Ashley's wailing and chat for a few minutes. When the conversation closes, we're both smiling. The weight pressing down on my chest is gone.

At least this time when I leave, I'll know he doesn't hate me.

We hug, and they walk away. Ashley clings to the old man while he tries to shake her off. I feel… completely satisfied.

"Thanks for doing that," I tell Ender.

He smiles and slips his fingers into mine. "You just tell us whose been mean to you, and we'll take care of it."

I laugh. "Well, there is my ex…"

Grey speaks from beside me. "Oh, trust us, he's on our list."

I start to laugh again, but I stop when I realize that he's deadly serious. I'm not ashamed to admit I'm strangely turned on.

They lead me into an alley, and then Journey's gaze locks with mine. "Is there anything else we need to do here before we go?"

I shake my head. "Not a thing."

"So, where should we head next?" Ender asks, running his hand through his beautiful hair.

Which is completely natural, the lucky asshole. I know because I asked.

"New Zealand?" Grey asks.

"Uh," I hesitate. "I'm not sure I can handle that flight."

Ender smirks. "Since when?"

I take a deep breath. This wasn't how I planned to tell them, but I guess now's the right time. "Well, since I found out I'm pregnant."

My words are met with complete silence.

After an awkwardly long time, Grey finally speaks. "That's impossible. Do you have any idea how rare gargoyle pregnancies are? There's been a handful of them between humans and gargoyles, ever. There's been a handful of them between gods and gargoyles, ever. This is… just not possible."

I put my hand on my belly. "Well, like ten pregnancy tests and a doctor's visit confirmed it."

"They must be wrong." Journey sounds breathless, almost in pain.

Hand trembling, I pull the picture from my pocket and unfold it. I'd gone to the doctor alone, without telling them, because I wasn't sure. I knew how badly they wanted kids, and I didn't want to be wrong.

They gather closer and stare at the ultrasound.

"That's our little bean," I tell them.

Ender takes the picture from my hand really slowly. "They're sure."

I nod.

"Holy fuck," Ender whispers.

Journey's hugging me in an instant, babbling like a fool.

And Grey? He's just staring at the photo. Unmoving.

He's happy, right?

It's Ender's turn to hug me. He's going on and on about what he'll do if it's a boy or a girl. How they're going to have so much fun, his words spilling out in his excitement.

Grey finally meets my gaze. "From now on, you do nothing. Not so much as walk. You're going to lie in a bed, and we're going to stand guard until our baby is born."

I laugh. "Not a chance."

He moves closer and Ender and Journey step back. "You don't understand, this is a miracle."

I stroke his arm, trying to reassure him. "I'll be fine. The baby will be fine. We don't have to change everything, just… how far we fly. A lot of shifters have to stop shifting when pregnant, so—"

"All right," he says, the word choked, and then he's hugging me too.

There's so much hugging, and kissing, and touching of my belly. I'm so happy I feel like I'm going to burst.

How could I have ever known that gargoyles and monsters could come together? Not only to fall in love, but to have a family together?

I guess, I couldn't.

But it doesn't matter. All that matters is that I'll never be lonely again.

The End

~ Want to read the next exciting book in this world? Then, pick up Cerberus Unleashed. It's the story of a hellhound finding love with her sexy gargoyles.~

Also by Lacey Carter Andersen

Mates Of The Realms

Renegade Hunter *audiobook*

Cursed Hunter

Betrayed Hunter

Rebel Lover

Rebel Lies

Rebel Loss

Rogue Demon

Box Set I: Demon Hunter

Box Set II: Rebel Angel

Monsters and Gargoyles

Medusa's Destiny *audiobook*

Keto's Tale

Celaeno's Fate

Cerberus Unleashed

Lamia's Blood

Shade's Secret

Shorts: Their Own Sanctuary

Shorts: Their Miracle Pregnancy

The Firehouse Feline

Feline the Heat

Feline the Flames

A Villainously Romantic Retelling

Worthy

Alternative Futures

Nightmare Hunter *audiobook*

Deadly Dreams *audiobook*

Mortal Flames

Twisted Prophecies

Box Set: Alien Mischief

The Dragon Shifters' Last Hope

Stolen by Her Harem

Claimed by Her Harem

Treasured by Her Harem

Collection: Magic in her Harem

Harem of the Shifter Queen

Sultry Fire

Sinful Ice

Saucy Mist

Collection: Power in her Kiss

Standalones

Beauty with a Bite

Shifters and Alphas

Collections

Monsters, Gods, Witches, Oh My!

Wings, Horns, and Shifters

About the Author

Lacey Carter Andersen loves reading, writing, and drinking excessive amounts of coffee. She spends her days taking care of her husband, three kids, and three cats. But at night, everything changes! Her imagination runs wild with strong-willed characters, unique worlds, and exciting plots that she enthusiastically puts into stories.

Lacey has dozens of tales: science fiction romances, paranormal romances, short romances, reverse harem romances, and more. So, please feel free to dive into any of her worlds; she loves to have the company!

And you're welcome to reach out to her; she really enjoys hearing from her readers.

You can find her at:

Email: laceycarterandersen@gmail.com

Mailing List: https://www.subscribepage.com/laceycarterandersen

Website: www.laceycarterandersen.wordpress.com/

Facebook Page: www.facebook.com/Lacey-Carter-Andersen-1940678949483316/

Printed in Great Britain
by Amazon